whelp's been counting money and writing letters all his life."

"Nonetheless, we're two men down," Ondego said. "And he volunteered."

"Where'd you find him?" the dwarf snarled. "Looks like you scooped him out of the gutter."

"Close," Hirk said. "We locked him up last night. He beat the cack out of a couple of stevedores, both a lot bigger and meaner than the prince here."

"Is that right?" the dwarf asked. He still seemed incredulous, but that incredulity was tempered now.

"So, you can't find Freygaf?" Ondego asked.

The dwarf huffed and shook his head.

"Well, then, that works out just perfectly."

Rem realized what was about to happen. He looked to Hirk. Hirk w stubbly face.

"Re is is Rem—
your p

THE FIFTH WARD

WARD

FIRST WATCH

DALE LUCAS

www.orbitbooks.net

ORBIT

First published in Great Britain in 2017 by Orbit

1 3 5 7 9 10 8 6 4 2

Copyright © 2017 by Dale Lucas

Excerpt from *Kings of the Wyld* by Nicholas Eames
Copyright © 2017 by Nicholas Eames

The moral right of the author has been asserted.

A CIP catalogue record for this book
is available from the British Library.

ISBN 978-0-356-50936-5

Printed and bound in Great Britain by CPI Group (UK) Ltd, Croydon CR0 4YY

Papers used by Orbit are from well-managed forests
and other responsible sources.

MIX
Paper from
responsible sources
FSC® C104740

Orbit
An imprint of
Little, Brown Book Group
Carmelite House
50 Victoria Embankment
London EC4Y 0DZ

An Hachette UK Company
www.hachette.co.uk

www.orbitbooks.net

For Lili

CHAPTER ONE

Rem awoke in a dungeon with a thunderous headache. He knew it was a dungeon because he lay on a thin bed of straw, and because there were iron bars between where he lay and a larger chamber outside. The light was spotty, some of it from torches in sconces outside his cell, some from a few tiny windows high on the stone walls admitting small streams of wan sunlight. Moving nearer the bars, he noted that his cell was one of several, each roomy enough to hold multiple prisoners.

A large pile of straw on the far side of his cell coughed, shifted, then started to snore. Clearly, Rem was not alone.

And just how did I end up here? he wondered. *I seem to recall a winning streak at Roll-the-Bones.*

He could not remember clearly. But if the lumpy soreness of his face and body were any indication, his dice game had gone awry. If only he could clear his pounding head, or slake his thirst. His tongue and throat felt like sharkskin.

Desperate for a drink, Rem crawled to a nearby bucket, hoping for a little brackish water. To his dismay, he found that it was the piss jar, not a water bucket, and not well rinsed at that. The sight and smell made Rem recoil with a gag. He went sprawling back onto the hay. A few feet away, his cellmate muttered something in the tongue of the Kosterfolk, then resumed snoring.

Somewhere across the chamber, a multitumbler lock clanked

and clacked. Rusty hinges squealed as a great door lumbered open. From the other cells Rem heard prisoners roused from their sleep, shuffling forward hurriedly to thrust their arms out through the cage bars. If Rem didn't misjudge, there were only about four or five other prisoners in all the dungeon cells. A select company, to be sure. Perhaps it was a slow day for the Yenaran city watch?

Four men marched into the dungeon. Well, three marched; the fourth seemed a little more reticent, being dragged by two others behind their leader, a thickset man with black hair, sullen eyes, and a drooping mustache.

"Prefect, sir," Rem heard from an adjacent cell, "there's been a terrible mistake..."

From across the chamber: "Prefect, sir, someone must have spiked my ale, because the last thing I remember, I was enjoying an evening out with some mates..."

From off to his left: "Prefect, sir, I've a chest of treasure waiting back at my rooms at the Sauntering Mink. A golden cup full of rubies and emeralds is yours, if you'll just let me out of here..."

Prefect, sir... Prefect, sir... over and over again.

Rem decided that thrusting his own arms out and begging for the prefect's attention was useless. What would he do? Claim his innocence? Promise riches if they'd let him out? That was quite a tall order when Rem himself couldn't remember what he'd done to get in here. If he could just clear his thunder-addled, achingly thirsty brain...

The sullen-eyed prefect led the two who dragged the prisoner down a short flight of steps into a shallow sort of operating theater in the center of the dungeon: the interrogation pit, like some shallow bath that someone had let all the water out of. On one side of the pit was a brick oven in which fire and coals glowed. Opposite the oven was a burbling fountain. Rem thought these additions rather ingenious. Whatever elemental need one had—fire to burn with, water to drown with—both were readily provided. The floor of the pit, Rem guessed, probably sported a couple of grates that led right down into the sewers, as well as the tools of the trade: a table full of torturer's implements, a couple of hot braziers, some chairs and manacles. Rem hadn't seen the inside of any city dungeons, but he'd seen their private equivalents. Had it been the dungeon of some march lord up north—from his own country—that's what would have been waiting in the little amphitheater.

"Come on, Ondego, you know me," the prisoner pleaded. "This isn't necessary."

"'Fraid so," sullen-eyed Ondego said, his low voice easy and without malice. "The chair, lads."

The two guardsmen flanking the prisoner were a study in contrasts—one a tall, rugged sort, face stony and flecked with stubble, shoulders broad, while the other was lithe and graceful, sporting braided black locks, skin the color of dark-stained wood, and a telltale pair of tapered, pointing ears. Staring, Rem realized that second guardsman was no man at all, but an elf, and female, at that. Here was a puzzle, indeed. Rem had seen elves at a distance before, usually in or around frontier settlements farther north, or simply haunting the bleak crossroads of a woodland highway like pikers who never demanded a toll. But he had never seen one of them up close like this—and certainly not in the middle of one of the largest cities in the Western world, deep underground, in a dingy, shit- and blood-stained dungeon. Nonetheless, the dark-skinned elfmaid seemed quite at home in her surroundings, and perfectly comfortable beside the bigger man on the other side of the prisoner.

Together, those two guards thrust the third man's squirming, wobbly body down into a chair. Heavy manacles were produced and the protester was chained to his seat. He struggled a little, to test his bonds, but seemed to know instinctively that it was no use. Ondego stood at a brazier nearby, stoking its coals, the pile of dark cinders glowing ominously in the oily darkness.

"Oi, that's right!" one of the other prisoners shouted. "Give that bastard what for, Prefect!"

"You shut your filthy mouth, Foss!" the chained man spat back.

"Eat me, Kevel!" the prisoner countered. "How do *you* like the chair, eh?"

Huh. Rem moved closer to his cell bars, trying to get a better look. So, this prisoner, Kevel, knew that fellow in the cell, Foss, and vice versa. Part of a conspiracy? Brother marauders, questioned one by one—and in sight of one another—for some vital information?

Then Rem saw it: Kevel, the prisoner in the hot seat, wore a signet pendant around his throat identical to those worn by the prefect and the two guards. It was unmistakable, even in the shoddy light.

"Well, I'll be," Rem muttered aloud.

The prisoner was one of the prefect's own watchmen.

Ex-watchman now, he supposed.

All of a sudden, Rem felt a little sorry for him…but not much. No doubt, Kevel himself had performed the prefect's present actions a number of times: chaining some poor sap into the hot seat, stoking the brazier, using fire and water and physical distress to intimidate the prisoner into revealing vital information.

The prefect, Ondego, stepped away from the brazier and moved to a table nearby. He studied a number of implements—

it was too dark and the angle too awkward for Rem to tell what, exactly—then picked something up. He hefted the object in his hands, testing its weight.

It looked like a book—thick, with a hundred leaves or more bound between soft leather covers.

"Do you know what this is?" Ondego asked Kevel.

"Haven't the foggiest," Kevel said. Rem could tell that he was bracing himself, mentally and physically.

"It's a genealogy of Yenara's richest families. Out-of-date, though. At least a generation old."

"Do tell," Kevel said, his throat sounding like it had contracted to the size of a reed.

"Look at this," Ondego said, hefting the book in his hands, studying it. "That is one enormous pile of useless information. Thick as a bloody brick—"

And that's when Ondego drew back the book and brought it smashing into Kevel's face in a broad, flat arc. The sound of the strike—leather and parchment pages connecting at high speed with Kevel's jawbone—echoed in the dungeon like the crack of a calving iceberg. A few of the other prisoners even wailed as though they were the ones struck.

Rem's cellmate stirred beneath his pile of straw, but did not rise.

Kevel almost fell with the force of the blow. The big guard caught him and set him upright again. The lithe elf backed off, staring intently at the prisoner, as though searching his face and his manner for a sign of something. Without warning, Ondego hit Kevel again, this time on the other side of his face. Once more Kevel toppled. Once more the guard in his path caught him and set him upright.

Kevel spat out blood. Ondego tossed the book back onto the table behind him and went looking for another implement.

"That all you got, old man?" Kevel asked.

"Bravado doesn't suit you," Ondego said, still studying his options from the torture table. He threw a glance at the elf on the far side of the torture pit. Rem watched intently, realizing that some strange ritual was under way: Kevel, blinking sweat from his eyes, studied Ondego; the lady elf, silent and implacable, studied Kevel; and Ondego idly studied the elf, the prefect's thick, workman's hand hovering slowly over the gathered implements of torture on the table.

Then, Kevel blinked. That small, unconscious movement seemed to signal something to the elf, who then spoke to the prefect. Her voice was soft, deep, melodious.

"The amputation knife," she said, her large, unnerving, honey-colored eyes never leaving the prisoner.

Ondego took up the instrument that his hand hovered above—a long, curving blade like a field-hand's billhook, the honed edge being on the inside, rather than the outside, of the curve. Ondego brandished the knife and looked to Kevel. The prisoner's eyes were as wide as empty goblets.

Ingenious! The elf had apparently used her latent mind-reading abilities to determine which of the implements on the table Kevel most feared being used on him. Not precisely the paragon of sylvan harmony and ancient grace that Rem would have imagined such a creature to be, but impressive nonetheless.

As Ondego spoke, he continued to brandish the knife, casually, as if it were an extension of his own arm. "Honestly, Kev," he said, "haven't I seen you feign bravery a hundred times? I know you're shitting your kecks about now."

"So you'd like to think," Kevel answered, eyes still on the knife. "You're just bitter because you didn't do it. Rich men don't get rich keeping to a set percentage, Ondego. They get rich by redrawing the percentages."

Ondego shook his head. Rem could be mistaken, but he thought he saw real regret there.

"Rule number one," Ondego said, as though reciting holy writ. "Keep the peace."

"Suck it," Kevel said bitterly.

"Rule number two," Ondego said, slowly turning to face Kevel, "Keep your partner safe, and he'll do the same for you."

"He was going to squeal," Kevel said, now looking a little more repentant. "I couldn't have that. You said yourself, Ondego—he wasn't cut out for it. Never was. Never would be."

"So that bought him a midnight swim in the bay?" Ondego asked. "Rule number three: let the punishment fit the crime, Kevel. Throttling that poor lad and throwing him in the drink...that's what the judges call cruel and unusual. We don't do cruel and unusual in my ward."

"Go spit," Kevel said.

"Rule number four," Ondego quickly countered. "And this is important, Kevel, so listen good: never take more than your share. There's enough for everyone, so long as no one's greedy. So long as no one's hoarding or getting fat. I knew you were taking a bigger cut when your jerkin started straining. There's only one way a watchman that didn't start out fat gets that way, and that's by hoarding and taking more than his fair share."

"So what's it gonna be?" Kevel asked. "The knife? The razor? The book again? The hammer and the nail-tongs?"

"Nah," Ondego said, seemingly bored by their exchange, as though he were disciplining a child that he'd spanked a hundred times before. He tossed the amputation knife back on the table. "Bare fists."

And then, as Rem and the other prisoners watched, Ondego, prefect of the watch, proceeded to beat the living shit out of Kevel, a onetime member of his own watch company. Despite the fact that Ondego said not another word while the beating commenced, Rem thought he sensed some grim and unhappy purpose in Ondego's corporal punishment. He never once smiled, nor even gritted his teeth in anger. The intensity of the beating never flared nor ebbed. He simply kept his mouth set, his eyes open, and slowly, methodically, laid fists to flesh. He made Kevel whimper and bleed. From time to time he would stop and look to the elf. The elf would study Kevel, clearly not simply looking at him but *into* him, perhaps reading just how close he was to losing consciousness, or whether he was feigning senselessness to gain some brief reprieve. The elf would then offer a cursory, "More." Ondego, on the elfmaid's advice, would continue.

Rem admired that: Ondego's businesslike approach, the fact that he could mete out punishment without enjoying it. In some ways, Ondego reminded Rem of his own father.

Before Ondego was done, a few of the other prisoners were crying out. Some begged mercy on Kevel's behalf. Ondego wasn't having it. He didn't acknowledge them. His fists carried on their bloody work. To Kevel's credit he never begged mercy. Granted, that might have been hard after the first quarter hour or so, when most of his teeth were on the floor.

Ondego only relented when the elf finally offered a single word. "Out." At that, Ondego stepped back, like a pugilist retreating to his corner between melee rounds. He shook his hands, no doubt feeling a great deal of pain in them. Beating a man like that tested the limits of one's own pain threshold as well as the victim's.

"Still breathing?" Ondego asked, all business.

The human guard bent. Listened. Felt for a pulse. "Still with us. Out cold."

"Put him in the stocks," Ondego said. "If he survives five

days on Zabayus's Square, he can walk out of the city so long as he never comes back. Post his crimes, so everyone sees."

The guards nodded and set to unchaining Kevel. Ondego swept past them and mounted the stairs up to the main cell level again, heading toward the door. That's when Rem suddenly noticed an enormous presence beside him. He had not heard the brute's approach, but he could only be the sleeping form beneath the hay. For one, he was covered in the stuff. For another, his long braided hair, thick beard, and rough-sewn, stinking leathers marked him as a Kosterman. And hadn't Rem heard Koster words muttered by the sleeper in the hay?

"Prefect!" the Kosterman called, his speech sharply accented.

Ondego turned, as if this was the first time he'd heard a single word spoken from the cells and the prisoners in them.

Rem's cellmate rattled the bars. "Let me out of here, little man," he said.

Kosterman all right. The long, yawning vowels and glass-sharp consonants were a dead giveaway. For emphasis, the Kosterman even snarled, as though the prefect were the lowest of house servants.

Ondego looked puzzled for a moment. Could it be that no one had ever spoken to him that way? Then the prefect stepped forward, snarling, looking like a maddened hound. His fist shot out in front of him and shook as he approached.

"Get back in your hay and keep your gods-damned head down, con! I'll have none of your nonsense after such a bevy of bitter business—"

Rem realized what was about to happen a moment before it did. He opened his mouth to warn the prefect off—surely the man wasn't so gullible? Maybe it was just his weariness in the wake of the beating he'd given Kevel? His regret at having to so savagely punish one of his own men?

Whatever the reason, Ondego clearly wasn't thinking straight. The moment his shaking fist was within arm's reach of the Kosterman in the cell, the barbarian reached out, snagged that fist, and yanked Ondego close. The prefect's face and torso hit the bars of the cell with a heavy clang.

Rem scurried aside as the Kosterman stretched both arms out through the bars, wrapped them around Ondego, then tossed all of his weight backward. He had the prefect in a deadly bear hug and was using his body's considerable weight to crush the man against the bars of the cell. Rem heard the other two watchmen rushing near, a flurry of curses and stomping boots. Around the dungeon, the men in the cells began to curse and cheer. Some even laughed.

"Let me out of here, now!" the Kosterman roared. "Let me out or I'll crush him, I swear!"

Rem's instincts were frustrated by his headache, his thirst, his confusion. But despite all that, he knew, deep in his gut, that he had to do something. He couldn't just let the hay-covered Kosterman in the smelly leathers crush the prefect to death against the bars of the cell.

But that Kosterman was enormous—at least a head and a half taller than Rem.

The other watchmen had reached the bars now. The stubble-faced one was trying to break the Kosterman's grip while the elfmaid snatched for the rattling keys to the cells on the human guard's belt.

Without thinking, Rem rushed up behind the angry Kosterman, drew back one boot, and kicked. The kick landed square in the Kosterman's fur-clad testicles.

The barbarian roared—an angry bear, indeed—and Rem's gambit worked. For just a moment, the Kosterman released his hold on the prefect. On the far side of the bars, the stubble-faced watchman managed to get the prefect in his grip and yank him backward, away from the cell. When Rem saw that, he made his next move.

He leapt onto the Kosterman's broad shoulders. Instead of wrapping his arms around the Kosterman's throat, he grabbed the bars of the cell. Then, locking his legs around the Kosterman's torso from behind, he yanked hard. The Kosterman was driven forward hard, his skull slamming with a resonant clang into the cell bars. Rem heard nose cartilage crunch. The Kosterman sputtered a little and tried to reach for whoever was on his back. Rem drew back and yanked again, driving the Kosterman forward into the bars once more.

Another clang. The Kosterman's body seemed to sag beneath Rem.

Then the sagging body began to topple backward.

Clinging high on the great, muscular frame, Rem realized that he was overbalanced. He lost his grip on the cell bars, and the towering Kosterman beneath him fell.

Rem tried to leap free, but he was too entangled with the barbarian to make it clear. Instead, he simply disengaged and went falling with him.

Both of them—Rem and the barbarian—hit the floor. The Kosterman was out cold. Rem had the wind knocked out of him and his vision came alight with whirling stars and dancing fireflies.

Blinking, trying to get his sight and his breath back, he heard the whine of rusty hinges, then footsteps. Strong hands seized him and dragged him out of the cell. By the time his vision had returned, he found himself on the stone pathway outside the cell that he had shared with the smelly, unconscious Kosterman. The prefect and his two watchmen stood over him.

"Explain yourself," Ondego said. He was a little disheveled, but otherwise, the Kosterman's attack seemed to have left not a mark on him, nor shaken him.

Rem coughed. Drew breath. Sighed. "Just trying to help," he said.

"I'll bet you want out now, don't you?" Ondego asked. "One good turn deserves another and all that."

Rem shrugged. "It hadn't really crossed my mind."

Ondego frowned, as though Rem were the most puzzling prisoner he had ever encountered. "Well, what do you want, then? I can be a hard bastard when I choose, but I know how to return a favor."

Rem had a thought. "I'm looking for work," he said.

Ondego raised one eyebrow.

"Seeing as you have space on your watch rosters"—Rem gestured to the spot where they had been beating Kevel in the torture pit—"perhaps I could impress upon you—"

Ondego seemed to appraise Rem honestly for a moment. For confirmation of his instincts, he looked to the elf.

Rem suddenly knew the strange sensation of another living being poking around in his mind. It was momentary and fleeting and entirely painless, but eminently strange and unnerving, like having one's privates appraised by the other patrons in a bathhouse. Then the elf's probing intellect withdrew, and Rem no longer felt naked. The elfmaid seemed to wear a small, knowing half smile. Her dark and ancient eyes settled on Rem and chilled him.

She knows everything, Rem thought. *A moment in my mind, two, and she knows everything. Everything worth knowing, anyway.*

"Harmless," the elfmaid said.

"Weak," the stubble-faced guardsmen added.

The elf's gaze never wavered. "No."

"You don't impress me," Ondego said, despite the elf's appraisal. "Not one bit."

"No doubt I don't," Rem said. "But, by Aemon, sir, I'd like to."

The watchman beside Ondego leaned close. Rem heard the words he whispered to the prefect.

"He did get that brute off you, sir."

Ondego and the big watchman continued to study him. The elf now turned her gaze on the boisterous prisoners in the other cells. A moment's eye contact was all it took. As the elfmaid turned her stone idol's glare on each of them, they fell silent and withdrew from the bars. Bearing witness to the effect the elf's silent, threatening stare had on those hard, desperate men made Rem's skin crawl.

But, to his own predicament: Rem decided to mount a better argument—he certainly couldn't end up in any more trouble, could he?

"You're down two men," Rem said, trying to look and sound as reasonable as possible. "That man you were beating and the partner he murdered. Surely you can give me the opportunity?"

"What's he in here for?" Ondego asked the watchman.

Rem prepared himself to listen. He was still trying to reason that part out himself.

"Bar brawl," the stubble-faced watchman said. "The Bonny Prince here was casting dice with some Koster longshoremen. Rolled straight nines, nine times in a row. They called him a cheat and he lit into them."

It was coming back now. Rem remembered the tavern. He'd been waiting for someone. A girl. She hadn't shown. He'd had a little too much to drink while waiting. He vaguely remembered the dice and the longshoremen—two tall fellows, not unlike the barbarian he'd just tussled with in the cell.

He couldn't recall their faces, or even starting a fight with them...but he did remember being called a cheat, and taking umbrage.

"I wasn't cheating," Rem said emphatically. "It was just a run of good luck."

"Not so good," Ondego said, "seeing as you're here in my dungeon." To the guardsmen beside him: "Where are the other two?"

"Taken to the hospital, sir," the big man said. "Beaten senseless by the Bonny Prince here."

"And a third Kosterman, out like a light on my dungeon floor. What is it with you and these northerners, boy?"

Rem shrugged. "Ill-starred, I guess."

Ondego seemed to appraise Rem anew. Three Kostermen on their backs was bold, and he couldn't deny it. "Doesn't look like much," the prefect said, as if to himself, "but he can hold his own in a fight."

Ondego was impressed with Rem—no thanks to the stone-faced watchman laying that damned "Bonny Prince" label on him. Rem guessed that Ondego's grudging respect might work in his favor.

"I don't like being called a cheat," Rem said, "first and foremost because I don't cheat. Ever."

Ondego nodded toward Kevel, limp in his chair. "Neither do we," he said.

"So I see," Rem answered.

A long silence fell between them.

"Get him on his feet," Ondego said. "We'll try him out."

Without another word, the prefect left.

Rem looked to the tall man. He felt a smile blooming on his face, then suddenly felt the pain of his brawl the night before. A swollen, split lip; a bruised nose; at least one missing tooth, far back in his mouth; the taste of old blood.

The big man offered a hand and yanked Rem to his feet. Upright, Rem swooned for a moment, his vision briefly going black again before finally clearing.

"Don't look so pleased with yourself, my bonny boy," the stubble-faced watchman said. "You've no idea what you're in for walking the ward."

CHAPTER TWO

This, Rem thought, was a stroke of good fortune, indeed. He'd been in Yenara for almost a week now, his purse was growing dangerously light, and he had yet to find paying work. He thought himself qualified for a great many things—he could read and write in three tongues, he was good with horses and strong enough to put in an honest day's labor—but somehow, employment in Yenara had eluded him. Each day, as his coin dwindled, he tried to tell himself that it was just a matter of time, that he would find something suitable if only he kept searching. But what could he hope for when even the carpenters and stonemasons of the city seemed to have too many strong backs on their payrolls? When he was told, time and again, that there was not enough paying, unskilled labor to be had in the city? And unskilled labor was, by and large, all that was open to him: trading on his courtly, lettered background might expose him, and he could not risk that, even so far from home.

In truth, that's what had gotten him into trouble the night before. He'd been in that tavern for one purpose and one alone—to meet a young lady he had spoken with in the market that very afternoon—but when those Kostermen asked if he'd like to join their dice game, Rem couldn't resist. Why not try to turn his last half dozen silver andies into a full dozen, or two dozen? Why not let fate decide his future?

He probed the empty space where a tooth once rooted with

his tongue. Clearly, throwing dice was not his game. Despite his winning streak.

But here, at last, was an opportunity: he would join the wardwatch! He could certainly make a go of that, couldn't he?

Two flights of stairs took them from the dungeons back up to the ground floor of the watchkeep. The watchman leading Rem, called Hirk, was the sergeant-at-arms and second-in-command after Prefect Ondego. He didn't speak much, so when he did, Rem paid close attention. In his experience, taciturn men rarely wasted their breath on chit-chat.

"Did you understand what was going on down there?" Hirk asked.

"I think so," Rem said. "Kevel was skimming off the fines he collected."

"Bright boy," Hirk said grimly. "You understand why that's a bad idea?"

"Because it throws off the natural order of the world, denies resources to those in need of them, and undermines the chain of command?"

Hirk stopped on the stairs and turned. Rem couldn't tell if he was pleasantly surprised or simply incredulous. "Where are you from, boy?"

"Up north," Rem said. "From Hasturland, around Great Lake."

"You a lordling?" Hirk asked.

Rem shook his head immediately. "No, sir," he lied. "Though, I was raised in a lord's house. My father was a groom. For a lord, that is."

Hirk stared, eyes narrow. "So you're good with horses?"

Rem nodded. "Very good, sir."

"Not much use for horses on this job," Hirk countered, then continued up the stairs. Rem followed.

When they reached the ground floor, the world was suddenly full of air and light that Rem hadn't realized he missed being down in those dungeons. The inner walls of the watchkeep were thick and solid, like a castle redoubt, but their arrangement and the windows at the front and back of the building allowed air to flow through and kept the place from seeming stuffy. Granted, the air had the slightly fetid tang of low tide, horseshit, and human sweat about it, but it beat the moldy drear of the dungeons any day.

The place was full of activity. They passed a chamber redolent of onions and hot bread that Rem assumed to be a mess hall. Beyond the door to the mess, Rem saw a corridor crowded with dozens of petitioners held back by stout ropes looped through iron rings in the walls. They all cried about this or griped about that—looking for locked-up loved ones, trying to collect debts from prisoners they identified by name, demanding that confiscated property be returned to them. A knot of watchwardens—including the familiar elf from the dungeons—stood on the inside of the rope barricade and held the public at bay.

From that corridor, they passed into a vast chamber, this one more administrative. There were desks like those used by monks in a scriptorium, shelves chock full of scrolls and ledgers, along with piles and piles of papyrus, parchment, and vellum. A portion of one wall was crammed with hundreds of portraits, some hand drawn, some printed by woodcut, a select few even painted in full color on vellum or some other sturdy surface. Rem could not be sure, but he guessed those might be the likenesses of fugitives. In the administrative chamber, the watchmen were just as hard and unflappable as those holding back the rabble in the outer hall, but they had an ease about them, being out of the public eye. Rem heard

one fat watchman being ribbed about his penchant for whores
with rich taste and few teeth, while in another corner a trio of
hard-faced watchwardens interrogated a sickly old man who
might have been a witness or a prisoner. At a desk near the
wall, a red-haired, querulous dwarf told a rather shocking joke
to a dour-faced prisoner in irons. Near the back wall, he saw a
pair of female wardens—one tall, frowning, with red-brown
hair cropped close to her head, the other smaller and far more
feminine but just as severe in countenance—trying to extract
a coherent story from a trio of rather genteel male prostitutes.

Hirk led Rem into a dark and narrow back corridor. At the
mouth of the corridor was a strange little alcove, in which stood
a cage of sorts, the kind of fortified booth that a moneylender
might hide inside of. A few watchmen stood in line at the
booth. As they stepped up to the little window therein, they
handed over all manner of items—torques and necklaces, fine
leatherworks, shiny daggers and flashing rings. Each of these
the man inside the cage inspected, made note of in a bound
ledger, then set aside before drawing coin from an unseen cash-
box within arm's reach.

"Our treasurer, Welkus," Hirk said as they passed the little
booth. "When you collect fines, you might sometimes have to
do so in goods, not coin. When that happens, you come here to
Welkus. He records the fine as paid, then gives you your cut."

Rem nodded. A fine system, if a little cumbersome. He
wondered how effective he would have to be in appraising the
items offered by lawbreakers in lieu of payment. If he took a
gold bracelet in lieu of a six-andi fine, and this Welkus only felt
the bracelet worth four andies, would Rem then be responsible
for the balance? All because he didn't have a pawnbroker's eye
for an item's trade value?

"Keep up," Hirk said. Rem realized he had fallen behind,

lingering to study the trade unfolding at the treasurer's window. He quickened his pace and followed Hirk down that dark, close little hallway to their final destination.

That destination turned out to be a storeroom or armory of sorts, crammed with shelves and drawers full of bric-a-brac: daggers, maces, and jewelry; swords, spears, axes, and dented shields; old Wanted posters faded by time, piles of strange old books that were clearly not ledgers (given their hasps of bone or gold and the bizarre writing on their covers), even a few stuffed beasts of strange lineage—creatures that Rem had probably read about in fairy tales and forgotten the names of long ago. Rem had seen a cabinet of curiosities in a duke's castle once that looked something like this, although in place of swords and spears, that duke had displayed dragon bones, rare gems or crystals, and orreries of brass and tin. In both cases, Rem guessed that the keeper of the chamber was the only one capable of finding anything, with a filing system as puzzling and arcane as his holdings.

The keeper of the ward's armory was a droopy-faced old fellow with smiling eyes, a frowning mouth, iron-gray hair, and thick whiskers on his cheeks. He was bent over a desk, comparing ledgers, line by line, and mumbling to himself.

"Eriadus!" Hirk barked.

The old man looked up from his figures. "Sergeant," he said in greeting, then returned to his ledgers.

"Official business, Eriadus," Hirk said. "We need a standard kit. New recruit."

Eriadus, whom Rem assumed to be the quartermaster, raised his eyes again from his ledgers. He studied Hirk for a moment—as though he thought the sergeant-at-arms was joshing him—then turned and noted Rem. He looked rather upset by Rem's shoddy appearance.

"Aemon's wounds, what happened to him?"

"Barroom brawl last night," Hirk said, "joining the ward-watch today. Neat and tidy, eh?"

"Does that hurt?" Eriadus asked.

Rem nodded and managed a smile. The smile pained him, but he wanted both of these men to know that a swollen eye, a split lip, and a missing tooth wouldn't keep him down for long. "Just bruises," Rem said. "They'll heal."

"That's the spirit," Eriadus said.

"Eriadus?" Hirk prodded.

Eriadus went rifling through the drawers nearby, then slowly started to work his way back into the stacks of detritus. Rem allowed his eyes to dance about the room, taking in all the flotsam and jetsam around him, following the tumbling lines of old sabers, blunt polearms, seized cuirasses and leather armor, cartloads of scrolls and fragments of old sculptures that looked long past their prime and strangely incomplete. At last his gaze came to rest on an enormous, three-dimensional bas relief laid out on a vast table in an alcove to his right. His mouth fell open.

It was a map of Yenara, so detailed that it was a work of art. The packed earth looked like real earth, dusted here and there with patches of grass; certain streets were paved with tiny cobbles; and the waters of the harbor and the bay looked like ice, vaguely transparent, but frosted in their immobility. There were even little wooden ships stuck in the cresting waves. Rem reached out to touch it.

"Don't," Hirk said quietly. "Eriadus will have your hand. He built that himself, and he keeps it up-to-date. Every time there's a fire, every time a new tower or manse goes up, he goes out, sketches the altered space, then comes back here and makes changes. Ondego wanted it out in the main chamber, but Eriadus won't let it out of his sight, so we sometimes have meetings in here, just so we can refer to the map."

"It's fine work," Rem said, honestly amazed. He'd always had a soft spot for quality modeling. His father's architects, with their scale models of the manses or strongholds they intended to build, always fascinated him.

"Pay attention," Hirk said, stepping up to the map. "How well do you know this city?"

Rem shrugged. "I've been here a few days."

"Not at all, then," Hirk said. "This bitch is far too complicated to reveal all her secrets in such a short time. So, look here—"

Rem watched, as he was told. The city was more or less ovoid in shape, longest from northeast to southwest, roughly bisected along its length by the meandering line of the Embrys River. There was a great bite out of the northwestern quadrant of that oval, where twin harbors—one to the north of the river, one to the south—cut into the cityscape.

"Here's the city," Hirk said, indicating the whole of the map. "It's broken up into five wards, and each ward has a prefect. Ondego, he's ours. This is the Fifth Ward." He pointed to the fork of land at the northeastern quarter of the city that wrapped around the northern harbor like a loose fist. "Our ward's got the most land area and the densest population, but we've got the same hundred-odd watchmen as the other wards."

Rem raised an eyebrow. "Not sporting, is it? I'll bet the city magistrate's always on you because the other wards have lower crime rates and make more arrests, per capita."

Hirk stared at Rem like he'd just sung the holy psalms in orcish.

"Am I wrong?" Rem asked.

"No," Hirk said. "You're bloody clairvoyant. Now shut up and listen."

Hirk went on to point out the other wards: the Fourth, just southeast of the Fifth; the First, which incorporated the oldest parts of the city and its municipal center; the Second, where the rich made their homes; and the Third, which covered the waterfront on the south side of the harbor.

"In every ward, the watchmen keep the peace and levy fines on lawbreakers. That's what you'll be doing: walking patrol, finding lawbreakers, and levying fines from them. When it's a serious crime—a violent one—or they can't pay the fine on the spot, you bring 'em in and lock 'em up."

"On the spot?" Rem asked.

"Well, where else?" Hirk asked. "D'you think they're likely to come here to the ward station and hand their coin over once you've called them out and convicted them?"

"Don't they see the judges?"

Hirk shook his head. "The judges only handle cases involving capital punishments. Anyone in danger of hanging, burning, beheading, or gibbeting gets to see a judge. Everyone else pays up when we call them on the cutting floor."

"And what if they don't have coin on them?" Rem asked.

Hirk smiled a little. "You didn't have sufficient coin on you," Hirk said. "Where did you end up?"

Rem nodded. "Dungeons. Right. Do I get a sword?"

As though prepared for his question, Hirk turned, snatched a wooden stave up off a nearby table, and laid it right in Rem's hands.

"You get that," Hirk said.

"A stick," Rem said. "But wouldn't a sword—"

"Can you *use* a sword?" Hirk asked.

"I can," Rem said proudly, because, in fact, he could. Not to brag, but he thought himself quite good with a blade, based on what he'd seen of the men running around in the world.

"Do you *have* a sword?" Hirk asked.

"Not presently," Rem said. In truth, he'd sold it to pay for his journey south, almost four hundred miles and forty days ago.

"Then you're welcome to buy one after you save your coin. As you can see, we've got many here in the armory, and they're available at very reasonable prices. But, at present, we don't provide swords to neophytes."

Rem looked around the armory. "There are enough swords in here for an army. If you've only got a single company of watchwardens, why can't you spare a few?"

Hirk took him by the tunic and shook him. "You sassing me, boy?"

Rem shook his head. "No, sir. Just puzzled."

Hirk thrust him away and gestured toward all the swords on display in the armory. "Those swords are property of the ward. We keep them handy for emergencies and we issue them to the watchmen as needed. Sometimes we bring in duffers off the streets and sell surplus. Get a pretty penny, too."

"Well," Rem asked, "when might I need one?"

"Live through your first ninety days," the sergeant said. "Then we can talk about it. I'm sure we can work out a payment plan—take some coin right out of your wages, until the pigsticker's paid for."

That's when Eriadus returned, bearing with him a bundle of equipment. He laid down the bundle and unrolled it. Before Rem could even take stock of the items laid before him, Eriadus named each.

"Cuirass," he said, displaying a roughened old boiled-leather breastplate that was probably already old when Rem's grand-father had been a lad. "Flint and steel, brass whistle, torches in shoulder scabbard, stave, and badge of office."

Rem studied the badge. It was made of lead, shaped roughly like the city itself, and had a bas relief of the number five in old imperial numerals on it. Although the badge was compact—small enough to be held in one palm—it was still heavy.

"Why lead?" he asked, honestly puzzled.

Eriadus snorted and chuckled to himself. He threw a mirth-ful glance at Hirk and Hirk just shook his head. He laughed as well, although even his laugh sounded like something grumbly and dangerous. Rem's eyes darted back and forth between the laughing pair.

"What's so funny?" he asked.

"'Why lead?'" Eriadus muttered, as though he couldn't believe he'd been asked such a silly question.

"Because it's of no value whatsoever," Hirk spat, "so you'll be in no danger of having it stolen."

Rem was about to ask how many golden or silver badges had to be stolen from the city watch before the watchwardens made the switch to lead, when Eriadus interrupted.

"And," he said, "lead deflects black magic."

"Does it?" Rem asked.

Eriadus shrugged. "So I've heard. Can't hurt, surely?"

Rem shrugged. "Suppose not," he said, and slid into the cuirass. It was stiff as lumber and smelled like a wet aurochs. Once the cuirass was on and the signet chain latched around his throat, he shoved the flint and steel into his pocket, then slung the scabbard with the three torches over his shoulder. He looked to Sergeant Hirk for approval.

The big man nodded. "Look at that," he said. "Almost a watchman."

"And what makes me a watchman at last?" Rem asked good-naturedly.

Hirk scowled as though that were the dumbest question he'd ever heard. "Watching," he said, and marched out of the room.

Rem turned to Eriadus. "Should I follow him?" he asked.

Eriadus threw out his arms. "How should I know?" With that, the old man and his muttonchops went back to their ledgers, and Rem scurried to follow the sergeant back out to the administration chamber.

CHAPTER THREE

Hirk next took Rem to Ondego's office. There, Rem was told
to sit on a very hard and uncomfortable wooden chair and submit himself to a line of questions that Ondego asked with a
strange mix of boredom and intensity. Clearly, they were questions he had asked before.

"What's your name?"

"Rem."

"Short for?"

"Remeck."

"And you're from?"

"Up north. Hasturland, near Great Lake."

"Whereabouts?"

"Lykos Vale, on the north shore."

Rem wondered if perhaps he should have lied about that
part, but it was too late now.

"Hirk tells me your pappy was a horse groom for a lord."

"True."

"What brings you to Yenara?"

Rem shrugged. "I wanted a change of scenery."

Ondego sighed at that. "Are you now, or have you ever been,
engaged in a criminal enterprise that would interfere with the
prosecution of your duties as a watchman of the Fifth Ward in
this city?"

"No, sir. None whatsoever."

"So you ran away from home," Ondego said, "but you stole nothing in the process?"

Rem started to answer, then paused. "Pardon me, sir?"

"Well?" Ondego pressed. "That's it, isn't it? You ran away from home?"

"Children run away from home," Rem said. "I'm twenty-five years old and bound by no obligations." Not entirely true, but true enough so far as he was concerned. "I didn't run away. I left."

"You wanted a change of scenery," Ondego finished. "Certainly. What horseboy from the north wouldn't want to just leave all that wide-open space and fresh air for a shit-hole like Yenara?"

Ondego was baiting him. Rem kept from arguing. "On the contrary," he said, "I think your city's one of the fairest and most impressive I've ever seen. If there are any to rival it in the world, I've yet to see them."

"Traveled much?" Hirk asked.

"Admittedly, no," Rem said, though he had always wanted to, despite his father's admonitions that there were more pressing matters at home. "But she's a gem, Yenara is."

"A dirty gem," Ondego said. "A crowded, festering, unpolished gem rife with dens of iniquity and overcome by her own blind lust for power and gold and the indulgences of vice. She's a crossroads where Koster reavers from the north, Isolian merchants from the south, orcs and dwarves from the mountains, and elves from Aadendrath in the west all come to trade. And while they're here, they have a knack for drinking too much, whoring too much, gambling too much, or digging a little too deep for their vice of choice. Many end up drawing steel or coming to blows. Some end up dead. That's your gem, boy. She likes to make promises she'll never keep, drive men toward collision, and sit by laughing as her victims bawl and bleed. That's Yenara, and don't you forget it."

"As you say, sir," Rem answered. And he meant this part down to his bones: "Right here, right now, there's no place I'd rather be."

Ondego stared at him for a long time, appraising him. At last, that appraisal seemed to conclude. The older man smiled and nodded, the weariness never leaving his dark eyes. "She *is* a splendid, foggy old wench, isn't she?"

Rem smiled broadly. "I've never seen her like," he said, "and wager I never will again."

"Any objection to catchpole work?"

Rem blinked. "Catchpole...?"

"Chicken chasing," Ondego said. "Nabbing debtors. In addition to bracing burglars, busting brawls, catching cutpurses, fettering footpads, and stirring stewmaids, we sometimes roust out debtors for the more up-and-up moneylenders of the city. I trust jackbooting for coinmongers doesn't offend your delicate sensibilities?"

Rem shook his head. "I suppose not. Every man should pay his debts."

"Glad to hear it," Ondego said. "That's why we'll be withholding your brawling fine from your first pay purse."

Rem's mouth worked, but no words came out. Maybe this hadn't been such a good idea after all.

Ondego looked to Hirk. "I like him," he said. Then he looked back to Rem and leveled a finger. "That's provisional, you understand. I can revoke my admiration at any time, given the right circumstances."

"Entirely understood," Rem said. "When do I start?"

Ondego looked to Hirk again. "Who should we hand him to? Djubal? Klutch?"

Hirk shook his head. "Those two are attached at the hip," he said. "They won't want a third, and they won't separate. Bad idea."

Ondego seemed to prickle slightly. "Well, fine, then. Varenus?"

"Too stiff."

"Sliviwit?"

"Not stiff enough."

"Hildebran?"

"For this one? Hildebran'll tear him apart."

"Queydon?"

"Too elvish."

"So I wasn't seeing things," Rem interjected. "You actually have an elf among your watchwardens?"

"Indeed we do," Ondego said. "Gone to the roads, that one. Their own kind don't take to them much once they've turned their backs on their dainty little treehouses and made their homes among us."

"Quite the pain in my backside," Hirk answered. "She's a great watchwarden, but poor company. You know elves. Aloof. Prone to skulking."

"They say they don't do it on purpose," Rem said. "Skulking, that is. It just comes naturally."

"We've got two dwarves as well," Ondego said. "Say, what about—"

And that was when the door to Ondego's office burst open on its hinges. It swung into the little room with such a racket that all three men—Rem, Hirk, and Ondego—were taken aback and expelled gasps from their gaping mouths. A small broad figure stomped into the room, swept right past Rem, and hove up to Ondego's desk.

The newcomer was a dwarf—and not the jocular fellow that

Rem had seen earlier. He was four feet tall and almost as wide at the shoulders, but in the manner of dwarves, not fat—just stout, like a stunted oak tree. This one had shaved his pate bald, but had long mustaches and muttonchops that arced over his ears and ended in foxtails at the base of his round, bald head. His drooping mustaches were tied into tails as well.

The dwarf threw up his long, thick arms and roared, *"Where the bloody hell is he?"*

"Who would that be?" Ondego asked, nonplussed.

"That no-good, wayward, wine-besotted partner of mine, that's who!" the dwarf roared. His voice was deep and raspy, like a rusty old hinge or a dull saw working on dense lumber.

Ondego looked to Hirk. Hirk just shrugged. "Been busy with the Bonny Prince," he said, nodding toward Rem. "I haven't seen Freygaf this evening."

The dwarf suddenly turned and looked at Rem, as though just realizing that a stranger was in their midst. His face twisted up in seeming disgust. "Who's he?" he asked.

Rem offered his hand. "Call me Rem," he said. "I'm new to the watch."

The dwarf's right hand struck. Rem thought he was about to strike Rem's offered hand aside, but he did something else: he grabbed his hand and turned it palm upward, eager for a good look at Rem's flesh. After a long examination, the dwarf tossed his hand away.

"Scrivener's hands," he said. "Bonny Prince, indeed. This whelp's been counting money and writing letters all his life."

"Nonetheless, we're two men down," Ondego said. "And he volunteered."

"Where'd you find him?" the dwarf snarled. "Looks like you scooped him out of the gutter."

"Close," Hirk said. "We locked him up last night. He beat

the cack out of a couple of stevedores, both a lot rougher and meaner than the prince here."

"Is that right?" the dwarf asked. He still seemed incredulous, but that incredulity was tempered now.

"So, you can't find Freygaf?" Ondego asked.

The dwarf grunted and shook his head.

"Well, then, that works out just perfectly."

Rem realized what was about to happen. He looked to Hirk. Hirk was fighting the bloom of a broad grin on his stubbly face.

"Rem," Ondego said, "this is Torval. Torval, this is Rem—your partner for the evening."

The dwarf, Torval, looked like he'd just been handed a leper and told to wipe its backside with his bare hands. "The hell you say," Torval growled.

"Thank that no-good partner of yours," Ondego said, his tone announcing that there would be no discussion. "Maybe if he'd shown up for work instead of sleeping one off, I'd have handed the Bonny Prince here to someone else."

Torval glared at Rem for a good, long while. Finally, scowling, he turned and marched out of the office. Rem looked to Hirk, then to Ondego. "Are you sure about this?"

"Better get going," Ondego said, smiling a little.

"He hates to get a late start," Hirk added.

Rem hurried after his partner.

Before leaving the watchkeep, Torval snagged a sentry's lantern made of wrought iron and tin and made sure its wick was lit. This was, he told Rem, one of the most basic requirements of being a watchwarden: each patrol pair carried such a lantern, so that they could easily find their way, even down the darkest of side streets, and likewise, be easily recognized.

"If we've got the lantern," Rem asked, "what are these torches for?" He pointed to the three pitch-smelling sticks in the scabbard slung across his back.

"Emergencies," Torval said, and picked up a last piece of gear in his free hand. It was a maul—a long steel shaft with a hammerhead on one side and a nasty-looking spike on the other. Lantern in one hand, maul in the other, Torval led Rem into the streets outside the watchkeep.

Since he did not remember being brought to the watchkeep in the first place, Rem studied his surroundings carefully upon emerging. Night had fallen, but the square just outside the keep was still lively and full of people. The centerpiece of the square was a fountain built around a weatherworn marble statue of some ancient dictator on a rearing horse. Some of the people milling about the square came to collect water from the fountain, others took it from the well that stood nearby. Many more lingered, standing on the flagstones surrounding the fountain or in the muddy streets that led away from it. Already the air was cool, a wan fog crept up from the waterfront, and a lone flamebearer made his rounds in the square, lighting the post lamps that ringed it.

Rem quickened his pace, since Torval was already halfway across the square. Opposite the watchkeep Rem saw a glowering gray temple with stone columns carved to look like trees and a high pitched roof covered in iron-gray slate. Rem recognized the gloomy edifice as a temple to the Gods of the Mount, the gloomy, ancient deities of fire, ice, stone, and storms worshipped by most of the barbarian sorts from Kosterland to the Ironwall Mountains.

Squatting beside it was a sporting house, appropriately marked by a little red lantern out front, complete with scantily clad men and women shimmying on its terrace, while the sound of lute music tinkled within. As he crossed the square and the wind changed, he smelled fresh-baked bread, then hay and horseshit.

"What is this place?" Rem asked the dwarf when he caught up to him.

"Sygar's Square," Torval said, cocking his head toward the statue atop the fountain.

Rem studied the statue again. "That's Sygar?"

"Sygar the Dynast," Torval said, as though repeating a tiresome lesson he'd been required to cover before. "Succeeded Decicus the Bloody, almost thirteen hundred years ago. Couple decades back, some rich twat decided Yenara needed to be reminded of its bravest and boldest forebears and commissioned statues for every ward."

"It's a lively spot," Rem noted. "And at least there's bread and water nearby."

"Yeah, whores and horseshit, too," Torval added. "Convenient. So, what's your name, longshanks? What do the soft-haired ladies of the north call you?" He led Rem out of the square, marching evenly and with purpose, broad little shoulders swinging.

"Rem. Short for Remeck. How did you know I was from up north?"

"Think I can't hear the lilt of the north in your speech? Rem'll do," the dwarf answered. "What brings you to our fair city?"

Rem shrugged. It wasn't that he didn't know what brought him; it was, rather, that he hadn't worked out a suitable answer yet for the curious who asked him. "Change of scenery, I suppose."

Torval hawked and spat a wad of phlegm onto the muddy street. "No fair meadows and rolling hills hereabouts," Torval growled.

"Well, the city's got her own charms," Rem countered.

Torval shrugged. "Some say so."

In the distance, Rem heard bells ringing. They were sono-rous and groaning and they sounded at regular intervals. Those would be the hourly bells from the Great Temple of Aemon, toward city center. Rem had grown accustomed to them since his arrival. Every hour, regular as the turning of a wheel, they clanged mournfully to keep Yenarans apprised of the progress of their days and nights. This time, Rem counted nineteen ala-rums. It was an hour past sunset. The workday was done and the city's nightly revelry was just under way.

From the muddy street that curved out of the square, the dwarf led them onto a broad, winding cobblestoned avenue. Rem's memory of the night before returned slowly, clearer and brighter, and he realized that he recognized this path. He knew, for instance, that there was a long line of mummeries and minstrel halls behind them, and ahead on their right, they would pass a tavern that he now recalled—the Knobby Gobby, sporting a colorful shingle of a goblin with a knotty head and crossed eyes. Rem had snickered at that shingle the night before. Beyond the tavern, he knew they would find an intersection of several streets ringed with post lamps and more alehouses, the five streets that met there all unraveling in dif-ferent directions, like the far-flung points of a star. The widest avenue of that pentangle square would empty onto one of the several stone footbridges that spanned the North Canal. From there, the main paved avenue would lead them down toward the waterfront.

"Stop it," Torval barked. He tucked his maul under the arm that held the lantern.

"Stop what?" Rem asked.

"Admiring the scenery," Torval said, shaking one thick

sausagelike finger in Rem's face. "Your gob's hanging open and your eyes are everywhere but where they should be."

"Where should they be?" Rem asked.

Torval cuffed him a good one behind his left ear.

"Ow!"

"Watch the street," Torval snarled. "Don't gawk and window-shop. You're looking for criminal enterprise, domestic disturbance, and sundry upsets to the well-being of this district in our fair city. Got that?"

"You didn't have to hit me," Rem said, trying to maintain some sort of dignity.

With lightning speed, the dwarf gave him another cuff—this one on the right side. They were quick like that, dwarves. Deceptively so, considering their bulky construction and short stature. Rem supposed he should be glad Torval didn't use the lamp he held as a bludgeon.

Torval leveled a finger in Rem's face. "There," he said. "I just hit you again. The question is, why? Why was I able to smack you twice headwise when you're supposed to be a watchwarden on duty? When you're supposed to have your eyes peeled and your gob shut? Where's your ugly stick, anyway?"

Rem brandished the stick, gripped in his right hand, swinging at his side. Despite his failure to use it to defend himself, Rem was about to give Torval a perfectly good explanation for why he'd been admiring the scenery—he was reconstructing the night before—when Torval's left hand struck once more, whistling toward Rem's cheek for an openhanded strike. Rem caught the hand in midair and stared down into Torval's burning gaze.

The glare of condescension never left the dwarf's eyes. "There now," he said, "the Bonny Prince is learning."

"I'm not a prince," Rem spat back. "And I don't care to be called one."

"And what would you like to be called, boy? Longshanks? Freckles? Gingersnap?"

Rem considered his answers carefully. "Rem will do, you obstreperous pickmonkey."

He expected another strike. Dwarves didn't generally care to be called pickmonkeys—just like orcs didn't care to be called huffers or mudknuckles and elves didn't care to be called fauneys or gawkylumbers. But it was a measured response: Rem had to see if this unpleasant little fellow really was hostile, or if he was just trying to bait him. If he was truly hostile, then he'd strike again, proving he could dish it out but couldn't take it.

But Torval didn't strike. His eyes finally started smiling, even though his mouth didn't move. He took his maul back in hand again and nodded approvingly. "That's better," the dwarf said. "No more of this wide-eyed country mouse in the big city cack. Come on, then."

Torval turned and kept walking. Rem followed, shocked that his ploy had worked.

"You know I didn't mean it," Rem said. "That 'pickmonkey' thing."

Torval waved him off. "Sure you didn't," he said. "That's the attitude you need hereabouts, though. Cultivate it. And just so you know, I haven't hoisted a pick in years. Not since you were a wee lad, most like."

"You've been here that long?" Rem asked. It really *was* unusual. Dwarves who came down out of the mountains, leaving behind their clans and guilds and smithies for city life were few and far between—or so Rem assumed.

"Aye," Torval answered. "Tired of the mines. Tired of the whole bloody mess."

Rem caught something in Torval's voice. Regret, perhaps a little sadness. For just a moment, Rem considered pressing for more information. Then he decided he had neither the right nor had he earned the respect of this dwarf to go digging into his past. Thus, he simply nodded and kept pace beside him. Soon they crossed the canal.

After a few moments of silence, Torval spoke. "Tell me about the brawl," he said. "Were they really both bigger than you?"

CHAPTER FOUR

Rem told Torval the story, as best he could remember it. In the telling, it seemed to reconstruct itself. He remembered that he had been in a tavern—the Pickled Albatross—to meet a young lady whom he'd noticed at the market earlier that afternoon. He'd struck up conversation with her among the greengrocers' and costermongers' stalls and asked where he could meet her, and the girl had told him—with a little embarrassment, but no attempt at a bald-faced lie—that she was slinging ale most nights at the Pickled Albatross. Her name was Indilen, and his short but pleasant conversation with her in the market had told him that she was far too polished and well-spoken to be just a barmaid.

"I'm actually trying to get scrivener's work," she had explained, brandishing a leather case hanging from a strap at her side—a beautifully tooled secretary set, adorned with an elegant silver seal. "It's not easy, though. People don't seem to see the purpose or value in a lettered woman trying to make a living."

When Rem had simply stared, not understanding what a fine leather purse would have to do with scrivener's work, Indilen had undone the binding buckle and opened the satchel so that he could see its contents. There was a lacquered writing board, some scraps of blank parchment, a few bottles of ink, even a lovely wooden box—which he assumed contained a writing stylus and various high-quality ink nibs—stained dark cherry and bearing inlaid silver filigree and what Rem recognized as both the stylized first letter of Indilen's name as well as an ancient family sigil of some sort. Clearly, the girl had been given the scrivener's set as a gift, meant for her and her alone.

She continued with her lament. "No one who needs a steady pen and good letters seems to believe I can do it," she said, shrugging and closing the satchel again. "They all want to get free work out of me, just to see what I'm capable of, but then they never ask for me to work again. Can't seem to countenance paying me at all, let alone paying me the same wage as a lettered young man."

Rem was truly taken aback by that. While he'd met a number of lettered ladies in his twenty-odd years—the kind who were taught simply as a matter of course, because noble husbands didn't want illiterate wives—he'd never met a working-class one. As they meandered among the stalls, Rem questioned Indilen further and learned that she was from a moneyed merchant family in Wothris, one of Yenara's sister city-states, farther south. As was custom, her elder brother would inherit control of the family's mercantile interests, and her sisters—being of a more provincial stripe—were content to be married off to other well-coined, trade guild–affiliated sons with their own fine villas and cash allowances.

"But not you?" Rem asked, an admiring grin on his face. "The thought of that sort of life—comfort, ease, to be well cared for—doesn't appeal to you?"

Indilen had turned and studied him with a curious look then, eyes narrowed, mouth half smiling, half smirking. She seemed to have something to say to him, but in the end she did not say it. She only shrugged. "Perhaps after I've been out in the world a bit, seen what there is to see and grown weary of it."

"A little intimidating, isn't it?" Rem added. "Traveling to a new place? Being all alone? I know I feel so—sometimes, anyway."

She nodded and studied the wares in the market stalls around them, playfully refusing to look at him again. They were engaged in a bit of a game now—Rem knew the rules well enough—and he was rather enjoying himself. "Perilous, certainly, but I'd like to think I'm reasonable and cautious. I came here with a pilgrim's caravan, just to make sure I arrived in one piece."

She punctuated the statement with a coy look thrown back over her shoulder. "But if strange men in the market keep harassing me, I might just have to hie homeward."

Rem decided to challenge her. "Say the word, miss. I'll leave you be."

Indilen shook her head. "You'll do no such thing, sir. However shabby you might appear, I'm sure you're keeping the groundlings away. I'll keep you close so long as you're useful."

Rem couldn't resist. He smiled. "I can be very useful."

Indilen gave him that strange, crooked grin again. "No doubt—a man with soft hands and courtly speech and fine manners like yourself? Let me guess: you're also a fine rider and handy with a sword?"

That question caught Rem off guard. He felt his hopeful smile flag slightly. She continued.

"If I weren't mistaken, sir," she said, "I might assume I weren't the only well-raised runaway slumming it in this great, grimy city."

For a moment—just a moment—Rem was certain that he'd

lost her; that her astute reading of him meant that she was done with him and ready to be shut of his company.

But no. She kept smiling. Kept staring. She wanted an answer.

"Not me, miss," Rem said, letting his grin widen. "I'm just a humble groom's son from the north."

Indilen raised one thin eyebrow. "That would have been my first guess, certainly."

But, of course, she did not mean that. Rem saw it plainly in her level gaze, her droll, understated half smile: she saw right through his adopted persona and knew well that he was just as out of place—and delighted to be so—on Yenara's streets as she.

That had clinched it. He needed to see Indilen again. And when she finally said that she must be going, she only had an hour before she was expected at work, Rem assured her that he'd be at the Pickled Albatross that evening. When they parted, she seemed happy with that arrangement.

But then, curiously, when he'd come to the tavern that night, she'd been nowhere in sight. He asked about her and everyone had a different answer: no, they hadn't seen her; yes, they'd seen her and she'd been sent on an errand; yes, she'd come in, sold her cunny to a sailor, and was probably in some alleyway, getting poked up against a splintery old fence. Rem decided that all he could do was to wait, and give Indilen a fair chance to show herself. It was possible she didn't want his attention and would avoid the place tonight to keep him from glomming onto her, but it hadn't felt that way at the market. So, he spent a few brasses—nearly his last—on a heel of bread, some salt pork, and a mug of ale, then sat himself down at a corner table to wait.

The longshoremen came after his fifth or sixth mug. Rem was determined to wait all night if need be, but in retrospect, he probably should have paced his guzzling. He'd been getting all warm and fuzzy inside, bleary-eyed, and found himself vaguely annoyed by the whole situation, when those two stevedores sidled up to the table and asked if he'd like to play a round of Roll-the-Bones. It was more fun with three, after all.

Rem accepted their invitation, knowing well that they probably took his relatively clean jerkin and trimmed hair as a sign that he was a toff with coin ripe to be lost. He didn't even mind losing a little coin to them—though he hoped he might win some, seeing as his reserves were getting low. But, truth be told, the main reason he accepted their invitation was that he was bored. He needed to get his mind off Indilen before he lost his patience and left altogether.

"Hopeless," Torval said, interrupting his story yet again. The tale unfolded in episodes as they patrolled the near waterfront— an area just on the far side of the great canal that cut the Fifth Ward in half. Barely two hours into their patrol, Rem felt he had already had a lifetime's education imparted to him. As they meandered through fog-choked, half-lit streets, past grogshops and peculiar dealers, they broke up street brawls, chased a would-be burglar from an alley behind a customs warehouse, stopped two pickpockets and one purse-snatcher, cited a priest of Nasca for proselytizing without a license, and levied an indecency fine from one troubled fellow who'd attempted to hold conjugal congress with a stray goat.

Torval collected all the coin and collateral, for when those cited and fined could not pay, he would gladly accept an item from their person of sufficient value: a torque, a cuff, a ring, or the like. This was Torval's way of educating Rem—showing him how to approach two men (a catcatcher and a dogcatcher) who seemed to be beating up a third (a ratcatcher); how to chase whores and their jacks out of back alleys (because whoring wasn't a crime, but getting tupped in public was, so they needed to go find a room or a darker, more deserted alley); and how to mark a man leading a horse and decide when the horse was too good for the man riding it (muddy breeks and disintegrating shoes bound up with rags were a good indicator), and then, how to challenge that man and make him prove the horse was his.

Most of these stops had yielded neither coin nor crime, but Rem knew what Torval was on about and let him do as he saw fit. He was the veteran, after all, and Rem the student. It wasn't Rem's job to question the lessons Torval thought pertinent.

But, at the moment, Torval was calling horseshit on Rem's insistence that he had been willing to wait in the Pickled Albatross all night, if need be, for the chance to see Indilen again.

"You were really going to sit there from dusk 'til dawn, waiting for this lettered little bint to show herself?" Torval asked. "She made that deep of an impression on you?"

"She did," Rem insisted. "You should've seen her, Torval. Auburn hair. Big brown eyes. And well-spoken, too. I can't tell you what a turnoff a dull-witted woman is."

"You don't have to tell me," Torval said. "On that, we're in agreement. Continue."

So Rem continued with his story, knowing that at any moment, Torval might drag him into a tavern to eyeball cutpurses or lead him down some winding back alley to search for creeping footpads or burglars. Rem covered the dice game, made it clear that he was just as surprised as his opponents that he kept rolling nines, and finally got to the part where things were both abundantly clear and still fuzzy.

"So," he concluded, "they called me a cheat. I took umbrage. I guess after that we traded blows and I ended up in your dungeons with no ken of how I'd gotten there. A lousy hangover, too."

"You're from Hasturland," Torval said. "That's close enough

to Kosterland to know why your dice mates would be put off by a run of nines."

"Sure," Rem admitted, "They might have been Kostermen, and I know the Kosterfolk are superstitious sorts. They think nine is sacred, but what could I do? It really was just dumb luck."

"Dumb, indeed," Torval said.

Torval led them to the door of a new tavern. "Shall we step in for a look about?"

Rem raised an eyebrow, not sure what Torval was getting at. Torval lifted his chin, suggesting that Rem look upward. Rem did so, and saw that the shingle above them was for the Pickled Albatross. He looked to Torval, shocked and grateful all at once.

"Taking pity on me, Old Stump?"

"Pity's the word, for you're a pitiful lad," Torval said. "Besides, I could use a quaff of something before we hit the waterfront."

The tavern was more crowded tonight than Rem remembered it being the night before. Almost every table was filled, and much of the standing room as well. A quick survey of the room told Rem that the clientele were of a shockingly broad cast. Among Koster sailors and stevedores, Estavari bravos and drovers from Hastur and outer marches, he saw a sprinkling of elves gone to the road and more than a few knots of squat, bearded dwarves—most likely not residents but just in town to trade wares or purchase pig iron. Through a low doorway, Rem even thought he saw some orcs in the dooryard beyond, swilling ale beside the horse troughs and tether posts. He wasn't sure if that was because the brutes found the tavern too cramped, or because the owner of the Pickled Albatross urged them to stay there.

He remarked on it to Torval.

"Not so unusual," the dwarf said. "Orctown's just outside the North Gate, not far from here. They'll drink where they can, providing the proprietors let them."

"Hardly sporting," Rem muttered. "If they're not causing trouble."

"Oh, they will," Torval said, perhaps a little too bitterly. "They always do, the mouth-breathing bastards. Save your pity, boy. They don't deserve it."

"What do they come here for, then?" Rem asked. "If they're so unwelcome—"

"Coin," Torval sneered. "Always coin. Up in the mountains, they cultivate poppy, witchweed, and berserker leaf. Eyefever mushrooms, too. They come down to the cities to sell them, or trade them for weapons to go a-butchering with. Hang the lot of them. If I had my way, they'd not be within a hundred miles of any civilized city."

He spat on the sawdust-strewn floor.

Rem was intrigued. He knew well that orcs were considered by most to be ancient enemies of both man- and dwarf-kind, and this is why one seldom encountered them in human settlements outside of cities like Yenara—the largest, the richest, and the most likely to ignore ancient enmities if it meant free trade and fresh coin. But he had seen evidence on the road south— human caravans willingly engaging with roving orc warbands who offered no threat in order to barter for furs or other forest produce—to suggest that, even outside the cities, the necessities and practicalities of everyday commerce often overcame even the most deeply held assumptions about who was or was not worthy of being treated with.

Torval, however, seemed thoroughly committed to his hatred

of orc-kind. The bitter tone of his words alone was enough to convince Rem of that.

A barmaid passed near them. Torval reached out with one long, muscular arm and flagged her down before she could move past. "Oi, lass. You know a girl named Indilen? Auburn hair? Big brown eyes?"

Rem felt himself turn red. The barmaid scrutinized him for a moment as though he were the lowest form of life she'd serve this evening, then shrugged a little. "She never came back. Cupp's in a twist about it."

Torval's tongue worked inside his mouth. "Send Cupp out," Torval said, then tossed a pair of brass coins on the girl's wooden serving tray. "Two Double Drakes. The coin's yours."

The girl smiled, said she'd see to both requests right away, and bustled on.

Torval looked to Rem. "Watchwardens drink free, but it's always good to throw some brass at the barmaids."

Rem glared at Torval. "Was that necessary? Making me out to be some heartsick suitor?"

"Because it embarrassed you?" Torval asked, mouth twisting into an impish grin. "Absolutely."

Soon enough, Cupp appeared. Rem assumed he must be the owner of the place, since he had the imperious nature and permanent air of distraction that marked every tavernkeep Rem had ever known. He was a large man, once muscular, now gone to fat, his arms still strong, but his belly thick.

"I know this one," Cupp said upon seeing Rem. "Do you have any idea what a mess you made in here last night?"

Rem tried to remain cool. He surveyed the room. "Looks like you cleaned up nicely, sir. Many thanks for a memorable evening."

"What's he doing here?" Cupp asked Torval. Clearly the two knew each other. "I hope he's to be whipped! Or at least spend some time in the stocks?"

"Actually, his punishment's far worse," Torval said. "Rem here's now a member of the wardwatch."

"You're joking!"

Torval shook his head. "Dead serious, Cupp. Don't worry—his fines will come out of his first pay purse. What can you tell us about a girl named Indilen?"

"She's fired," Cupp said.

"You fired her?"

"I will when she shows up. Two nights in a row she hasn't. If she's not dead in a ditch or hied to the hills, it's my grave intent to toss her into the street without so much as a copper of her last week's pay. You don't just stiff me like that. I gave her a job when nobody else would and let her get good when she clearly wasn't to start. Some thanks I get..."

Torval looked troubled. "The nerve," he said distractedly.

"What's your interest in her?" Cupp asked.

"The boy here's smitten."

"Is that what kept you here all last night?" Cupp asked Rem sneeringly. "You were waiting on that hoity-toity little bitch?"

"I think you can stop there," Rem said. Why he should take offense over a girl he only met once being called a bitch by her boss was beyond him. Still, something in him rebelled at the thought of Indilen being so named, and he couldn't keep his mouth shut, in spite of his better judgment.

Cupp loomed over him. "See here, boy," he snarled. "I don't give a tin tinker's fart that you're in a cuirass and sportin' the signet. You don't come in here and dictate a thing to me."

Two things happened then that kept Rem from offering a pithy—and potentially provocative—response to Cupp. First, the barmaid returned with their Double Drake ales. Second, there was a sudden row from the far side of the room—the doorway that led out into the livery yard where the orcs drank. An orc stood in the door, nearly filling it, barking at an older barmaid who was doing her best to talk the beast back out into the night. It was no good, though—the orc kept snarling at her, clearly insisting that he had a right to sit in the Pickled Albatross and swill his mead, the dearth of open space notwithstanding.

Torval, quaffing a great mouthful of his ale, looked to Rem. "Well?" he asked.

"What?" Rem said. Torval still hadn't passed him the other mug of Double Drake. Rem felt his mouth watering in anticipation.

"Disturbing the peace," Torval answered. "Go see to it, watchman."

"You're joking," Rem said, snatching another look at the belligerent orc in the doorway, who was now shoving the barmaid aside and stomping into the tavern as though he owned the place.

"Here," Torval said, finally offering Rem the other cup of ale. "A little courage, then off you go."

"This should be good," Cupp snorted.

"I can't," Rem began.

"Then you can slough back to the watchkeep and turn in that cuirass and signet," Torval said, no longer amused by Rem's refusal. "Get your ass over there, fledgling!"

Rem snatched the cup from Torval's hand, gave himself a refreshing mouthful, then handed the cup back and crossed the room. He tightened his grip on the wooden stave in his hand.

CHAPTER FIVE

The orc seemed to grow as Rem approached. It was quite disconcerting. Rem had never seen an orc up close before—he'd grown up too deep in the low country of the north to ever catch more than a fleeting, distant glimpse of one, and he had certainly never treated with them directly. It had a broad, flat face, wide nostrils, beady eyes deep-set beneath a heavy, sloping brow, and a prominent underbite. Its skin was somewhere between the color of a green olive and tarnished steel. It smelled like wet mud and horse dung. Finally drawing up close, Rem realized the orc was a full head taller than he, its shoulders as wide as two of him.

"Excuse me," Rem said, stepping right into the orc's path. It was shoving its way through a tightly packed knot of tables, leaving in its wake a trail of very unhappy patrons. Worse, those patrons were hard men—sailors and horsemen and rogues and cutpurses and gamblers, all more than a little offended that some knuckle-dragging orc from the mountains would dare to shove itself into the midst of their nightly revelry. Rem saw the flash of daggers here and there in the mulling crowd, and realized the moment that he stepped into the orc's path that he smelled sour mead on its breath.

A look into the beast's deep-set, beady little eyes convinced him that the orc was smashingly drunk.

Bollocks.

"I think there's been a misunderstanding," Rem said, the

orc's little pale eyes now focusing on him. "What say we step outside and talk it over, eh?"

The orc snarled, showing its crooked—and very large—yellow teeth. One fist shot out with blinding speed and clamped around Rem's throat. Before Rem could make even the smallest sound of surprise, he'd been lifted off the floor, legs pinwheeling. Both of his hands fell onto the orc's wrists and he struggled to free himself. Already his sight was going bleary, filled with whorls of shadow and bursting stars. Worse, the patrons weren't objecting to the orc's abuse of a watchwarden. They were laughing.

But then a low dark form moved in on Rem's right. He saw that form take up a chair, swing that chair in a wide arc, and shatter it on the orc's left shoulder. The sound the chair made when smashing was so deep, so blunt, that Rem realized it was a stoutly made little chair, and that it took great force to swing it, and greater resistance still to break it.

The orc let Rem go. Down he went, landing on his ass and thumping his head on the rush-strewn plank floor. As his vision cleared, he saw that it was Torval who'd swung the chair.

The dwarf—barely half the size of the drunken orc—lunged right up toward the beast. He raised his maul for emphasis and shook it in the orc's face.

"Oi!" he barked. "He was talking to you, you bloody knuckleback! Get your green arse outside!"

The orc swung at Torval, but the dwarf ducked, then swung his maul and planted a series of savage blows in the creature's abdomen and flanks. The orc roared and bent double. Without hesitation, in a movement so swift it could have been the envy of any Estavari sword master, Torval drew the maul back and brought it arcing down on the orc's bent shoulders. With a *whoof*, the beast went down.

The orc's companions lingered in the doorway, watching their comrade struggle to rise but making no move to assist him. Rem skittered away from the beast, moving crabwise across the floor and dragging himself to his feet on a table some ten feet away. He looked back just in time to see the situation spiral out of hand.

The orc reached out with one long arm to find purchase somewhere, to help itself regain its feet. Unfortunately, it grabbed the lip of a table where two men sat swilling ale and gambling, a pile of throw-down cards and mismatched coin between them. The orc's haphazard groping brought the table down. Both men leapt to their feet, furious that half their deck and all of their money now littered the floor. A few nearby patrons dove for the floor to scoop up the strewn coin. One of the gamblers threw himself at that lot, to keep their grubby hands off their swag. The other gambler shouted curses at the downed orc and lunged toward him, knife sliding out of a sheath at his belt.

When the man attacked the orc, the orcs at the door stomped into the room and beset him, eager to help their companion. More men saw orcs attacking their fellows and decided that could not stand. In moments, a pile of writhing, struggling bodies roiled stormily above the downed orc—who, so far as Rem could see, never managed to regain his feet. Torval, likewise, was buried in the melee. That localized brawl knocked over more tables, and more patrons joined it. New brawls then broke out all across the quaffing floor, the opportunistic orgies of violent men in search of a night's entertainment.

Rem blinked in disbelief. Everyone, it seemed, fought everyone.

Then Torval emerged from the fray above their orcish prisoner. He didn't leave the melee—he simply backed away from it for a moment, got a sense of what was unfolding, then dove in again. Rem watched, amazed, as the dwarf swung his maul to the left and right in broad, flat arcs, stunning men and orcs twice his size with strike after strike, ducking punches, kicks, and whistling blades meant for him, hauling men bodily off the battling orcs then shoving them aside like children, snatching knives out of eager fists and tossing them haphazardly aside to stick in support beams or wooden wall paneling nearby. Torval was a small but vicious storm of steel and fury, and the businesslike way that he tore into the crowd and neutralized each protesting fighter, one by one, took Rem's breath away.

Unlike with orcs, Rem had some experience with dwarves, for they traded in his homeland often. He knew they were fierce adversaries. He'd heard the stories they would tell around the hearth fires of local inns, as well as the tales told by older men who had seen them in action or fought alongside them. But Rem had never seen—nor heard of—one dwarf taking on such an enormous crowd of adversaries before—and winning—with only a steel club in hand.

Surrounded by a gaggle of defeated drunks, beaten brawlers, and delirious bleeding orcs, Torval was at last without impediment. He stood above the drunken, beaten orc that he'd sent Rem to subdue. The beast quivered and thrashed on its back, trying to regain its feet after being trapped beneath the dog pile of angry drinkers. Before it could get upright, Torval was on it. He straddled the beast and leaned right down into its foul face to snarl at it.

"I'm implementing a new policy in your honor, you slope-headed bastard!" Torval shouted. "No huffers in this winesink! Do you hear me, you knuckle-dragging piece of cack?"

The orc roared defiantly. Some of its dazed friends responded in kind.

Torval gave it a mighty head butt that broke its upturned nose. The orc wailed like a child. Its wide nostrils oozed blood. The other orcs fell silent.

As the orc wailed, Torval proceeded to shatter its teeth and jaw with his fists. By the time he was done, the orc was no longer roaring or wailing...it was sobbing, begging for mercy.

Rem's stomach turned. He wasn't sure what sickened him more: the sound of Torval's bare fists striking the orc's thick flesh, again and again, without relent, or the ferocity of Torval's hatred. His broad face was a mask of fury and contempt, but there was an infernal light in his eyes—a sort of feral satisfaction. For the first time that evening, Rem found himself fearing his new partner's wrath.

Torval leapt off the orc and reeled away. The other orcs strewn about scurried out of his path. He wended through the litter of beaten drunks and overturned tables—no easy task amid all that chaos—and made straight for Rem.

Rem managed to stand upright. He opened his mouth to tell Torval how astounded he was. To think that Torval—little Torval, all by himself—could put so many men and orcs on their backs—

Torval punched him. Rem hit the floor.

"Next time," Torval growled, "hit first, ask questions later. Now tie that one up and bring him along."

Away he went. Rem, tasting blood in his mouth and sensing that his lip would be swollen again within the hour, looked to the whimpering, bloodied orc on the tavern floor. He didn't relish approaching the beast, let alone trying to use one of the double sheepshank binders at his belt to immobilize its great, apish hands or urge it along, but he'd already made a mess of it all, hadn't he? Best not to make things worse by balking now.

★   ★   ★

Surprisingly, the orc submitted to being bound and followed Rem out of the Pickled Albatross without resistance. When they emerged into the cool, foggy night to find Torval waiting outside, the beast quailed at the sight of the dwarf and actually cowered. He wasn't afraid to go with Rem, it appeared—just Torval. The orc could sense the dwarf's latent animosity, his unbridled hatred for the whole of the orcish race. Rem tried to calm the brute, but when Torval saw the orc's resistance, he strode to them, grabbed the coils of rope round the orc's wrists, and yanked.

"Not another word," Torval growled, looking up into the orc's broad, flat face like the beast was half his size and not the other way round. Torval then proceeded to search all the pouches at the beast's belt, as well as a leather purse slung across its back. He found a few handfuls of coin, along with two or three morsels partaken-of but wrapped in hanks of roughspun for later—a stale crust of bread, some very smelly salt-cured meat, and a wedge of cheese that was already showing the first signs of green mold.

Torval pocketed the coin, tossed the victuals, and continued his rooting. Just when Rem thought he should end his search—what more was there to find, after all?—Torval suddenly produced a wrapped bundle bound up in cheesecloth from the depths of the orc's deep purse. Torval sniffed the bundle, then tugged at it to open one twine-bound corner. When the bundle was open, Rem immediately got a whiff of something coarse and pungent, a stench like funereal incense, burnt cloves, and cooling pitch.

"Is that witchweed?" Rem asked.

Torval glared up at their sheepish orc prisoner. "It most

certainly is, and a rather large parcel of it as well. Where was this headed, mudknuckle? Planned to sell it off, pinch by pinch, to sailors on the waterfront? Or maybe you had a single buyer willing to part with a bag of gold for such a stash?"

The orc shook its head vehemently. Rem was relieved it didn't bother to deny any of the charges—it simply didn't want to offer specifics, either. Finally, Torval handed the bundle to Rem. Rem wasn't sure what to do with it. If he held it too long, breathed in its strange, mephitic odor too deeply, would he start to see things? Feel strange? Have the vasty deeps of the angels' planes opened before him?

Torval addressed their hulking prisoner again. "Stay quiet and don't give us any trouble. We're off to Gorn Bonebreaker's, then we'll be shut of you. Savvy?"

The orc didn't seem to like the sound of that name, either— Gorn Bonebreaker—but nonetheless it nodded and assented. When Torval handed the lead line on its wrist bonds back to Rem, the orc made no further attempt to overpower them.

"Hold that," Torval said, then marched away.

"Where are you going?" Rem asked.

"The same place you are!" Torval barked. Rem started to follow, but Torval rounded on him again. "Bring the bloody prisoner, you daft knob!"

Rem supposed that was quite a rookie mistake. He circled back to where the bound orc still stood, beside a horse trough and tie post in front of the Pickled Albatross, and yanked at the lead line on the orc's bindings. The brute fell into step behind him. Rem hurried to catch up once more with Torval.

"Aren't we going the wrong way?" Rem asked, trying to catch his breath. "The watchkeep is back the other way, isn't it?"

"We're not going to the watchkeep," Torval said.

Rem waited for an explanation. It felt like a very long time before Torval finally offered one.

"Any orcs we shackle we're obliged to offer up to the ethnarch," the dwarf said, sighing impatiently. "So he can dispense his own justice."

Rem quickened his pace to draw up abreast of Torval. He gave the trailing orc's lead line a yank. "Ethnarch?"

"Babe in the bloody woods," Torval muttered. "In bygone days, treaties were made to protect each race from arbitrary justice by the others. In places like Yenara, where we all mingle, you'll usually find ethnarchs—members of each race whose job it is to dispense justice among their own folk in that city. The orc ethnarch, Gorn Bonebreaker, holds court outside the North Gate, in Orctown. He's little better than an outlaw baron, and we often catch the orcs we deliver up to him later running his nasty little errands. Still, treaties are treaties: if we don't want to risk anarchy and war, we keep them."

"Are there others?" Rem asked. "Ethnarchs?"

"Of course," Torval said. "For us dwarves, there's Eldgrim and Leffi, a husband-and-wife pair, who first came to the city as trade ambassadors. Elves pay homage to a pointy-eared witch with a pleasure garden over in the Second Ward, Ynevena. And, of course, Yenaran law was written by men, so your sort are covered by it."

"How is it," Rem asked, "that you're not subject to Yenaran justice, yet you can enforce it?"

"Ah, but I am," Torval countered. "When one of the elder races joins the wardwatch, we're required to swear an oath and renounce our right to the justice of our ethnarchs."

"Complicated," Rem muttered.

"Not really," Torval said. "Just an expedient. Now hurry up and keep quiet. I'm tired of answering your questions."

Rem shut his mouth and kept pace. At one point, he stole a quick glance over his shoulder to check on their orcish prisoner. The brute shook its head, as though it, too, could not believe how little Rem knew of the ways of the world.

Rem answered the orc's silent impertinence with a belligerent tug on the rope. It followed where they led, docile as a gelded bull.

By and by they reached the North Gate and were waved through by the city guards on duty there—a resplendent bunch compared with the wardwatch, fully armored and liveried in crimson, black, and gold, Yenara's traditional colors. Just outside the North Gate, Rem saw a cluster of dimly lamp-lit buildings huddled in the fog, corralled by a low wall of rough-hewn stones and lorded over at its center by a squat castle keep that he assumed was the home of Gorn Bonebreaker. Torval led Rem and their prisoner down the wide, muddy North Road from the gate, closer by the moment to that haphazard little gathering of hovels and taprooms dubbed Orctown. As they approached, Rem realized that he could hear new sounds emanating from that little enclave—sounds unlike any he'd heard as yet, even on Yenara's crowded, cacophonous streets.

In addition to the guttural dialogues, coarse and boisterous laughter, and foreign curses he expected, Rem heard songs sung in the rough, consonant-heavy tongue of their prisoner, barked into the night like the canticles of warmongering bears. A few humans lingered inside and outside the Orctown gates, men on missions, eager to gather coin or spend it. Smiths hawked arms and armor, fur traders haggled for fresh pelts and hides, and, of course, furtive, shifty-eyed street-corner apothecaries held quiet congress in whispers and grunts with orcs selling narcotics. Witchweed, Rem assumed, along with poppy milk, magic mushrooms, and wake-leaves.

Torval did not seem concerned with the trade going on all around them, so Rem pretended not to care either. Secretly, of course, he was amazed, not so much that the city folk dealt so openly with orcs—considered by most of mankind to be ancient, divinely ordained enemies of the human race—but rather, that the orcs had managed to find for themselves an unassailable business niche in Yenara's rich economy. Who better than woodland vagabonds and mountain bandits, after all, to gather the psychotropic produce of the Ironwall Mountains and the deep, broad forests in their shadows and transport those eagerly sought goods to places where men could buy them? It was a sharp and bitter lesson in just how willing all the races were to put aside their ancient enmities when there was money to be made or vice to be indulged.

Beyond the square they entered a series of narrow, winding streets lit only by the dim lamps flickering outside the alehouse doors they passed. Rem didn't care much for those surroundings, as it was unnervingly dark and impossible to see what cutthroats or marauders might lie in wait for them. Still, Torval seemed to know where he was going, so Rem just tried to keep up, kept a tight hold on the lead line tied to their prisoner's bonds, and kept sweeping his gaze from side to side, in hopes of catching any would-be thief or assassin before he (or it) was right upon them.

Finally, they came to the threshold of Gorn Bonebreaker's squat, foreboding little keep. Two orcs guarded the main door—stout, carven tree trunks bound by thick iron and long-tarnished brass—but Torval's badge instantly silenced their challenges. The great door opened, the watchwardens and their prisoner were admitted, and a hunched, limping orc runt in what Rem took to be house livery scurried off ahead of them to announce their arrival to his master. The narrow vestibule they waited in was dim and close and smelled of old moth-eaten furs and smoked meat. Rem did not care for it. Their orc prisoner seemed to like it even less, constantly shuffling from foot to foot, furtive eyes darting around the low, shadowy chamber in search of some lurking attacker, some promised ambush. Rem almost asked Torval just what they should expect, but the dwarf seemed to be lost in a reverie of his own—mouth set in a stony frown, eyes narrowed and suspicious. Seeing the grave seriousness of Torval's countenance, Rem opted to keep his mouth shut.

In short order, the door was opened, courtesy of the liveried, limping orc again, and Rem, Torval, and their prisoner were ushered into the great hall beyond. It was not much larger than the vestibule in terms of length or breadth, but at least the ceilings were higher and it didn't feel so claustrophobic, like a tunnel leading from one subterranean prison to another. Along the length of the great hall, sputtering torches that stank of pitch guttered in rusty iron wall sconces on the chamber's sentinel pillars.

The room itself was adorned in haphazard fashion with all manner of weapons, fragments of armor, and trinkets of every odd sort: here a hilt attached to a broken sword, there a hammer-dented breastplate that looked, to Rem, like something from the *Scrolls of Bygone Ages*, a pile of ratty, matted old rodent furs, an old moss-stained forest stone, once carved in the countenance of an eldritch god, now so worn and smooth that it was basically just a rock again. The great hall looked less like a proud nobleman's seat of power and more like a long-unused stable filled with junk that its owners should part with, but just could not seem to.

And there, slouching in what seemed to be an undersized throne at the far end of the chamber, was the orc that Rem took to be Gorn Bonebreaker, the ethnarch of his people in Yenara. As the three of them approached, passing in and out of shimmering pools of torchlight and gloomy shadow, Rem tried to study the brute without being seen to study him. Gorn had the same broad, flat face, pronounced underbite, forward-thrust head, and wide shoulders of his race; he seemed big to Rem, for orcs always gave that impression, but perhaps not so big, his wide shoulders and long, muscled arms giving more of an impression of size than any actual height or mass.

But what Rem noted most keenly—and disliked, almost instantly—was not any sense of physical intimidation or threat. It was, rather, a sense of being in the presence of a cunning, deceptive, and proudly disingenuous adversary. For all his muscles and grimness and malevolent little eyes, Gorn's most striking feature was what a deep sense of untrustworthiness he radiated. Rem had known men in his time to possess that same quality, and he almost always hated them, instantly, even without cause for feeling so. Here, now, he hated Gorn Bone-breaker, and suddenly realized he wanted to be out of the orc's court as soon as possible.

"Rather late for gifts, neh?" Gorn rumbled. His voice was deep and sonorous—the sound of a great man-sized war drum or rolling thunder. Rem found himself surprised by Gorn's exacting use of the common tongue, though—how carefully the orc sought to form each syllable and sound, despite the fact that his underbite-heavy jaws were not formed by the gods to speak such words.

"Business as usual," Torval replied. "We serve the law in this city, we honor our treaties."

Gorn's inhuman mouth formed something like a smile, apparent only by a slight curling at the edges of his mouth. "You forget yourself, Watchwarden. Make your obsequies."

Torval actually growled, like a street cur cornered by a suspect stranger. He exhaled, a long, weary sound, then finally said, "Hail, thee, great Gorn, called Bonebreaker, Bane of the Minefolk, Scourge of Men, and Chosen Harbinger of His People's Destiny. I present to thee this prisoner, for his mercy or his wrath, however His Majesty the Bonebreaker sees fit to use him."

Rem caught himself staring. Really? All that? For this second-rate diplomat holding court over this shabby little enclave in this great city? Rem wagered speaking those words made Torval's hackles rise and stomach churn, yet there must be some established ceremony in it. A rote tribute paid to an officious, self-serving monster made of smug arrogance and delusions of grandeur.

Gorn, for his part, seemed very satisfied indeed with Torval's words. He waved his great, shovel-like hand. Torval, in answer, grabbed the lead line from Rem's hand, yanked the orc prisoner forward, then shoved him toward his ethnarch with no attempt at subtlety. The orc landed on its knees. He stole one glance at Gorn, but otherwise kept his head down.

"I salute you, master dwarf," Gorn said. "There is so little to you, yet any of my folk in your care are always so ... tractable. So cowed."

Rem saw Torval smile venomously. "You are a breaker of bones, Gorn. I am a breaker of orcs."

That nasty little almost-smile curled the corners of Gorn's lips again. Clearly, there was no love lost between Gorn and Torval—and yet, Rem wagered there might be some sneaking admiration.

"What is his crime?" Gorn finally asked, indicating the prisoner.

"Failure to follow the lawful commands of a watchwarden,

resisting arrest, disturbing the peace, and carrying on his person a very hefty cache of unlicensed witchweed."

Torval brandished the bundle they had seized from the orc's purse. If Rem wasn't mistaken, he was almost certain that he saw Gorn's face—his beady little eyes—register something like shock and worry at the sight of all that witchweed in Torval's hands and not his own. A moment later, the ethnarch glared down at his arrested subject, and Rem knew that he'd been right: somehow, Gorn knew exactly where that parcel had been bound, and that whoever expected it would not be happy when it failed to reach them.

But, experienced dissembler that he was, the orc managed, in the next instant, to hide his true designs. Once more, his face was a mask of mock courtesy and haughty composure. He harrumphed and shifted in his cramped seat.

"Leave this pile of ambulating offal with me, good watchwarden, and I'll see to his punishment forthwith."

Torval hawked phlegm and spat it unceremoniously onto Gorn Bonebreaker's flagstones. "As is your wont, great Bonebreaker. We bid you good night."

Torval turned and headed back toward the door. Rem bowed a little to dismiss himself, received a magnanimous wave of the great orc's hand, then hurried after his partner. They did not speak again until they were outside, tromping swiftly away from the ethnarch's palace.

"You don't care much for him, do you?" Rem asked.

"Had I my wish," Torval muttered, almost not to Rem at all, "we'd toss the lot of the knuckle-dragging sods into the Fires of the Forge Eternal and swill mead as they slowly burned."

A knot of orcs stumbled from the doorway of what Rem took to be a tavern. They were all reeling, imbalanced, clearly drunk, and as loud as a stampeding herd of aurochs. They loped right into Rem and Torval's path. Just as Rem was about to snag Torval's tunic and steer him sideward, the dwarf suddenly shouted at them.

"Away!" Torval roared, his voice splitting the otherwise quiet night and actually freezing the orcs in their tipsy tracks. For just an instant, they all sought the source of the sound, their faces masks of gathering fury and indignation.

Then when they saw that compact four-foot-tall engine of flesh and muscle moving toward them, recognized him, and realized that he'd given them an order, they moved away without a word. All the resistance drained from them, and their party split, retreating to either side of the narrow street. Torval and Rem marched right through them.

Breaker of orcs, indeed.

Torval wasn't very talkative the rest of the night. Rem couldn't decide if it was because the dwarf's mind was elsewhere, Rem had offended him, or the Stump simply didn't like him. The dwarf performed his duties, guiding Rem along his normal beat, showing him where the artisans clustered (all together, like four-leaf clovers) and which shops were likelier to draw thieves than others (tinkers, for their valuable metals; tailors, for their precious silks and fabrics; greengrocers, for their rare, imported spices). They broke up three brawls and collected a smattering of coin and cheap jewelry for fines, chased two would-be burglars without catching them, told at least half a dozen whores and jacks to find more suitable environs for their coupling, and foiled one purse snatcher, returning the coin-filled pouch in question to an old bakerwoman who had left her shop late after a very good business day. Torval not only returned the coin purse to its owner, he also dug whatever coin he could find from the snatcher's pockets. Derisively, he told the thief that his fine was paid and sent him running. Through it all, Torval only spoke when necessary, and seemed evermore distracted.

When the distant bells of the Great Temple of Aemon sounded the fourth hour of the morn, Rem finally offered his apologies.

"I'm sorry," he said, "for the orc."

They were sitting on a stone horse trough just a block or two from the bridge that crossed the North Canal. The smell of low tide was strong, the air chill, the fog thick, the boisterous city finally dark and still.

Torval didn't look at him. "I shouldn't have been surprised."

The silence that fell between them was inscrutable, almost painful.

"You don't think much of me as a partner, do you?" Rem asked.

Torval turned a penetrating, burning gaze upon him. "You seem a good sort, lad—honestly, you do. But maybe this isn't a job for good sorts. Maybe it isn't a job for you."

Rem felt a rage rising in him. "If you start with that Bonny Prince rubbish again—"

"Forget that!" Torval said, leaping to his feet. He was still a foot and a half shorter than Rem, but his presence and his conviction were absolutely overwhelming, as though he were a full head taller than Rem, looking down his nose at him.

As though he were Rem's own self-righteous father.

"There are two hundred thousand people in this city," Torval said, "and our sort are the only thing standing between the bad intentions of those hundreds of thousands and total, bloody chaos. The Council of Patriarchs can fill a hundred Halls of Justice with laws and good intentions—in the streets, on the ground, *we* are the only bastion against savagery. *We* impose order where there is no law. If you're not up for that challenge—if you're not willing to give yourself the authority to call out anyone, anywhere, at any time and *put them down* when they challenge you, then you cannot do this job, boy. Not now, not ever."

"You think I'm a coward?" Rem asked.

"I think you're a babe in the woods," Torval said. "And if you're not careful, you'll get one or the both of us killed."

Torval turned and strode away, shaking his head as he went. Rem wanted to follow him, but couldn't quite manage to. His feet were rooted where he stood. He heard his father's voice in his head.

Abroad? What makes you think you could keep yourself safe outside these domains? Without my protection?

Your place is here, Remeck. Your purpose is here. Out there, you'd be eaten alive.

A babe in the woods, Torval said. *And if you're not careful, you'll get one or the both of us killed.*

Torval was a good distance from him now. Rem finally put one foot in front of the other and followed, but he made no attempt to catch up. *Give Torval some space for a time,* he thought. *Myself, too.* He maintained a steady distance from the dwarf, but never closed it.

The sound of singing drew his eyes off toward the shadows on his right. There he saw two swaying inebriates stumbling out of an alleyway, joined in a raucous, badly harmonized chorus from an old Loffmari ship's ballad. They leaned on one another as they reeled off into the night.

Rem suspected the dwarf was right. He wasn't cut out for this work. Wielding authority and imposing his will had never been his strong suits, had they? How many times had his father scolded him for the same offense, something that Rem saw as no offense at all? *Do not ask the servants, command them,* his father would say through clenched teeth. *And stop thanking them. It sets a bad example.* He was fooling himself if he thought he could do this. He had only jumped at the opportunity because he was desperate. His rent was due and he was dead broke. He'd made it all the way to Yenara on the coin from a hocked sword and a traded destrier—but now he was in danger of ending up destitute, desperate, homeless, and hungry.

Just as his father said he would, if left to his own devices.

Perhaps that was why it meant so much to him. He did not simply want to start anew, to make his own way in the world—he wanted to *earn* his way into something. A trade, a fraternity or guild, a noble pursuit. Almost by accident, he'd found that fraternity, that noble pursuit, in the wardwatch. If he could succeed here, now, and make a place for himself, that would prove that his father—that everyone who had ever assured him that he was only a creature of the court—was wrong.

Perhaps that even he had been wrong about himself. Everything he'd ever owned or called his own—including his doubts about his ability to stand alone, to make his own way—had been handed to him, not earned. Some mad part of him had decided that the only way to banish those inherited assumptions was to divest himself of them and go find—go earn—new truths that contradicted them.

Or maybe he was just lonely. He'd been in Yenara for almost a week now, and he'd been on the road for a month before that. He couldn't really say that he'd made any friends. He usually thought of himself as a loner, but the realization that, for weeks, he hadn't shared a friendly word with anyone, hadn't caught up with anyone or been caught up on, hadn't seen a familiar face or looked forward to a meeting . . . it was startling, strange, yet completely undeniable.

Yes. He was lonely.

And desperate.

And, truth be told, he did like Torval, even if Torval was not so fond of him. He sensed that there was no lying in the dwarf, no guile. He judged things purely by his gut instincts and his observations, and he would challenge Rem at every turn.

And that was precisely what Rem needed.

Because he wasn't giving up.

"Hey!" he called, and hustled to after the tromping dwarf.

Torval threw a glance back over his shoulder. He did not slow his pace. "It's nothing personal, lad—some can do this work and some can't. I'm sure there's something out there for you to—"

Rem slowed as he hove up abreast of the dwarf. "Shut your gob," he said.

Torval stopped. He turned to Rem, scowling. "What did you say?"

"I said shut your yapping gob," Rem answered. He half expected to suddenly feel Torval's maul crack him headwise. When that didn't happen, he plunged on.

"Fine," Rem said, "I underestimated the gravity of that situation and I fouled up royally. I've learned from it. You're not going to dismiss me that easily."

Torval cocked his head. "And what makes you think you have a choice in the matter?" Torval asked. "If I say I'm done with you, Bonny Prince, I'm bloody *done* with you—"

"Call me 'Bonny Prince' again," Rem snarled, "and I'll shove that maul up your cack-hole, headfirst."

Torval was silenced by the threat. Rem decided he should press on, before Torval realized it was all bluff and bluster.

"I erred; I've begged your pardon. Let's move on. You can hold whatever opinions you might of my abilities, you bloody little stump, but you will not judge my potential on a single blundered arrest. You can ask Ondego to shove me at someone else when we get back to the watchkeep, but I'll tell you right now—"

Torval punched him. It wasn't a teasing knock upside the head as he'd offered earlier in the night, either—it was a full force, hard-fisted battering-ram job that knocked Rem onto the hard-packed mud of the waterfront street. Rem hit the earth hard, tasted blood. He spat out a mouthful of red, bubbling saliva. He dared a glance up at Torval.

The dwarf stood over him, sausage-fingered hand extended. He was offering Rem help back onto his feet.

Rem accepted. "You bloody little..."

"You made your point," Torval said. "Now shut your sauce box before I crack you again."

The dwarf offered a sly little half smile. Rem offered his hand, a show of peace.

"Partners? If only for the night?"

Torval took his hand and shook it. "As you say," Torval answered. "And if you call me 'Stump' again, I'll break every bone in your body and throw you into the bay for the sharks."

Rem nodded. "Fair enough."

"Now come on," Torval said after a persistent silence. "Let's head back. Shift's almost done." The dwarf started on his way. Rem followed. His jaw felt like a piece of cracked sculpture.

The two of them trudged back up the gentle slope of the hill, toward the cut of the canal and the bridge that crossed it. Rem couldn't believe how silent and empty the streets now seemed, after a long night of warm bodies, activity, and noise. Somewhere between the third and fourth bells, everyone seemed to feel their exhaustion and return to where they slept. He guessed it would stay like this for another hour or so, until the city's shopkeepers, stall men, and workers rose for another day of labor. When the first light of dawn appeared on the horizon, the brother of the watch at the Great Temple of Aemon would ring the morning bells to herald the day. An hour after that, the city gates would open, horse- and ox-carts would trundle across the cobbles, and life would return to the streets.

They crossed the bridge over the canal that snaked down toward North Harbor. As they did, Rem saw some people moving below, down by the waterside—washerwomen and tanners' wives carrying buckets of water back to their hovels, a drunk singing himself to sleep, a few thin cats, and one scrawny stray dog. The canal and the city were all shrouded in a thin mist, and that mist made the world soft and dreamy, like something one imagined, not like something that was actually there.

They were well over the bridge, two or three blocks past, trudging uphill back toward the watchkeep, when someone screamed far behind them. Rem and Torval both spun toward the sound. They waited, and were rewarded with yet another scream. Exchanging only momentary glances, they took off running back the way they'd come. To Rem's surprise, Torval's thick little legs carried him quite swiftly.

Before they reached the bridge, they saw a woman come tottering out of the morning fog. She was old and bent, and Rem guessed that she was one of the washerwomen he'd seen down by the canalside. When she saw them running closer, she threw out her bony old arms and waved them frantically.

"A dead man!" she shouted. "A dead man down by the water!"

"Shut it!" someone called from a dark alley off to their left. "Some of us are trying to sleep!"

"Dead!" she carried on. "All the gods, he's dead!"

Rem and Torval reached her. "Where?" the dwarf demanded.

"Down there," she said, pointing toward the canal with one shaking finger. "Right down there, on the near bank, just under the bridge!"

Torval nodded and led the way. Rem followed the dwarf down a side street that ran parallel with the winding canal until they found a flight of stone steps that led down to the water. As they descended, the smell of dead fish and mold grew stronger. Rem nearly choked. He hadn't noticed the stench coming off the canal when crossing it, but down here—right beside it—it was unmistakable. He sincerely hoped no one drew their drinking water out of that turgid stream.

The drunk who'd been singing to himself was tottering on the far bank now. "What's all the commotion?" he shouted across at them. "What's that old fishwife on about?"

Torval ignored him. Rem saw that someone else lingered farther upstream on the near side of the canal—another woman by the look, with a basket of laundry lying beside her, barely visible in the moonlight.

They trudged toward the base of the bridge. Already, though dark, Rem could see the body. It lay at the mouth of a large circular sewer drain that emptied into the canal. The dead man's legs lay toward the water. The upper half of his body was shrouded by the shadow of the drain.

"You ever seen a dead man?" Torval asked.

"He's not my first," Rem answered, though he supposed the body he was about to see would be a far more shocking sight than his mother or his grandparents, washed and well attired and arrayed with some dignity on their funeral biers.

"Nor your last, on this watch," Torval replied.

They reached him. The dead man lay still and silent, half in and half out of the drain, a brick-lined cave as wide as a man's spread arms from fingertip to fingertip. Their lantern had stopped burning hours ago. Torval looked to Rem and gestured toward the torches slung across his back.

"Light up," he said. "You never, ever want to step into one of these drains—not even right in the mouth of it—without ample light."

Rem drew out a torch. "Why is that?" he asked as he clamped the torch under one arm, then fetched the flint and steel from his pocket.

Torval was grave. "There's not just life on Yenara's streets," he said. "There's plenty more under it. Always be wary when you get near these outlets."

Rem nodded. He would take Torval's warning to heart. In moments, he'd summoned sufficient sparks to light the torch's pitch-soaked head. He handed the torch to Torval and knelt beside the body.

Rem didn't notice any stench above and beyond that of the canal itself and the drain that trickled into it, so he guessed the dead man was fairly fresh—perhaps just a few hours old, and recently washed up on this muddy bank. The roiling gold-red flames of the torch cast a bright, flickering light upon the corpse and a short distance into the black maw of the sewer drain. Satisfied that nothing lurked in that darkness to snatch him, Rem edged closer.

"Turn him over," Torval said.

Rem nodded. He reached out, took two fistfuls of the dead man's jerkin, then heaved backward. The body turned over easily.

The first thing Rem saw was the horrid, red-black grin drawn across the dead man's pale, hairy throat. It was a deep slash. In all likelihood, he'd bled out fast—perhaps in as little as ten or twenty seconds.

But then Rem noticed a few other unpleasant details. The

dead man had two broken fingers on his right hand. The front of his leather jerkin was punctured and torn in at least three places, indicating that the fellow had been cut and poked before finally being slashed and bled. Finally, there was the fellow's strange tattoo—a five-pointed star inside a circle that enclosed his right eye.

"Looks like they worked him over before they killed him," Rem said.

Torval said nothing. Rem turned, ready to argue with the dwarf if he claimed that Rem was being too hasty in his judgments, too concerned with details. That would be just like the stubborn little bastard, wanting to deflate Rem's still-emerging sense of competence.

But Torval seemed to have nothing to say. Even in the golden light of the torch, Rem saw that the dwarf was pale, his eyes wide, his mouth slack. Apparently, the sight of the dead man was quite a shock to him.

"Torval, what is it?" Rem asked, honestly concerned. It was the first time all evening the dwarf had been speechless.

"That's my partner," Torval said. "That's Freygaf."

CHAPTER SIX

Torval used the little brass whistle that all watchwardens carried. The shrill note it sounded seemed to ring far and wide through the close quarters of the Fifth Ward. In no time, Rem heard the sound of bootheels slapping walk boards and cobbles as any watchwardens within hearing of the whistle came running. Likewise, many a sleeping resident woke to the urgent call and cursed the watchwardens for the bloody noise they made. Torval did not even have the belligerence left in him to dress these complainers down and urge them back to their beds. He simply stood by the canal bank and waited. Rem, meanwhile, took the opportunity to examine the site where Freygaf's body had been discovered.

He lay in a wide-open sewer outlet, a broad, dark passage that led back into the bowels of the city at a vaguely sloped angle, no doubt to allow the outflowing water to run downward and gain momentum before joining the flow of the great canal. Rem, trying to heed Torval's warning about lingering too close to the open sewer passages, only leaned forward to study the interior of the outlet at one point, and when he did so, he was careful to keep his torch well ahead of him, so that its flickering orange-gold light filled the passage for a few spear lengths. That, at least, would allow him to see anything that might come scurrying out of the dark at him.

There was very little to see in the immediate vicinity of the corpse save the normal detritus that one might find at a sewer outflow: old branches and refuse, a few drowned rat carcasses, and soft piles of who-knew-what droppings. Rem imagined that after a heavy rain, or during the spring thaw, when the river that fed Yenara's sewers was swollen with meltwater from the distant mountains to the east, the outflow down here could be quite heavy, washing just about anything caught in its flow down into the canal, and along the canal's final length into the harbor, the bay, and the sea beyond. But presently, there was only a trickle, meaning the waters that flowed under Yenara's streets and washed away her piss and shit and secrets were at low ebb. That could work to their advantage, he supposed, because the runoff would not have washed away all the clues they could find.

His search of the inner mouth of the outflow tunnel completed, Rem stepped over Freygaf's body and lowered his torch to the ground. He began a slow, laborious search of the stone drainage trough that led from the mouth of the tunnel down the bank to the canal, and the damp gray mud that stretched away on either side. Almost at once, he saw his own tracks and Torval's approaching from the south along the bank, still freshly depressed in the mud. But as he studied the soft bank, he realized that he saw something else as well.

There were other tracks that his and Torval's had crossed and, in one spot, trampled. There were two sets, one close to the mouth of the tunnel, the other set apart slightly. The tracks set apart were clearly human—leather boot of a good make, with solid heels and soles, the sort that only a well-to-do dandy or proud soldier on holiday might wear. The other set of tracks were pressed deeper into the mud, indicating a person or creature of greater mass. These tracks were barefoot, and, if Rem was not mistaken, not human.

"Torval?" he called.

The dwarf, lost in a grieving reverie no doubt, grunted from his vigil at the canal bank. Rem caught Torval's gaze, and jerked his head sideward to urge him nearer.

"You might want to see this," he said. Rem was fairly sure that he knew what he was looking at. He'd spent ample time hunting in the forests near his home ever since he was a child, both from horseback and on foot. He might not have many useful skills outside of a royal court, but he knew spoor, sign, and tracking like a lifelong ranger. However, he was still new here, and new to Torval. He wanted Torval to reach the same conclusion he had so there was no chance of the dwarf dismissing his observations through the fog of his grief, or out of pride.

Torval dragged his way over to the mouth of the tunnel. He studied the tracks in the mud that Rem indicated. Rem pointed at the outer set.

"Those are clearly human," Rem said. "But these—"

Torval's face was red. His broad, muscular little body seemed to be shaking with a rising internal fury. "Orc," the dwarf grunted.

"That's what I thought," Rem said. "Barefoot, too, so probably not a well-to-do sort."

"Some of 'em wear boots," Torval said, "but not all. Many prefer to go barefoot when they can—bloody savages."

Rem heard a definite tone of bitterness in Torval's already raspy voice. It was the voice of a man fighting a flood of emotions, most of them unpleasant and totally beyond his control. Rem thought he would continue with his surmises so that Torval could concentrate on information and not his feelings.

"Look here," Rem said, pointing to the place where the tracks turned and moved away from the mouth of the sewer outlet. "The orc tracks are deeper over there, upon approach, then shallower here, as they move away."

"The orc was heavier on approach," Torval said, nodding in understanding. "The orc was carrying something?"

"That'd be my guess," Rem said, standing.

Torval studied him for a moment. His expression of grief and fury never changed, but his eyes narrowed and he seemed to appraise Rem anew.

"Not bad for a horse groomer's son," Torval said.

Rem shrugged. "I've done a lot of hunting in my time. Read a lot of sign. I've never seen orc tracks in the wild before, but we were shown casts when we were young—me and the other house brats—so that we would know when to call off a hunt and come home."

"Good work," Torval said, then turned and wandered away again.

It was, Rem thought, feeling a dull glow of pride despite the grim circumstances. *It was, at that.*

It wasn't long before they heard heavy feet moving on the bridge above them. Rem and Torval looked upward, toward the sound, and someone up there leaned over the railing and peered down through the fog into the cut of the canal.

"Who's that?" the newcomer called. "Is that Torval down there?"

"Get down here!" Torval barked. "Double-time!"

The newcomer only nodded, then Rem heard the thump of pounding feet again. In a few more moments, the new arrival and a companion were hurrying down the stone stairs that led from the street above to the canal bank below. One of the new arrivals was a tall, well-made fellow with the dark skin of a Maswari native, while his companion was as pale as Rem, shorter than the tall fellow, but still well-muscled. These two hurried to join Torval and Rem where they stood by the great outflow passage from the sewers. Both of them slowed when they were finally close enough to see the body that lay in the mud.

"Sundry hells," the dark-skinned one muttered.

"Is that—" the other one began.

Torval nodded, turned, and wandered away from the corpse. "Aye," he said. "It is."

Torval was clearly going to make no introductions. Rem stepped forward to make his own. He offered his hand to the two watchwardens. "I'm Rem," he said, "new to the force. Tonight's my first night."

"Djubal," the dark one said. "I remember you. We saw you following Ondego around the keep like a pup earlier. Didn't we, Klutch?"

The light-skinned fellow, Klutch, nodded and offered his hand to Rem. "We did, indeed. And here we thought you were just some nobleman's son, posting bail and begging the prefect to keep your arrest quiet."

Rem smiled. Perhaps that wasn't too far from the truth—but these two didn't need to know that. Now, with introductions made, Djubal and Klutch both drifted nearer. Each knelt beside the body and examined it. Rem made them quietly aware of his observations—especially the orc footprints in the mud—then withdrew, content to let them make their own examinations and surmises.

"Well, now," Djubal muttered as Rem withdrew. "This is a rank state of affairs..."

Rem looked to his partner. Torval now stood beside the lapping waters of the canal, lost in thought, his back to the rest of them. Rem noted that the wind seemed to have been knocked out of the dwarf: this was the first time all evening that he had not been dominating the conversation, barking orders, or laying out combative challenges. A grave silence and air of distraction hung on him like a pall. Finding his partner dead on the canal bank had turned him inward. Rem didn't know the dwarf well, but what experience he'd had of him in the last twelve hours suggested that this was anything but normal behavior for him. Granted, he understood the why of it—he just didn't care to be a witness to it. No doubt, somewhere deep inside himself, Torval would resent Rem—a stranger—seeing him so vulnerable.

"You should go," Klutch offered from his place beside the corpse. "Both of you. Your watch is finished for the night."

"We can stay," Torval said halfheartedly.

"No need," Djubal answered him, getting to his feet and daring an approach. "We've got him now, Torval. We'll see him handed over to the crones, with all due respect."

Torval turned. He was still arguing, but Rem noted that the dwarf's heart didn't seem to be in it. He simply could not tear himself away, perhaps felt that he would somehow betray Freygaf if he left him. "What about—"

The dark-skinned watchwarden, Djubal, did something then that surprised Rem: he laid a hand on Torval's shoulder. It was a friendly gesture—a brotherly one.

"We'll take good care of him," Djubal promised. "On my honor."

"Mine as well," Klutch offered.

"You have none," Djubal said to his pale partner, his neutral expression curling into a wry half smile. His eyes never left Torval's. "Go," he said again. "Give Ondego the news, then call it a night."

Torval had no argument left. He simply nodded and trudged away from the corpse. Rem followed. They did not share a word all the way back to the watchkeep.

The brothers of the Great Temple of Aemon were ringing five bells when they arrived back at the watchkeep. It was Torval himself who gave Ondego and Hirk the news. Both men, prefect and master sergeant, were still on the premises, still "in character" even now, so early in the morning. Rem idly wondered if the two slept at all, or if they had chambers in the keep itself. Both seemed genuinely saddened by the news of Freygaf's demise, but Rem noticed that, strangely, neither seemed surprised.

"Now I guess we know why he didn't show up last night," Torval said hollowly. He threw a strange, accusatory look at Rem, then went back to moping.

Rem didn't care for that look. It told him he was a poor substitute for a good man. It told him he was a thief and a vulture, for taking that man's place without realizing that the man in question wasn't just sleeping off a drunk or late for work...he was dead beside a Fifth Ward canal.

"Go home," Ondego said to Torval. "Take tomorrow night off. We'll partner Rem here with someone else. Pour out some libations for Freygaf and make offerings, if need be. He prayed to the Gods of the Mount, yes?"

"When he prayed," Torval said. "Which wasn't often."

"Still," Ondego said, "best to keep with custom. The gods of the dead get prayers for their dead. I know you'll see to it."

"I'll see to it," Torval said, sounding hollow again.

A long silence fell. Torval lingered there in Ondego's office. Rem didn't want to leave until Torval did. Ondego stared at them both, awaiting their departure.

"Go home, Torval," he said.

Torval nodded, rose, and wandered out of the little office. Rem threw a worried look at the prefect, then followed the dwarf out of the chamber.

Outside the keep, first light was bleeding into the world and the people of the Fifth seemed to be slowly yet surely retaking the streets they'd abandoned a few hours before. Rem called to Torval and struggled to catch up, but the dwarf trudged on, slumped shoulders swinging, as though he didn't hear. Rem finally drew abreast.

"I'm sorry," Rem said.

Torval grunted.

"I mean it. I can tell he was a good mate and that he meant a lot to you."

Torval grunted again.

"I could help you, if you needed assistance."

Torval glanced at him—glared really. "What assistance?"

"I know you're thinking you should find his killers. Bring them to justice. I could help—"

"No, you couldn't!" Torval suddenly exploded. He stopped, swung into Rem's path, and leveled one thick finger at him. "You couldn't help even if you wanted to, and I know you don't want to. You just feel guilty. Obligated. As though we share something. Well, listen to me, you northern ponce: we don't share anything. The very fact that you're getting all sentimental about me after one lousy night of walking the ward tells me this isn't the job for you. There's no room for sentiment here. There's only the job, and getting it done. Now get away from me and don't even flap your gums in my direction again!"

CHAPTER SEVEN

With that, Torval turned and stomped away again. Rem wavered over whether to follow him or not. Thus far, the dwarf had exhibited a tendency to esteem confrontation, not withdrawal. Whether they were partners or not, they'd be walking the same ward, and Rem wanted the dwarf's respect. That answered his quandary for him, and he followed. Once more, he hove up alongside the striding dwarf.

"Look," Rem said. "You don't have to like me, but I could be of assistance just the same. People don't know my face around here. They don't know I'm part of the watch yet. Maybe I could work undercover for you? Try to roust out some information..."

Torval stopped, turned, and shoved Rem with all the strength his little body could muster—which was considerable. Rem went sprawling in the mud, narrowly avoiding a pile of still-steaming ox turds.

"You're not my friend or my partner," Torval snarled. "Freygaf was my partner, and he was twice the man you could ever hope to be. So just take yourself back to your rented rooms, you sot—you tourist—and find yourself something else to do. This is a game for grown-ups, not spoiled stable whelps who've run away from home."

With that, the angry dwarf turned and strode away. Rem couldn't even pull himself up off the ground, he was so shocked, so humbled. The dwarf had him dead to rights...at least, the running-away-from-home part. Rem thought he was being sold short in the matters of his dedication and capabilities, but what did he really have to show the dwarf to claim otherwise? How could he convince the squat bastard that he really did want to help, and that he really did want to bring Freygaf's killers to justice?

At the end of the street, just before he should have turned a corner and been lost to sight, Torval stopped. He stood for a long time, as if contemplating something. Rem still sat in the mud. He hadn't made any attempt to rise. When Torval turned and marched back toward him, Rem finally did so, and did his best to scrape the mud off his kecks and jerkin.

Torval's face was softer now—as soft as that hard, broad countenance could be, anyway. He looked lost and sword-shocked again. For a moment, his mouth worked, but no words came. Rem didn't rush him.

"I'm sorry," the dwarf finally said. "That wasn't fair of me."

"Understandable," Rem said. "You've had a shock."

"I don't know you," Torval said. "I shouldn't judge you. But judging is what we watchwardens do. Every night, again and again and again, we walk into situations we know little of and we have to read those involved. We have to guess if they're dangerous or not, if there'll be trouble we can handle or trouble we need help with. Judging wrong gets us killed. So, it becomes habit."

Rem shrugged. He wasn't angry. "It makes sense," he said.

Torval was silent for a time. Finally, he nodded, the apology given and accepted. "Come break fast with me," he said. "We can talk a bit. Maybe...well, maybe if you want to help me, I could use your help."

Rem nodded. "I'd be honored. Lead the way."

*   *   *

Torval led Rem into the Third Ward. Rem didn't ask where they were going and Torval never said, but Rem trusted the little fellow now and knew that Torval was probably still sword-shocked from the revelation of Freygaf's murder. If he was quiet, it was because he needed quiet. Rem decided to let that contemplative silence persist.

The Third Ward—where Rem kept his rooms—was nowhere near as crowded or as hoary as the Fifth. While its streets seemed just as labyrinthine and its quarters as close, there was an underlying orderliness to it all that made Rem feel far more at ease than he did while walking the Fifth the night before. At this early hour—just after sunrise—the streets were starting to show signs of activity, with food stalls and grocers' carts nabbing prime real estate at the edges of the cobbled or muddied streets, while blacksmiths, carters, wheelwrights, stevedores, and day laborers all slumped off into the morning mists toward their labors, or in search of paying work. Generally, Rem got the impression that the Third Ward was more middle-class, an impression that hadn't fully taken hold when he simply rented his rooms there, before knowing how the city's wards were divided, or what another of those wards looked like.

At last they came to a nicely sized tavern near the East Gate of the city. Its shingle named it the King's Ass, and it sported a rather charming caricature of a loutish, happily knackered monarch swaying atop a grim-faced, put-upon donkey. Even at this early hour, the doors were wide open and the buzz of conversation spilled out into the still, quiet morning air.

"My place," Torval said by way of introduction.

"Charming," Rem answered.

The inside was as warm and inviting as the humorous sign

suggested. The rushes and sawdust on the floor were fresh, the tables and chairs lacquered and in good repair, and the clientele a fine mix—neither hoity-toity nor drawn from the dregs, but mostly made up of laborers, shopkeeps, and artisans on their way to or from work. Torval sauntered through the thin crowd like he owned the place. He led Rem up to the bar and they took stools there.

There was no one behind the bar when they hove to, but in moments, a handsome woman just shy of or into her forties appeared from the door to what Rem presumed were the kitchens. Her face brightened when she saw Torval and she made a beeline toward the pair, wiping grease from her hands on the apron that hung around her waist.

"Bless me and keep me," she muttered, "it's my very best customer. Just off duty, Torval?"

Torval nodded. Rem saw something strange on the dwarf's broad face now: a sort of discord where the smile that the woman brought to Torval's mouth clashed with the still-ruminative sadness in his hazel eyes. "Aarna, my love, you're a sight for tired eyes."

The sight of her really did seem to light him up from within, silly as that sounded. But still, the fresh reality of Freygaf lay upon him like a sodden mantle.

"And where's Freygaf this morning?" Aarna asked, clearly familiar with the dwarf's former partner. "Did he leave you for the brothels again, or were there prisoners in need of tenderizing?"

The mention of Freygaf's name brought the trace of tears to Torval's eyes. He was still struggling to smile, still putting on a show for the woman, but the show was fading, and the truth of his grief pressing through.

"Alas," Torval said, "our dear Freygaf's no more."

His voice broke when he spoke. Rem didn't know the dwarf very well, but he wagered it took a great deal to make him show emotion so baldly, so publicly, to anyone that wasn't a blood relation.

Aarna, for her part, seemed to understand this. Immediately, her face was a mask of worry and concern and she rounded the bar. Without a single word—with all the simple, honest sincerity of a true and longtime friend—she threw her arms around Torval and held him. To the dwarf's credit, he didn't try to throw off the embrace or shun it—as many a dwarf might—but put his own long, thick arms around Aarna and held her, too. It was a good thing he was sitting on his stool, otherwise, his head would've been buried in her ample bosom. Then again, maybe that would've assuaged his grief further.

Rem didn't say a word while Torval sought his solace in the arms of the bar matron. When their embrace finally broke, Torval gave a single, punctuating sniffle, wiped his eyes with his wrist, then slapped the bar.

"Enough," he said. "I'm famished, and so's the lad."

Rem noted that Aarna beamed with something like pride at this subtle display of self-control from Torval. Clearly, she knew the little fellow well and understood that he would let no more of his grief color the morning. When more tears came, they'd come in solitude, without anyone—friend or family member—bearing witness.

She turned her bright eyes and broad smile upon Rem. "And who is the handsome lad, Torval?"

Rem found himself touched. The woman was neither flashy nor what one would call beautiful, but her large brown eyes and broad grin and comfortable curves suggested she was a woman of singular charms and distinctions. Perhaps not highborn or polished, but lovely in her own way nonetheless. To be called handsome by her, to be smiled at by her, made a man feel all the more manly.

"This is Rem," Torval said gruffly, "a poncey whelp who was arrested the night before last for disturbing the peace but whose good looks and quick tongue got him a place on the watch. I've been forced to deal with his easy incompetence all night long, and now I need a tankard of ale just to wash his taste from my mouth. Can you help me?"

"I can always help," Aarna assured him, and gave Rem her hand. "Delighted, young sir."

Rem took her hand and kissed it. "My pleasure, madame."

"Sundry hells," Torval chuffed. "Bonny Prince Remeck, kissing hands and collecting favors..."

Aarna slapped Torval's broad shoulder playfully. "You're just jealous. Shall you be breaking fast, as well?"

"Aye."

"Ale and repast, then, on the way." She left them with a flourish, and Rem delighted in the silly, self-indulgent grin that bloomed on Torval's face as he watched Aarna disappear into the kitchen.

Rem heard something off to his left, a sound that drew his gaze and begged his attention. It was laughter—high, musical, completely unselfconscious. That laughter belonged to a young barmaid on the far side of the room with flaxen ringlets and bright-blue eyes. She, too, had Aarna's natural brightness and charm—evident from a distance—although there was no way the two could be related, so different were they. Nonetheless, Rem suddenly found himself staring, watching the young lady as she smiled and flirted and freely laughed with a group of stonemasons as they placed their orders.

For a moment, he smiled. The girl's laugh reminded him of Indilen, and their brief afternoon together. She had a laugh like that, as well—a laugh as bright as sunlight on a rippling pond. In an instant, his smile had fallen.

"Oh ho, see here," Torval said beside him. "Some bull's had his lead yanked."

Rem threw a glance at Torval, tried to force a smile and sound nonchalant. "Just admiring the scenery."

"What you see doesn't seem to be pleasing you," Torval said.

Rem shrugged. He thought he might speak, as well, but no words came. Thankfully, Torval did not press him for any.

Rem had been so sure that Indilen would be there, working at the Pickled Albatross, to meet him. Why in all the sundry hells of the Panoply hadn't she deigned to even show up and speak with him that night? Had their brief but memorable afternoon together really meant so much to him and so little to her? Had she lied to him? Forgotten about him?

Or had something terrible befallen her? Something that kept her from her appointed shift, and their intended meeting.

"I could introduce you," Torval said.

Rem finally found the words that had escaped him moments ago. "I should learn my lesson where barmaids are concerned."

"Come now, lad," Torval said, "You can't stop petting the pups just because one bit you and ran away."

"If she'd deigned to bite me," Rem said, "I'd have counted myself lucky. She skipped right to the running-away part. And, honestly, Torval, I really thought there was something between us. Some spark, like tinder and flint—"

"Such is the way of things," Torval said wistfully. Aarna returned with two tankards and thumped them down in front of the pair. Torval lifted his and Rem followed suit. Before he drank, Torval paused, held out his tankard, and poured a small measure of the ale onto the rush- and sawdust-strewn floor.

"A draught for Freygaf," he said quietly. "May his ascent of the mountain be smooth and his welcome in the Halls of the Undying a warm one."

Rem gave Torval an approving nod and poured out some of his own ale. Then he lifted his tankard in toast. "To Freygaf."

"To Freygaf," Torval said.

They drank.

The ale in the tankard was some of the finest Rem had ever tasted—fruity and fulsome, big and malty, with some mild hoppy bitters to temper its sweetness and a whorl of mouth-tempting spices. The brewers of the Lycos Vale were renowned throughout the north, but Rem honestly couldn't remember ever tasting an ale to compare with what he now quaffed.

"Hell's bells," he muttered, licking his lips. "Where on earth did they find this stuff?"

Torval smiled. "*Aaaah*, another satisfied customer! That'd be Joedoc's hand. He's the brewmaster. Doesn't work the mornings, so he's not around at present—but he's a genius with barley and malt, isn't he?"

Rem settled onto his stool. "I think I've just found my new favorite watering hole," he said.

Torval made a mock-serious face. "I saw her first, Longshanks!"

"Didn't your mother ever teach you to share, you obstreperous little man?" Rem asked, laughing.

For the first time since being thrust upon Torval, Rem felt like the two of them might make good partners after all. When their laughing tapered off, the food arrived—cheese, some dried plums, and salt pork—and the two ate. Rem found the fare simple but satisfying—and the quality of the ale more than made up for the simplicity of the food that accompanied it. When they had finished, Rem felt the weariness of a long night upon him and begged his leave of Torval.

"I've got to sleep," he said, feeling as though he might conk out at any moment, right there at the bar.

"On your way, then," Torval said, pulling coin from the little purse at his belt.

"Wait a minute," Rem said, "I'll not have you paying for my ale just yet—"

"Shut your cake hole," Torval snarled. "This one's on me. 'Sides, they only charge us for the ale here. Food's free for watchwardens. You can buy for me after you get your first pay purse."

Rem was touched. "Very generous of you. Thanks, Torval."

"Get out of here," Torval said. "Go get some sleep. We'll have another long night ahead of us come sundown."

Rem stood and swayed on his feet. The combination of the ale and his weariness was working on him. Hard. He steadied himself on the bar.

Aarna emerged from the kitchen again. "Leaving us already, good sir?" she asked.

"For the last time, Aarna," Torval said, almost growling, "this little snot's no 'sir.' He's just another dumb watchman walking the beat, like the rest of us."

Rem felt a bloom of warmth in the center of him. Strange as it might be, he liked the sound of that. Of all the things in the world that he could be—that he might have been—a watchman walking a beat sounded good enough for him.

Rem bent over the bar, took Aarna's hand again, and gave it another kiss. "Until the next time, milady."

"You can bring him back whenever you like," Aarna gushed to Torval.

"Bloody hells," Torval grumbled.

CHAPTER EIGHT

Although he was exhausted, Rem slept fitfully. True surrender to sleep was hampered by a storm of thoughts swirling and racing through his exhaustion-addled brain—thoughts that he could not entirely make sense of or banish. He worried about acquitting himself well in his new position. He wondered what sort of strange encounters he might have in the days and weeks and months to come, walking the ward. He idly built scenarios in which he—with Torval's help—stepped in to alleviate tense or dangerous situations and did so with a combination of guile, luck, and occasionally physical violence that he was not even sure he was capable of.

You are skillful, his father had said after many a tournament melee or sparring session with blunted swords, *but you are not ruthless. In tourney, that will cost you a cup. On the battlefield, that could cost you your life.*

Could he survive the perils of Yenara and her close-packed wards by being skillful but not ruthless? He truly wondered . . .

That led him to entertaining all sorts of unpleasant worst-case scenarios in which minor scuffles and routine calls for order escalated quickly into uncontrollable blood feuds, usually ending with him taking a dagger in the belly or a dirk point in the throat.

So much could happen. In an instant. Over nothing.

Was he equal to that? Could he face that, night after night?

His father would have said no. And somewhere deep inside himself, Rem probably agreed with him—which was why he was here now, in a shabby little rented room, in search of a new life to live, a new Rem to be, and not back in his bedchamber in a castle in his father's dukedom.

Stop it, his mind snapped. *Stop letting your father's words—anyone's words—define the person you want to be. If you want to do well here—to thrive here, despite all the danger and uncertainly—you can, and you will. Sleep now, you fool—you're tired.*

And so, he slept. He woke at intervals, wondering if the day had passed, dimly hearing the bells from the Great Temple of Aemon announcing that it was only midmorning, midday, early afternoon.

Just as frustrating, dreams plagued him throughout his fitful sleep, all of them centered on Indilen. There were several variations, but they all amounted to pursuits. He would see her from a distance in the market, then call to her. She would turn toward the sound of his voice, acknowledge him with a smile and wave, then turn and amble away. As Rem tried to follow, the press of the crowd and the flow of foot traffic would, inevitably, keep him from overtaking her. Always, she disappeared into the milling throng, and he was left alone, with the nagging feeling that he was being followed as well, just as he was following her.

He had that same dream—or some variation of it—at least three times during his slumbers. Each time, he found her in a different location—the marketplace, the waterfront, the Pickled Albatross—and each time he lost her in the crowd, finally realizing that he, too, was being followed. The last time this rather unpleasant nightmare awoke him, he would even have sworn that he felt a heavy hand fall on his shoulder just as he awoke.

Somewhere, Aemon's bells rang. It was the middle of the afternoon. His shift would not start for several more hours, but after that last replay of the familiar dream in which he lost Indilen, over and over, Rem didn't feel much like rolling over and going back to sleep. It wasn't simply that the dream troubled him, or reminded him that he had, somehow, lost something (rather, someone) quite special—there was also the vague sense that he knew something that should suggest a puzzle waiting to be solved, but what that something was and just why it should trouble him he could not say.

He pondered. First, he considered Indilen herself: auburn-haired, dark-eyed, pale and vaguely freckled, her smile both merry and world-weary, idealistic and experienced. Clearly, she was smart, and she had an independent streak—otherwise, what would she be doing here, in a city not her own, trying to make her own way in the world? But she was also cautious—neither naïve nor foolhardy. She had been drawn to Rem, just as Rem was drawn to her—he honestly believed that—but, like any smart girl in a new place, she would have wanted to be cautious about him. He assumed that's why she had invited him to meet her at her place of work, the Pickled Albatross: it was public, and if he gave her any trouble there, she could have him ejected.

Thus their meeting was low- to no-risk on her part. She had control, and she was on safe ground.

Therefore, could Rem really assume that she had simply quit her job and stood him up, without something important having waylaid or drawn her away? True, she might have simply decided both that she hated serving ale to drunken louts and that she had nothing to gain by getting to know Rem, but somehow—foolishly or not—he did not think that would be the case with such a girl. She seemed the sort to keep her promises, and so he regarded her failure to keep those promises—both to him and her employer—as more than a little suspect.

All right, then. Perhaps something had happened to her, he thought, staring up at the knotty wooden ceiling beams above his bed. What? What could have become of her between the time Rem saw her at the morning market and the time he arrived at the Pickled Albatross and Indilen failed to report for her shift?

Answer: quite a bit. Yenara was a bustling city full of very shady characters with all sorts of bad ideas about how to entertain themselves or make a living. Indilen could have been snatched by cutpurses, who saw her regal bearing and the fine scrivener's set she carried and instantly marked her as easy prey. They might have stolen everything of value in her possession and left her strangled or bleeding out in a back alley.

He shuddered. What a horrible thought.

And how doubly horrible that he could easily imagine it, in all its vile detail.

Perhaps, he thought, *I should seek her out.*

The sensible part of him balked at that thought. What if she simply didn't want to see him again? What if she had purposely avoided him? What if his assumptions that she liked him, that she wanted to know him as desperately as he wanted to know her, were all wrong? Would it be fair of him to hunt her down and confront her and make her tell him that, face-to-face? Shouldn't he simply leave her be, wherever she was and whatever had become of her?

No, he thought. *No, I shouldn't. Something terrible may have befallen the poor girl, and wouldn't your heart be broken, your honor impugned, if you had suspected as much and not tried to learn the truth? You need not put any pressure on her if you find her—simply make it clear that you were worried, and you wanted to make sure she was safe. That is all that you need to know, and no more.*

That thought—that determination—got him out of bed. In moments, he was dressed. He bounded down the stairs of his boardinghouse, splashed water from a nearby public fountain on his face to refresh himself, then headed off in the direction of the Fifth Ward and the Pickled Albatross.

He had a couple hours before his shift began. He could squeeze in a little investigative work of his own before he reported for duty...

Rem arrived at the Pickled Albatross in the early evening. Outside, the sun was falling and the shadows in the street grew long, but inside, the night had not yet begun. It was still too early for the longshoremen and laborers who toiled on the waterfront to be released from their daily labors so that they could get about the important business of a night's drinking, thus the tavern was largely empty, the normal midnight roar declined to a dull hum of muttering voices, occasional coarse laughter, and the scrape of chair legs on the rush-strewn floorboards.

Rem stood near the doorway, searching the great room for his quarry: that brusque, unflappable blond barmaid that he and Torval had been served by the night before. Something she had said to them lodged in Rem's mind and kept repeating itself like the only phrase known to a Maswari parrot. Her words echoed, again and again, while Cupp's own, in sharp contrast, were interjected between them. It might mean nothing at all, but their two explanations seemed to vaguely contradict each other, so Rem thought a polite follow-up couldn't hurt.

When she hustled past him, emerging from the kitchens and on her way to a table with a tray loaded down with bread, beer, and wedges of very smelly cheese, Rem nearly missed her. He raised his hand and tried to flag her down, but she was on a mission. Thus, he followed, scurrying across the room in her wake, deciding that calling out for her and making a spectacle of himself probably wasn't the best approach.

She delivered her goods, took coin from the men at the table who received it, then turned to career toward another waiting table of cardplayers who had flagged her down. That's when Rem struck, inserting himself into her table-to-table path and offering a winning smile to try to reassure her.

"Hello there," he said. She nearly fell on her bottom, having to work entirely too hard to stop her forward trajectory when Rem blocked it. Rem caught her before she could fall. "I'm very sorry. Do you remember me, by any chance?"

"No, sir, I don't," the girl said. "But don't take it personally, I serve a great many fellows on a daily basis, so if we've just met once, you were unlikely to make an impression."

Rem motioned to his watchwarden's cuirass and signet. "I was in here last night, with my partner, a dwarf."

"Ah," she said, smiling a little. "The Double Drakes, followed by the brawl."

"Precisely," Rem said.

The girl bent close, speaking in a conspiratorial whisper. "You'd best not let Cupp catch you here all by yourself. He's likely to give you a pass if Torval's with you, but alone? He'll chew you up and spit you out."

"That bad, is he?" Rem asked.

The girl shook her head. Her manner was resigned, almost disinterested. "You have no idea."

"Well," Rem said, "I'll be brief, then. Do you remember us asking you about another barmaid? Indilen?"

"Oi, girl!" the cardplayers at the neighboring table called.

"I've got to go," she said to Rem.

"Just a quick question or two," Rem said. "Do you remember what you told us?"

"She's not around."

"Right," Rem nodded, "you said—"

"She arrived for her shift on Saturday," the barmaid said impatiently. "Cupp sent her on some errand, and she hasn't been back since."

"So she was here on Saturday, but—"

"Wax in your ears, love?" the barmaid asked, looking at Rem like he was a stray, underfed puppy. "She was here, Cupp sent her off, she never came back."

Rem nodded. That's what he feared she'd said. "All right, then. Thank you, er...what's your name?"

The girl cocked her head a little. Her eyes narrowed. A crooked smile livened her soft face. "Planning to ask after me when I flee this roach hovel?"

Rem reached into his pocket, pulled out his last few coppers, and handed them over—an offering. "No, ma'am—I just want to thank you by name for helping me."

"Jhonna," she said. "Now, if you'll excuse me..."

Away she went to take the cardplayers' orders. Rem slowly extricated himself from the seating area, moving in a slow, driftwood fashion back toward the main entrance.

She came in on Saturday. Cupp sent her on an errand. She never returned.

That wasn't what Cupp had said.

Should he ask the tavernkeep again? Should he challenge his story in light of the one Jhonna told? No. That was foolish. Accused of lying, Cupp would only take it out on the barmaid.

It could all be a simple mistake, of course. Maybe Cupp spoke out of turn? Chose his words lazily? Maybe he didn't really mean that he hadn't seen her in two days, but that she simply failed to return from the errand and work her Saturday-night shift?

"What in the sundry hells do I have to do to be rid of you?"

Rem was snapped out of his reverie. Cupp had found him. The big, thick-bellied tavernkeep had just emerged from the kitchens, and he didn't look pleased to find Rem in his foyer. Rem decided to play it like a professional: cool, collected, indifferent.

"Evening, sir," Rem said, as cordially as he could manage. "Seems a quiet afternoon hereabouts?"

"You may be a watchwarden," Cupp said, "so when you're on your shift, I may be forced to be polite to you and give you your free bloody beer, but if you're not in here on official business, then I don't want your troublemaking arse in the place, do you understand—"

"I do," Rem interrupted. "And I apologize, profusely, for any trouble I've caused you, either before or after acquiring this signet."

Cupp sneered. He seemed to sense sincere regret in Rem's voice—indeed, Rem was trying to offer some—but the tavernkeeper was belligerent nonetheless. "Fine, maybe in the future I won't consider you a bloody pox on this place. For now, get out."

"A quick question," Rem said, "and I'll be on my way. About Indilen."

Cupp's eyes rolled. "Bloody hells, lad—are you still on about that little twist?"

Rem tried to look lovestruck and ridiculous. He probably didn't have to try very hard, but he needed Cupp to believe he was a fool after a piece of tail, and not a watchwarden questioning him to test the veracity of his story.

"Sad to say," Rem answered.

"I told you, she missed two bloody shifts. She's fired. If I see her, I just might chain her back in the scullery and make her wash mugs for a few nights, just to teach her what it means to run out on a contract with me."

"So she never showed up for her shift on Saturday at all? Ever?"

"What did I just tell you?" Cupp snapped. "No. I ain't seen her since the night before that. Now take your eager prick somewhere else, Mr. High-and-Mighty Watchwarden, before I tear it off and feed it to the alley mutts."

With that, Cupp spat at Rem's feet and lumbered away. Rem watched him go for a moment, satisfied that he was onto something.

According to Jhonna, Indilen showed up for her Saturday shift, was sent on an errand by Cupp, then never returned.

According to Cupp, Indilen never showed up at all.

Someone was lying. The question was who, and why?

It was Golden Hour—the sun below the horizon, but light still in the sky—as Rem trudged back to the watchkeep from the Pickled Albatross. The activity in the streets was a strange reversal of all that he'd seen that morning, after he and Torval had gotten off work: vendors closing up their stalls and carts for the night, shopkeepers closing their windows and doors, laborers coming home from work and children playing out the last light of day in the streets before their mothers ordered them home for the night. Rem felt a strange, familiar peace among all these humdrum daily activities. He almost felt as if he were home—or in a place he could call home.

The walk to the watchkeep in the Fifth Ward took him less than a half hour. When he reached his destination, there was only a narrow band of pale red-gold light in the western sky, beyond the harbor and the great lighthouse, the sun having finally slipped below the horizon. A sliver of moon rose out of the east. Mounted torches burned all around the little square that fronted the watchkeep, and little tin lamps hung on posts, keeping the square alight even though night was now upon them. It felt a little strange when Rem showed his watchman's signet to the guards at the main entrance and was immediately granted entrance.

I guess they haven't changed their minds, he thought. *I'm really here, really a part of the city watch.*

In he went, to start his second night on the job.

All the watchwardens on duty—sixty or seventy, perhaps—were crammed into one corner of the administrative chamber, all jostling for a view into one of the side chambers. As Rem pressed nearer, trying to elbow his way through the crowd to see what had them so fascinated, he heard a man shouting, apparently in pain, swearing and cursing himself and everyone around him. Little by little, Rem crept nearer the front of the crowd, catching only a few sour looks along the way. At last, he could see through the archway that led into the side chamber and had a view of the chaotic scene therein.

It looked like some sort of little infirmary, hosting a wooden table, a couple chairs, bundles of wadding and bandages, and all sorts of strange probing implements and apothecary jars. Presently, a man lay on the table—bearded, long-haired, voice low and gravelly. It was he that kept cursing himself for a clumsy fool, for having let such a thing happen. Rem saw plainly, even from his imperfect, crowded vantage, that the man's right ankle was swollen terribly, horrible, livid bruises already blooming beneath the puffed-up flesh. Another man—thick and round as a barrel, bearded and florid of face—stood at the injured watchwarden's side, trying to get the cursing injured man to lie still.

"Stop mewling, Sliviwit!" he coaxed. "Just lie still and hold your tongue and—"

"What in the sundry hells was I thinking?" the injured man, Sliviwit, howled. "That was a bloody, buggered rookie mistake—"

"It'll be all right," the fat one said, trying to get his partner to lie still.

"Hold him, Demijon," someone said. "The healer's coming!"

Then, off to Rem's left, the crowd parted. A young woman with silver hair and puzzling, ancient eyes moved through the crowd without hindrance and arrived at Sliviwit's side. She studied the swelling ankle for only a moment before holding one hand out to Sliviwit's thick-waisted partner, Demijon. Demijon, without hesitating, laid his hand in the girl's. She pressed it down on the swollen ankle, her own palm atop, and Sliviwit howled at the pain of their touch. Without anyone having to ask, two more watchwardens stepped forward and held Sliviwit on the table.

Rem guessed what he was about to see, and had to remind himself to breathe as he awaited it. He had heard of such wonders as he was about to witness, but never seen such a thing firsthand.

Everyone grew silent, as if all understood what was about to unfold. The strange girl with the silver hair muttered words in some ancient tongue that Rem could not identify. As she did so, Sliviwit, the injured man, began to gnash his teeth and growl, clearly in a great deal of pain, now using every ounce of strength he could muster to bear it and resist the urge to buck. At the same time, Rem saw that Demijon, his partner, with his thick hand pressed down on Sliviwit's broken ankle under the silver-haired girl's own palm, grew pale and sickly. It was like watching someone succumb to seasickness or food poisoning. His eyes lost focus. His skin blanched. Fine beads of sweat broke out on his brow. There was not a sound in the room apart from Sliviwit's snarling against the pain and the desire to thrash away from it.

Everyone stared. No one made a sound. After a time, Rem realized he was holding his breath.

Then it was over. The silver-haired girl removed her hand and Demijon's. Sliviwit, suddenly free of the pain of whatever healing spell the girl enacted, fell backward onto the table, panting, desperate for breath. Demijon reeled backward, dazed and in danger of toppling. One of the two watchwardens who had rushed forward to brace Sliviwit leapt to Demijon's side. The fellow helped the heavy watchwarden lean back against the table behind him. Rem looked to Sliviwit's ankle. Already, the swelling subsided and the bruising faded as though the injury were weeks old and not minutes.

Just like that, the spell was broken. The crowd around Rem turned from the scene and began to disperse. Rem was surprised to find Torval at his elbow, having apparently watched the whole thing unfold in silence, never once making Rem aware of his presence.

"Ever seen such a thing?" Torval asked.

"She's a healer," Rem said, indicating the silver-haired girl as she glided away again, silent, swallowed by the milling crowd of watchwardens.

"Aye," Torval said, nodding. "One of our Mage Squad."

"She drew energy from the healthy man to help her heal the injured man—is that right? That's why the big fellow ended up so white-faced and woozy?"

Torval nodded. "When your partner's in need, you give, be it coin or blood or the very life force that animates you."

Rem shook his head in astonishment. "Extraordinary," he whispered, then joined Torval and the rest of the crowd as they milled away from the little infirmary chamber and spread out through the administrative area.

Across the room, Ondego and Hirk stood just outside Ondego's office, conferring with each other apart from the others. Rem also saw what he believed to be more milling bodies, pressed into Ondego's office—but he could not be sure. Since Ondego and Hirk blocked the doorway, it was hard to see. Outside, the gathering seemed loose and at ease, with watchwardens sitting on desks, chairs, or just standing about. Rem found himself a chair and sat. Torval stood.

It took only a moment for the watchwardens to come to their comrade, one by one, and offer their condolences about Freygaf. Rem overheard almost all of the muttered offerings, and they generally consisted of, "He was a good man," "We'll all miss him," or "The gods of the mountain are probably wishing they could give him back about now." Rem supposed Freygaf must have been blustery and a brawler, but, on any given day, a solid man to have on your side.

Hirk whistled. Everyone quieted down and gave Ondego their attention as he moved to the center of the room.

CHAPTER NINE

"You've all heard about Freygaf," Ondego said, his voice completely without sentiment. "Offerings and libations can be poured out at the Temple of the Gods of the Mount, just across the way. The crones there will see to Freygaf's preparation and immolation. The fire should be lit midweek. Details to follow.

"That being said, we've still got jobs to do in the here and now. What happened to Freygaf—be it murder with intent or a simple accident of being in the wrong place at the wrong time—could happen to any one of us. Since it happened to him when he was alone, that's all the more reason to remind yourselves why you've got partners, and why you need them. We can't afford to lose anyone else off this watch, so believe me when I say you do not—I repeat, *do not*—have my permission to die.

"Now, if I may, I'd like to introduce a new member of the crew. Show yourself, lad."

He looked to Rem and indicated that he should stand. Rem felt suddenly abashed, but managed to get to his feet anyway. He hated being the center of attention. The watchwardens all turned their hard, world-weary gazes on him. Not a one smiled or offered words or gestures of welcome.

"This is Rem," Ondego continued. "Fresh in from the north."

One burly northerner screwed up his face. "Didn't I arrest him the other night?"

"That you did, Hildebran," Ondego said. "But the lad and I had a talk while he was in the stir, and I decided he might make a fine addition to our iniquitous little band here. So, extend him every courtesy, make him feel like a brother, and try not to leave bruises or lacerations where they can be seen."

They all smiled and chuckled at that. Rem didn't like the way they were looking at him, like sailors who'd been at sea for months looking on the first maiden to cross their path—even the few females among them, whose gazes were just as vicious and predatory as the men's.

"Now, then," Ondego continued. "We have a special visitor, and I should like you all to extend him every grace as he treats with us."

There were, indeed, people waiting in Ondego's office. A small retinue emerged, led by a slender, sad-eyed, richly appointed elf. Accompanying the woodlander was a swarthy but handsome sort in much more modest apparel—probably a bodyguard, Estavari by the look of him—and a doughy, powdered eunuch that was, in all likelihood, the steward of this affluent elf's household.

The elf's expensive and showy attire struck Rem as rather bizarre. He imagined that city elves would, on occasion, enrobe themselves in fine silks and damasks, because they appreciated craftsmanship and comfort—but there was something in the elf's ensemble that suggested to Rem something more than understated appreciation. It seemed actively showy: slightly crass, even. His robes were silk, of a bright, colorful crimson weave that might have been more at home on the body of a rich merchant or high-priced courtesan. Enriching the fine, well-spun silk garments were a deep purple sash hanging across his thin body from his right shoulder, a shiny ornamental leather belt cinched around his narrow waist and chased with both silver and gold filigree, and a heavy, glittering neck torque around his slender throat, offset by a gaggle of bejeweled rings on his long, elegant fingers. Had Rem not seen the high cheekbones, pointed ears, and vaguely enlarged eyes that marked all elves as elves, he would have assumed this was just the spoiled son of some first-generation merchant's family enjoying a recent inheritance. Perhaps the sight was not such a strange one in a vibrant cosmopolitan city like Yenara, but it was utterly alien to Rem's admittedly limited prior observations and assumptions about elves and how they might appear or behave in person.

"This," Ondego said, introducing the grim and slender sylvan in his well-embroidered robes, "is Mykaas Masarda, an emissary of one of this city's most prominent citizens, Kethren Dall, of the most ancient House of Dall. Citizen Dall has asked that his honorable emissary be given the privilege of addressing us directly, and I've granted it, so keep your ears open and your gobs shut. Citizen Masarda?"

The elf stepped forward. Rem was amazed at how familiar his bearing and countenance were: growing up in a noble court, he had seen a thousand men with that same stiff back, that same proud profile, the same grim set of mouth. It was as if all the rich and powerful folk of the world were, in some sense, the same—even if they were elves.

"Citizen Dall is my friend," Mykaas Masarda began, his voice melodious and calm. "So long as I have made my home in this city, I have been welcome in his household, enjoyed the company of his wives and children, and supped at his table. Now, in his hour of need, my good friend has asked that I bring a message to you. His daughter, Telura Dall, just seventeen years old, seems to have disappeared, and Citizen Dall fears for her safety. She was last seen yestermorn, in their own home in the Second Ward, by her mother, her tutor, and a brace of family servants. She went out in the afternoon, and she has not been seen since. Because she is child of privilege and not well versed in the cruel and deceitful ways of the world, her father fears, to say the least, that something terrible has happened to her."

Mykaas Masarda paused. Rem saw the vague glint of tears in his eyes, a barely perceptible trembling in his lower jaw. Clearly, he was a close family friend, for the girl's disappearance seemed to trouble him as deeply as it might a blood relative. The men in the administrative chamber, if they noticed this subtle but clear display of emotion, all seemed to listen without judgment. So far as Rem could see, there was not a single sneer, nor any unkind whispered word in answer to the elf's clear if covert grief.

"My good friend has asked this," Masarda said, pressing on, "that I, and all of his business associates, visit all the watchkeeps of the city tonight to make it known that a great reward awaits the one among you who uncovers some news of our Telura's whereabouts. Your reward will be greater still if she can be found and returned to her family alive and unharmed."

Masarda then handed a hand-sized portrait to Ondego, who took a quick look at the portrait and passed it around. It was painted on a thin sheet of wood, no bigger than a quarto volume. When the picture arrived for Rem to study, he saw that it was a fine and realistic likeness of a young lady with dark hair, brown eyes, and a proud, aquiline profile. She was clearly a nobleman's daughter—he saw patrician blood and manners in the extension of her long, graceful neck, the slight lift in her chin, and the challenging, even playful fire in her deep brown eyes. After committing the image to memory, Rem offered the portrait to Torval. The dwarf only gave it a summary glance, frowning as he did so, then passed it along.

The watchwardens rumbled, whether in answer to Telura's plight or the promise of a reward, Rem could not tell. When the portrait had made the rounds, Hirk finally reclaimed it. He walked it to the wall of portraits that Rem had assumed to be a rogues' gallery of fugitives and used an iron nail to affix it there.

Rem stared at Telura's picture, one among hundreds—not part of a rogues' gallery at all, but a portrait gallery for the missing and displaced. Staring at the wall now, he could finally see clearly what he had failed to notice before: how many of the most recently hung pictures and sketches were of beautiful youngsters, male and female.

Beautiful youngsters...just like Telura Dall.

"Find her," Mykaas Masarda was saying when Rem finally returned his attentions to the elf's address. "Return her to her family. Do so and you shall have the eternal gratitude of the House of Dall and all their compatriots, in addition to a fortune of your own."

No one spoke. Not a sound came from the gathered watchwardens, nor from Mykaas Masarda's embassy. After a long, pregnant silence, Ondego finally stepped forward, shook Citizen Masarda's hand, and indicated that he could now be on his way. Masarda and his richly appointed companions nodded, whispered thanks, and took their leave. Ondego did not speak until they had left the administrative chamber.

"And with that," Ondego said, "our evening's business is complete. Carry on, gentlemen. Keep your eyes open, your fists clenched, and your back to the wall. Dismissed."

The gathering broke. Men separated into small knots, all

discussing Telura Dall and the possible reward for her safe return. Torval did not join any of the conversations, though. He broke from the group instead and went stalking off toward the armory at the back of the keep. Halfway there, he stopped and looked back at Rem.

"You coming?" he barked.

Rem leapt out of his seat and followed.

When Rem arrived at the armory, Torval was already conferring with Eriadus, ticking off requests on his fingers. Rem did not hear what Torval had asked for clearly, but he saw Eriadus nod agreeably, then bustle away to go rooting through a series of cells stuffed tight with scraps and scrolls.

Rem studied the many weapons on display. Torval stood silently, staring into the middle distance, a scowl on his broad little face.

"Is the maul always your weapon of choice?" Rem asked, by way of making conversation.

Torval glanced at him, seemingly annoyed that he'd broken his reverie. He grunted. Shrugged. "Mostly. Sometimes the ax. Handy with a short sword when necessary."

"I'm best with the sword myself," Rem said. "Used to practice all the time. Hours upon hours—"

"Sparring with the horses?" Torval asked.

Rem didn't know what to say to that. Truth be told, he probably shouldn't let on to Torval just how good he actually was with a blade. He *was* supposed to be just a groom's son, after all. Never mind that he had won any number of planting and harvest festival tourneys since turning fifteen, the youngest age of competition. He would just have to keep his skill with a blade—just like his aristocratic origins—quiet until such time as they were called for.

Eriadus returned. He had an armload of scrolls and he offered them to Torval. Torval indicated that Eriadus should hand them to Rem, and Rem dutifully took them, nearly losing the whole load in the transfer. There were quite a few, and none seemed of uniform size.

"What's all this?" Rem asked.

"Arrest records," Torval said. "Six months' worth."

Rem raised an eyebrow.

"You can read, can't you?" Torval asked.

"I can," Rem confirmed.

"Then come on. You can read them to me." Torval turned and led the way back out of the armory.

"And why are we doing that?" Rem asked, trailing after him. He didn't need to ask whether the dwarf was capable of reading them himself or not; he clearly wasn't.

"Looking for suspects," Torval answered without even turning back. "There's a good chance that whoever offed Freygaf is someone that he and I have dealt with on the streets before. Thought a perusal of the records might jog my memory a bit."

They set up at an unused desk in a quiet corner of the room, lit a number of lamps and candles to provide good light, then dove in. Rem's eyes nearly crossed when he studied the first scroll he unrolled—the crabbed script, the lines upon lines of simple entries, the many columns illuminating the nature of each arrest, its date, its particulars, and the like. Rem's momentary, slack-jawed disbelief and squinty perusal of the records made Torval impatient.

"What's the problem?" the dwarf snarled. "I thought you said you could read?"

"I can," Rem said. "I'm just trying to orient myself. There's a lot going on here."

"Well, hurry up," Torval said, shifting on his chair. "We've got a lot to go through and I don't want to spend all night doing it."

Rem looked at the dwarf. He could tell now that the little fellow wasn't upset with him—he was simply impatient, and still a little angry over his partner's ignominious end. More than anything, he looked worried and preoccupied. Rem wanted to broach the subject of Indilen with Torval, to discuss the strange lie that he'd caught Cupp in at the Pickled Albatross—but he could see that this moment was the wrong one. He licked his lips, studied the pages before him.

"Do you have any solid ideas?" Rem asked quietly. "Someone the two of you brought in? Or an accomplice?"

"None," Torval said. "So, let's get started."

"All right, then," Rem said, and dove into the scrolls.

It took close to three hours to comb through the arrest records, neatly arrayed in chronological rows upon the scrolls like monetary entries in a ledger. Torval sat beside Rem and stared off into the middle distance, listening with a frowning, implacable face, occasionally telling Rem to make a note of one of the arrestees before urging him to carry on with this peculiar trip down memory lane. Finally, when they'd made it back seven or eight months, Torval bade Rem stop reading from the scrolls and reread the list of suspects they'd compiled.

Rem did as he was told, mumbling the names and their attendant crimes: Grummon, trading in stolen goods; Larga, illegal blood sport; Valek, burglary; Haerken, pickpocketing and purse-snatching; Eldred, illegal trade in narcotics; Nerva, prostitution and theft. Once more, Torval revealed little of what he thought. His mouth remained in that unmoving frown; his eyes kept staring off into the distance. Rem waited silently for a definitive response.

He waited for quite some time. He got none.

"Well?" he prodded. "What now? Do we go roust them out?"

"Three names on that list have one thing in common," Torval said, almost to himself.

"And what's that?" Rem asked.

Torval finally looked at him, a frown on his face. "They all pay tribute to the same guild master." With that pronouncement, Torval leapt onto his feet and swaggered across the administrative chamber toward the door.

Annoyed, Rem stood as well. "Where are we going? Do I return these to Eriadus?"

"Leave them," Torval called back over his swinging shoulder. "Eriadus will take them back or we can return them later. We've got places to go now."

Rem hurried after the dwarf, only catching up to him on the far side of the room, nearer the entrance. Already there was the nightly flock of petitioners in the vestibule outside, awaiting audience with watchwardens or Ondego himself. Torval bypassed the vestibule and crowds of citizens and made for a side entrance that allowed easy exit.

"Do you have your stick?" Torval asked.

Rem checked his belt. "No, I seem to have forgotten it, seeing as you're in such a blasted hurry—"

"Well, go get it," Torval growled. "You'll need it."

Rem doubled back to the armory, snatched up one of the many nightsticks lying around there, then hightailed it into the street. Torval was waiting in the square outside, maul in hand, smoldering and impatient. He didn't say a word when Rem approached. He simply started off again, leading them out of the square and deeper into the Fifth Ward.

"Do you mind telling me where we're headed?" Rem asked.

"While there are all sorts of criminal lordlings in this city, great and petty," Torval answered, "there are five primaries, each controlling a different ward. We arrest them when we can, but generally, we look to them to keep some semblance of order among the pickpockets, mollies, and gambling hounds that pay them tribute. Most of the time, we manage an uneasy peace of sorts—but every now and again, when we've pinched their earners once too often or these thief lordlings feel unduly targeted, they might try to retaliate."

"So you and Freygaf, you rousted this fellow you're speaking of, or people who worked for him, once too often?"

Torval nodded grimly. "He's a proud sort. Takes wardwatch interference in his affairs as a personal slight. We've always maintained an uneasy peace with him, but it's not beyond the bastard to suddenly decide a lesson needed to be taught."

"Wait a minute," Rem said, suddenly realizing that Torval was probably leading him into a very dangerous situation. "Is this stick really all I get to protect myself? Or do I need something else? Something a bit more . . . persuasive?"

"No," Torval spat. "If you walk into this place armed, you'll be dead before you take three steps or get your sword from its sheath."

"But you've got your maul."

"They know me," Torval said.

That didn't fill Rem with any confidence. Where the hell were they off to?

Torval led them deep into the labyrinthine streets of the Fifth Ward, closer and closer to the waterfront. Finally, after taking so many corners that Rem thought they were walking in circles, they came at last to a boisterous tavern bleeding acrid poppy smoke and the sounds of rumbling revelry into the night. Beyond a dooryard arrayed with modest gardens, a pair of burly bouncers flanked a single narrow door under the dusky light of a tarnished old tin lamp. As Torval approached, both sentinels drew upright, their shoulders squaring, their faces growing dark with belligerence.

Torval was barely half the size of either, but he stared them down nonetheless. "I'm here for a chat with your boss," he said. "Stand aside."

"You're not on the list," one bouncer said. He was a thick-necked Hasturman, with greasy hair the color of fresh-churned mud.

"Turn around and march your stunted little arse back to ward headquarters," the other urged. He was thinner but still muscular: a swordsman perhaps, muscles corded, eyes aloof.

Torval sighed, looking deferential. For a moment, Rem thought the dwarf might just turn around and go back the way they'd come. Then Torval struck.

Using his bald head as a battering ram, Torval drove his body into the belly of the whipcord bouncer on his left. The strike stole the man's breath and doubled him over. Before his fellow could leap to his aid and yank Torval aside, the dwarf had seized the thick-necked bouncer's scrotum through his filthy breeks and squeezed. The Hasturman dropped to his knees, howling in agony. When he was down, Torval hit him with a powerful uppercut and sent him reeling. By that time, the slender bouncer was recovering from being head-rammed in the belly, but he was still too slow. Torval grabbed his tunic and head-butted the thin-but-muscular bouncer so soundly that the man's nose exploded with a sickening crack, cartilage crumpling and blood squirting out of either nostril. Down he went in a heap atop his companion.

Torval still had his maul in hand, but he had never employed it. A broad splash of blood from the bouncer's exploded nose lay on Torval's forehead. Rivulets of the red stuff cut tracks down his broad, flat face.

The entrance to the house of ill repute lay open and unguarded before them.

Rem stared at the bloody-faced Torval. Torval just cocked his head toward the door. "What are you waiting for?" he said, and pushed through. Rem followed.

CHAPTER TEN

It was, indeed, a den of iniquity, but quite a stylish one. There were Estavari tapestries depicting jousts, hunts, and grand old battles long forgotten, finely carved imperial tables and plush, comfortable chairs, even little storybook lamps from the Far East—Shimzari, if Rem was not mistaken—gracing all the tables and pillars. The lamps, along with numerous banks of half-melted burning candles and tapers, filled the common room with a smoky, golden glow that struck Rem as rather warm and welcoming.

Games of all sorts unfolded around them—card games like Burning Bridges or Turnslip, dice games like Roll-the-Bones or Swallowtail, even parlor games like Trinary and Malice. The more reckless guests were engaged in other contests, some involving venomous snakes or scorpions, others based on strength or skill with a blade. Every game played was played for money, and almost every contest attracted watchers, who placed their own bets on the one who might walk away from the table victorious. Rem was taken aback instantly by the openness and variety of vice on display. There were beautiful youths—female and male, scantily clad, well-oiled, and, no doubt, perfumed—serving drinks and attending the customers, while prostitutes of equally diverse stripe moved ghostlike between the tables, casting coy glances and tempting laughter toward their would-be marks, expertly manipulating any and all who caught their eye toward a conversation, a few drinks, then promises of sweet favors for solid coin. There were hard-faced, hard-lived men with beautiful young maids in their laps, and, perhaps more surprising, equally hard-faced, hard-lived women with young men on leashes. If one could imagine a pleasure or an indulgence that could be undertaken for sport or profit, it was here, out in the open, on vivid display. Even the most notorious of grogshops in his homeland would not hold a candle to the blithe decadence and cheerful lechery unfolding before him.

Rem felt a slight twinge of jealousy. Though such a hive of villainy would, more likely than not, never be his chosen outlet for an evening's entertainment, part of him yet admired and even envied the people he saw before him. Their openness. Their complete disregard for social conventions or the expectations of polite society. He secretly hoped that someday he too could learn to care so little about what other people thought, what others expected of them.

A cursory glance around the room revealed that they were being watched by house security. Furtive sellswords and bravos with scars and oiled beards and blades at their belts were stationed all around the common room as plainclothes security. They all eyed Rem and Torval with a strange sort of incredulity. No doubt, they saw the blood sprayed across Torval's face from his head-to-head collision with the bouncer outside, and they knew that something was amiss.

Their suspicions were verified moments later when Torval the dwarf gave a loud, bellowing battle cry, leapt toward the nearest gaming table, and brought his maul crashing down on the jug of wine in its center. Wine splashed everywhere and ceramic shards went flying. Torval followed that by upending the entire table. The players gathered around it scattered in a flurry of oaths and curses. The table flipped sideward, spilling ale steins, coin, and dice. Some of the girls screamed. The little band playing in a back alcove—a piper, a harpist, and a fellow with a squeeze-box—fell silent.

Torval turned to Rem and eyed the nightstick at his side. "Time to use that," Torval said.

Before Rem could ask what Torval meant, a pair of bravos charged them. Torval shoved the first aside—right into Rem's path—and lit into the second with his maul. Rem, suddenly face-to-face with what looked like a swarthy Sartoshi pirate with a lazy eye and a glittering short sword in his hand, raised his nightstick like a fencing blade and prepared himself for a match.

Torval's act of belligerence set off a chain reaction. Card-players leaping clear of the upturned table collided with the tables around them. The players at those tables took umbrage and demanded satisfaction. Blades slithered from scabbards. Fists flew. Brawlers fell to fighting and cowards ran for cover. In moments, the common room was in chaos.

Rem had no time to curse his rotten luck or try to talk his way out of the situation. The bravo immediately set about sticking him with his sharp little poniard, and Rem was forced to defend himself with only his nightstick. Thrusting and slashing with a blunt piece of wood was not so useful, but he acquitted himself well enough, parrying most of his piratical opponent's blows and never once feeling the sting of the blade. After some dancing back and forth, Rem finally managed to force his opponent into a knot of brawling gamblers. When the Sartoshi pirate slammed into a pair of wrestling Blighters, the Blighters joined forces and attacked the pirate. Rem thought his escape was made.

But before he could flee, Rem found his path blocked by

a burly Kosterman with long, flaxen braids and only half the teeth he was born with. The Kosterman wielded a great, knotty club—most likely fashioned from a limb off a gnarly old oak. Rem set himself on guard with his nightstick. The Kosterman attacked. The brawl continued around them as they sparred.

From time to time Rem managed to catch sight of Torval, four feet of hellfire toppling men twice his size, upending tables, cracking skulls and shattering bones with his maul, even employing stray bric-a-brac—ale steins, pewter plates, footstools—as improvised weaponry. The dwarf's gnashed teeth seemed to form a grin, but Rem could not be sure. Perhaps that was just Torval's war face?

In either case, the truth was clear: Torval was in his element. "I want the Creeper!" Torval shouted. "Where's the gods-damned Creeper!"

He was a miniature bull stomping through a field of adversaries and making each pay dearly for whatever blows they landed, whatever insults they dared. Were he not so busy defending himself, Rem would have been eager to stop and bear witness to the swath of destruction that Torval left in his wake, far more impressive than his stunted stature suggested possible.

And then, just as suddenly as the brawl began, it stopped. Someone on a high platform blew into a hunting horn. The long, bellowing thunder of the horn drew everyone's attention—a collective pail of cold water on the proceedings—and all eyes were drawn toward the deep and droning sound. When the horn's sounding ended, Rem followed all the eyes in the room toward a balcony at the far end, where stood a thin pale man with dark, fiery eyes and lank, oily black hair. He looked like an underfed pickpocket—a shifty-eyed, thieving sort whose longevity was the result of nothing more than skill, luck, and ruthlessness.

"Torval," the fellow on the balcony called down. "What the bloody hell are you doing to my gaming room?"

Torval leveled his finger at the fellow on the balcony. "Was it you, Creeper?"

The fellow on the balcony—Creeper—said nothing for a long while. "This is about Freygaf, isn't it?"

"Yes or no!" Torval demanded. "Was it you?"

"It was not," Creeper said. "Now get up here and let's talk over cups like civilized men."

Torval's face, a blood-spattered mask of fury, didn't suggest that he was interested in civilized discourse. Rem not only saw the fury in it, but also the sadness. All of these bruised and blinkered patrons had paid a price this eve for Torval's grief. In that moment, Rem felt profoundly helpless. He wished there was something he could do or say to assuage Torval's loss.

But there was nothing. He could only follow when the dwarf broke off from the Hasturi bruiser he'd been brawling with and picked a careful path across the ruined space toward the stairs that led up to the Creeper's loft.

For the private den of a gambling baron, the loft struck Rem as surprisingly cozy and welcoming. There were plush Maradi carpets, sofas and divans draped with colorful linens and silks, a number of impressive mosaics in the old imperial style mounted on the walls, and a number of candles and brass lamps about, filling the homey space with a warm, golden light. Creeper himself, slight, bony creature that he was, seemed out of place in such plush environs—but his comfort level was apparent as he sauntered across the room, rounded a large mahogany desk, and bent to pet something lingering behind it. Rem had to crane his neck to see clearly what strange pet the Creeper was greeting.

It was a black panther on a bronze chain. The beast purred and swished its long, dark tail. Rem saw the glint of white, sharp teeth behind its black lips.

Torval seemed unimpressed. His baleful stare and squared shoulders suggested that he was a man on a mission, indifferent to both dangers and pleasantries. He stood in the very center of the room, allowing Creeper to greet his pet and dispense with well-mannered greetings and obsequies.

The Creeper didn't strike Rem as particularly friendly, but neither was he unnecessarily combative or unwelcoming. He came across, rather, as a dedicated businessman whose interactions with others, even when cold and calculated, were always calm and cordial.

"Ale or brandy?" he asked. Whole casks were on hand, along with a number of cups and glasses. Clearly, the robber baron was used to entertaining in his private sanctum.

"Neither," Torval said. "This is business, not personal."

"And I never conduct business," Creeper countered, "without a drink in hand. It's uncivilized. If you're worried about me poisoning you, you needn't be. I could've had my guards and patrons tear you to pieces out in the gamesroom if I'd wanted."

Rem bit his tongue. He was desperate for a drink about now, to take the edge off, but he'd let Torval run this his way, and show no signs of eagerness.

"Fine," Torval said. "Ale. What'll it be for you, lad?"

"Brandy," Rem said.

Creeper tapped the appropriate casks. Torval got a mug of frothy brown ale and Rem was handed a glass of brandy. A taste told him it was made from apples, not grapes, and he resisted the urge to compliment their host on the quality of his liquor. No need to embarrass Torval by making the Creeper feel too superior.

Creeper lifted his own glass of brandy. "To Freygaf," he said, poured out a measure right on the fine carpet, then drank himself. Torval followed suit with his ale.

Once more, Rem was embarrassed. They'd been pouring out libations for Freygaf for at least three or four days. Why did he keep drinking before the offering? Though the pouring of libations for the recently deceased was not common custom in the courts of Hasturland, it was certainly not unheard-of—especially among the common classes. He should have known that. He resolved never to put a cup to lips again in Torval's presence unless Torval had already done the same.

Torval swallowed his first mouthful of ale, stared into his cup. "Was it you?" he asked.

"No," Creeper said flatly.

Torval seemed to study the bony little apparition for a moment, before finally nodding and exhaling through his nose. "He'd owed you money in the past. I thought perhaps—"

"Freygaf hasn't been in hock to me for a year," Creeper said. "Not since you stepped in and settled his last debt. He's been in here a few times—the cards and the dice still called to him—but he hasn't gotten himself in trouble again with my sharks the way he did before. For all that time, he'd been smart and sensible. With me, at least."

Torval frowned. "What does that mean?"

The Creeper swirled his brandy. Rem took a sip of his own. Gods, it was good stuff! He hadn't had a taste of apple brandy this good in years!

"I'm loath to speak ill of the dead," Creeper said, "but you shouldn't be so surprised that Freygaf ended up a corpse, Torval. His best quality was his friendship with you and his insistence that he was a man of the law. Other than that alignment, he wasn't a nice man, and he wasn't into the most savory of midnight activities."

Torval was clearly controlling the urge to throttle the Creeper where he stood. He swirled his ale but wouldn't take another sip. "Just what is that supposed to mean?"

"I have no intention of saying any more," Creeper answered, "not because I'm trying to make it hard on you, but because you'll be incredulous and you won't believe me. Suffice it to say, Freygaf kept odd company and was guilty of some dirty deeds. Dig deep enough and you'll find evidence of it. Then, you can come back and tell me that I told you so, and I was right."

"You don't think I'd know my partner better than you, you scheming little spider?"

"No, I don't," Creeper countered, a tad bitterly. "You only knew one side of Freygaf, Torval. The best side. All the naughty bits were exposed when he ran in my circles. Those are the bits you never knew of... or at least, never cared to see."

"Why don't you tell me?" Torval demanded.

"Aren't you a wardwatchman? Go root it all out for yourself." Creeper answered. "You'll believe evidence and your own eyes more than you would my words. Now, if you don't mind, I'd like you to introduce me to your new partner."

The Creeper turned his dark gaze on Rem. Suddenly, Rem felt violated. There was something in the robber baron's eyes that made him profoundly uncomfortable. Rem felt naked... leered at. Desperate to avert his gaze, Rem looked to Torval, silently asking if an introduction was in order.

"His name's Rem," Torval said, before Rem could introduce himself, "and if you make any move to get your hooks in him, I'll burn this place to the ground. With him inside."

Those words struck Rem like a sucker punch to the gut. The meaning was clear: Torval wouldn't brook Rem spending any of his off-hours in the Creeper's gambling and pleasure den. Clearly, this fellow and his particular brand of vice were above and beyond—or rather, below and beyond—the everyday vice that Torval could countenance in a partner or a friend.

"Do you like the brandy, Rem?" the Creeper asked.

Rem stared into the glass and nodded. He did his best to sound flippant and casual. "I do. It's good."

"Well," Creeper offered, "it's my pleasure to both entertain and accommodate the brave men of the city watch when they're not busy watching. Despite your partner's harsh words, you're welcome here for a game or a tumble any time you like. First round's always on the house."

"No, he's not," Torval said. "Welcome, that is. Come on, lad. Time to go."

Torval set aside his ale cup and Rem did the same. The dwarf had him by the arm and was leading him toward the door like a callow youth when Creeper spoke behind them.

"Seek, and ye shall find, Torval," Creeper cooed. "Just as the sages say. Just don't be surprised if you don't like what you uncover."

"Thanks for the ale," Torval growled, and shoved Rem out through the loft door. Rem half expected to see everyone in the common room waiting for them, bravos and sellswords with their blades at the ready, whores sporting sharp dirks and garrotes, patrons eager for the show of two watchwardens being rushed and trounced by the criminal colluders in Creeper's court.

But in fact everyone in the common room seemed to have forgotten about them. At some tables, the games of chance went on apace, while others went about the work of putting their tables and chairs and contests back together again. Songs were sung along with the minstrel band, and the whores and their jacks made googly eyes and cooed like doves and bartered for their preferred currencies. Rem led the way down the stairs from Creeper's loft and Torval followed. His silent fuming was like a bed of banked coals at Rem's back, pulsing, waiting to be stirred and taste the air before once more becoming a raging fire.

They left Creeper's Court with little more than they started with. When they were about a block away from the place, Rem turned to Torval. The dwarf was lost in thought, eyes downcast, mouth set in a thoughtful frown. Rem reminded himself to hold his tongue—he was the junior half of this partnership, after all—but his anger got the better of him.

"What was all that about?" Rem demanded.

Torval's trance was broken. He looked at Rem like he'd just spoken Quaimish. "What?"

"I asked you a question," Rem snapped. "Just what was all that about? You walked me into that place completely unprepared, you almost got us killed, and on top of that, I didn't even get to finish my drink!"

Torval's face screwed up, his own anger rising. "Now see here, Ginger—"

"Don't call me that!" Rem said. "Not Gingersnap, not Freckles, not Bonny Prince. The name's Rem—or have all those head butts you doled out rattled your memory?"

"Our only chance to get straight answers from the Creeper was to force him to treat with us and unbalance him. Pure shock and awe. It worked, didn't it?"

"Did it?" Rem asked. "We have nothing more now than when we started."

Torval hove up into Rem's face and snarled his reply. "That's one name off the list," Torval growled. "You don't like the way I work, slither back to Ondego and beg for another partner. Otherwise, shut your gob and follow my lead."

Rem almost responded, then realized he had nothing to say. The dwarf was right. Unorthodox his methods might be, but they did get results. Rem took a deep breath, calming himself. He waited, expecting directions from Torval. None came.

"Well?" he asked.

"Well what?" Torval retorted tartly.

Rem threw up his hands in surrender. "Where to next? I'm guessing that the Creeper didn't tell you anything you didn't already know?"

"No," Torval said shortly. "No, of course he didn't. Surely..."

Rem knew that Torval was lying. Creeper's insinuation— that Freygaf was not the man Torval thought him to be, and that if Torval dug deeper, he would find irrefutable proof—was still working on the dwarf. Clearly, Torval really had thought Freygaf's worst secret was his gambling problem. The idea that there might be more to learn—more hiding beneath the surface, to be learned only now, when Freygaf was dead—clearly didn't make Torval happy.

Rem would say nothing of it. First and foremost, he didn't know Freygaf, and therefore, wouldn't assume that whatever terrible things the Creeper said of him were true. Beyond that, though, there was just the issue of being right and honorable: you didn't defame the dead when you hadn't known them in life, no matter what they were guilty of. Thus, Rem could only make suggestions about their investigation, or posit lines of inquiry. He didn't want to blight Freygaf's memory, nor did he want to try to replace him.

Thus, Torval had to lead the way.

"Partner," Rem said gently. "Where to now? I'll follow wherever you take me."

Torval seemed to awaken from a daydream. He eyed Rem suspiciously for a moment, then seemed to look sad. Finally he shrugged and cocked his head northward.

"Come on," he said, and set off. "Let's search Freygaf's chambers."

CHAPTER ELEVEN

Freygaf had kept quarters in a rather gloomy courtyard tenement on the north side of the Fifth Ward, near the city walls. His neighborhood was quite lively, even now, after dark, with market stalls, sidewalk winesinks, curbside dice games, and all sorts of after-dark revelries keeping the streets full and the air thick. Pine torches crackled and bled inky smoke. Post lamps were lit. Residents in upper windows and apartments called down to those in the street and vice-versa, some to complain, some to greet, others to issue challenges or invitations.

"Charming neighborhood," Rem said to Torval as they marched through.

More than once, locals recognized Torval, stopped him, and offered their condolences. Clearly both the dwarf and his partner were well-known here, and given at least some measure of face-to-face respect. Torval took all offered condolences with few words and little apparent interest. He was on a mission now, and he couldn't afford to be slowed or distracted.

"This is the Knot," he explained to Rem. "One of the roughest neighborhoods in Yenara, but also one of the liveliest."

"Seems to be a spirited locale," Rem offered, scanning the boisterous street before him.

"You have no idea," Torval snorted. "They're all hustlers—every mum, every da, every grandmother and babe on feet.

They see to their everyday tasks, then spend their off-hours reveling and working odd angles in pursuit of a little extra coin or fair trade. They're good people, all in all—just don't trust them farther than you can throw them."

Rem nodded. Duly noted. Still, he could see how this neighborhood could seem attractive to someone after a while. There were friendly shadows and a welcoming closeness amid all the buzzing and bustling—it was the sort of place that only city locals might know of or appreciate, and that could leave a mark on anyone who stayed there long enough, engendering their affection even as their pockets were picked.

Torval led them off the main avenue and through a series of winding alleys. Even here, in the narrower quarters of the Knot, there were street hustlers and gamblers and open doors leading into cellar taprooms. Finally, they came to Freygaf's shabby, crowded tenement, with its long, narrow courtyard and rising tiers of rooms and colonnades.

"I would assume the wardwatch has already searched Freygaf's rooms?" Rem asked as they mounted the stairs.

"Aye," Torval answered. "But I'd like to poke about a bit on my own, if you catch my drift."

Of course, Rem understood. Torval was Freygaf's longtime friend and partner, after all. Rem wagered Torval would note any number of clues or strange indicators of interference that an indifferent watchwarden might not have caught upon their own inspection of Freygaf's quarters.

They climbed three flights of stairs, strolled down a lengthy, narrow hallway open to the air, and finally, Torval stopped before a certain door. He waited for a long time, staring, as if unsure whether he should enter or not. Rem hated to see the blustery little fellow waver so, and tried to offer him a way out.

"Torval...are you sure you want to do this?"

Torval looked to him, as if startled that anyone stood beside him. "What do you mean?"

Rem shrugged. "If Freygaf was your friend, what does it matter what he may or may not have been involved in? Does that really affect your friendship, such as it was?"

"Don't be daft, boy," Torval spat back. "If my so-called best friend has been lying to me for years about whatever rotten pies he's had his dirty fingers in, I need to know, because everything he did reflects on me."

"How—"

Torval raised a finger. "Shut up and listen," he hissed. "We're watchwardens, boy. It might not mean much to many, but that means something to me. I only keep my share, I always watch my partner's back, and I never break my word. That's the source of all my honor, such as it is. That's my code. Without it, I'm nothing. And if anything Freygaf did in life sullied that, or made it seem as if I was compromised, well...I can't let that stand. I can renounce a dead friend as quick as I can a live one—but first I've got to know the truth."

Rem nodded. "All right, then. But what about revenge?"

Torval seemed to smile a little—a grim and deathly smile that only warriors and killers were capable of. "Revenge comes either way. Even if Freygaf was dirty, he didn't deserve to be beaten and broken and left by the bloody canal."

He turned toward the door, then offered as an afterthought, "At the very least, I should've had the chance to beat and break him myself, if he was lying to me."

With that, he raised his stout little leg and kicked in Freygaf's door.

The first thing Rem noticed was how dark and cramped Freygaf's chamber seemed—a narrow room with only a bed, a chair, a small corner brazier, and a slop jar. Then Rem saw something else: a fleet black form, stark against the slate-gray darkness of the little room and its dearth of light. The form was bent over a banded chest on the floor near the foot of the bed, rifling through the contents and holding something that flashed in its hands.

Torval saw the form, too. Likewise, the form saw them. Rem heard it draw a shocked breath and mutter a curse.

Then it ran for the window.

"Oi! Stop right there!" Torval shouted, and barreled into the room after the absconding thief.

Rem followed for three steps, then skidded to a halt. He saw the thief go leaping right through the narrow window at the far end of the room. Rem was about to clap Torval on the back, to assure him that they could catch the thief if they turned and hurried back down the outer steps now and wasted no time, but Torval had another idea.

Torval leapt through the window after the thief. He sounded a throaty battle cry (or was that a surprised curse?) all the way down. Rem hurried to the window to see what had become of his partner.

He saw two forms moving in dark blurs in the shadowy, benighted alley below. The first was the thief, tearing out of the alley and onto the main street they'd come from. The second was Torval, rolling off a large refuse pile (which had broken his fall), getting his feet under him, then sprinting off on his stumpy legs after the fleeing burglar.

Rem cursed, turned, and hurried out of the room. He ran into a laundress hauling an enormous basket of linens in the narrow hallway, knocking her sideward. Her laundry basket spilled over the railing of the walkway and went raining down into the courtyard of the tenement, three stories below. The woman laid into Rem with a stream of invectives, but he didn't wait to hear just what she had to offer.

He pounded down all three flights of stairs, skipping several at a time when he could and sometimes even leaping the rail. When he hit the ground floor and thudded out into the street, he searched. He saw nothing but a pair of boys tying a pair of cats together by their tails.

"A dwarf? Running?" he asked.

The boys pointed up the street, the way Rem and Torval had come from. Rem nodded and took off at a brazen pace.

When he reached the main thoroughfare—which was crowded with stalls and barkers and gamers and children starting their own nightly games—he saw his quarry far off to the right: the thief, wending this way and that through the crowd, knocking over tables, chairs, and anything else he could to make his path more laden and harder to follow, and stocky little Torval, thumping along behind at a speed that Rem would never have attributed to his short legs.

"Stop that son of a whore!" Torval cried as he went. "Watchwarden coming through! Someone bring that bastard down!"

No one listened. Rem debated which way he should go—follow directly or try to head them off—and finally decided on the latter. He ran forward to the first side street, took a right, and plunged headlong up another narrow lane between tenements, all the while scanning the alleys off to his left for signs of the fleeing thief.

There! He saw him! The thief had turned right as well and was flying up a street that ran parallel to Rem's own. Already feeling the strain of his speed, Rem willed his body to give him a little more strength, a little more stamina, and tried to pull ahead of the thief. When he felt he'd gained some advantage, he cut left down another alleyway.

He watched, knowing with certainty that he'd see the thief barrel by at any moment, missing him by just a few seconds. Closer and closer to the mouth of the alley onto the thief's street he ran—harder, faster, panting, a stitch in his side.

Then someone bounced off the corner of the building to Rem's right and came barreling into the alleyway.

Right at him.

There was no time to stop. Barely time enough to utter a startled scream. Then Rem and the newcomer in the alley ran right into each other, head-on. Rem saw stars, reeled backward, bounced off a brick wall, and collapsed hard onto the filthy alley floor. Vaguely, he heard the person he'd run into do the same. He blinked and blinked, trying to clear his vision. It was all constellations and fireflies.

"Well, now!" he heard, and knew that Torval had found them. "What have we here?"

Finally, Rem's vision was clear. He managed to sit up, his head aching. Torval was snatching Rem's collision partner to his feet and slamming him hard against the nearest brick wall. It was the thief, after all.

Rem struggled to his feet and leaned against the wall. Although the alley was dark and his vision still muddled, he saw that the fellow they'd stopped was slight, wiry, and red-haired—although his hair was far more of a copper gold than the auburn red that Rem sported. The little man's impertinent face boasted an upturned little piggy nose and a wealth of freckles. He had something clutched in his hand.

"Ginger Joss!" Torval harped. "How long's it been, you little freckled frog?"

"Torval, mate!" Joss offered, not sounding in the least bit happy to see the dwarf. "It's a good thing you happened along. This cheeky bastard"—he pointed to Rem—"he ran right into me in this here alleyway. Like he was lying in wait or some such. Ask me, he's up to no good."

"That's my partner," Torval said. "New to the wardwatch. For once—and in more ways than one—the lad used his head to bring you to heel. Now, what's in your hand?"

Joss tried to stuff the thing he clutched in his pocket, but Torval had his hand in an iron grip. He twisted and Joss whined and the object fell free onto the alley floor. Rem bent and picked it up. His head reeled when he did so.

"Well?" Torval asked.

Rem studied it. "Some kind of pendant. Don't recognize the markings. You?"

He offered it to Torval. Torval studied the little bauble, but seemed equally puzzled. He turned back to Joss. "Talk," he commanded. "What is it?"

"Heirloom," Joss said. "Freygaf was keeping it for me—"

Torval planted a fist in Joss's gut. Before Joss could double over in pain, the dwarf had him pinned to the wall, one thick arm wedged across his throat. "Freygaf's dead," Torval snarled. "So pardon me if I find you rifling through his goods at this particular instant more than a little suspicious."

"I think you'd better tell him what he wants to know," Rem said, throwing up his hands. "I barely know him, Joss, but I'm here to tell you, he's not to be trifled with when he's in such a mood."

"You shut your sauce box!" Torval barked. "You don't know what a scheming, scummy, scurrilous little spider our Ginger Joss is! Freygaf and I busted this little twat at least half a dozen times, and he never took the bloody hint..."

"Look," Joss said, "I can tell this business with Freygaf has you a bit on edge—"

Torval shoved the pendant into Joss's face again, shouting as he did so. "What? Is? It?"

"I can't tell you!" Joss shot back, "And if I did, we'd all be dead, so stop bloody asking! Take me in to the watchkeep if you want, but forget you ever saw that thing!"

Then screams sounded out of some nearby alley. They echoed up and down the little brick and plaster canyons of the Knot and brought cries of impatience and consternation and pleas for quiet. They didn't let up, though. Whoever the woman was, she just kept screaming and screaming and screaming.

Rem moved to the mouth of the alley and peered out into the street. There was a commotion just a few blocks down. Something on a side street. A crowd was already gathering.

"Torval, you'd better come see this," Rem said.

Then, someone in that crowd cried the magic word. "Watchman! Somebody call a watchman!"

Torval released Joss—a move more reflexive than deliberate. "Bloody hell, now we're bound to answer…"

And that was all Joss needed. He threw all his weight against Torval, forcing the dwarf backward against the opposite wall. Torval got the breath knocked out of him. Joss got a good head start and went pounding down the alley in the opposite direction.

Torval growled and started after him, but Rem stopped him. "They're calling us, Torval. I think we should answer. At least we've got the pendant, right?"

Torval looked at the strange little bauble in his hand. "Aye. That we do."

They went to see what the commotion was about.

Under another of those high, foul rubbish piles so common in the alleyways of the Knot, a girl hauling out the family dinner scraps for the night had come across something not usually found in a trash pile.

It was a dead girl.

Rem and Torval both recognized her from the oil painting that had been handed around the watchkeep earlier that night.

It was the missing girl, Telura Dall.

CHAPTER TWELVE

Once word of Telura Dall's fate spread around the watchkeep, a palpable gloom settled in. Those watchwardens on hand—filing their arrests, ending a shift or starting one, engaged in some investigation that took them off the streets—all became silent and morose, as though the girl were one of their own wives or daughters, as though her family's mourning was a departmental duty of the city watch. Rem found this level of reaction puzzling. Surely, these men could not mourn for every dead body they found on the streets—in no time, their hearts would be too heavy, their duties too burdensome to undertake. He asked Torval about it.

"It's not the girl's death," Torval muttered, lost in his own reverie, "so much as the fact that now, there's no reward for anyone...nothing to look forward to or hope for."

That stunned Rem to silence. These watchwardens were a hard-hearted bunch indeed, their cynicism as deep and dark as a coal mine.

Torval made Rem fill out the report, since he had his letters and Torval had none. The report covered their journey to Freygaf's chambers in search of clues as to who might have murdered him, their discovery and chase of Ginger Joss, and finally, the alarm sounded by the citizens of the Knot that led them to poor, dead Telura Dall. Rem read the written report back to Torval for his approval, but the dwarf only grunted and nodded. Rem supposed that was all the approval he would get, and filed the report.

Torval sat in pensive silence when Rem returned to the scrivener's desk they had settled at. Rem tried to respect Torval's reticence to speak, but after a few minutes, he found himself restless. He was not only eager to share what he had learned at the Pickled Albatross, he was also desperate to fill the uncomfortable lull with some conversation—any conversation, really—so that he could stop thinking about what a horrible end young Telura Dall had come to: the daughter of a rich, proud family, murdered and buried under a slum rubbish heap.

Are you really so different from her? a part of him wondered. *Rich, pampered, out of your depth on these streets and subject to all manner of random disaster? You're lucky that wasn't you under that trash heap. But, of course, there is no one here to offer a reward for your whereabouts, is there?*

Rem shuddered. He decided to speak with Torval in an effort to quiet his mind.

"I went back to the Pickled Albatross," Rem said. He waited for some pique from Torval.

All he got was a grunt.

"Do you put much stock in what people say?" Rem asked. "The little things? The details?"

Torval looked at him now. The dwarf cocked his head, raised his eyebrows, and offered an answer.

"There's on old saying among the wardwatch in Yenara: 'Knotted words tie the hangman's noose.'"

Rem nodded. "Fair enough. Well, some things that Cupp and his barmaid had said when we were in there the other night seemed at odds, so I wanted to ask them a few more questions."

Torval smiled a little. "Investigation. I'm impressed, Bonny Prince."

Rem couldn't help but smile at the compliment. "I think I caught one of them in a lie, and my coin would be on Cupp being the liar."

Torval stared at him intently now. He was clearly intrigued.

"The barmaid, Jhonna, told us—and confirmed to me—that Indilen had come in on Saturday for her shift, but that Cupp sent her out again on an errand she never returned from. Whereas Cupp—"

"He told us he hadn't seen her in two days," Torval said.

"Precisely," Rem said. "Jhonna has no reason to lie to us about Indilen's whereabouts. But if Cupp sent her somewhere dangerous and she never came back—"

"That might incriminate him somehow, meaning he'd be best off saying nothing about her at all," Torval finished. "Good work, lad. For what it's worth, I agree with you. I think it's worth assuming that something unusual happened to keep your little market girl from her appointed rendezvous with you—but the question is, what? And how does Cupp figure in?"

Rem shrugged, at a loss to explain. "I can't say. That's why I shared it with you."

Torval nodded. His eyes slid away, as if seeking something neutral to gaze upon, to allow him time and repose to ponder what Rem had offered him.

That's when Eriadus and Hirk appeared. They had taken it upon themselves to examine Telura Dall's body, their senses of honor and violation pricked by news of the young woman's murder. They delivered a summary of what they found to Rem and Torval, just so the two of them would know what a state the girl had been in when she was finally murdered. The girl was largely untouched, her body free of any indications of significant trauma or struggle. She had seawater in her lungs, though, indicating that she had probably drowned in the waters of the harbor.

"That's ridiculous," Rem blurted. "How could she drown in the harbor and end up under a rubbish heap a far distance from the harbor?"

"A puzzle, indeed," Eriadus said helplessly. "I'm simply the messenger. Answers are your purview, watchman."

Rem looked to Torval. Torval nodded. "It's rotten, all right," Torval agreed. "But the very strangeness of it might make uncovering the truth that much easier."

"Gentlemen," Rem asked, his throat closed to the size of a reed, "I just have to ask, do you see this often?"

Rem could keep the peace, see justice done, protect the innocent from wanton predation, all without once fearing for his safety or his sanity... but all this death? Two bodies in two days—murdered, not simply unlucky—and he, on the force for the same brief span? What sort of a snake pit had he stumbled into?

"The dead are no stranger to us," Hirk offered, "Men and women, young and old. But for some rich man's daughter to end up drowned, then buried in a rubbish heap? That's beyond the pale. That's the sort of thing we don't encounter every day. As you can tell, lad, it throws us."

Eriadus cleared his throat. "The family are Panoplists," he said. "I'll see the young lady's body delivered to the House of Rest for preparation."

Rem, Torval, and Hirk all nodded absently at Eriadus's statement. Without another word, he left them. Business as usual carried on in the administration chamber, but the pall remained. It blanketed the whole room like a cloud of sooty smoke belched from an uncleaned chimney.

Their triune silence didn't break until Ondego emerged from his office and approached them. "Well," he said, looking dog tired and sounding like he hadn't slept in days, "let's see it."

"See what, sir?" Rem asked.

"The bauble Ginger Joss stole from Freygaf's chambers. Your report said you had it."

Rem nodded. Torval had given it to him for safekeeping. He drew it out of his pocket and offered it to the chief watchwarden. Ondego studied the strange little pendant on its cheap chain for a long moment. When his examination was complete, he offered it to Hirk. Hirk studied it, but didn't seem to recognize it, either.

"Never seen its like," Ondego said, handing it back to Rem.

"Neither have we," Torval said. "Neither has anyone. We passed it all around the room. Nothing. I'd like to run it by Queydon—since the runes are obviously elvish—but she's nowhere to be found."

"Strange," Rem mumbled. "Elves aren't known for being great lovers of jewelry, but here we have a trinket with their runes upon them..."

"That's not so unusual," Ondego corrected. "People who can't read elvish wear jewelry with elvish inscriptions on them all the time. They think the lines of the runes are decorative. I've even known jewelers who admitted their elvish inscriptions were pure gibberish, simply because people want the script designs and don't care what they say, if they say anything at all."

"Not to mention the fact that it's cheap silver on an even cheaper chain," Hirk said, inspecting the pendant for himself. "If it were the property of an actual elf, I'd wager coin it'd be of finer make."

"Fair assumption," Ondego offered. Somewhere in the distance, the temple bells began to toll. Rem counted six.

"That'll be the sunrise and the end of your shifts," Ondego said wearily. He wagged a finger at Rem and Torval. "Give me a moment before you two knock off. I'll write you letters of introduction. Before you return this evening, I want the two of you to pay the Lady Ynevena a visit and have her offer her thoughts on this bauble."

"The Lady Ynevena?" Rem asked.

"Elven witch," Torval grumbled. "Remember what I told you about the ethnarchs? She's our elven ambassador. On the rare occasions that we have trouble with our city elves, it's Ynevena who's ultimately responsible for straightening out our pointy-eared perpetrators."

"You think she might know something about this?" Rem asked Ondego.

The prefect shrugged. "Can't hurt to ask, can it? Wait here."

He disappeared into his office. Rem and Torval sank into a pair of chairs and waited, the night's exhaustion finally starting to set in as the minutes slipped by. Finally, Ondego emerged again, two folded letters on paper in his hands. He handed Rem and Torval their missives.

"There—those should smooth things over with any Second Ward watchmen who might challenge your presence in their ward, and the Lady Ynevena herself. Now go home. You've uncovered a clue and located a missing girl, dead though the poor wretch was. I'd say that's a full night for anyone."

Rem stood, ready to be on his way. Torval's movements were much slower, as though he had grown heavier since planting himself in his chair. As they slowly withdrew, Ondego offered them a last admonishment.

"Gentlemen," the prefect said. "Please, try not to stop at any more gambling houses to make a mess on the way home?"

His voice was light, even whimsical, but Rem heard the implicit order in it. Torval started to speak. Ondego stopped him.

"That's right," he said, "I heard all about your little tantrum at the Creeper's. That's not even your beat. I had to hear it from Djubal and Klutch."

"Call it a hunch," Torval grumbled.

"Well, call this a censure," Ondego countered. "I don't mind rousting out the criminal element of this city when we've got probable cause, but in this case, you went wading into the Creeper's domain, stomping like a highland ox in a porcelain shop, all based on a wild notion gleaned from Freygaf's past. This city can't stand too many upsets of that sort, Torval, do you understand? Even scum like the Creeper can have powerful friends. You go stirring him up, make sure it's for a reason, not just because your kecks are in a twist."

Torval nodded. Ondego looked to Rem to make sure he understood as well. Rem nodded and lowered his eyes.

"Fine," Ondego said. "Get out of here, both of you. I'll see you on your next shift."

Ondego left, and Hirk with him. Rem ran his hands down over his face. It was true—although their night was not complete, it had been a long one. He was ready to go home and crawl into bed. He clapped Torval on the shoulder.

"Come on, partner," he said. "Don't think of it as censure. Think of it as two days of watch-work in one night. We'll get behind the mule again come sundown."

Torval nodded. He seemed preoccupied. Finally, he looked to Rem. "Would you join me for breakfast again?" he asked. "I've a new place in mind."

Rem nodded. "Lead the way."

Once more, the city seemed to awaken as the predawn gloom became the silvery, mist-laden light of a new morning. Now that the sunrise bells had been rung from the tower of the Great Temple of Aemon, the city's quiet, glowering tenements and boardinghouses quietly extruded their residents into the streets. Piss-mongers collected slop barrels from the tenement dooryards for their clients at the tanneries, the smells of fresh-baked bread wafted warm and inviting from the open windows of bakeries and sweet shops, and animals snorted and lowed in their separate stables from the many liveries that lined the main avenue through the heart of the ward. It was a new day, and life went on apace, even though poor Telura Dall was not—and would never again be—there to witness it.

Though he was exhausted, hungry, and eager to collapse into his bed, Rem enjoyed this time of the morning. Already, he had come to think of this as a special privilege of his position: with each dawn, he got to watch the sleeping city awake, its hard-working denizens stirring to meet their daily destinies, what-ever they might be. It gave him a strange feeling of conspiratorial warmth, as if he and Torval and all the men of the night's watch shared a secret with Yenara herself, and could count themselves part of some strange inner circle.

Few words passed between them. Rem was not sure if Tor-val was thoughtful or simply tired. But since the soft sounds of the waking city brought him such comfort, and since their walk would not be an overly long one, Rem decided that enjoying that blessed silence, that glorious absence of all need or imposition, was best for them both. Torval knew where they were going. Rem would simply follow and eagerly await the surprise at the end of their journey.

They were nearing the great intersection of Harbor Avenue and West Gate Street when Rem heard someone moving up quickly behind them. The streets were soft and muddy, and they had not reached West Gate Street yet, which sported cob-blestones, so the sound that he noted was not precisely foot-steps, but more of a strange, fast-approaching sucking sound.

When Rem was sure that he was not imagining it, he threw a sideward glance at Torval.

The dwarf heard it too. He nodded.

The footfalls reached their sloughing crescendo. Rem and Torval turned toward them. They found themselves staring at a pair of big, broad men—bruisers, leg-breakers—flanking a wispy fellow between them, a familiar, smirking little apparition with red hair, ruddy skin, and bad teeth.

Ginger Joss.

CHAPTER THIRTEEN

Rem understood immediately what was about to happen. Clearly Torval did, as well. He sighed and shook his head slowly.

"I believe you have something that belongs to me," Joss said. "You've got five seconds to hand it over."

"You've got three seconds to beat feet, Joss," Torval countered.

Three seconds. Five at the most. Rem assessed the situation, trying to formulate a plan of attack. He wouldn't be caught unawares again, like he was with that drunken orc in the Pickled Albatross.

Joss was a known quantity—small, wiry, cunning, and quick, perhaps, but certainly not strong. His companions, however, were of tougher mettle. The one on Rem's right looked like he might have once been Tregga, one of the horse-mounted steppe nomads that wandered the frosty plains beyond the Ironwall Mountains. His hair was shorn now, lacking the many braids and knots so common in Tregga culture and showing that he'd surrendered at least some measure of his identity to civilization, but his face still sported the familiar ritual scars in strange geometric whorls and patterns that made the nomads so easy to identify. He wore a longsword in a scabbard slung across his back. As yet, the blade had not been loosed.

His partner, by contrast, had swarthy olive skin, dark hair, and gray eyes—clearly a southerner, perhaps from as far away as Isolis or Ferosus. He was armed with a farmer's mace—a cheap piece of steel on a hickory shaft, inelegant, but definitely effective. Each of the brutes towered at least half a head above Rem, and looked like they tossed aurochs and felled trees with single ax swipes in their spare time. Torval was exactly half the size of either of those big men, and despite his ferocity and bravery, Rem guessed that those hired hands could—given the opportunity—make mince of Torval and leave the dwarf bleeding in the middle of the muddy street without breaking a sweat.

Was there help coming? Rem scanned the street in all directions. People carried on about their business. He caught a few passersby and shopkeeps noting the tense standoff in the middle of the muddy avenue, but that was simple curiosity. There would be no one to assist them if it came to a fight.

Rem then stole a glance at Torval. The dwarf had already sized up their opponents and marked their weaknesses—Rem could tell by the way he stared at them with neither fear nor fury, only cold appraisal. Torval had his maul in his hand, but what could that one blunt instrument do against these two, with their own weapons and their long reaches? Rem himself had a few ideas of his own about how to fell these giants if they started a fight, but he couldn't count on either strategy until the fight was truly joined. Rem didn't fancy trying to disarm them with nothing in hand, but he hoped that their size and very clear overconfidence—neither of them seemed to be in a guarded stance—would work against them.

Those five seconds were up now. Rem drew a long, slow breath.

Joss snorted, tired of waiting. "Cripple them," he said.

The moment the words were out of Joss's mouth, Rem

lunged for the scar-faced nomad before him. The big man grabbed Rem's tunic and tried to lift him. Rem, going in for a low, hard tackle, collided with the horseman, head in his gut, one arm wrapping around his muscular waist. Before the horseman could yank him free, Rem grabbed the nomad's testicles and squeezed.

The horseman roared.

Rem managed to get just a moment's image of what was happening beside him. Joss had withdrawn, eager to let his hired hands fight it out. Torval, meanwhile, matched blows from the southlander's mace with his maul, drawing the dark-skinned man away from where the fight began. Rem was relieved: so long as each of them kept their own man busy and separated from his partner, it would keep the two of them from working in concert.

The horseman seized Rem's tunic, trying desperately to tear him loose from their grappling. Rem let go of the nomad's balls, tore himself out of his grasp, then spun sideward. The steppe rider tried to stand, still half-hunched over in pain, and reached out with one hand to snag Rem again. Rem evaded his clumsy snatch with a quick step, took aim, and kicked hard, aiming squarely for the outer crook of the bruiser's knee joint.

With a sickening crack, the joint collapsed inward. Once more, the horseman screamed. He fell, face forward, right into the mud.

Rem looked to Torval, who was still engaged with his opponent, their melee having drifted onto the boardwalk along the edge of the street now. A crowd gathered to watch the duel. No one seemed eager to call for a watchman to break it up.

And Joss? Where was Joss?

No matter. Rem turned back to his opponent in the mud. The nomad was trying and failing to raise himself on his disjointed leg. He screamed again and shifted his weight, trying to support himself on his three good limbs instead of his single damaged one. The sword on his back passed within a foot of Rem's grasp.

Rem reached out, yanked the blade from its leather sheath, then moved in to end the duel before it started. He kicked the Tregga hard in the ribs—once, twice, four times, six times—and when he felt the nomad well and truly tenderized, shoved him sideward with one boot so that he would roll onto his side. The horseman lay fetal, shaking, howling in pain, cursing as well, making all sorts of promises about what he would do when he was on his feet again. One hand hovered over his balls. The other grasped at his right leg, the one that Rem had dislocated. He made one halfhearted swipe at Rem, as though he could simply grab him by his breeches and yank him down into the mud with him.

Rem evaded him. He chanced another quick look behind him. Torval was still dancing around in the street, avoiding some very violent attacks from the swarthy, mace-wielding southlander. He no longer had his maul. *Blast!* He must have lost it in the midst of their fight. That meant that Rem was needed—his partner was outmatched and unarmed. He had to make sure the nomad wouldn't rise or cause further trouble so that he, Rem, could speed to Torval's aid.

A few knots of citizens had gathered now, all transfixed by the unfolding drama.

"Call the wardwatch!" someone finally shouted.

"We *are* the wardwatch!" Torval replied, still evading his attacker but, without arms of his own, unable to truly engage.

Rem looked to the horseman again. The nomad glared up at him. Mud and tears streaked his scarred face. He looked furious and terrified all at once.

Rem thought he recognized that look. It was unbridled rage. It showed no self-regard or self-control.

And where was Joss? The thief could be sneaking up behind him at that very moment, a sharp little dagger in his filthy hands, ready to strike—

"Stay down," Rem said to the wounded nomad, "or you'll only make it worse."

The horseman reached out, lightning-quick, one big hand seeking Rem's ankle, probably to yank him off it and send him toppling into the mud.

Rem regarded the fast-moving hand as a striking snake. Pure reflex took over. He stabbed downward with his stolen sword. The blade passed right through the horseman's grasping hand like a crucifixion nail and pinned it to the muddy street. The horseman roared and bled.

"I warned you," Rem said. Then something else was upon him—a writhing, smelly form that he vaguely recognized as Ginger Joss. The little thief was trying to wrestle Rem to the ground. Rem, having both height and muscle on the lithe little bastard, managed to curl one arm around Joss's throat and lock it in place. As Joss bucked and sidled and struggled to free himself, Rem used the only weapon left to him. He punched Joss in the face several times, until he heard the crunch of nose cartilage and felt hot blood and snot pouring out onto his crooked forearm. When Joss's struggles grew weak and haphazard, Rem spun him around, kneed him in the gut, then tossed him aside. He looked again to Torval.

"Sundry hells, you poncey bastard!" Torval shouted. "I could use some help here, if you're done toying with those two!"

Rem drew a deep breath to steady himself. Without warning, he yanked the sword from out of the horseman's pinned hand and hurried to meet Torval's attacker. Presently, the mace wielder had his back to Rem. Rem prayed that would remain the case, just until he could close in.

The macer struck at Torval. Torval leapt backward—and buffed up against a stone horse trough, half-full with green, scummy water. The swipe carried the macer around so that, suddenly, he stood face-to-face with the approaching Rem.

The swarthy southerner, seeing Rem's approach with sword in hand, only hesitated for a moment. Rem knew what was about to happen. It made his stomach turn a somersault in his belly. But his years of training in his father's courtyard took over. He slid backward into a low, defensive stance, sword point leveled. He caught the southlander's wild gaze and tried to reason with him.

"Stop," he said, as loudly and clearly as he could. "Drop the mace, walk away, and that's the end of it."

The southlander clearly had his blood up. He was panicked, wild-eyed. Rem felt something coil up in the center of him. Was it really about to come to this? Here? Now? Early on such a fine morning, after such a long and sorrowful night?

He knew what had to be done, but he didn't want to—he had never *not* wanted a thing so much in all his life . . .

But he knew what these men would have done to them if they had not managed to overpower them. He knew, instinctively, that there were no rules in this fight, only victory.

The southlander drew back the mace for another hard arc, aimed right at Rem's skull. He loosed a throaty battle cry.

That moment—that tiny, infinitesimal moment, when the swarthy southerner decided to sound his intentions and draw back farther for an all-or-nothing killing blow—gave Rem the opening he needed. He lunged, using all his weight to drive the sword point forward, pushing himself inside the arc of the southlander's blow. The sword passed through the man so smoothly that Rem had to glance down to make sure that it had hit home.

It had. The blade was sheathed, hilt-deep, in the southlander's gut. Blood welled out in a hot sheet, filling the sword's shallow fuller groove and burbling over the hilt onto Rem's hand.

Rem looked into the man's gray eyes. The fellow looked confused, surprised, almost comical.

But Rem could not laugh. Rather, he wanted to weep, the way this man would weep, if he had more time to devote to his tears before all the life bled out of him.

The southlander sagged to the street with the Tregga horseman's sword in his gut, Rem still standing above him. Rem watched as light left the sellsword's eyes and the swarthy killer expelled a last, hoarse breath.

The street was silent and still.

Torval stared at Rem, clearly shocked that the young man had gone for the kill.

Elsewhere, over Rem's shoulder, Joss scrambled through the mud. When he gained his feet, he burst through the clotted onlookers and fled the scene.

Rem bent double and vomited beside the man he'd just killed.

His first.

Rem remained in a stunned daze. He heard the shrill cry of Torval's little brass whistle. He noted, after a time, that some watchwardens had arrived—dayshifters, men he didn't recognize. They listened to Torval's report of the incident, then set about cleaning up the mess. Throughout, Rem thought he heard whispers passed among the onlookers and passersby, all of them murmuring about how that young, red-haired watchwarden had simply murdered that southlander in cold blood, without any real provocation or justification. If he was so good with a sword, why couldn't he simply disarm the poor man, instead of slaying him in the street? And what sort of contest was that—the deadly point and cutting edge against the simple blunt strength of a farmer's mace?

Rem heard these whispers—or imagined he heard them— as all those workaday Yenarans milled past and stole glances at him: a stout baker's wife with rosy cheeks and dark eyes; a pair of grizzled, gray-bearded dwarves who had carried their morning ale mugs out into the street to watch the fray; a burly longshoreman, all muscle and bulk, leading his child to their morning labors; a slack-faced albino orc in a tattered cloak, its red eyes blinking out of its bestial face with only dim under-standing. Though he knew it was impossible, Rem felt that he could hear what they were all saying about him—*thinking* about him—as they lingered around the periphery of the bloody brawl and studied its pitiful aftermath. The many voices all sounded like one voice, after a time—the voice of his own conscience, persecuting him for taking a man's life when, per-haps, he had not truly needed to.

Or was that his father's voice? *I hope you're proud of yourself, Remeck. You left the safety and ease of the court and came all the way down here to prove something to yourself, and look what you've proven. You're a brawler and a killer, just like any of those illiterate fools who crew a merchant's barque.*

Well, he'd proven something about himself at last, hadn't he, however unpleasant it might be to face it? Finally, he had some-thing that he could claim as his own, for all time and beyond.

"Lad?"

Rem snapped out of his reverie. He was thankful for the interruption. Those voices were starting to sicken him.

Torval stood before him, staring up into his face with a true and probing concern that Rem had never seen before. Slowly, the dwarf reached up and laid one thick hand on Rem's shoulder.

"How are you?"

Rem started to answer in the affirmative but lost the words. It occurred to him to ask a question of his partner, but an instant later, he lost that question as well. After a time, he managed a resigned shrug.

Torval pivoted and moved in beside Rem. Rem was sitting on the broad lip of the stone horse trough that had almost trapped Torval during the fight. Now the dwarf leaned against it beside his young partner. He laid a hand on Rem's back, a gentle reminder that, whatever Rem felt at that moment, he wasn't alone.

"You've never killed a man before, have you?" Torval asked.

Rem shook his head.

"You gave him a chance to run," Torval said, "and he failed to take it. You did your duty, lad, clean and true, and the fool left you no options."

"I suppose," Rem muttered.

Torval stood again and slid right into Rem's line of sight. He glared into Rem's haunted eyes and made sure that Rem was looking at him.

"Listen to me," Torval said, a little more forcefully, "his blood was up. He tried to kill me. He would have killed you. You did nothing wrong here."

"It just seems so..." Rem choked. He couldn't find the word. *What was the word?* He should know the word, because it was right on the tip of his tongue. Why was his mind suddenly all a-muddle? Was this the price of killing a man?

"Cheap," Torval said. "Cheap and tawdry. Is that it?"

Rem nodded, amazed that Torval knew the word he had been searching for.

"Well, it is," Torval said, moving closer to him. "When a man dies in the mud over a second-rate trinket like that bloody pendant we're carrying—dies for no good cause, and meets no good end—it *is* cheap and tawdry. But you gave him a choice, lad. You gave him a choice, and he failed to take it. His death might as well have been by his own hand, and not yours."

"That doesn't help," Rem said.

"Well, it should," Torval snapped. "You didn't just save your own life, boy, you saved mine! My children still have a father because of you. For that, I'm eternally grateful."

Rem raised his eyes to Torval. "Children?"

The dwarf carried on, ignoring Rem's inquiry. "Now come on. If this bloody pendant we lifted from Freygaf's room is so important that a weasel like Joss'd be willing to spend coin on hired killers to retrieve it, I say it could be important to us. Shall we go visit the Lady Ynevena and pick her haunted elven brain forthwith—first thing in the bloody morning—instead of letting the day waste away?"

Rem drew a deep breath. He thought his heart rate might be slowing at last. He looked at his hands and saw that they were no longer shaking. "Let's do it," he managed, and stood. "Let's get out of here."

Torval set out, and Rem fell in beside him.

CHAPTER FOURTEEN

Their walk was a long one. The gradually gathering light of the morning, softened by the thinning fog and enlivened by the vague chill that still clung to the air, acted as a balm to Rem's conscience after a time. By the time they moved through the outskirts of the Third Ward into the First, Rem could almost justify his opponent's death to himself; by the time they passed across the borderline between city center and the richly appointed Second Ward, Rem could almost convince himself that he hadn't killed anyone at all—that had been the act of some other young man (he told himself) that he had merely borne witness to. An altercation turned deadly. A misunderstanding spiraling quickly out of hand.

He had a choice, he kept telling himself, just as Torval had insisted. *He had a choice and he failed to take it.*

That would have to do, for now.

The Second Ward was, according to Torval, where the moneyed and well-to-do of the city made their homes. There were a few crowded tenements and dodgy side streets laden with vice and populated by members of the unwashed masses at its periphery—where else should the servants and artisans who served the rich live, after all, but close at hand?—but the concentration of lovely, well-maintained villas on winding, hilly streets behind high, ivy-covered walls and well-manicured hedges was unmistakable. They climbed into the gently slop-

ing hills of Yenara's southern quarter, those hills like colorful steps carved into a mountainside, and they gazed down on
the sprawling city below as the well-heeled patricians of that
neighborhood would—askance, aloof, down the long, sloping
bridges of their proverbial noses.

As they entered the ward and climbed a not-too-steep cobbled street, Torval explained that the Lady Ynevena, Yenara's
sole elven ethnarch, ran a sort of posh hostel for her kind and
any others who might desire to sojourn among them (provided
those others—human, dwarf, or otherwise—met Ynevena's
undefined and ever-mutable social standards and could pay the
price of admission). Some muttered that unnatural things went
on behind those walls, but Torval assumed that was just the
gentry offering jealous gossip about the activities of a person
they could not understand, inside a pleasure palace they would
never be allowed to explore. Everyone knew elves were dec-
adent, sensuous, carnal sorts, in love with every last sensation
to be drawn from the world, from the quiver of flesh under a
bare fingertip to the sublime movement of the soul provided
by espying a lovely and monumental piece of architecture or
looming, cyclopean mountain summit. But from what little
Torval had seen, and what more he had heard, Lady Ynevena's pleasure palace was not so much a pulsing, torrid den of
iniquity as a strange, particular sort of inn and museum where
guests sometimes dallied with themselves or one another. So
long as they kept their peculiarities within their bloody walls,
Torval reasoned, he didn't give a tin tinker's fart what they got
up to.

"But you said she's the ethnarch," Rem interjected. "So that
means she wields some sort of authority?"

Torval nodded. "Aye. When some fauney of her pointy-
eared persuasion runs afoul of the law—and while it's a rare

occurrence, it's not unheard-of—we're obligated, by ancient treaty, to deliver the perpetrator to the Lady Ynevena and her personal tribunal and guard. Between them, said elven perp is then judged and convicted, and shipped out on the next caravel to Aadendrath, or perhaps by supply wagon to one of the larger sylvan enclaves to the north or east."

"So, those elves that break Yenaran law never face Yenaran justice?" Rem asked.

Torval shrugged. "As I said—the treaties are ancient. Such is the way of things."

"Will she even treat with us?"

Torval made a sudden left, marching down a narrow alley between two high stucco walls covered in bright-purple bougainvillaea and white roses. Rem nearly kept on up the canted street they climbed, but he caught Torval's change of direction out of the corner of his eye and turned to follow.

Torval didn't turn and respond to his question until he had come to the very end of the narrow alley, to a stout, well-seasoned door set into the wall covered in bougainvillaea, a strange brass facing bearing a door-knocker upon it, in the semblance of some long-forgotten, half-beastly elven wood deity.

"She may or may not treat with us," Torval said. "But leave no stone unturned, yes?"

Rem shrugged. "Fair enough."

Torval indicated the great brass knocker. Rem grabbed it and gave it three hard thumps. They seemed to resound on the other side of the wall, inside the compound, like wallops on a drum. After a long, patient silence, they heard faint footsteps approaching from the other side of the stout door. A small wicket opened before them and a smooth, well-chiseled face gazed out at them from beyond. The eyes in that face were languid, all curiosity dulled.

"Your business?" the smooth-faced porter demanded, voice a dull whisper.

Torval brandished both their signets. "Watchwardens, come for the Lady Ynevena on business from the Fifth Ward." Now he lifted the sealed letters of introduction that Ondego had given them. "We have warrants for the Lady's review, if it pleases her."

The porter studied them through the wicket—a long, bored consideration that struck Rem as either the product of hard narcotics or a thoroughly bored and jaded intellect. Finally, the porter stepped back and closed the wicket. They heard bolts thrown, hinges gave the faintest, well-oiled squeal, and the door was opened for them.

The porter was an elf, as Rem had suspected. He had the smooth, lovely face of a youth and the bored, ancient gaze of a man nearing the end of many scores of years. He wore no top—which struck Rem as rather strange on a morning with such a pronounced chill upon it—but only a long, flowing silk sarong of sorts, and sandals with silken cords and soles of the softest kid leather. For a moment, the indifferent elven porter studied them—a nobleman, studying something that he found amusingly common and prosaic—before finally closing the garden gate behind them. He set off on a slow walk up a path of spaced flagstones that wound deeper in beneath the foliage.

"This way," he said. Rem barely heard him. He threw a puzzled glance at Torval.

Torval only raised one bushy brow, as if to say, *yes, that's right—that's how they comport themselves*—then the two of them followed their lackadaisical greeter.

The elven porter led them on a meandering path through a dense, mist-shrouded little jungle of well-manicured shrubs, flower beds, and stunted trees, never saying a word, never looking back to check on their progress. There were thickets of whispering pines and weeping willows, giant beds of ferns and cycads lording over plots of poppies, winter roses, and blazing-purple rhododendrons.

As brilliant as the hue and blush of the flora were the smells. They teased and tortured Rem's olfactory senses like dancing wenches in a tavern, alive and frolicking feverishly in his nostrils. He detected lilacs and jasmine, roses and scarlet sage, mint and apple blossoms, even currants and apricots. It was heady, intoxicating, and it seized him with the strangest of sensations.

There, walking along the path with Torval at his side and that glum elven porter leading the way, Rem suddenly realized that he wanted to crawl in among the brush—yes, to just step off the path, and lie down on a bed of white jasmine, strip off his boots and tunic, and sleep. And what dreams might find him here, in the shadows of this very special garden, an island of peace and rest and reverie in the heart of a teeming, unwashed, indifferent city? Just crawl in beneath the welcoming canopy of a willow and—

Torval suddenly stood at his side, shaking him. Rem blinked. He hadn't been walking at all. He was standing stock-still at the edge of a colony of winter roses. In the misty morning light, their thorns gleamed hungrily under their soft white petals.

"Torval, I—"

"Shhh," the dwarf hissed. "Just step back onto the path and keep moving."

Up ahead, nearly lost around a gentle curve, the elven porter stopped.

"Is there a problem?" he purred.

"None whatsoever," Torval said, then jerked his head sideward again. Rem obeyed and stepped back onto the path. They fell in step once more behind their host.

"What happened?" Rem whispered.

Torval sighed. "Not sure. I turned to ask you a question and you were gone. I found you back there, drifting into the flower beds, staring like a loon."

Rem shook his head, rubbed his temples. "Gods, what a strange feeling."

"Magic, boy," Torval grumbled. "It's rife here, and hungry. Try to keep your wits about you. If you feel yourself drifting, just put your eyes and ears back on something more prosaic"—he gestured toward his own face—"like this ugly mug, if you must."

Torval punctuated his jest with a sour little smile. Rem, thankful for his partner's vigilance and concern, patted his shoulder in agreement.

As they walked on, Rem grew ill at ease. The garden was lovely, aye—no doubt about that. It was a place to get lost, a place lovely enough to lie down and die in. But it was also haunted. His little fugue state and the strange, insistent murmuring of a breeze that wasn't there in the dense, deep foliage assured him of that. Clearly, people came to the Lady Ynevena's private pleasure garden to lose themselves, or submit themselves to some sylvan, floral power older and more preeminent than their own mortal wills. Gods, what a sublime and dangerous place. Rem had never seen a grotto more welcoming or, concurrently, predatory. Truth be told, it frightened him.

At last, they emerged from the greenscape into a bounded yard with a manicured lawn, a rock-bordered pond full of fish and turtles, and a number of stone seats and benches strewn about in a haphazard pattern. Just across this yard was a broad, paved terrace and upon that terrace, half reclining on a lovely old imperial divan, was a woman of such delicate mold and exquisite beauty that the very sight of her made something deep within Rem ache and coil. Her hair was a bewildering tangle of scarlet, copper, and gold curls, framing a face so perfectly proportioned and molded as to be the work of an artist, for life, chance, circumstance alone could never fashion such a stunning work of art. Only the mind of a single visionary, fever-racked painter or sculptor could imagine such perfect, ageless, unrivaled beauty. Her body, to Rem's great chagrin, was no less impressive, the smooth, lithe shape of it readily apparent under the sheer, loose gown that she wore, a garment that almost wasn't, beautified and embellished with pearls set in crimson-gold inlays or finely wrought brocades of silver and opalescent thread. Far from being thin and willowy, as Rem might have expected of an elven matron, the Lady Ynevena's body was a pale temple displaying perfect, sensuous curves beside taut, translucent stretches of smooth white flesh. Rem thought he saw a pearl stud winking beneath the sheer transparency of the lady's gown, embedded in her stout pink nipple—but he couldn't be sure. The moment he thought he saw that pearl flashing above her erect areola, he forced his eyes away from her.

A man bearing a cup and a polished silver pitcher stood just behind the Lady Ynevena's divan—tall, human, olive-skinned, and raven-haired. He was darkly handsome, exceptionally muscled, and wore only two items of clothing: a colorful silk sarong, wrapped about his middle, and a small, almost dainty leather collar round his throat. A leash of black silk cord was attached to the collar. Its opposite end was gripped lightly in the pale hand perched on the Lady Ynevena's curving hip. Rem noted that the man's eyes never left his beautiful mistress. He simply stood, staring down at her, expectant and impossibly patient, as if the only thing in the world that would give him pleasure was to pour her a fresh cup of wine and offer it.

Rem realized then that if he wasn't careful, he would end up drifting right into the arms of the Lady Ynevena just as he had almost drifted into that thorny rose bed. And who knew what sort of thorns this elven maid concealed beneath her soft white petals?

The porter approached his mistress, bowed, and whispered into her perfect pointed ears. How Rem wanted to nibble on one of the soft, pale lobes at the base of those perfect, tapering ears...

Stop that! Get hold of yourself, you fool!

Rem coughed, cleared his throat, and shifted on his feet. He looked to Torval. Torval's glare suggested that, telepathic or not, the dwarf could clearly read his thoughts—and he wasn't pleased by them.

The Lady Ynevena nodded to her porter. Without raising her eyes, she reached out to the table before her, took up a plump, candied apricot between two lithe, delicate fingers, and bit from it. Rem felt a shudder move through him.

She turned her gaze upon them. Under that gaze—those almond-shaped honey-colored eyes, ageless, penetrating—Rem suddenly felt naked and ashamed. She could see right into him—right through him—and she knew exactly what sort of lascivious thoughts her beauty and complete lack of embarrassment awakened in him. Moreover, he thought he saw a slight smile at the corner of her lips—silent acknowledgment that she knew what he wanted, and that perhaps—just perhaps—the right words, the right entreaties, might grant him the keys to the proverbial kingdom.

"Good watchwardens, I bid you welcome," she said. Her voice was music. Rem sighed, growling a little in disgust with himself. "What business can I aid you with on this fine, lovely morning?"

Torval looked to Rem. *Would you like to speak to her?* he seemed to ask. Rem, completely uninterested in speaking to the Lady lest he make an utter fool of himself, deferred with a nod to Torval. The dwarf stepped forward and presented the letters from Ondego.

"Introductions and entreaties for aid, milady," the gruff little dwarf said. "We've come to an impasse in an investigation, and the aid of someone of your—one who is, that is—"

"Elven?" the Lady Ynevena offered.

"Just so," Torval conceded.

"Call me elven, then, Watchwarden," the Lady said with a smile. "That's what I am, and I am not ashamed to be so."

"As you say, milady," Torval answered.

The Lady took the offered letters but immediately set them aside without reading them or breaking their seals. She sat up on her sofa now, and Rem lowered his eyes. Gods help him, she really was naked beneath that sheer gown. Now that she was upright, he could see *everything*.

Torval, the little monk, didn't seem to note this or to be troubled by it at all.

"We've come into possession of a pendant," Torval began, "found among the effects of a murdered watchwarden—"

"Someone close to you," the Lady Ynevena said.

Her sensitivity gave Torval pause. Rem wagered the dwarf should have been ready for that—everyone knew that elves could read thoughts and feelings, after all. "Just so," the dwarf said, his voice ever-so-strangled, then coughed to clear his throat. But before he could carry on, the Lady Ynevena spoke for him.

"Show me the bauble and I shall identify the rune upon it if I can."

Torval searched his pockets—then realized that it was Rem

who had the pendant. The dwarf turned to him, and Rem suddenly felt like a little boy forced to recite the holy psalms before the local Priests of Aemon—scatterbrained, nervous, completely unprepared. But nonetheless, he forced himself to step forward, rooting in his pocket for the pendant on its chain. He handed it to the Lady Ynevena, and forced himself to look into her eyes as he did so.

There was a smile in them now—knowing and warm, the smile of a holy sister trying to show peaceful acceptance and a complete lack of judgment at a child's confession, or an experienced whore amused by a virgin's clumsy reticence. Either way, the elf maiden's knowing gaze did nothing for Rem's composure or confidence.

The Lady Ynevena took the pendant on its chain with her free hand, then gave her manservant's leash a gentle tug. Eagerly, her muscled cupbearer poured fresh wine into her goblet and handed it over. The Lady Ynevena sipped and let the pendant swing before her eyes, studying it in the gradually brightening morning light.

"It's of cheap make. Workmanlike, as one might find in a market for travelers and green folk. The material is probably nickel, alloyed with tin and a little real silver for a nice shine in direct sunlight."

"And the inscription?" Torval pressed.

The Lady Ynevena studied it quietly. Despite her clear disregard for its origins and craftwork, she seemed fascinated, even amused by the little charm on its cheap chain. Her stare, beyond that mild amusement, was otherwise unreadable. Her gaze remained fixed on the pendant for a long time, and brought with it a long, uncomfortable silence.

Finally, she raised her eyes. She looked first to Rem, then to Torval, then handed her cup back to her leashed companion.

"The rune is *yethred*, the ninth letter of our alphabet, intertwined with another letter, *qhwur*. The flourishes on the design suggest some sort of family crest, but I could recite for you the names of five thousand separate elven families living now in various corners of the continent, or west, upon Aadendrath, and I can assure you that none of them ever employed this particular runic combination in their family sigils."

"What could it be, then?" Rem managed to ask.

The Lady raised her mesmerizing eyes to him. He felt something stroke the center of his consciousness—a strange, entirely inward sensation, like one's fingers idly sliding along the furry spine of a meandering cat. Rem's breath caught and he had to remind himself to inhale again.

"Perhaps," the Lady suggested, "it's the sigil of a bloodline that no longer exists? Many have been lost to war, disease, and slavery in the last thousand years. Even if that's the case, there are no guarantees that this sigil's presence on a hotly contested piece of evidence suggests any elven involvement in your present investigation. As you both well know, humans are fond of adopting the detritus of elven culture at whim for purely decorative purposes, devoid of all understanding of the stolen marker's true meaning."

Rem nodded, as did Torval. Yes, they both knew that. Ondego had said as much earlier. Torval wanted more, though.

"Do you have any inkling of what this could be used for, milady? Any at all?"

The Lady Ynevena studied the pendant once more. "No pointed observations, certainly."

She offered the pendant to Rem. He took it, catching a glimpse of the gorgeous swell of her white bosom beneath her sheer morning gown as he stared down at her. This time, he made no attempt to hide his object, or his lust. The Lady Ynevena offered him another of those knowing half smiles. Her eyes never left his.

Torval cleared his throat. *Enough of that, lad. Time to go.* Rem tore his eyes away, drew a deep, centering breath, and forced himself to look once more upon the Lady Ynevena's man-toy. He was staring at his mistress again, eager, expectant.

Please, that look said, *please, ask me for just one more cup of wine.*

Rem shuddered and moved away from the Lady, drifting back toward the edge of the terrace.

"I'm sure I need not remind the two of you," the Lady began, "that if, in point of fact, one of my kind is somehow involved in this nefarious little plot you're trying to uncover, said criminal should be delivered to me, unharmed, for the swift expedition of justice."

"Per the treaties," Torval assured her.

Rem threw a glance back over his shoulder. The Lady was leaning forward now, addressing Torval directly. She was wearing the same knowing half smile and had leveled her unnervingly direct gaze upon the dwarf, but Torval's stance suggested that he wasn't subject to her enchantments as Rem had been. She knew this, Rem thought, but she sought to unbalance him by being brazen anyway.

"I find that outcome most unlikely, in any case," the Lady said, tilting her head slightly. "I would imagine you watchwardens only rarely encounter criminal enterprise undertaken by my people. We are poets and artists, after all, not malefactors."

"As you say, milady," Torval replied. "But there are wormy apples on every tree in the orchard, aren't there?"

"What a colorful metaphor," the Lady said, without a hint of mirth in her voice.

"We'll be on our way," Torval said, and broke off from her. The glum porter who had shown them in was waiting by the path to escort them out again.

Just before they disappeared into the thick growth of Lady Ynevena's enchanted garden, Rem heard the Lady speak from her divan on the terrace.

"It was a delight making your acquaintance, Watchwarden Remeck. Do call again, even if you have no particular business to transact."

Rem forced himself not to look back. He kept moving, as though he had not heard her—but of course, he knew that she knew that he had.

He and Torval did not speak again until they were back on the cobbled street outside the compound walls and some distance from the gateway. They rejoined a bustling avenue that cut through the hoity-toity Second Ward, an avenue loosely crowded with foot and litter traffic, sporting flower vendors and hungry solicitors on almost every major corner. Finally, when they had reached this seemingly safe haven—out in the world, away from the Lady Ynevena's enchanted garden and its temptations—Torval broke their silence with an incredulous snort.

"You've never been around them, have you?" he asked.

Rem threw up his hands. "Of course not. Why would a—a—groom's son from the north have any commerce with elves?"

Torval shook his head. "Bloody witch, skulking around inside your head. Don't you dare go back there, do you hear me?"

"I would never—" Rem began. "Of course not."

"Don't give me that cack," Torval said. "You were eyeing her like she was your last supper before the gallows, and she knew it at well as I did. I've seen it before—those bloody tree fuckers cast strange spells on human hearts. For you, it's an immortal and everlasting love, for her kind, it's an afternoon's tryst. I'm telling you, lad, if you let her into your head and heart, you'll never be right again. Trust me on this."

Rem nodded. "You have my word."

They heard a commotion and turned toward it. A stone's throw away, a pair of well-dressed Second Ward watchmen were rousting an orc in a threadbare old cloak from the stretch of cobbles where he crouched, no doubt begging alms. There were other beggars on the street—where better to beg than at the doors of the rich and well-appointed, after all?—but these watchmen seemed to have no interest in the others. The orc was their only target.

"We should go," Torval said quietly. "We've got letters from Ondego, so we're in this ward on business, but that may not stop them from asking questions and dragging us back to their watchkeep for an official report."

Rem nodded and they set out, heading down a side street away from the main thoroughfare, a more direct shortcut back toward the northeastern quarters of the city.

"I would've expected more cooperation between the ward-watches," Rem said as they walked.

"Maybe once upon a time," Torval said, shaking his head. "Perhaps at some point far beyond us. But presently, the wards are all fiefdoms, and the lords of the fiefs don't much care for footsoldiers from the others stomping on their turf. Being forced to pay a toll for unmolested passage through the ward isn't unusual, and four times of five, that toll comes out of your own purse."

Rem shook his head. "There's no authority over the pre-fects, to settle such disputes?"

Torval nodded. "Of course there is. That's Black Mal, the

chief magistrate, who reports to Essarhadden, the high justice. But Black Mal's only concern is maintaining the semblance of order, collecting fines, and getting a steady supply of convicts that the Halls of Justice can sell to slavers or lease to mining companies for profit. He'll only settle disputes between prefects if he thinks doing so will result in greater order or increased coin for the Halls' coffers. Truth be told, I think he likes the competition between the prefects and their men—it lets him see plainly who's got real sack and who's merely a quailing bureaucrat."

Rem shook his head once again. "Senseless," he muttered.

"Call it tradition, however foul," Torval said. "Now let's get back to our side of town and break fast. I'm starving."

CHAPTER FIFTEEN

Rem kept pace beside the dwarf as they marched out of the Second Ward, across the breadth of the First and back into the Third, into the narrow, winding streets where early morning was already rousting out the carters, the grocers, the merchants, and the shopkeepers for another day of business and toil. In the east, the sun was just above the city walls and lowest rooftops, shining down into the narrow streets obliquely, creating deep pools of shadow in the lee of the temples and tenements. Far from invigorating Rem, the low glare of the morning sun made him even more weary. He thought a few times that he might bow out on Torval's invitation to break fast, but something in the dwarf's preoccupied manner and knit brow told him that Torval needed company right now, so he stuck with him.

After stopping by a cheesemaker's to buy a flagon of goat's milk, they came at last to their apparent destination—not a tavern at all, but an apartment house in the heart of the Third Ward, with an arkwright's shop on the ground floor and a narrow stairway leading to the rooms above.

"Is this your home, Torval?" Rem asked.

Torval nodded. "Such as it is. You've no objections?"

Rem was about to shake his head—indeed, he was more than a little curious to see what kind of home the little ball of muscle and obstreperousness made for himself—when a commotion in the street at their backs interrupted him.

A costermonger leading the way for a heavily laden two-wheeled cart dragged by what appeared to be his overlarge teenage son had encountered a hindrance to their progress in the form of a tall, huddled beggar blocking a rather narrow corner where the street bent sharply. Now that same costermonger stood shouting into the face of the beggar in question, but surprisingly, the beggar was neither begging pardon nor backing down.

Rem studied the big vagabond in the tattered, stained old cloak that stood his ground against the foul-mouthed costermonger and realized suddenly why the panhandler wasn't backing down or begging pardon. It was an orc—his bare, corded arms and the jut of his lower jaw beneath the cowl of his cloak made that clear enough. But more puzzling to Rem was the orc's complexion. It wasn't the typical olive green or slate gray of most of its kin, but of a pale sort: bone white, with a tinge of blue green, an albino of some sort.

And that realization sent a strange, uneasy tremor down the length of Rem's spine, because he had seen that pale-skinned orc before. Just an hour or so ago, the same beast had been rousted out by the Second Ward watchmen for begging at some inappropriate crossroads near the homes of the rich. And just two hours ago, Rem would be willing to lay coin on the fact that the very same orc had been part of the milling crowd that swirled around the scene of his and Torval's deadly street duel with Joss's sellswords.

"Torval," Rem began, ready to offer his observations.

"I know," Torval said, clearly having suffered the same realization. "Let me handle it."

These last words were spoken with a terrible undercurrent of malice and acrimony—growled almost, like an animal's snarl when it realizes it's being trailed by a predator. Torval then shoved the flagon of goat's milk into Rem's hands and headed toward the bend in the street where the orc and the peddler traded their heated words. As he approached, Torval reached over his shoulder and drew his iron maul out of its sheath.

Rem took a few steps forward, trying to figure out just how, if it came to pass, he could join the coming fray. And what should he do with the milk?

Torval was almost upon the orc and the peddler. He shouted, "You!" and both of them turned toward his booming voice. The peddler looked annoyed, as if he had asked for no assistance and would now refuse any offered, but the orc was a different matter. When it turned and saw Torval, Rem got a clearer look at its shadowed face. He saw the glint of small red eyes deep in the shade of its cowl, and he had the fleetest, barest impression that those eyes glinted with something like surprise, even fear, when the orc saw Torval approaching.

No, neither surprise nor fear exactly—*recognition*.

Torval shook his maul at the orc. "Get your huffing, humpbacked arse out of my dooryard, you filthy, scurvy, begging beast, you!"

"Carry on, Old Stump," the peddler said. "I can handle my own altercations, thank you—"

Torval didn't relent. He never even acknowledged the costermonger. "Yeah, I'm talking to you!" the dwarf snarled. He was in a state unlike any Rem had seen him in thus far: more angry than he had been at Creeper's, more fearsome than he had been when questioning Ginger Joss. His whole body shook with rage and the veins on his neck stood out like guylines on an oak mast. Before the costermonger could utter another protest, Torval shot forward, poked the orc with the blunt end of his maul, then kicked the begging brute repeatedly, his stumpy little feet driving the towering beast into retreat.

"Move! Move! Move!" Torval shouted as he kicked at the orc and swung his maul. "Get your milk-white carcass back to Orctown and keep it there, you mouth-breathing, knuckle-dragging piece of dried-up old pigshit!"

The orc looked surprised, hurt, a little angry, but mostly just shocked. It shrank from Torval's blows, tried to mutter some apology or curse, but managed only to growl and howl, then drew its tattered cloak about it and went loping up the street. Torval stood his ground until the orc was well out of sight. Only when he knew it was gone and not returning did he turn and acknowledge the peddler.

"I could have handled it," the peddler said.

"Da," the strapping lad carrying the peddler's cart whined. "This is heavy."

"Shut your sauce-box," the peddler snapped. "And you, Old Stump—I see that badge. You're of the Fifth. This isn't even your ward—"

Torval leaned into the costermonger's fat face. "Move this cart now, or I'll have you in stocks by sundown."

The peddler was clearly shocked. "Why, you can't talk to me that way!"

Torval lunged at the boy dragging the cart. "Now!"

The boy lurched forward, dragging the laden cart and all its second-rate bric-a-brac with him. He almost ran down his father as he made the effort to move along and clear the narrow bend in the street.

Torval withdrew from them, scowling bitterly. The peddler called after him.

"I'll report this!"

"By sundown!" Torval shot back, and continued on to where Rem waited. When he reached Rem, he neither acknowledged him nor stopped, just snatched the flagon of goat's milk from him and kept on marching, right toward a little door next to the entrance to the arkwright's shop. Beyond the door, he mounted some steps.

"Come on," he spat back at Rem. "Bleeding mudknuckles…"

Rem, thoroughly amazed by the level of Torval's ferocity for a single, begging orc on the street—even if that orc had been familiar and suspicious—followed without a word.

Torval led Rem up a flight of steps, down a short corridor, and came at last to a door that he knocked upon. The knocks came in code—four, then two, then three. From within, Rem heard an explosion of laughter and childish voices.

"Papa!" they all exclaimed.

"Auntie Osma!" he heard. "Papa's home!"

Papa?

Rem studied Torval in the gloomy little corridor. The dwarf had a strange look on his face, part eager excitement, part mild embarrassment. Rem tried to smile in such a way as to put Torval at ease, but before any words could pass between them, a bolt was thrown back on the door, the door swung inward, and three small figures poured out into the corridor to latch onto Torval like lampreys on a shark. Their laughter was infectious. Rem heard himself joining in after only a moment. A matronly dwarf woman stood in the doorway with her hands on her hips.

In the tangle of limbs and laughter, Rem thought he counted three children: one, a girl, probably in her teens, a boy slightly younger, and a little one that barely came up to Torval's thigh, leaping again and again with arms in the air, begging for his father to scoop him up and hold him. Torval, assaulted by these little miscreants and clearly happy to be so, handed the flagon of goat's milk to the woman (Aunt Osma, Rem supposed), then did as he was bade. He scooped his little boy into one arm and threw the other long arm around his daughter and older son.

"All night walking the ward," Torval growled, "and I come home to an ambush. Poor, dear, unlucky me! Remeck, lad, have you ever seen such a gathering of rowdy, rambunctious ragamuffins in all your life?"

Rem shook his head. He felt an unbidden smile on his lips. "Surely, Torval, I haven't."

The little one in Torval's arms pointed at Rem. "Who's this?"

"He's tall," the girl said, and Rem could tell by the way she studied him and said that it was meant as a compliment. He turned red and hoped the shadows of the corridor hid the fact.

"Inside," Osma said. "Inside, inside. We've got to be off to school and the market soon!"

Torval and his little ones tromped back into the little apartment. Rem followed.

The ceiling was low, but not so low that Rem couldn't stand up straight. It didn't seem like an apartment made specifically for dwarves—just a small one made for humans. From where he stood in the forward room, Rem saw there were three chambers: the forward room, adjoining the hall, an aft room, facing the street, and a long side room off to the right. In the aft room lay a brick oven and chimney full of white, ashy coals from the previous night's fire. Osma bent over these, raked them to bring some life back into them, then threw another piece of cordwood on the ash pile to rekindle a fire. She then drew out a pot that had been hanging on an iron hook just outside the fire and carried it to the family table in the forward room, where Torval and his miscreants were all a tangle of arms and legs and chattering mouths and bright eyes and ruddy young faces. Clearly, the children didn't always get to see their father before they were taken to their lessons or went with their aunt for the day, to do whatever it was they did in the market.

Seeing them—a family, each beloved of the other, each happy to see the other—gave Rem a slight pang of homesickness. He thought he even felt the sting of tears in his eyes. But he couldn't allow such maudlin sentimentality—surely!—so he pinched the bridge of his nose, drew a deep breath, and concentrated on just enjoying the moment. If he missed being missed—being loved—he would just have to bask in the glow from these four.

"I'm sorry to offer so little," Osma said, placing half a loaf of barley bread on the table beside the iron pot and the goat's milk. "Since my brother failed to tell me he was bringing company home to break fast."

"And how could I have warned you?" Torval asked, snarling as his littlest one yanked on his fox-tailed mustaches.

"Is he a watchman like you, Papa?" the middle boy asked.

"He'd like to think so, Tav," Torval said, throwing Rem a wink. Rem appreciated the good-natured joshing and decided to play it further.

"In point of fact," Rem said, "I was a criminal before your father reformed me. Spent a night in the dungeons and everything."

The middle boy's eyes grew wide and shone like jewels in the gloomy little apartment. "Untrue!"

Rem laid his hand on his heart. "I swear. Your father found me in the dungeons and beat some sense into me."

"More like," Torval broke in, "Longshanks here was handed to me. 'Make something of him,' the prefect said, 'or it's your hide, Torval!'"

"And how's he shaping up so far?" the middle boy asked.

"Tavarix!" the elder girl hissed. "Don't be rude!" She threw Rem a solicitous look, suggesting that she understood his plight and respected his privacy, even if no one else did.

"Well, all's well, Ammi!" the boy shot back. "He's here eating with us, so he can't be all bad!"

"Strictly amateur," Torval grumbled with a grin, then drew a bowl near and poured some of the goat's milk into it. "He's harmless." He snagged the barley bread next, tore off a piece, dipped it in the milk, and ate.

Osma set a bowl in front of Rem, along with a wooden spoon. "Help yourself, sir. We don't stand on ceremony here."

"Many thanks," Rem said, bending forward to look into the pot. It was a stew of some sort, still steaming a bit and smelling delicious. "Lamb?" he asked her.

"Mutton," she said with a shrug.

Rem scooped out two portions—plenty would be left for Torval—spiked his stew with some of the goat's milk—just as he would've done back home—and dug in. It was simple, but hearty and good, even this early in the morning. He instantly liked Torval's sister, this Osma. Anyone who could take a few chunks of tough mutton, a turnip and an onion and turn it into some homey, enjoyable fare was to be celebrated.

Torval drew the pot to himself and spooned out the rest of the stew. Together, the watchmen ate as the children swarmed and laughed and cavorted around them. Ammi kept doting on Rem in a most motherly fashion, despite her youth, offering him some wild strawberries to go with the goat's milk and even using the hem of her own dress to wipe some stray stew off Rem's chin. The middle boy, Tavarix, wanted to know all about Rem and what villains he and their father had been busy thumping the night before. He might be small of stature, but Tavarix was as full of boundless energy and enthusiasm as any human child Rem had ever known. Then there was the young one—little Lokki—who looked to be about five, but who was probably more like ten—dwarven children growing at a much slower rate than their human counterparts. Lokki was a delight, all smiles and laughter and body-rocking giggle fits, clearly adoring his father and being the apple of his family's collective eye. He climbed on Torval, monkeylike, as the dwarf ate his breakfast.

To Rem's great delight, Osma laid a pitcher before them along with small mugs. "That's the last of it," she said to Torval. "I expect you'll bring more home with you on the morrow?"

Torval nodded absently and filled their mugs. He and Rem toasted in silence—in truth, their mouths were full—and swigged. Rem had expected ale, but instead tasted a wonderful, pleasantly sour hard cider. He relished it and drank his entire mug in a single draught.

"All right," Osma finally said when the light outside had gone from gray to frosty blue, the morning creeping up on them. "Time for us to go, so your father can get some sleep."

"And where are you going, if I may ask?" Rem inquired, trying to make it clear he was simply curious.

"We have a stall in the east market," Osma explained. "While the boys go to school in the dwarven quarter, Ammi and I sell greens, fruits, and any sundries that fall into our path."

Torval raised a finger, reached into his tunic, and pulled out a small parcel wrapped in rag. He handed it to Osma and she unwrapped it. Within were a pair a bracelets, a torque, and some good leather gauntlets—all, Rem knew, taken as fines from routine watch stops. He had seen Torval give the best of his take to the watchkeep treasurer, so he knew well that what remained here was Torval's true property—his by rights as a member of the watch. "See what you can get for those," Torval told her, and Osma nodded that she would indeed.

"Come now, little ones," Osma urged, indicating the door. "Time to go, and go we must. Ammi."

Ammi moved behind the boys, ushering them toward the door. In that instant, the girl seemed very grown-up, and Rem imagined that someday, if she ever had children of her own, she would take very good care of them. She threw Rem a last, reassuring look, then helped her aunt get the boys out the door. When the door shut and the last of their footsteps faded from the stairs outside, the silence that fell was strange and oppressive. It reminded Rem of his own bedchamber back home: spacious, stone-walled, filled with beautiful things and all the hallmarks of privilege and comfort—but heartless, utterly devoid of warmth or charm. Instantly, Rem wished the children were back again. He liked the life and light they gave this little room.

Torval was staring at him, as if awaiting some round of teasing and bracing for it.

"They're lovely," Rem said simply. "You have a fine family, Torval."

"Aye," Torval said, his voice softer and more nakedly sincere than Rem had ever heard it. "That I do. Did you really like the stew?"

"I've been eating in taverns for the past month, and I've had nothing as tasty," Rem said. "Honestly, your sister's quite a cook."

Torval nodded. He picked at the heel of the barley bread before him. The long silence that fell between them was pregnant and uncomfortable. "Go ahead and ask," he said.

Rem swallowed. "About their mother?"

Torval nodded. "I'll tell if you ask."

"You don't have to," Rem said. "If it pains you."

"It does," Torval said, smiling wistfully. "But that's no reason not to tell you. And it's not so grand, really. Just one more banal disaster in a rather bland life." He sniffed. Rem couldn't tell if it was derisive or sad.

"What happened to her?" Rem asked.

Torval nodded, and began to tell the story.

CHAPTER SIXTEEN

"What do you know of my people, Gingersnap?" Torval asked, and for the first time, Rem thought he heard something like affection attached to that epithet in the dwarf's lowered voice.

"I know they're renowned miners and warriors," Rem said. "That they tend to prefer the company of their own kind to outsiders, and that the clan-groups aren't just family units, but act as trade and craft guilds."

"Very well, then," Torval said. "That's a good foundation. Did you also know, though, that we are, among ourselves, forbidden from undertaking work of any sort outside of the clanguild that we are born into?"

Rem raised an eyebrow. "I wasn't aware of that."

Torval nodded gravely, eyes down. He sipped his cider. "Mine is the Grimwandel clan—the Bloodstones—and we hail from the Ironwall Mountains. For five hundred years we made a good life there, carving new mines out of the mountains and trading with the human principalities on the slopes and in the lowlands. Certain families within our guild were given license to smith and tinker and make jewelry from the ores and gems we mined, but by and large, ours was a mining and a home-trade guild, neither roving merchants nor machinists nor warriors."

"So you weren't raised as a warrior," Rem interjected. "Based on what I've seen of your skill and your ferocity, I'm astonished."

Torval shrugged. "We are all taught the way of the ax, the sword, and the shield in our childhoods, but that's seen more as ceremonial training—something to harden our minds and our wills to any task at hand. When we come of age, we take our place in the work of our guild, and if that work isn't blade work, then our blades are stowed away and rust."

"No matter how much prowess one of your youngsters shows?" Rem asked.

Torval raised his eyes. There was something like bitter irony and wan humor there. "Correct. No matter how good any of us proves to be with the blade or the bludgeon, we are still obligated, by accident of birth into our clan, to take up our picks and hammers and descend into the mines when we are fully grown."

Rem nodded. He thought he understood a little more of Torval now—had glimpsed some hidden corner of his soul that he had never realized created a kinship between them.

Torval sighed and sipped his cider again. "When I was a young dwarf, I married my sweet Olian. From the time I was old enough to know I had to marry, I knew she'd be the one—at least, I hoped she'd be. I don't know if you have an eye to appreciate dwarvish womenfolk, young master, but if so, I can assure you, Olian would have impressed you. Gorgeous flaxen hair, long and flowing down her back, blue eyes as deep as pools and bright as sapphires. She was more beautiful than an ugly little stump like I could have ever hoped for, but somehow, when I made overtures, she chose me. She told me often when I would ask her that she chose me because there was no lying in me—not even boasting—and that was something that few dwarven men could attest to. At least, none that she'd ever known."

"She recognized quality of character," Rem said. "As do I."

Torval shrugged. "Perhaps. She was my treasure. The only

thing that I ever loved as much as her were the five little ones we made, each one more polished and precious than the last. By the gods of the mountain, lad, we were a merry pair. We were never well-to-do, or influential, or possessed of power- ful friends, but we were happy. I made sure she had all she required to take care of those children, and likewise, did my best to always be honest and true. That was why she loved me, after all, thus I considered it the best part of myself. Certainly more honorable than my temper..."

Already Rem sensed the story about to take a melancholy turn. Torval mentioned five children, but Rem had met only three.

"Did they teach you of the Ironwall Wars in your schooling?"

"I was young," Rem said. "No older than your little Lokki— but I yet remember talk of the wars in the mountains. The orcs and the Tregga horse nomads joined forces, didn't they? Started pressing through the passes and threatening the western slopes?"

"Precisely," Torval said, nodding. "We're not sure what made those two bands start to coordinate their bloody activi- ties, but they did, and they ran our warrior clans a merry chase. All through the summer and fall our forces harried them where they found them, chased them into the snowy heights and the rocky redoubts. When they couldn't slay them to the last, they made it clear that the brutes weren't welcome in those climes. They marked the pass roads with orcish or Tregga heads on pikes and they made them pay dearly for every village they raided, every settlement they put to the torch. All of this news returned to us weekly, sometimes daily, via messenger birds and the occasional wounded warrior who came limping home to take his respite and tap a replacement to go join the rov- ing band. And though most of us were just simple miners and tradesmen, we all thrilled to their exploits and felt that we, too, were on the front lines, doing battle with those ancient enemies of ours for the common good of our homes.

"But while our forces were out on campaign, in the dead of winter, a band of orcish raiders slipped past them. They made their way down the mountain, unchallenged, until they came to the mining settlement where my clan—and my family—made their home."

He sipped his cider. His eyes were dewy and unfocused now, staring into an agonizing past that Rem could only begin to imagine. He almost wanted Torval to stop his story, to avoid the dread end that Rem knew was coming...but he couldn't do that now. He had asked. Torval would tell it.

"While I was deep in the mines for my daily shift, Olian, Rinnit, and Gedel—my wife, my son, and my daughter—died under orc iron. The way some of the survivors told it, Olian was defending Lokki—he was just a babe then—and screaming for Rinnit and Gedel to run. Gedel made sure Rinnit ran, because she was older than he, and thought she should defend him, then doubled back to help her mother. Gedel was murdered en route to Olian's side. Rinnit was cut down as he fled. Olian, she...she died and fell on Lokki. It was a miracle he survived. Osma found him after...after the orcs were gone and the fires all dying. He was wailing and hungry, pinned beneath his dead mother."

The dwarf sniffed. No tears came, though. Dwarves were not immune to showing their emotions, but they did not do so lightly, and usually not in front of strangers. Only family got to see the true depths of their passions and pains.

"I could not stand by any longer," Torval said, and looked to Rem with eyes holding a pain so deep and desperate that Rem could barely hold the dwarf's gaze. "I went to every clan elder, every lord commander of every warrior company that had returned to regroup or that formed in answer to that surprise raid. I begged each for the right to lay down my pick and my hammer and take up the ax and join them on campaign. Once, when I found a legendary band of orc slayers in their clan great house, swilling mead and pouring out libations for the dead, I even went so far as to challenge them. 'Send four against me,' I said, 'No—five! Nay, six! If I can put six of you on your bloody backs, then let me join you! My wife and my children are owed no less!'"

He fell silent, shuddering a little, as if the memory itself left his very body and mind distressed.

"Six?" Rem asked. "That's a daring challenge, Torval— dare I say, even a little foolhardy."

"They thought so as well," Torval said, "but they seemed eager to teach me a lesson. As it turned out, I put nine of them on their backs before another half dozen dog-piled upon me and put me down. They disarmed me and beat me bloody, and when the strongest of them asked their lord commander what punishment a haughty little pickmonkey deserved for daring to challenge men born and sworn to the sword, the lord commander decided that I should be shorn. So—away went my long, braided locks and my beard. I fought every step of the way and probably have more than a few scars on my head from their daggers that I wouldn't have if I had just taken the punishment they meted out to me with deference—"

"I don't think you owed them any deference," Rem said.

Torval smiled. It was a bitter smile—a damned, lost devil's smile—and it made Rem's heart ache. "No. No, I didn't either."

Silence fell. For a long time, all Rem heard was his breathing and Torval's and the distant noise from the street outside the shuttered windows.

"So," Rem said, "you challenged them again, yes? You made them let you join the fight?"

Torval shook his head. "No, lad. They had beaten me, and they had branded me when they took my hair and my beard, and all the clans—mine own and all those born and sworn to the sword—made it clear that I was to cease my campaign to join them on the battlefield forthwith. I was born to a mining clan, after all, thus it would be an affront to nature—and the gods themselves—if I stepped outside the bounds of my true purpose in life to take up arms in vengeance for my dead wife and children. Let fighters fight, they said—in the meantime, I could drown my grief in hard work underground, mining ore and gems to trade to men for weapons and foodstuffs and gold to support the ongoing war against the orcs and their Tregga allies. Labor, not warfare, was the trade the gods had chosen for me—I courted ruin and damnation if I took any further action to undermine that divine ordinance."

Rem studied the dwarf. Torval emptied his ale cup down his gullet, then reached for the nearby pitcher to pour himself some more.

"So?" Rem finally prodded.

Torval shrugged. "So, I gathered my children, and my sister—who had lost her own husband in the same raid—and we left. We left our clan, we left the mines, we left the mountains. And as we did, we were warned by any and all who saw us, trudging out of there with our meager belongings on our backs like a bunch of stump-legged vagabonds, that if we left, we would never, ever be welcome to return. But what did I care? Why should I submit myself to the will of a people who will give me no choice in my own destiny? Who would not even let me take up arms to avenge the deaths of my precious family, simply because I was born into one clan and not another? I spat on their curses and admonitions and silly divine ordinances and I spit on them still."

And then, he did just that—turned and spat right on his own floor.

Rem decided to broach a rather intimate question—one that he probably had no business asking the dwarf. "So, you don't believe in your gods anymore?"

Torval raised his eyes. He shrugged, shook his head, fiddled with his cider cup. "I don't know. If the gods were as the elders said they were, then they were slavers and despots, and I should not bow to them. And if they were other than the elders always said—kinder, freer, more benevolent—then they were also lazy, because they did not save my Olian and my children when they could have, and they further denied me the honor of avenging them when I sought it. So, those seem to be my choices—the gods are tyrants, or the gods are fools."

"Some say the gods are mad," Rem offered. "Others say there are no gods at all."

"And what do you say?"

Rem was about to answer—then suddenly realized he had no answer at the ready. What *did* he believe, so far as the gods were concerned? In all his years of attending services and participating in rituals and learning the holy scriptures from both the *Book of Aemon* and the *Scrolls of the Panoply*, no one had ever asked him what he believed.

And though he could have served Torval some evasive pap, he decided that he should not. Torval had shared a deep and terrible wound with him; the least Rem could do was repay the dwarf's trust with his own.

"I say praying gives me comfort," Rem answered, "even when it does me no good. Believing that there is a plan, an endgame, gives me the same sort of comfort. I suppose I would say that, even when I don't trust them or fear they're nothing but smoke, the gods deserve some ration of courtesy and respect—the same courtesy and respect I'd give any stranger, at any rate."

Torval waved his thick hand, as if waving away a swarm of bothersome flies. "Cack, all of it. I know that the gods have nothing to offer me, so I offer them nothing in return. When my children ask, I still tell them the old stories and urge them to say their prayers and make offerings as tradition demands. That's why I finally put the boys in a dwarven school here in the city. They should know who they are, where they come from, who their ancestors prayed to. I took their home and their clan from them, but I shan't take their gods. Let them throw off the yoke of those watchful old ghosts in their own time, according to their own hearts."

"Just so," Rem said. "Because everyone deserves a choice, don't they?"

Torval met his gaze, and Rem thought he saw real kinship and understanding in the dwarf's blue eyes. "Aye—everyone deserves a choice. That's why we left. That's why we eventually settled here."

"Why here, specifically?" Rem asked.

Torval took a moment, seeming to honestly consider his answer before offering it. "Because here, at last," he said, "I found what I sought, for myself and for my children. For good or ill, come salvation or perdition, Yenara always offers us a choice. That, I think, is the great gift she has given the world, and the main reason that men still fight to possess her and are possessed by her. Whatever your fate when your mother whelped you, when you come here, it is all erased. Yenara strips us of what we were, and demands that we become what we truly are."

"Or what we want to be," Rem said under his breath.

"One and the same," Torval said. "One and the same."

Torval smiled, then Rem smiled in answer. Without a word, Rem raised his cup and Torval raised his own. Their cups touched and man and dwarf drank.

"Your children love you," Rem said. "I saw it on all their faces. I felt it."

Torval nodded and finished his ale. "Aye, they do. Never mind I let their mother die because I wasn't there to protect her."

A silence hung between them then. It was as if Torval intended to say something else, but didn't. And Rem, though he was not close to the dwarf and could not know him well, thought he could guess what it might have been.

Never mind I let their mother die because I wasn't there to protect her . . . and Freygaf.

"I'm truly sorry," Rem said. "Not just for your wife but for Freygaf as well. I know I've benefited from your loss. I know that may color me in your eyes—"

"Bah!" Torval barked. "It's the chance we take. As watchmen."

But he didn't seem convinced.

"Do you believe him?" Rem asked. "The Creeper? About Freygaf's . . . secrets?"

Torval considered that question long and hard. He didn't raise his eyes before answering. "I don't know. I thought I knew Freygaf as well as anyone could, but . . . well, maybe I didn't. Maybe you never can." Then he raised his eyes. He glared at Rem, his gaze piercing right through the young man like a spear through a straw target. "I don't know you, but something tells me I can trust you."

"You can," Rem said. He meant it.

"Don't make me sorry," Torval said.

"I won't," Rem said.

Torval stared at him for a long time, studying him, trying his best to wheedle out any weaknesses or secrets. After a time, he seemed to give up, finding none. His face softened.

"I'm tired," Torval said.

"As am I," Rem offered, starting to rise.

"You look it," Torval said.

"I should go," Rem said, offering his hand. "Thank you, Torval."

"You don't have to," Torval said. "Go, that is. The children sleep in a man's bed. It should fit you."

"No, I couldn't—"

"Come on!" Torval barked. "You're dog-tired and I've got a place for you to sleep. It's the least I can do after dragging you here and plying you with ale and mutton."

Rem considered. He really didn't feel like walking home at present. Falling right into a bed sounded rather appealing.

"And here," Torval said, leaning forward a little and whispering conspiratorially. "On our way into the watchkeep, what say we swing by the market where you first met her and ask after your missing lady friend?"

Rem was taken aback by that sudden offer. Torval, however, seemed delighted to make it, as if the search for Indilen were not simply Rem's obsession but Torval's own, as well.

"Fine," Rem said, working very hard to suppress his gratitude and his eagerness. If he were not so bone-weary and bleary-eyed, he would insist they take to the streets at that very moment. "Show me the bed, and quickly, before I fall on my face."

CHAPTER SEVENTEEN

While Rem slept, he dreamt of Indilen. She found him in the Pickled Albatross and whispered in his ear. He turned to meet her, to finally draw her into his lap and see what those soft pink lips of hers tasted like, but in the short breath that it took him to turn, she had already stolen away across the room. A sea of patrons well in their cups and rowdy gamblers stood between Rem and his prize. Still, Rem chased her. Always, Indilen was far ahead of him, moving across the room from this corner to that in the blink of an eye, never where he thought she would be, always just out of reach.

From that unpleasant dream, Rem woke. He felt a deep pang of disappointment and loneliness within him—worse than any he'd ever known, a strange assurance that now and forever, he would always be alone, unloved, and most likely, unremembered. It was a strange feeling—deep and sure and biting and entirely unlike him—but he could not deny it. He chalked it up to being tired and still being new to the city, then turned over in the children's bed.

Across the room he saw Torval asleep on his little wooden cot. The dwarf lay on his back, snoring, one hand on his slowly rising chest, the other hanging off the bed beside him.

A man stood beside Torval's bed. He wore a dark cape and cowl, and held in his right hand a gleaming, well-honed dagger.

That wasn't right.

Rem searched for his watchman's stave and saw it, just beyond his reach, hanging from a hook on the adjacent wall. He was reasonably sure he could take the intruder if he were armed, but he wasn't eager to challenge the cloaked man with the dagger empty-handed. And there was no time to waste—in two breaths, maybe three, that dagger would be at Torval's throat.

Rem rolled himself out of bed, tottered upright, then dove for the stick.

"Torval!" he shouted.

The intruder spun.

Torval woke.

Rem had his hand on his stave now. He yanked it off the hook and turned to face the armed intruder. It had to be late afternoon, because the light had shifted in the little sleeping room and the shadows were deep. He tried to get a good look at his adversary, but he couldn't see any more than the barest suggestion of a face and the glitter of eyes deep inside the dark cowl. Nonetheless, the figure's stance and the gleam of his blade suggested that he was a brave fighter with ample experience.

"Sundry hells!" Torval shouted when he saw the armed intruder towering over him.

The stranger struck with a fist, smacking Torval right in the face and sending him reeling back onto the little cot. The dwarf, stunned, let loose a string of colorful curses.

Rem turned his body sideward to make himself a narrower target and put the wooden stave out before him, as though it were a sword on guard. Surely, with this solid, arm-length piece of oak he could take a man with a knife.

The assassin silently accepted Rem's challenge and went on guard as well. He then surprised Rem by reaching under his cloak and drawing another blade—a full-length sword. It whispered from its scabbard and the point bobbed low in Rem's vision, looking entirely too sharp, too lethal. By its grace and fine workmanship, Rem marked the blade as mostly likely Estavari in make. A man who owned a blade like that probably knew well how to use it.

And here Rem stood, with nothing but a stick.

He shifted backward and his foot hit something. There was a clatter and a thump. Rem dared only a moment's glance to see what he'd almost tripped on.

It was Torval's maul.

The assassin took the opening. He lunged forward and thrust with his blade—a full-arc cut being impractical in the tight space of the long, narrow sleeping room. Rem threw his forward shoulder back and brought the stave up in a clumsy parry. Clumsy it may have been, but it worked. The blade was pushed aside by the blow—but the assassin recovered and struck next with the dagger in his other hand. The little blade whistled through the air just inches from Rem's face.

Torval was up now. He threw himself on the assassin with a bullish battle cry and tried to get his thick little arms around the assassin's throat. The assassin avoided being so encumbered, spun, and threw Torval off with a shrug. The dwarf went crashing to the floor in the far corner, smashing the cot as he landed.

That was Rem's chance. He dove, snatched up the iron maul, then turned to face his opponent again. Now they were more evenly matched—sword and dagger against maul and stave. The long, narrow bedroom would keep the assassin from making full use of his long blade, but the unbalanced weight of the maul could easily make any attacks Rem attempted with it clumsy and irregular. He choked up his hold on the maul to better balance it, then lunged forward.

He surprised the assassin, as he'd hoped to, unleashing a fierce bevy of strikes with the stave that the assassin was forced to block with his dagger arm. When the assassin tried to thrust with his sword again, Rem swung the maul around and blocked the strike, sending the point of the blade wide and saving himself from another bleeding wound. He hoped to shatter his opponent's blade with the heavy bludgeon—but no such luck.

They fought on, Rem parrying the thrusts and slashes of the sword with stave and maul, deep notches being hacked into his nightstick as he fought, the point of the blade coming dangerously close several times to his rolling shoulder, his striking arm, his bobbing head. He couldn't keep blocking the sword with the stave forever—sooner or later, the blade would hack right through it. He had to disarm his opponent or unfoot him before that happened.

In the corner, Torval was just recovering. Doing his best to keep his eye on his opponent, Rem saw the dwarf take up some piece of the cot as a makeshift bludgeon and come charging at the assassin from behind. The assassin saw the charge as well. He thrust with his sword, the point this time slipping right through Rem's defenses and piercing his left shoulder, then spun to meet Torval and tried to skewer the charging dwarf on his dagger.

Torval met the dagger with the cot leg in his hand, thrust the assassin's knife hand aside, then tried to plunge the blunt end of the wooden cot leg into the assassin's gut. He didn't see that the sword was high and ready to come crashing down on his bald head.

Rem charged, throwing down his stave and laying both hands on the long handle of the iron maul. He held the maul horizontally before him and slammed right into the assassin's undefended right flank, staving off the fall of the sword and driving his opponent into the back wall of the bedroom, nearest the little door that led into the front chamber. Close by, Rem heard a tear and a clatter of coin. He dared a glance and saw that the sharp, broken end of Torval's makeshift bludgeon had ensnared a small pouch at the assassin's belt and torn it open. The clatter Rem heard were the pouch's contents, spilling onto the floor. Rem redoubled his efforts to immobilize their opponent.

The assassin was in a frenzy. He fought with Torval, still attacking him from one side, as Rem pressed him hard against the chamber wall. As Rem and the assassin struggled, the spike on Torval's maul dipped and cut a long, shallow, bloody wound into the assassin's left bicep. Rem heard a startled growl, then a muttered curse, then felt the assassin's knee in his groin. The blow was stunning and he doubled over in agony. The assassin then sent Torval reeling with a clumsy blow from the pommel of his sword, broke from the pair of them, ducked through the doorway, and fled.

Torval tried to give chase, leaping right over Rem—but his trailing foot caught on Rem's bent shoulder. Torval went sprawling on his face. In his teary-eyed discomfort, Rem saw the assassin rushing right out of Torval's door and heard his boots go pounding down the stairs in the hall outside.

Torval rolled off Rem and scurried to his feet. "Are you all right, lad? Did he stick you?"

"I wish he had," Rem gasped. "Aemon, I wish he had..."

"Walk it off, son," Torval said, patting his shoulder. "Hurts like the sundry hells, I'm sure, but it's better than being dead. Which I'd be if you didn't wake me when you did and hold that bastard off."

Rem was regaining himself. He managed to sit up but couldn't quite stretch out his legs. "You're welcome," he muttered. His hands were still clasped around his aching family jewels.

Torval shook his head. "I mean it, boy. That was quick thinking. And fine stave work! I reckon you weren't lying when you said you were good with a sword. If you'd been so armed here and now, you'd have probably ended that son of a whore where he stood. As it was, he only almost had you because you didn't have a blade to match him with."

"I appreciate it," Rem said, Torval's praises falling on pain-deafened ears.

"That bastard," Torval growled, pacing the room now like a caged tiger. "Stalking me here, in my gods-damned own home! The nerve! I'll have him flayed for that bit of villainy, I swear it!"

Rem managed to get on his feet again. It still hurt, but at least he could stand to be upright now. "We've got to catch him first," he said. "And I didn't see his face."

"Me neither," Torval said. "But no matter. We know we're onto something now."

"And how do we know that?" Rem asked.

Torval smiled. "Why else would someone try to hunt and kill us?"

He had a point, at that.

Torval now lowered his eyes and studied the mess of detritus that had come raining from the assassin's torn belt pouch. Rem studied the mess as well. Mostly, it was coin—brass stars, a few large and small silver pieces, a handful of brass and coppers thrown in. There was a sterling-silver broach in the shape of a rearing stallion, a simple and lovely little bauble that looked both antique and expensive. Also, there were a few broken wooden chits with numbers carved into them, the sort used by pawnbrokers as checks for pawned merchandise.

But Torval seized upon a single item: a wooden disk, a little larger than a coin, painted in bright shades of blue, purple, and yellow and bearing upon it a bright, pale-yellow "500" in old Horunic numerals.

"What is that?" Rem asked, moving closer to examine it.

Torval had a satisfied smirk on his face. "It's a gambling mark. Some of the gaming houses in the city use them on their gaming floors so they can keep all the real coin under lock and key. Tends to cut down on men getting into desperate and fatal contests at their tables, or likewise, trying to rob the place blind."

"Well, where's it from?" Rem pressed, excited that they had such a concrete clue as to their assassin's recent whereabouts.

Torval turned the chip over. On the opposite side was a crude icon in the form of a black bird, like a raven or a crow.

"That's the sign of the Nightjar," Torval said. "He's the thief prince of the Fourth Ward—wealthy, powerful, and all but untouchable thanks to his partnership with the Fourth's prefect, Frennis."

"So, he'd probably be unlikely to talk to us, wouldn't he?" Rem asked.

Torval's smirk became a smile. "Talk? Lad, we'll make that bastard sing. Come on."

They left word with the arkwright downstairs that the rooms had been compromised, and that neither Osma nor the children were to sleep there. Torval instead steered them toward the King's Ass and told them to ask for Aarna. Then all that remained was for he and Rem to swing by said tavern and leave word that Torval's family would need a room for the night. Torval didn't want to waste time on in-depth explanations, but Aarna was more than willing to help, and swore she would see personally to their safety.

After that, Torval led Rem elsewhere. This time, they tromped through a tangle of back alleys, inns, and taverns, meandering down toward the Fourth Ward waterfront to a rather imposing-looking warehouse guarded by a pair of burly, well-armed, swarthy southerners—Tsauranian or Ferosi, Rem couldn't tell which. The shabby, muddy square that the warehouse fronted was swathed in unfriendly shadows and had a haunted, gone-to-seed look about it, while the warehouse itself held court over the largely empty crossroads and bled chaotic noise from within.

Torval paused for a long time, watching the warehouse as hard and desperate men of all sorts meandered in and out, all challenged by the burly doormen but eventually gaining their entry. After a while, the dwarf's hesitation started to make Rem uneasy.

"What are we waiting for?" he asked.

Torval turned and eyed him suspiciously. "I'm having second thoughts, lad."

"About what?"

Torval suggested the warehouse with a jerk of his head. "This is someone else's ward—someone else's watch. By rights, we shouldn't be here without warrants from our prefect or the tacit permission of this district's prefect."

"Do we need to circle back to the watchkeep, then?" Rem asked.

Torval shook his head. "No. Ondego won't allow it. He's a good commander, but he's learned that keeping the peace and staying out from under the feet of the other prefects is the best way to get along. And Frennis, prefect of the Fourth, is the most territorial among them. He's a hard man, not to be trifled with."

"You said he had some sort of partnership with this Night-jar," Rem said. "That tells me he's not just a hard man—he's a corrupt one as well. Shouldn't a man like that be challenged?"

Torval stared at Rem, his face suggesting something like pity. "Maybe in the north, lad...but this is Yenara. The rules are different here."

Rem studied the warehouse. Studied Torval. Considered all of their options. "It's me, isn't it?" he finally asked. "If you were alone, you'd do this without hesitation, but because I'm a whelp in these woods, and new to the watch, you think I have to be protected."

Torval sighed and gave a reticent nod. "That might have something to do with it. If we go in there and start making trouble, asking questions without a by-your-leave from Frennis himself, we could be leaping into a snake pit without a ladder."

Rem stared right into Torval's eyes. He wanted to be sure the dwarf saw his seriousness. "I'm your partner, Torval. Someone just tried to kill us, and we've got evidence suggesting they were here, in this place. Considering no one was trying to kill us before we started investigating your former partner's murder, I'm willing to guess that the information we glean here will carry us a little closer to some answers. You can worry over my well-being all you like, but my life is on the line in this, too.

"So, what's it going to be, Old Stump—go it alone, or let your partner do his job and watch your back?"

Torval, to Rem's great surprise, smiled. He was beaming with an almost fatherly pride. "Into the snake pit, then?"

Rem swept his arm. "After you, sir."

They stowed their watchwarden badges under their shirts and crossed the square under the gaze of the many darkened and empty houses and storefronts that gazed out blankly upon it. It seemed that the warehouse was the only business still operating in this quayside corner of the Fourth. The closer they got, the louder the warehouse became. It was as if an entire spring tournament were being held beneath its ancient rafters and sagging shingles, for Rem picked out intermittent cheers, exhortations, and cries of despair amid the generalized roar of an excited crowd. In moments, they had made the door.

The bouncers didn't balk at letting Torval through the front door, despite the fact that he never flashed his watchman's signet. Either they recognized him for who he was or they had mistaken him for someone else entirely. Either way, they made it easy. They stepped aside in deference and urged him on. Torval led the way. Rem followed.

Inside, Rem was overwhelmed by a pandemonium of noise and activity. The warehouse's fringe regions and upper gallery were filled with tables and chairs, a vast and bustling sporting house where games were played, whores plied their wares, and men drank vast quantities of liquor at dark corner tables all alone. But beyond these staid borderlands lay the real attraction of this strange place. Deeper into the warehouse, there were pits dug into the earthen floor. Those pits were surrounded by screaming, cheering patrons whose faces were masks of lust and fury. In those pits were fighting animals, and by their savagery and scars, Rem guessed they fought to the death.

In the first pit they came to, the contest was between a big brown bear and a trio of snapping, drooling mastiffs. By the look of things, the bear was winning, one hound already lying to the side and bleeding its last while its two fellows continued to charge the bear, snap at its swiping paws or spread legs, then retreat before it could end them. But the bear was chained in place and could move no more than a few feet in any direction. Gradually, even in the few fleeting moments that Rem watched, the mastiffs seemed to sense this. They were testing the bear's boundaries and area of movement, preparing for a final, coordinated assault. Rem guessed that if one of them could take the beast from the rear while the other dove in to tear at its gut, the bear would not survive.

But that wasn't the only contest on display. Torval led Rem past the bear pit, through the roiling crowd, and deeper into the warehouse's cavernous bowels. Along the way, Rem saw more pits with more animal contests—albeit some much smaller and simpler than the bear baiting. There was a staked pit wherein cockfights unfolded; another depressed pit where a terrier snapped at a brace of hungry, red-eyed rats; and another pit of similar size to the bear pit, where an orc fought a pair of angry, toothy, bristling boars. The orc was making a good show of it, but even in the fleeting moments that passed as Rem and Torval circled the pit, Rem saw one of the boars charge and knock the huffing orc right off its feet and onto its back. It would only be a matter of time before the orc's entrails littered the fighting pit, courtesy of the tusks of those two angry, cornered boars. Rem didn't care to be present when that outcome came to pass.

He leaned toward Torval.

"Who are we looking for?" he asked, having to shout to be heard above the din in the great gaming house.

"Watch the gallery," Torval said, suggesting the wooden catwalks above them, lined with patrons and gamblers. "The Nightjar's an ebon Maswari chap. Handsome, with green eyes."

Rem nodded and started scanning the milling crowd above and around them. Certainly, here in the west, a fellow from Maswari, far to the south, would stand out like a shadow on a white shroud. Rem did not see many southlanders about them—there were not many in Yenara—so surely, locating one couldn't be too troubling for them.

But no matter where he looked, how deeply he concentrated, he saw nothing. There was no sign of an ebon fellow anywhere in the milling crowd that met Torval's description. Worse, that orc in the pit off to their left was in trouble now, down on his knees, wrestling with the boars. He wouldn't last long.

Suddenly, Torval grabbed Rem's wrist and yanked him close. His grip was so hard that Rem cried out and instinctively yanked his arm away from the dwarf. Torval offered no apologies. He just pointed.

Rem followed the invisible line suggested by Torval's pointing finger. There, in the crowd, was a familiar, pug-nosed, red-haired thief: Ginger Joss, the very same villain they'd discovered the night before in Freygaf's chambers and stolen the strange pendant from; the same rogue who'd hired a pair of sellswords to gut them in the street earlier that morning.

Torval waved Rem close. "Circle around him. I'll approach from the front. When he tries to run, you be ready to stop him."

Rem nodded and separated from Torval. He went jostling through the crowd beside the boar pit. A sudden roar went up, along with cries of incredulity and disappointment. Rem stole a glance and saw the orc in the pit holding a handful of his own ropy entrails as one of the boars tore into his gut, swinging its head from side to side as though it were snuffling for truffles. The orc tried to beat the beast back with its bare fists, but the fight was over. Already the light was leaving the knuckle dragger's dark-green eyes.

Money changed hands. Bets were won and lost. On to the next contest.

Rem kept Ginger Joss in his sights. Off to his left, Torval slowly pressed through the crowd, in no hurry, trying to get as close as he could before Joss saw him and bolted. Rem was nearing him rapidly now, only a few yards from the red-haired little thief as the knave collected coin from a nearby gambler and offered his sincerest condolences on the outcome of the fight.

Then Joss glanced up and saw Rem.

He recognized him instantly.

He ran.

"Torval!" Rem cried, but his voice was swallowed in the din. There was no way he would be heard in the noisy warehouse. He tried to press after Joss, but suddenly the crowd was moving against him. They wouldn't part, and they all seemed to be flowing in another direction, toward the back of the warehouse, away from the blood-littered boar pit. Rem was fighting against the tide, and Joss was getting away.

He saw the shock of red hair bobbing above the crowd, zigzagging this way and that to find the path of least resistance. Joss was making better headway than Rem, and Rem was terrified he would escape.

Then, suddenly, something seemed to yank Joss under the human tide. Down he went with a cry that couldn't be heard from where Rem stood. A few of the people just around Joss seemed to take notice that there was a man suddenly underfoot, looked perplexed, then flowed on around him. Rem pressed on, trying to reach the spot where Joss had just collapsed.

When he reached it, he realized that Joss had not tripped or fallen: Torval had run right into him, yanked him off his feet, and now straddled Joss's heaving chest, holding him with his jerkin bunched up in his little dwarven fists, screaming into his face.

"Just where did you think you were going, Joss? Eh? Just where did you think you were off to, you slippery, slimy little eel?"

Joss struggled mightily, but Torval had him well pinned. There was no rising with the dwarf's concentrated bulk on top of him. Someone tried to bend to Joss's aid and help him to his feet, but Rem took the initiative and shoved them off.

"Wardwatch business!" he shouted. "Carry on!"

Joss jostled this way and that, doing his damnedest to buck Torval off him. It wasn't working.

Then, all at once, Rem was aware of a strange silence having fallen. All the movement around them stopped. All eyes turned toward the two watchwardens and their prisoner. Torval didn't notice right away, still too busy subduing the wriggling Joss, but Rem noted the change and it filled him with fear. He scanned the crowd.

Just a stone's throw away from them, the crowd parted around two men like waters around a boulder in a rushing river. One was a tall, well-made ebon with skin the color of loamy earth and eyes like two flashing emeralds. Beside him stood a big, broad man made of equal parts fat and muscle, with a shaggy head of gray-flecked red hair and flashing eyes full of playful malice. The man wore a medallion around his throat, a lead likeness of the city of Yenara with a Horunic numeral "4" stamped upon it.

Rem nudged Torval, who finally stopped wrestling with

Joss and lifted his gaze. When Torval saw the newcomers, his eyes narrowed and his mouth set stonily.

"Nightjar," he said with a nod. "Prefect Frennis."

"This is, indeed, a surprise," Frennis said with mock amusement. "And, if I'm not mistaken, Watchwarden, I think you are well acquainted with my absolute disdain for surprises."

CHAPTER EIGHTEEN

"Well," Torval said, rising and planting one foot on Joss's chest, "We came here looking for the two of you, in fact. As it happened, I came across this suspect and decided I'd apprehend him before seeing to the business that brought me."

"And what's he suspected of?" Frennis asked.

"Murder," Torval said. "The murder of a watchwarden, too, if you must know."

The Nightjar's eyes widened, as though in surprise. He looked to Frennis. "Those are very serious allegations," he said, "I suppose we should accommodate these good seekers and answer their questions, and sooner clear our good names and the spotless reputation of this establishment."

"Aye," Torval said. "That you should."

"I have a better idea," Frennis said to the Nightjar, loud enough so that all could hear him. "What say we bring all of these miscreants into more private quarters and have a little palaver with the lot of them? After all, these two claim to be watchwardens, even though they don't wear their signets and they've clearly broken the rules of their office by pursuing suspects and prosecuting an investigation in a ward not their own."

The Nightjar gestured toward Joss and spoke to a pair of bodyguards lingering nearby. "Get him up. Take him to the salon. Make sure the other two follow."

The bodyguards—one a muscled, topknotted Kosterman,

the other sporting tight curls and ruddy, angular cheeks that marked him as Loffmaric—did as they were told, shoving Torval off Joss and lifting the little red-headed thief as though he were a rag doll. He fought, but their grip was ironclad. Frennis led the way and the guards followed. The Nightjar gestured again, encouraging Torval and Rem to follow the five of them.

"After you, gentlemen," he said.

Torval did as he was told and cocked his head, indicating that Rem should follow. Rem, not entirely sure he wanted to know what sort of salon this man was inviting them into, dutifully followed. The Nightjar did not join them. He simply stood in silence, among his customers, as Rem and Torval and Joss were led away by Frennis and those two burly bodyguards.

Rem shot an inquisitive glance at Torval. The frown carved onto the dwarf's face did not inspire confidence.

Frennis led them into a dark and cluttered sanctum at the rear of the warehouse. This was nothing like the Creeper's lair—no plush Shimzari carpets, no casks of ale or brandy, no friendly golden glow from a bevy of brass lamps and candles. No, the space that Frennis led them into was nothing more than a boathouse appended to the great warehouse, where the crime lord's animal gladiators fought their battles. It was high-ceilinged, drafty, and filled with strange, shifting light and shadows from the ripples on the water and the wan light of a few torches left burning in the great, cluttered space. On all sides were stacked crates and barrels and casks of gods-knew-what, and every inch of the floor seemed to be littered with something potentially hazardous: old coils of rope or rusty anchor chains, broken glass or splintered wooden planks. Rem disliked the space the moment they entered it, because it felt like the sort of space that might hide an ambush. There were too many nooks and crannies, too many recesses, too many shadows.

As they all traipsed into the great, cluttered space, hulking Frennis turned and spoke to Torval. "We've met before, haven't we?" he asked. "Your face and name both seem familiar to me."

"More than once, Warden, sir," Torval said, his voice devoid of all courtesy.

"You had another partner, didn't you? A northman?"

"Freygaf," Torval said.

"And what became of him?"

Torval shot a glance at Rem. He was clearly impatient, suspecting—if not entirely sure—that Frennis knew damn well who he was and who his partner had been and what became of him. "He was murdered," Torval growled through gritted teeth.

Frennis stopped at the edge of the dock, staring down into the murky-green waters beneath him. He searched his environs, seeming satisfied when he found a nearby bucket. It was too dark for Rem to see what was in the bucket, but whatever it was, Frennis bent, took out a morsel, and looked once more to the water.

"I'm surprised that knowledge escaped you," Torval said, with just a touch too much malice in his voice. "I would think that the death of any watchwarden, in any ward of this city, would be cause for a fellow watchman's grief."

Frennis tossed whatever he held in his hands into the water. Suddenly, there was a violent roiling as a pair of swirling, shining gray shapes leapt and tumbled and rolled, trying to get at whatever the prefect had thrown them. Rem saw rolling black eyes, snapping jaws full of razor-sharp teeth, and skin like rough gray leather.

Sharks—not so uncommon in the waters of Yenara's bay. The bucket held chum, and Frennis was summoning his pets for a feeding.

But what did he intend to feed them?

"Not my ward, not my problem," Frennis said, turning and smiling at them. "As you can imagine, master dwarf, I'm a busy man and can't afford to muddle my concerns with what goes on outside of my home ground . . . which leads me to the two of you and your interest in Joss here."

Joss struggled in the grip of his guardsmen. "Frennis, you know I can repay you, if only—"

"Be quiet, Joss," Frennis said calmly. "I'll get to you shortly. Let brothers-in-arms talk now, yes?"

"Clearly, not so brotherly," Torval muttered.

Frennis moved closer to them. "You know the rules, Torval. In this ward, I'm sovereign. If you wanted to operate here, you should have sought me out first and begged my aid."

"Let us question him, then," Torval said, nodding toward Joss.

"No," Frennis responded. "I'm afraid that's not possible. You see, these are my men on either side of Joss, so that means he's *my* prisoner. And I'd be quite remiss if I let the two of you question *my* prisoner before I had done so myself."

"Is it such a trial?" Rem asked, suddenly impatient with all of Frennis's childish posturing.

Frennis answered him by taking one long step toward Rem and punching him squarely in the gut. The prefect's fist felt like an iron mace driven deep into Rem's soft middle, and Rem doubled over under the weight of the jab, dropping to his knees. He couldn't breathe. His innards felt as though they'd been shattered and liquefied.

Torval shot forward and used all of his strength to shove Frennis away from his partner. Frennis retreated, but only by a single step. Without a word of warning, he snatched up Torval by his tunic and lifted the dwarf off the ground. Rem, watching from where he knelt, struggling for breath and some end to his agony, could not believe his eyes.

A man had just laid hands on Torval in anger, and Torval, instead of fighting him, just hung there in Frennis's grip, his feet a good arm span off the ground, his fists dangling at his side, white-knuckled.

"You didn't need to hit him," Torval spat into Frennis's face. "He's new."

"Then he needs to learn, doesn't he?" Frennis answered, and shook Torval as though he were a straw-stuffed scarecrow. "Just as you do, you bloody pickmonkey."

The prefect released Torval and he hit the floorboards beside Rem. Rem was starting to regain the ability to breathe. The agony racking his insides gradually subsided from a raging inferno to a dull, smoldering ache. He looked up at Frennis. He really hated the man, and he counted himself lucky that he had ended up in Ondego's dungeon and not Frennis's.

"What brought you here?" Frennis demanded.

"A gambling mark," Torval answered. "One of the Nightjar's."

"And who dropped this gambling mark?" Frennis asked.

"A knife man who tried to murder us while we slept," Torval answered. "Perhaps he's one of yours, Prefect, sir?"

Frennis bent closer, hands on his knees. "If he was one of mine, you'd be worm food, master dwarf," Frennis said. "Now, why would someone be trying to kill you?"

"Because we're trying to solve the murder of my partner," Torval said. "And we think we're getting close to the culprit because no one would be bothering to kill the likes of us otherwise."

"Do you suspect the Nightjar?" Frennis asked.

Torval didn't answer. Frennis grabbed one of the dwarf's

ears and twisted it violently. Torval roared and smacked Frennis's hand away, but made no further move to threaten him. Still, Rem could see in his partner's eyes the urge to murder the bulky prefect of the Fourth. Truly, Torval hated the man, as well.

"Answer me," Frennis said.

"He has motive," Torval said. "Ever since we broke up his little blood-sport ring in the Fifth Ward."

Frennis seemed to consider that for a moment. "Bygones," he said finally. "He's no longer active in your ward."

"But he's active in yours, isn't he?" Torval countered.

Frennis shrugged. "Ends and means, master dwarf. If I choose to maintain order in my district by issuing accomodations to specific business concerns, all in the name of peace and stability..."

Ginger Joss, thinking that maybe his captors had relaxed their grip, suddenly bucked and squirmed. The two bodyguards held him fast. The Loffmari even cuffed him headwise, then slapped his face in a most insulting fashion. Frennis wandered away from his prisoners, pulled another piece of chum from the bucket, and threw it into the waters below the dock.

"So, if you suspected the Nightjar, what's your business with this piece of offal?" he asked Torval and Rem, gesturing toward Joss.

Torval threw Rem a sour glance. He didn't like the fact that Frennis now had their suspect. There was no telling what he might do, or how he might make their lives more difficult.

"He's a suspect," Torval said. "We have reason to believe he knows something about Freygaf's death. He also tried to have us killed this morning, in broad daylight. The fact that we found him here, in your gaming house, bodes not well for the Nightjar, nor for you, Frennis."

Frennis nodded deferentially. "I suppose it wouldn't. Nonetheless, let me be frank—I had nothing to do with Freygaf's death. Nor, I suspect, did Joss here. Will you tell them, Joss?"

"Only if you get me out of this," Joss answered.

Frennis took another one of those long steps forward and drove one ham fist into Joss's jaw. Rem thought he heard the mandible joint crack. Joss spat blood and a few teeth. Frennis shook his now-aching hand and spoke quietly. "My goodness, Joss—do you actually think you're in a position to dictate terms?"

"He'll kill you for this, Frennis," Joss suddenly spat, mouth leaking blood and saliva in long, pink ropes. "He'll not just have your skin, he'll have your soul—"

That's when Frennis snatched Joss out of the two bodyguards' hands and, with a single, roundabout shove, sent the thief headlong into the shark-infested waters below the dock.

Rem and Torval shot forward, instinctually, without hesitation. Only when they came to a rough stop beside each other at the dock's edge did Rem suddenly realize that they were both now within easy shoving distance of Frennis. With barely an expenditure of energy, the prefect of the Fourth could reach out and send them both tumbling into the waters where Joss now splashed and screamed. Realizing this, Rem took a long step back—clear of the edge, but still close enough to see what unfolded—and silently urged Torval to do the same.

Joss, meanwhile, had regained some composure after the initial shock of hitting the cold water. With long, smooth strokes, he swam for the open entrance to the boathouse. No doubt, he thought if he could swim out into the open water and cut across the harbor, he might be able to drag himself back on shore and escape his captors.

But the sharks were, alas, too swift. There were two of them and they slid through the waters off Joss's left. One of them hove out in front, rolled, and let its maw gape wide. Joss had time for a single, terrified scream, then the shark's jaws closed on his rib cage and under he went. His hands and feet thrashed above the surface in short bursts, but in moments, there was no more than a swirling mass of pink foam floating on a crimson glut of blood.

The worst part, Rem realized, was how quiet it had all been; how silently those two sea monsters slid through the water and claimed their prey.

Frennis turned to Torval. "Oh dear," he said. "We seem to have lost him."

Torval lunged at the prefect, but once more, Frennis's size and strength gave him an advantage. He snatched Torval up in his fists, then heaved him bodily back away from the edge of the dock. Torval hit a stack of barrels and sent them all toppling with a great, thunderous crash. Though it occurred to Rem that he should, perhaps, come to his partner's aid—or at the very least, try to avenge his mistreatment—the simple fact was that Rem knew Frennis had every advantage: he was bigger, stronger, meaner, and most importantly, had no scruples regarding right and wrong. He was a petty but terrifying despot of a very small urban kingdom, and he ruled that domain with a smirk and steel fists.

So Rem simply retreated to Torval's side, and helped the dwarf back to his feet. Torval, once he regained his feet, slapped Rem's supporting hands away and lunged toward Frennis again, like a dog let off its leash. Rem threw himself bodily onto his diminutive partner and struggled mightily to keep him from once more engaging the red-haired prefect.

"You fat fool!" Torval growled, straining against Rem's embrace. "He was our best lead! Our *only* lead!"

"Rules, you belligerent pickmonkey," Frennis answered,

still haughty and composed. "This isn't your ward, so if you transact business here—*any business*—you come to me first. Being my ward, under my watch, I'll decide which witnesses are material to which crimes and which are simply...fish food."

"Regulations have nothing to do with this," Torval snarled. "You just killed a man to prove a bloody point that had nothing to do with his crimes or his guilt! I'll take this all the way to Black Mal and have your signet, you woolly bastard, I swear—"

Frennis looked to Rem now. "I suggest you see your partner out of my sight, boy, before I lose my temper and toss you both in the drink."

Rem decided it was time to intervene. "Torval," he said quietly, still using all his strength to keep the dwarf immobilized, "we should go."

The dwarf relented. With barely a shrug, he threw off Rem's iron-clad lock on his short, broad body, turned and marched away in sullen silence. Rem, a good distance from Frennis and well out of his reach, decided he couldn't leave without a word of his own.

"You made your point," he said, as calmly as he could. "And now we have nothing."

"It would appear so," Frennis said, as though he were teaching a lesson to a slow child. "Perhaps in the future, you'll think twice about snaring your prey in my woods."

The bodyguards, having been fascinated during this entire exchange with the still-tumbling sharks in the waters below and the roiling, spreading cloud of blood that engulfed them, finally seemed to snap out of their reverie and realize their leader was facing his enemies alone. One of them—the more muscled of the two—stepped forward. The other drew the sword sheathed at his side.

Rem slowly backed away from Frennis and his hired swords.

When he was far enough away to feel safe, he turned his back on them and walked speedily after Torval, who was just disappearing through the door into the main warehouse. Behind Rem, there was a strange *gloop-gloop* sound from the water, the slap of a wet tail. He quickened his pace behind Torval, eager to be out of Frennis's lair and far away from the dark waters of the bay.

CHAPTER NINETEEN

They were hours late for their shift when they finally arrived at the watchkeep. Torval assured Rem that Ondego would understand, what with the attempt on their lives and all, but that gave Rem little comfort. He was new to his position and he wanted to prove himself trustworthy. Showing up late for one's shift without a by-your-leave was a quick and easy way to get on the prefect's cross side. And who knew what sort of trouble Frennis would make for Ondego, after having to threaten his men and chase them out of his ward?

As it turned out, Ondego seemed pleased to see them. "Here they are, my wayward sons!" he exclaimed, crossing the administrative chamber with a very strange smile on his face and a stranger light in his eyes. Rem and Torval, embarrassed by this show of interest and sure that it must be some plot to publicly chastise them, stood stock-still in the doorway to the great chamber and tried to keep from turning red as all eyes followed Ondego on his long walk to greet them. Across the chamber, by Ondego's office, Hirk stood sentinel, his stony face an unreadable mask.

Ondego reached them. "Are you quite safe and sound, lads? Any trouble to report?"

"Someone tried to kill Torval," Rem said.

"Probably would've tried to kill you too," Torval said. "Don't flatter yourself."

"*Kill you?*" Ondego asked, brows rising. "Whatever for? Two such brave and resolute watchwardens as yourselves? Never errant? Always vigilant? Never *three fucking hours late* for their appointed shifts on the watch!"

There it was at last: the fury. Ondego's face was bright red. A pair of thick, ropy veins bulged at his temples. His eyes looked like two hot ovens, stoked and ablaze.

"Steady on," Torval countered. "You just heard our excuse."

"It took them three hours to try to kill you?" Ondego asked. "Please tell me they kidnapped you first and rode you out to the countryside..."

"Well, after slipping the assassin," Rem offered, "we had a lead we wanted to follow up on."

"A lead!" Ondego exclaimed. "Bless me, that's good news. Who was this lead, and pray, what did you learn from them?"

"It was the Nightjar," Torval said. "And in truth, we didn't learn a bloody thing from him."

"The Nightjar?" Ondego said, crossing his arms and nodding his head deferentially. "Well, then, that makes everything all right. Questioning the Nightjar would require the two of you getting official leave to operate in another ward, after all, and since you never came to me for any such leave, I can only assume you realized that pursuing your investigation in this manner was folly indeed, so you hurried here, to get the proper clearances and explain your gods-damned tardiness."

"All right, all right," Torval grumbled. "You've made your point."

"Have I, in fact?" Ondego said. "I'm still waiting for the stunning climax of your story. Spill it."

"We went to the Nightjar's and ran across that sneak thief again," Rem said. "The fellow we found in Freygaf's chambers. Ginger Joss."

"Well," Ondego said, planting his hands on his hips, "Just what did Joss have to say?"

"Nothing," Torval spat.

"Aye," Rem said. "Nothing. Once Frennis tossed him in with the sharks—"

"Frennis?" Ondego asked.

Torval raised his eyes, only briefly. "Aye."

Ondego studied them both. Rem saw that his jaw was clenched and his eyes were vibrating with a terrible, shuttered rage. Behind their prefect, Hirk simply hung his head, shook it, and retreated into the prefect's office.

"Frennis," Ondego said again, not a question this time.

"Aye, Frennis, you heard us!" Torval said, sounding rather annoyed. "Are you going deaf now, sir?"

"Secure that," Ondego shouted, and the entire room froze. "You're lucky I don't strip the both of you of your signets here and now and throw you in the stocks! Do you have any idea, either of you, the unholy rump-rutting I'm going to be liable for because the two of you tromped on someone else's turf? Transacted business in someone else's ward?"

"Aye, sir," the dwarf spat back.

"And Frennis's ward, no less! Bonny Prince, you're ignorant as an inbred mule in this, being new—but by all that's sacred and profane, Torval, *you know better.* You know that Frennis is a despot and a cunning toad and a cold-blooded killer. Why, why, why, knowing all of that, would you put yourself and your partner and *my ward* in danger by stepping on the toes of that rabid, slavering mastiff on his own turf?"

Torval lost his patience. "Because I'm trying to find out who killed my *dead* partner, sir, and in pursuit of that justice I will fear *no* man and step over *any* boundary that impedes my efforts. *Is that clear enough for you?"*

"Oh, well that's a relief," Ondego carried on. "That means that you dragged the Bonny Prince down there knowing full well what a fuck-all of hellfire and brimstone you were stirring up for me, since I could have sworn all my watchmen are expressly forbidden from operating in other wards without my clear permission!"

"It couldn't wait!" Torval protested.

"Everything can wait!" Ondego roared. "Someone else's ward, someone else's problem. Do you have any idea what kind of tributes we might have to pay if Frennis complains?"

"Well, I'm bloody well tired of repeating myself!" Torval shouted back. "We told you why we're late, but now we're here. Kindly step aside and let us get about our business—sir!"

Ondego looked like he was about to pick Torval up in his arms and tear him limb from limb. His whole body shook, the corded muscles of his arms were taut, and veins stood out on his throat and forehead. Then, just as suddenly as the storm arose, it dissipated. Ondego threw up his hands, shrugged, and waved off the two of them like they were a pack of annoying flies.

"Fine," he said. "Just get going."

"Get going where?" Torval asked.

Ondego looked puzzled for a moment, then seemed to remember something briefly forgotten. "Oh, that's it. I forgot to tell you, since you were so gods-damned late for work and I was put out about it and all. You two sodden bastards have been summoned to the home of our most eminent citizen, Kethren Dall. It seems that he learned you were the two who found his little girl in that dross pile and he wants to thank you personally for seeing her returned to the family."

"You're joking," Torval said.

Ondego raised one eyebrow. "Do I look like I'm joking, Torval?"

"Tonight?" Rem asked. "It's late and—"

"The family is keeping a vigil through the night and accepting mourners. It was made clear to me that no matter the time, the two of you should be sent to Citizen Dall's manse as soon as was possible. So, now that you've finally deigned to show yourselves hereabouts, what say you make my life easier and go see the man? Express the right obsequies and he might even offer a gift of some sort to the Fifth. So, remember, you're not just representing yourselves—you're representing all of us."

"We can't go into that man's home, with his daughter lying in state," Torval said. "You said it yourself, sir—all we did was answer a call and found the poor lass lying under the rubbish. Even Hirk and Eriadus were the ones responsible for seeing her cleaned and prepared—"

"Nonetheless," Ondego said, "Citizen Dall asked for the two men who found her, and the two men who found her are you and the Bonny Prince here. So, on your way."

"Must we?" Rem asked, horrified at the thought of facing the poor girl's grieving family with no leads, no indicators that they were any closer to seeing justice done on her behalf.

"Yes, you bloody well fucking must!" Ondego shouted.

The Dall manse, like many of the city's finer homes, was on the southeast side of the harbor, in the Second Ward, in a fine, well-heeled neighborhood of walled villas and gardens that climbed up the gentle slope of one of the city's three hills. Rem couldn't speak for Torval, but he felt strangely out of place the moment they entered the Second Ward and their surroundings became noticeably posh. Rem thought this a strange sort of irony, since he was from nobility himself, but it seemed that his month away from home, moving and living among the lower sorts, had truly changed him. The ostentation on display in the high walls, manicured gardens, and embossed front gates to all the estates they passed really did leave him a little sick to his stomach... especially since he now knew how simply the bulk of the city's people really lived.

Still, it was an order, and they would follow it, no matter how uncomfortable it made them.

"I hate this sort of thing," Torval confessed as they climbed the last rising street toward the Dall home.

"He just wants to say thank you," Rem offered, not sure if that meant anything.

"Perhaps," Torval said. "But honestly, what's he thanking us for? His daughter's dead and we just found what was left of her. For that we deserve thanks?"

Rem nodded. He understood what Torval meant. He didn't feel like he deserved thanks, especially considering that they had found Telura Dall almost by accident, while they were busy with a separate investigation. But Rem also knew—from personal experience—that the rich and powerful were keenly aware of how their capacity for largesse and gratitude could be later used to their advantage by cultivating their associations and calling in favors when special aid was required. Even if Kethren Dall's desire to show the two of them some gratitude was, for Dall himself, entirely genuine, there was probably some deeper, covert impulse in his character that quietly suggested that having a couple of good, reliable men on the city watch could, in the fullness of time, come in very handy.

Patronage. Favors for favors. Loans and obligations. These were the foundational relationships of the rich and powerful. Rem knew the game well, and had grown so weary of it that he had come all the way to Yenara to escape it.

But he offered none of that to Torval. He simply kept walking, mouth shut.

In time, a line of mourners appeared, some walking, some borne on servant-carried litters, all climbing the cobbled street toward the manse at the summit. Rem and Torval fell in with the many mingling parties and kept an even pace, eager to neither fall behind nor pull ahead.

As they stood in the long, snaking line of guests, Rem found his wandering gaze drawn to the servants that bore the finely chased litters bearing the richer acquaintances of the Dall family. All seemed foreign, their skin tones ranging from deep ebony to dusky olive, all of them had their hair cropped close to their heads, and all wore iron collars, as thick as a man's finger, that seemed to have neither joint nor latch chain. At first, Rem assumed it must be some bizarre fashion accessory, but as he started to note the prevalence of the strange collar among all the shorn-headed men bearing those colorfully lacquered litters, Rem began to suspect there was another explanation.

He bent toward Torval. "Are those slaves carrying the litters?" he whispered.

Torval drew up on his toes and rocked back and forth, trying to see around the press of bodies surrounding him. Finally, he nodded. "Aye."

"I thought," Rem said, "that slavery was proscribed in the west?"

Torval shrugged. "For the most part. Your countrymen, in the north, never had many to begin with—though the Kostermen used to keep them, in bygone days. The kingdoms and courts farther south let the Panoply and the Temple of Aemon talk them out of the practice. Most of the free cities, like Yenara, forbid the taking and trading of slaves, and make it clear that every citizen born within their borders is free—but these sorts, the rich, they're not forbidden from traveling east, to slaving cities, buying servants there, and bringing them back to Yenara with them. So long as they license their chattel and pay the proper taxes—"

Rem nodded, frowning. "The Yenaran way: it's perfectly legal if the right authorities are paid."

Torval shrugged. "Just so. There certainly aren't many of them. It's only the poshest of the posh that keep them, like some ugly trophy of their wealth and privilege."

Rem realized his stomach was churning. The realization that he stood in a crowd with human beings that other human beings claimed to own, as property, had caused his body to react with visceral horror. Suddenly, the smug courtly life that he'd soured on and left behind did not seem quite so repugnant anymore.

"I wonder how they'd like it," he muttered, "if foreign armies swept into their cities and villages and dragged their women and children away, to have their spirits broken and their bodies sold like farmstock on an auction block?"

"Give it time," Torval said. "The wheel always turns, doesn't it?"

Rem nodded. How very true.

As the mourners arrived at the main villa gate, their cavalcade slowed and the crowd gradually bunched up around them. Rem heard murmurs of sadness and reproach all around—rich families discussing how broken up poor Kethren Dall must be, how they couldn't imagine what a terrible shock it must have been...and in some cases, how they were simply glad it was a disaster that befell him and not them. Rem understood that sort of talk, but that didn't make hearing it any easier.

Torval seemed quite uncomfortable and far out of his element. There were no other dwarves on hand, for one thing, so even in his small stature, he stuck out like a sown-on thumb. He was not simply other than human, he was also a tradesman by training and humble by birth. Rem thought to try to put him at ease, but one glance at Torval's squared, tense shoulder and his downcast eyes told him that nothing was likely to make the dwarf feel better about his present surroundings. Thus, Rem let it rest, and the two carried on in the slow line as it drifted toward the gate to the Dall home and, little by little, the mourners trickled into the main house as other earlier arrivals trickled back out.

They were challenged at the door, but a servant standing within earshot vouched for them, assuring the overearnest porter who asked the names of all the incoming mourners that the master of the house had, indeed, summoned these two scruffy-looking, clearly low-class watchmen. Rem and Torval were apologized to, then shown into the main hall of the villa, where the young Telura Dall lay in state on a silk-draped bier surrounded by mounds of flowers, bundled herbs, and funerary offerings. Rem and Torval joined the line of mourners waiting to move past the corpse so that they, too, could pay their respects. It took almost a full half hour for that line to inch forward, snaking around the great room to finally place them before the young lady.

Rem thought that young Telura looked as beautiful as any maiden he'd ever seen, either back home or in the city. Even her pallor seemed healthy and alive, her skin gilded gold by the many candles burning all around her, her cheeks rouged red to give some semblance of life. There were no signs of the wounds on her scalp, or on her wrists. Rem knew nothing of the funerary arts, but he thought the widows at the House of Waiting sorceresses indeed to have taken this poor girl—whose body had been found beneath a pile of rubbish in a bad part of town—and turn her once more into something resembling a peacefully-napping princess.

Beside him, Rem saw that Torval seemed deeply moved by the sight of the young lady. Perhaps he was thinking of his own daughter—or even his wife. Rem had spent enough time with Torval to know now when the dwarf was struggling to keep his deep and powerful emotions bottled. Though his countenance remained stony, the glint in his eyes and the trembling at the downturned corners of his mouth were unmistakable. Torval might play at being inured to all the terrible things he was privy to as a wardwatchman, but Rem could tell that all those myriad sins, whether blasphemous or banal, still had a profound effect upon him.

Once their time before the corpse was done, they moved into the gardens, where the guests all gathered to quietly mingle, drink, and eat of the buffet set out for them, and (presumably) to discuss their own fond memories of the dear departed. True, Rem overheard conversations of all sorts around him—gossip, business deals, plans for illicit meetings, and demands for restitution of debts—but he knew what the funeral of a high-born young lady was supposed to consist of in theory, if not in practice. He tried to screen out all the venality around him and simply enjoy the fine wine and free repast. He hadn't eaten since he and Torval had breakfasted that morning, and he was quite hungry.

Torval did not mingle. He simply stood aside, waiting as though on guard, a stalwart little figure with squared shoulders and feet set apart. More than once, the guests turned and remarked upon Torval and Rem and their apparent crashing of the party, but Torval never seemed to hear them, and Rem never thought to make their conversations a topic of his own. He decided, instead, that it was best to wait. If Kethren Dall wanted to find them and thank them, he would do so. If he did not, then they could leave after a time.

Rem caught sight of a strange figure across the torchlit yard. He studied the figure for a moment, then bent to whisper to Torval.

"That one looks familiar," he said.

Torval raised himself up on his toes, to get a better view, then nodded in agreement. "Aye. That's the elf that delivered our watchkeep news of the missing girl."

Rem snapped his fingers. "That's it. The one who offered the reward. Strange company to find an elf among, isn't it?"

"And why is that?" Torval asked.

Rem shrugged. "I suppose I never thought of the wood folk as . . . well, mercantile."

Torval shot him a sideward glance, then let loose a heavy, exasperated sigh. "Just as not all dwarves live under mountains mining and polishing jewels, not all elves spend their lives smoking witchweed and snuggling trees. Look at this one's forehead—that should tell you all you need to know."

Rem did as he was told. It was hard to see clearly from a distance, but when the light hit the elf's high, pale forehead just right, he thought he saw a strange scar there—a sort of star, right in the center of his brow.

"Thorned," Torval said.

Rem waited for an explanation and got none. "What does that mean?" he finally asked.

Torval sighed. "In the old days, slavers sometimes snatched elven children for trade. The slavers didn't want the children using their mind magic against them, or communicating secretly with their fellows, so they would drive a cold-iron spike through their foreheads. Not deep enough to kill them—just enough to kill the part of their mind that allows them to speak without words and read thoughts."

Rem felt a chill run through him. It seemed a rather barbarous thing to do, considering elves were born mind readers—the terrible, irrevocable theft of a gods-given birthright. "Is it common?" Rem asked.

Torval shook his head. "Not so common anymore, as slavers rarely get their hands on elven children these days. But when they do, that's how they make them compliant. Worse, even if the thorned children ever get free, they can never get the gift back. It means that their own sort want nothing more to do with them."

"So they're outcasts among men because they're elves and former slaves," Rem said, "and they're outcasts among elves because they no longer have the gift that all their fellows share?"

"That's it," Torval said.

Rem sighed grimly. "That's fantastically cruel," he said. "I can't imagine what that could do to a person."

"I don't know his story," Torval said, referring again to the elf that had drawn Rem's attention, "but I'm willing to bet he's made a life among men because his own kind wouldn't have him back. Probably a merchant of some sort. A man—or elf—can yank himself out of any pit of despair if he can find the right merchandise to trade."

Rem studied the elf as he moved among the guests, speaking to some, being avoided and whispered about by others. "He dresses well enough. Those are Quaimish silks. And all those jewels..."

Torval shrugged. "Rare, to be sure. But there's all sorts under the sun, in't there?"

"I say," a fellow exclaimed, suddenly approaching them. He looked well-to-do in a dark tunic and toga, a cup of wine in hand and more of his stripe following on his heels. "I say, may I ask who the two of you might be?"

Torval started to open his mouth. Rem saw from the way his

eyes narrowed and his mouth twisted that it was bound to be something gruff and uncharitable. Rem intervened.

"Watchwardens, milord," Rem said, bowing the slightest. "Humble and out of place in these environs, I can assure you."

The rich man and his equally rich companions all looked puzzled. "Well," the fellow said, looking more embarrassed than indignant, "if I may ask, what brings you to the wake this evening?"

Rem smiled, trying to alleviate the tension in the air. "We were the men who found the young lady, sir. Apparently, his lordship Citizen Dall wanted to thank us personally for doing our duty and seeing the young lady returned to her family."

The rich man and his companions all seemed strangely amazed by this, as though thanking a civil servant were the most bizarre and wondrous thing they'd ever heard of. They grumbled and muttered among themselves for a few moments before their leader finally offered his hand to Rem in greeting.

"Othren Osk, of the ancient House of Osk. I am most delighted to meet you, Master...?"

"Remeck," Rem said, bowing again. "Of no particular ancient house. This is my partner, Torval."

Torval nodded gruffly. He seemed quite shocked that Rem had taken it upon himself to speak with these men, even annoyed. Still, he kept his mouth shut and Rem was glad of it.

"So, the two of you are watchmen," Othren Osk said, as though it were the most fascinating thing he had ever heard. "You patrol the streets, arrest criminals, that sort of thing?"

"Just that sort of thing, milord," Rem said with a nod.

"Then I would imagine," Osk said, "that such tragedies as this are part and parcel for you. All too common, I would think."

"Death and murder are common, it's true," Rem said. "But

the murder of one such as young Miss Telura Dall—one so
beautiful and well-to-do—well, sir, there's nothing common
in that."

"Is that right?" Osk said, looking to Torval for confirmation.

Torval's face remained stony. "That's right."

"Such fascinating work," Othren said, and he genuinely
seemed to mean it, even though the men at his elbow were
chattering among themselves now and ready to move on. Rem
knew the type: this Othren Osk was the sort of fellow who
had long been sheltered by his money and power. He honestly
enjoyed conversations with people from other walks, simply
because their lives struck him as curious and alien. If a flesh-
eating plant or white tiger could talk, he would probably be
equally as pleased to speak with them.

It was then that a servant approached, the very same bald and
powdered eunuch who had saved them at the door and gained
them admittance. "Good gentlemen," he said, bowing obse-
quiously, "the master has asked for you and will see you now."

"I beg your leave?" Rem asked Othren Osk.

"Freely granted. A delight, Watchman Remeck."

Rem nodded. "My pleasure, milord." Rem looked to Torval
then. "After you."

Torval scowled as though it were an insult and followed the
eunuch out of the gardens.

CHAPTER TWENTY

They were led once more through the great hall, down a side corridor, and into a spacious but cluttered room that looked to Rem like some sort of office. Cubbies filled with scrolls and shelves laden with books lined all the walls, a large desk stood at one end of the room under a pair of watchful hanging lamps, and opposite the desk stood a trio of comfortable couches, no doubt intended for leisurely perusal of all the reading material on hand. Currently, there were several men in the room, all congregating around a certain fellow of regal bearing and aquiline profile, whom Rem recognized as their grieving host, Kethren Dall.

"The watchmen you summoned, milord," the eunuch said with a deep bow, presenting Rem and Torval to the proud-looking patrician before them.

Dall studied them, looking down his nose with affected pride. The affectation did little to mask the ghost of grief apparent in his sagging, red-rimmed eyes and the deeply cut frown at the corners of his mouth. While Rem could not guess as to Dall's true character, his immediate impression was one of trustworthiness—though he knew well that first impressions were often proven wrong.

"What are your names, gentlemen?" Citizen Dall asked.

Rem and Torval each introduced themselves. Rem knew the drill with men of Dall's sort—he'd been one, hadn't he?—so he kept his eyes down and his head slightly bowed in the rich man's presence, feigning humility for the sake of his subterfuge. Torval, for his part, also kept his eyes down, but there was no subservient bow in his shoulders, no bend of his neck. The dwarf still stood straight, at attention, proud and mighty though he remained only four feet tall.

The men in Dall's company had grown silent when the two of them had been presented. Rem absently wondered if that was because they were discussing shady business, or because they simply didn't want to be overheard talking by a pair of roughspuns from the wardwatch. Dall himself seemed to take a great deal of time to study them, then gave a nod to his eunuch servant. The servant bustled away to a side alcove of the room to see to some unknown task, and Dall addressed the two of them directly.

"You are the watchmen who found my precious Telura?"

"We are, milord," Torval said.

"In a rubbish heap," Dall said.

Rem threw a glance at Torval. Should they acknowledge the truth? Did Dall know it, or was he asking for a more honest report than he'd previously been given? Torval, for his part, didn't seem too sure about which was the case either. After a long, uncomfortable silence, the dwarf finally spoke.

"That was where we found her, milord," Torval said, "sad as it is to report."

Dall studied the two of them then, his lip trembling, his eyes growing watery. Rem didn't look forward to what might come in the next moment. The fellow could become angry, slinging all the fury and hatred he felt for Telura's murderers at these two hapless public servants. Or he could simply break down with grief again, and they'd be forced to stand here and watch him sob until he thought to dismiss them. Either way, it wouldn't be pretty. Rem didn't care to be the brunt of the man's grief or anger. Right now, all of a sudden, he simply wanted to go, and go quickly.

"Do either of you have children?" Kethren Dall asked. His voice broke.

"I do, milord," Torval answered. "Three. And I've lost two in the past, so I know something of milord's pain at this present moment."

Rem looked to Torval. He hadn't imagined the dwarf would share such information with this rich stranger whom they may never see nor speak to again. Still, he understood the wisdom of it. If Dall was about to fall apart in their presence, it might bode well for them if he knew that one of the two men before him was also a father, and knew what a father's grief felt like.

"If that's true," Dall said, "then I daresay you do know what I'm feeling. What would you do in pursuit of the men who were responsible for your dear daughter's murder, master dwarf? What could stop you in your quest for justice?"

Torval's mouth was set stonily again. "Nothing," he said slowly. "Nothing in the world could stop me once I'd set my sights upon them and determined to hunt them down."

The eunuch appeared again. He handed something to Dall, which Dall then brandished for Rem and Torval: a pair of small leather pouches. They tinkled metallically. Rem knew they were filled with coin.

"Then I expect you to stop at nothing," Kethren Dall said, and flung one of the little coin sacks in his hand to Torval, the other to Rem. Each caught them and hefted them. Rem could not tell whether the coin within was gold or silver, but either way, the gifts were generous.

Not gifts, he reminded himself. *Bounties. This man expects his daughter's killers to be brought to justice.*

"These are tokens of my appreciation for all you've done thus far," Kethren Dall said. "For finding my little girl and seeing her returned to us. Now I beg you, gentlemen—find the men who stole her from us. Find them, and let me look into their eyes just once before they're brought to their final justice and sent to their gods for punishment."

"We can hunt these men," Torval said. "But we cannot accept this coin, milord. We were only doing our jobs and it wouldn't be right—"

"Then give the coin to the prefect if you must. Let it buy new armor or new swords for the men of the watch, or fill your buttery stores. It's out of my hands now and in yours, and I won't have it returned without being insulted."

Torval nodded. "Ours is but to serve, milord."

The sound of approaching footsteps presaged the opening of the study door. There stood the elf, Mykaas Masarda, looking quite surprised to find so many people crammed into Citizen Dall's den. He scanned the faces of all present and gave a barely perceptible bow of his head in greeting.

"My apologies for interrupting, old friend," Masarda said to Citizen Dall. "I had no idea you were speaking privately with anyone."

"No apologies, Mykaas," the patrician replied. "I was just expressing my gratitude to these good watchwardens—as you suggested."

The elf turned and studied Rem and Torval more fully, and Rem thought he saw something in the woodlander's smooth and angular face: an almost invisible flash of pretense that suggested that his surprise in finding them there was false. Rem took the opportunity—that extended moment when Mykaas Masarda seemed to study and size them both up—to do a little hasty consideration of his own.

The elf was youthful and pale, ears tapered and pointed, head bald save for a long flaxen topknot that fell down his back in a well-bound braid. Up close, the thorning scar on his forehead was much more apparent, slightly livid in the shadowy lamplight of the study. Lingering in the hall outside was a man in clearly low-class raiment that Rem marked as Estavari by his olive skin, dark hair, and well-oiled beard. He wasn't dressed to impress, nor for the funeral, so Rem assumed he must be the elf's bodyguard. Even at this distance, half-cloaked in the shadow of the hall beyond the elf, the Estavari looked equal to any adversary that would stand against him.

Strange, Rem thought, *that the elf would bring his bodyguard with him to a funeral vigil.*

Rem and Torval each made slight bows. Mykaas Masarda, their new elven acquaintance, offered his hand to each in turn.

"Watchmen," he said, not ungraciously. "It is my pleasure, and my honor."

"Citizen Masarda is an old acquaintance of mine," Citizen Dall offered. "Though in all our years of association, I don't think he's aged a day, while time has certainly heaped its whips and scorns upon my old countenance."

Masarda seemed embarrassed. "The curse of my kind, I'm afraid."

"And what brings an elf out of the woods and into this close, crowded city of ours?" Torval asked. "I thought it strange enough to see my own kind on these streets, let alone the kith and kin of your fair kind, good citizen."

Rem shot a puzzled glance at Torval. What was he doing? Was he *trying* to insult their host and get them kicked out? Of course, Rem had wondered those very things aloud only moments ago, but he never would have expected Torval to give them voice.

"Rare, indeed, to be sure," Masarda answered with a slight smile. "In all honesty, master dwarf, the forest was never for me. These streets, with their press and shadows and noise and colors, move me far more deeply. But if one considers, it's really just a forest of a different sort, isn't it?"

"Such a thought had occurred to me since my arrival," Rem said.

Masarda turned his ageless gaze upon Rem. "And where did you arrive from, good watchman?"

"Up north," Rem said. "Hasturland. The low country."

"Ah, the Hasturi low country," Masarda said. "Pastures and orchards and green rolling hills. What on earth brought *you* here, to this most oppressive and wanton of cities?"

Rem shrugged. He kept the elf's gaze locked with his own. "Just looking for a change of scenery, sir. I would imagine you know something of what I speak."

"I'm sure I wouldn't," Mykaas Masarda replied, his smile remaining but his eyes and voice gone cold. "I was taken from my folk and their forest home when I was but a child. By the time I could return there of my own accord...well, shall we say there was nothing for me to return to. It was only Yenara and her penchant for...we'll call it *reinvention*, that allowed me to once more find a suitable and welcoming habitat suited to my talents and moods. It was my home before I ever arrived, you might say, just waiting to welcome me."

For that one instant, Rem understood the elf perfectly. He, too, had known that curious feeling—the surprising realization that Yenara—new, alien, overwhelming, threatening—was, in fact, the home he had always yearned to return to, the place of belonging that his own homeland had never been.

"I'm sure this good dwarf knows of what you speak," Kethren

Dall interjected. "Yenara can't be much like the Ironwall Mountains, or wherever it is you hail from, eh?"

Torval looked weary with all the obsequies and banter. Clearly, mixing and mingling was not his strong suit. "No, indeed," he said. "Though I'd had my fill of mountains and mines by the time I came to Yenara, it most certainly was *not* what I was used to."

"There, you see?" Dall offered. "You gentlemen have something in common!"

Mykaas Masarda offered a forced smile and stared for a very long time at Rem and Torval. "Apparently," he finally said, then smiled unconvincingly. "How serendipitous. Carry on, good watchmen. Be ever vigilant and keep us safe."

He swept into the room, the assertiveness and swiftness of his movement making it clear that now that he had arrived in Citizen Dall's presence, Rem and Torval could leave.

"As you say, milord," Rem said, and stepped toward the door, hoping that Torval would take the cue and follow him.

At the door, Rem nearly ran into the elf's Estavari bodyguard. For just a moment, the two stood toe to toe on the threshold, eyes locked, quietly appraising one another, each waiting for the other to step out of the way.

Rem finally decided to relent and stepped aside, allowing the bodyguard to enter the room and linger at his master's elbow. Once he was in, Rem and Torval passed out again into the hall and quickened their pace, to be away from that cramped study and Mykaas Masarda's ageless, inscrutable gaze as quickly as possible.

"Can we go now?" Torval asked.

"With pleasure," Rem said. "And what are we to do with this?" He hefted the fat little pouch of coin that Dall's eunuch had handed him.

Torval shoved his own coin bag into a pouch on his belt. "Keep it. The regs say we can accept gifts for tasks already completed when said gifts are issued by private citizens. Still, don't forget to give Ondego a cut—just to keep him happy. A fifth should do."

Rem nodded. "Wouldn't want to end up down in the dungeons, like Kevel."

Torval shot Rem a narrow-eyed glance. "No. You most certainly would not."

CHAPTER TWENTY-ONE

Rem and Torval ended up back at the watchkeep. It was the middle of the night, but the administrative chamber was alive with arrested suspects and watchwardens on their way in from fresh arrests or heading out in search of more—an atmosphere of weary assurance. The two of them sat at an empty desk, hunched into themselves, and did their damnedest to piece the scattered shards of their investigation together. After almost an hour, they weren't getting very far.

"So," Rem offered, "to summarize, Freygaf ends up beaten and murdered by the North Canal; the Creeper claims innocence, but assures us that Freygaf had secrets that you won't be happy to uncover; Ginger Joss provides a promising lead, sneaking into Freygaf's apartment to steal this funny little medallion, but Joss ends up as shark food because Frennis didn't like us invading his turf. All we know, courtesy of the late Ginger Joss, is that he fears someone else more than he feared Frennis—at least enough to keep quiet before the fish ate him."

"That's about the size and shape of it," Torval agreed.

"So," Rem said, "we know little more than when we started."

"Little enough," Torval said. He was toying with the little sack of coin he had been given by Kethren Dall. Unexpected bonus aside, he was clearly glum and downtrodden at being no closer to Freygaf's killer than they were even a day or two earlier. Rem couldn't blame him. He felt like a failure himself—and he hadn't even known the late, mourned Freygaf.

"Then what's left to us?" Rem asked. "You've no other leads from the arrest records?"

Torval shrugged. "I've exhausted them. We had history with the Creeper. The Nightjar bore us a grudge, and the presence of one of his gambling chits—not to mention finding Joss on his property—seemed promising. But both of those leads led to dead ends, didn't they? All the other colorful sorts that Freygaf and I have arrested over the years were small-timers. I suppose we should leave no stone unturned, but I have a hard time believing any of those remaining in our personal rogue's gallery were capable of getting the drop on Freygaf, let alone killing him."

"Then we're at an impasse again," Rem said. "Barring miracles or necromancy."

Torval was silent for a long while. However, his incessant fidgeting with the little bag of coin had stopped. Torval's gaze had wandered off into the middle distance and his mouth hung open.

"Torval?" Rem asked.

Torval studied the young man then. He picked up his little bag of coin and brandished it. "How attached are you to this little bonus, lad?"

Rem shrugged. His own bag of coin was still in the inner pocket of his jerkin. "I suppose I couldn't miss what I didn't have a couple hours ago. What've you got in mind?"

Torval sat up straight. He stared at his coin bag again, as though trying to penetrate it with his gaze alone, in search of some secret or hidden clue. "I've an idea," he said, "but it's on the shady side. I don't want you joining me in it unless you're truly willing. Besides that, it might cost us."

"What is it?" Rem pressed. "Don't keep me in suspense."

Torval snatched up his coin bag. "You said it yourself. Necromancy."

Rem stared at Torval for a moment, not sure if he'd heard him right. Then, knowing that he had, he did the only reasonable thing: he shrugged and rose from his uncomfortable wooden chair.

Torval nodded. "Follow me," he urged, and off they went.

Torval explained on the way. In Yenara, there were a finite number of mages legally licensed to sell magical implements and wondrous works. The wards even kept several on the payrolls—specialized battle mages and diviners, employed for dangerous raids, incursions into hostile territory, and the reading of signs and portents. However, outright necromancy—summoning and speaking with the dead—was strictly forbidden by city law and the laws of several of the city's more powerful temple congregations, so no licensed mage—especially one on the wardwatch payroll, such as a member of the Mage Squad—would ever agree to such black and proscribed magic, lest they end up with their heads on pikes at the city gates.

However, since most of the city's working mages could not afford to be, or did not want to be, licensed, the fact was that there were many, many more in the wonder-working business who simply plied their trade illegally. They usually fronted their operations by owning curio shops or botanicals or apothecaries, but if one knew who one was talking to and what they were capable of, these same seemingly innocent shopkeeps could, for a price, work all sorts of magic for their customers in the name of commerce.

Most of them, according to Torval, held court in a dog-legged side street right there in the Fifth Ward, known as Mage's Alley.

"So, we're going to buy a miracle?" Rem asked as they marched through the winding streets of the Fifth, on the way to their destination.

"Something like that," Torval answered. "I don't know what these two little sacks of coin can buy us—black-market mages working blacker magic can more or less name their price for whatever operation you seek from them—but since we're out of options, short on leads, and newly coined—it seems worth a try."

"Have you got someone in mind?" Rem asked. "To handle the transaction?"

Torval threw a glance at him. "Of course. It's not the first time I've come down here looking for a little help on a case—though it has been a very, very long time."

Outwardly, Mage's Alley looked like any other narrow side street, chock full of shopfronts and twisting side lanes. The shop windows—dark so late at night—seemed entirely ordinary, the peaked rooves with their thatch and shingles just as prosaic as any other collection of buildings in the city. The street was deserted this late at night and shrouded in a fog even more perpetual than that which often graced the remainder of the city. There were very few post lamps here, so light was dim and intermittent, but Torval seemed to know where he was going and needed no guidance. Rem kept his mouth shut and his eyes open, quite uneasy for all the open alleyways and dark corners that lurked about them. If there was a place in the city where two watchmen shouldn't be after dark, Mage's Alley seemed to be it.

Finally, Torval found their destination—one more shopfront that looked no different from the many they had already passed, a little door next to a window crammed with the accoutrements of witchery on display. There was no light within, and no movement. Torval pounded on the door.

Rem looked for a shingle above the door, to mark the place. He didn't see one. None of the shops nearby had shingles or names. That struck him as decidedly odd.

Torval kept pounding on the door, pausing only for a few moments at a time, then resuming again. "Sheba!" he called, seemingly unconcerned with what neighbors he might be waking, or whose attention he might be drawing. "Sheba, get your ass out of bed and get down here!"

Suddenly, the window shutters just above the shop window opened. A woman leaned out, her hair hanging in a loose braid over her left shoulder. Her eyes flashing in the dim second-hand post lamp light. "What is it?" she hissed.

"It's Torval," the dwarf said. "We've need of you and we have coin. Get down here."

"Torval?" the woman sighed. "It's the middle of the bloody night—"

"Do you want the coin or don't you?" Torval demanded.

She sighed again. "Heel your hounds. I'll be right down."

It was only a moment before the woman, Sheba, was moving through the shop, throwing back the bolt on her door, and letting the two watchmen in. Rem tried to get a good look at the woman in the murky, uneven light. She had a head full of dark, disheveled hair and a vaguely annoyed air about her.

More like a bright-eyed pie baker than a powerful necromancer capable of trafficking with the forces of darkness, Rem thought.

"What is it, then?" she demanded. "It's the middle of the bloody night and I've had a long, trying day. Where's Freygaf? Who's this young sprout?"

Young sprout? Rem started to open his mouth and protest, but Torval stopped him.

"Freygaf, I'm afraid, is no more," Torval answered. "The lad's my new partner."

"Oh dear," the woman said, not sounding terribly upset about the state of things.

"No time for grief now," Torval cut in. "We're on the trail of his killer, and that's why we've come to you."

Sheba blinked. "Really?"

Torval drew out his own sack of coin, then held out his hand for Rem's. Rem obliged. Torval laid both sacks in Sheba's hands. "That's all we've got. We want to speak to Freygaf's spirit and find out who murdered him."

"You want me to summon a dead man?" Sheba asked.

"Yes," Torval answered.

"No," Sheba said.

"No?" Torval asked.

"No," she said again. "Absolutely not."

"What do you mean no?" Torval asked. "We've got money. We're willing to pay!"

Sheba handed back both sacks of coin. "It's not the money, it's the 'mancy,'" she said. "You know damned well how dangerous necromancy is, even for an accomplished practitioner."

"Which you are!" Torval countered. "Didn't you once tell me—"

She raised a hand. "I did. I have. That's not the point. The two or three times I've done it, the outcomes have been, shall we say, unpredictable. I wouldn't undertake it save for three times that much money and with far more time to study and prepare."

"Then we shall take our money elsewhere," Torval said, and turned toward the door.

"No, you won't," Sheba said, and threw a glance at Rem that said this was a dance that she and Torval had done before. "You know damned well that any other mage on the alley would tell you the same thing. And the one that doesn't tell you the same thing, that offers to conjure Freygaf's spirit *tonight*, while you wait, is a charlatan or a fool. Do you want Freygaf's spirit to end up wandering this plane eternally? Do you want him tied to you, to *your* person, following you around and skulking about in your bedchamber at all hours of the night—"

"Day," Torval said. "I work at night."

"Regardless," Sheba said impatiently. "Or consider this, Torval: the borderlands between the lands of the living and the dead are haunted by all sorts of things—things that were once alive and things that have never known the pleasures and pains of this plane. They hang about newly-arrived spirits like street-corner con men in search of new arrivals in the city, knowing that the recently dead are the ones most likely to be called back, to be questioned. And when you open those doors to let the spirit you're after through, *other things can slip through as well...*"

"But can you do it?" Torval pressed.

Sheba wasn't listening. "And just consider the expense—for me! Every implement and offering employed in a necromantic operation is tainted by its employ. Anything I put to use would have to be burned, melted down, or buried when I was done, and I'd expect my customer to pay me for the loss and replace-ment of all those articles—"

Torval threw up his arms. He was losing his temper. "What, then? We need a break in this investigation, lass, and we need it now, tonight! What do you recommend?"

She shrugged. "Something less dangerous, perhaps? Have you got any objects that I might read? Any leads I could try to illuminate?"

Rem was struck by a sudden inspiration. "We do!" he cried, and pulled the little medallion that they'd lifted off Ginger Joss out of his pocket. "Remember this, Torval?"

"Well enough," the dwarf grumbled. "But we could've

had the Mage Squad do that for us, and without the outlay of coin—"

Sheba shrugged. "You're welcome to be on your way, then. I'm sleepy and—"

"Oh, bugger it all!" Torval spat. "Give it to her, lad. We're here, we might as well let her do her work."

Sheba took the medallion and studied it. "Even a little piece of tin like this can absorb a lot of information, Torval. You know that."

"I was looking for something more direct," he said.

Sheba put a mock frown on her face. "Oh, Torval, I know. But just think—it might be this little tiny piece of information that leads you to the end of your investigation. And it'll lead you there down a safer path—with less coin spent! I promise, I won't gouge you."

Torval mulled it over for a moment, drew a deep breath, then sighed. "Get on with it."

"Very well, then," Sheba said. "Come in the back."

They followed her into a close, incommodious conjuring space at the rear of the shop—a chamber with laden shelves on every wall and no windows, and only a narrow chimney in the roof to allow smoke to exit. Rem and Torval waited in the gloomy little space as Sheba went about her preparations. She lit lamps that hung from the low ceiling, snatched a silver bowl off one of the shelves and set it on a waist-high wooden butcher's block complete with a meat cleaver stuck in its surface. She then disappeared out back for a few moments with a bucket. When she returned, her pail was half-filled with water, which she poured into the waiting silver bowl. Finally, she went rooting on her shelves again, drew off three phials of strange liquid, then returned to the bowl on the pedestal.

She held out her hand. "Pay in advance. Twelve silver andies, please."

Torval, still looking more than a little perturbed with the sorceress, opened one of the two coin bags, drew out a handful of the silver coins therein, then counted them out into Sheba's waiting palm. Satisfied, she slipped the coins into the pocket of her house robe, then held out her hand again.

"The medallion," she said.

Rem, ever the keeper of the little bauble, offered it. Sheba studied the little pendant and chain carefully under the light of her many hanging lamps, then gently laid it at the bottom of the silver bowl, beneath the water. "Silence while I work," she said, eyes falling on each of them in turn. "If the time is ripe for a question, I'll tell you, and you may ask one. But ask for nothing until I tell you it's safe to do so."

"I've heard this spiel before," Torval grumbled.

She indicated Rem. "He hasn't."

"Just keep your mouth shut," Torval said to Rem. "Let me ask the questions."

"Age before beauty," Rem countered with a crooked smile.

Torval frowned.

Sheba, to Rem's delight, smiled at his jest. "All right," she finally said. "Let's get to work."

A long, pregnant silence fell. Sheba closed her eyes, stretched out her hands over the bowl, and began to make strange and intricate hand signs above the water in the bowl. After a few moments, the hand signs were coupled with strange words in a language that Rem had never heard, and couldn't imagine being spoken by a human mouth. Nonetheless, Sheba seemed to know what she was doing. It was as if her hand signs and the strange words that tumbled out of her mouth were meant to

coax the latent information in the pendant into the open air—
pleas and beseeching to an inanimate object.

Suddenly, her chanting stopped. She reached for one of the
phials beside the bowl, uncorked it, and poured a strange, oily
red liquid onto the surface of the water. The liquid floated there
in bubbles and whorls, resisting dissolution. Next she took up a
second phial and poured out more oil onto the water's surface—
blue this time. The last phial's liquid was amber yellow.

Sheba then bent down and gently blew on the surface of the
water. The whorls of colored oil began to skate around on the
surface of the water under the weight of her breath, and as they
did so, she watched them. For a long time, as they swirled and
turned, she watched them carefully, eyes narrowing, seemingly
doing her best to read the signs she saw therein.

"I see girls and boys," she said. "Young, beautiful, unsuspecting girls and boys."

Torval threw a glance at Rem. Rem was probably thinking
just what the dwarf was: Telura Dall . . . and more like her.

But Rem saw another face in his mind, too, wholly unbidden: Indilen.

Young, beautiful, unsuspecting . . .

Could it be?

"I see satins and silks. I see billows of witchweed smoke
and the dulled, dreamy vision that comes from inhaling it. I
see darkened lamps and men with sharp swords and bare flesh
sheened in sweat."

There was a hypnotic quality to Sheba's voice that made all
the hairs on Rem's arms and the nape of his neck stand on
end. It was strange, how low and breathy and inviting her voice
sounded. He thought that he could listen to her read genealogy
tables for hours on end and count himself a lucky man, if only
he could hear more of that strange, low voice that she used to

recount what she saw in the whirling daubs of oil on the water's surface...

"I see a tavern or an inn," Sheba said suddenly. "Maybe a sporting house. Ask me a question."

"Where?" Torval demanded.

"I don't know," she said, shaking her head. "I can't see any signs that mark its place in the city. But I can see the shingle out in front. There's a crescent moon under a shimmering sea."

"You mean above the sea?" Torval asked.

"Shhh!" Sheba hissed. "I didn't give leave to ask a question. And no, I didn't mean above. I meant below, as I said. That's the name of the place, I think, though I can't read the words on the sign—"

"The moon under water?" Torval asked.

"Shhh!" Sheba hissed again. "Stop that! That's twice. You're going to dispel the visions." She sighed. "But you're right. That's it. The Moon Under Water. That's the name of the place that the bauble came from."

Torval looked to Rem and nodded. *At last, a lead!*

"That's where the bauble will gain you entry," she said. "I see newcomers. They show their medallions at the door and the doors are opened."

Torval opened his mouth to ask another question, then thought better of it. He shut his mouth.

Sheba lowered her head, no longer looking at the water. She took a deep breath, as though to gather herself after a trying undertaking or tiring conversation. She gave the surface of the water one more glance, then shook her head.

"That's it," she said. "That's all I see."

"That's what a dozen andies bought us?" Torval asked.

"It's more than you had," Sheba shot back, looking more than a little perturbed. She reached into the grease-strewn water and pulled out the pendant. She handed it back to Rem, who immediately pocketed it.

"Could we buy another?" Torval asked. "Another reading? A deeper reading?"

"I doubt I could get more out of that little thing," Sheba said.

The back door suddenly buckled on its hinges. With a terrible rending and cracking, it was torn from those hinges in a shower of splinters and sawdust.

Hulking there, broad shoulders filling the doorway, was a familiar albino orc, beady red eyes burning in their sockets like malicious stars.

CHAPTER TWENTY-TWO

Rem's first reaction was not one of fear, or even shock, but a strange sort of impatience at the sudden intrusion. Sheba screamed and leapt toward the inner wall of the shop. Torval, meanwhile, fell back a few steps and blinked in disbelief.

But there was no arguing the fact. There stood the big, hulking shape, the same albino orc that had eyed them after their deadly exchange in the street that morning and that had been haunting them just an hour or so later, right on Torval's doorstep. This time, the beast didn't seem inclined to simply tuck tail and run. Its red eyes flashed, it roared savagely, then it strode into the room, making tracks toward its nearest target: Torval.

Rem heard himself call out in fear, a warning, as though Torval did not see the beast, or was not equal to meeting it. But a moment later, Rem realized just how wrong he was. Torval raised his maul, gritted his teeth like a bear in a fighting pit, and beckoned the orc nearer with an open hand.

"Come on, you knuckle-dragging son of a whore!" Torval shouted. "Have at it!"

Then the dwarf stepped forward to meet the beast, even though it was twice his size and apparently quite upset with him.

Rem—suddenly realizing that Sheba had retreated right into his arms—tried to call out to his partner and warn him. "Get out of there!" he cried dumbly, even though he could see clearly that there was nowhere for Torval to go, and that Torval himself was already determined to take the fight to the enemy.

Then Torval charged, closing the space between him and the enraged orc. Rem saw the dwarf plunge headlong into the orc's midsection, trying to use his head as a battering ram, the same way he had with the Creeper's bouncers. His head impacted with the orc's abdominals, and the monster bent double, but it seemed more annoyed than injured or winded. Before it could lay hands on him, Torval landed two hard strikes with his maul, one to each of the orc's legs. Roaring, the beast snatched up Torval in both hands, lifted him as high as it could in the cramped, low-ceilinged little back room, and tossed the dwarf into one of the chamber's walls. Torval hit the wall—and the shelves it supported, and the bric-a-brac littering the shelves— then thumped to the floor in a mess of broken jars and bottles, old dried herbs, and magical implements.

Rem saw a chance to get Sheba to safety, since the orc—for that single instant—was occupied with Torval. He shoved the conjuress toward the door to the front room and urged her to make a run for it. A moment later, the orc closed in on Torval, shoving aside the butcher's block that supported the silver bowl full of water that Sheba had used for her reading. The monolith of wood hit the wall just inches from Rem with a thunderous crash and fell to pieces. Rem snatched up one of the broken legs of the butcher's block to use as a bludgeon and charged the orc.

He got in three good whacks with the broken table leg, but none of them seemed to slow the creature down. As Rem drew back for a fourth whack, the orc turned toward him and shoved him roughly aside. The gesture was one of complete, annoyed dismissal, but it carried with it enough force to send Rem tumbling across the little room, where he slammed into the opposite wall and fell into a heap on the floor.

Rem lay there dazed, trying to blink away the fireflies that filled his vision and get back on his feet. As his vision started to clear, he saw Torval scampering away from the orc's great, snatching hands, scurrying toward the broken butcher's block near where Rem lay. As the orc pivoted to give chase, Torval snatched something out of the wreckage of the butcher's block: the meat cleaver that Rem had noted earlier, probably used by Sheba to take heads off chickens for spell offerings and the like. Before the orc was even turned full around, Torval had laid into the beast with the cleaver, hacking and slashing with the square little blade as he might with a hand ax.

And if Rem wasn't mistaken, Torval seemed to be reveling in every minute of it. The dwarf, though clearly gripped by bloodlust and fit for war, was laughing and taunting the orc with every strike and every swipe. His blue eyes were alight with an unholy fire and his gritted teeth seemed one moment a grimace, one moment a grin.

"Come on, you bumbling blackguard, you!" he growled. "You milky monkey! You mouth-breathing, knuckle-dragging piece of sun-bleached cack! Come on!"

He had drawn blood. Rem could clearly see a number of deep lacerations now on the orc's right flank, shoulder, and arm, all made by Torval with Sheba's meat cleaver. The orc, for its part, roared and spat in answer, and reached out with its long arms and grasping claws to try to block each new strike of the blade, but it was clearly starting to shrink from Torval's onslaught, starting to feel the sting of those cleaver strikes and know fear for its own life.

"Rem!"

Rem turned. Sheba stood at the door to the front room. She had a broom in her hand and she threw it toward Rem. Instinctively, he caught the broom, but only stared at it.

"What am I supposed to do with this?" he asked.

"Use it!" Sheba snapped. "It's all I've got!"

Well, it was long and hard, wasn't it? In the absence of a spear or a stave, it would have to do. So, Rem leapt to his feet, vision clear at last, and charged the orc from behind. He shoved the broom's straw-tipped end toward the orc's legs and tried to sweep them out from under the beast, to get it on its back. It was no good—the broom gave him no leverage and the orc was well planted. It only turned toward him and roared, spewing spittle and foul breath into Rem's face. He tried a new tack and swept the business end of the broom up into the orc's bone-white face. It shrank a little from the dried tips of the reeds bundled there. That gave Torval a moment to charge again and hack into the orc's left flank with his meat cleaver.

Double-teamed and crowded, the orc bellowed and snarled, then summarily swept them both aside. It slammed its left fist into Torval's face and sent him sprawling, then reached for Rem. Rem shoved the broom handle forward, trying to block the orc's grip. The beast plucked the broom right out of his fingers and tossed it aside. For a moment, it seemed to be reaching for Rem as well—then a dim sort of realization flashed in its little ruby eyes, and the orc seemed to decide otherwise. Without another attempt at grappling, the beast shoved Rem back into the wall and went running for the door to the front of the shop. As it disappeared through the doorway, Rem heard Sheba scream.

Rem hurried to Torval. The dwarf was rolling right back up onto his feet again, completely unfazed by the orc's having swept him aside. His broad little face was ruddy and flushed, and he had murder in his eyes. Orc blood covered his face and arms and the edge of his makeshift blade, and Rem thought for that moment that he had never seen Torval look so fearsome and intent.

"You okay, partner?" Rem asked.

Torval shoved him aside with a strength almost equal to the orc's. "Out of my way!" Torval shouted, then regained his feet and went tearing out of the room on the orc's trail.

Rem, drawing a deep, exasperated breath, followed.

Just as Rem reached the doorway, he heard an enormous crash. The orc had skipped Sheba's front door and thrown itself right through her shop window into the street. Torval followed without hesitation, scratching himself on the jagged, toothlike shards of glass that remained around the frame of the window and not caring. As the orc rolled to a stop in the mud outside, Torval charged toward it and raised the cleaver with both hands, ready to bring it down on the orc's head for a killing blow.

But then the orc was up on its feet again. In one smooth movement it snatched up the charging Torval, spun around to gain some momentum, then hammer-threw the dwarf toward a shop window on the far side of the street. Torval cursed all the way, even when the window shattered and he went sprawling into a mess of broken glass and shop-window junk on display.

Rem needed a weapon. Seeing the wealth of broken glass, he knew that was his only option. Hastily, he tore a long swath of fabric from the edge of his tunic, snatched up a long, jagged shard of glass, then wound the fabric around one end of the shard to give him some protection from its edges. He leapt through Sheba's window into the street and charged the orc, shoving the glass shard deep into its lower back. The orc shrieked as the glass bit through its white flesh and penetrated its body. Before Rem could retreat or get clear, the orc swept around and backhanded him with an outstretched fist. Rem fell into the mud.

The orc towered over him, a milk-white beast draped in old rags, slashed and torn from head to foot but still murderous and malign. It had Rem, dead to rights. All it needed to do now was reach down and crush his head between its two great, shovel-like hands or simply stomp his skull flat beneath one square, heavy foot. Rem braced himself for what came next, assuming there would be no time to scurry to safety or concoct another plan of attack.

Then the orc howled and fell to one knee. Unsure of what was happening or why, Rem scampered backward in the mud, eager to be out of the brute's grasp. From his new position, he saw that Torval had beset their attacker, hacking right through the orc's heel tendon with Sheba's meat cleaver. That crippling blow had brought the beast literally to its knees.

The orc, unable to stand again, tried to pivot on its single good leg while still balancing on its knee. It failed miserably, toppled sideward into the mud, then flopped and rolled in a vain attempt to reach its little adversary and end him. Torval kept his distance, circling just out of reach of the now-crippled orc. As Rem struggled to his feet and wiped what mud he could from himself, he thought he heard something strange in the orc's huffs and grunts—evidence of worry, panic, fear. Circling opposite his partner, struggling to get a good look at the hobbled orc in the dim lamplight of Mage's Alley at midnight, Rem thought he even saw true worry and mounting fright on the orc's flat, pale face.

It still fought, still wished ill upon its adversaries...but it was also scared.

Torval seemed to relish the beast's mounting panic. He made a sound in his throat—halfway between a laugh and a barbaric grunt—and kept circling, brandishing the meat cleaver whenever the orc's haphazard attempts to grab him threatened success.

Sheba was at Rem's elbow now. He looked to her, asked

after her safety with a silent look that she clearly understood. She held up her arms and stood, as if for inspection—*All safe, Watchwarden. Many thanks.*

Then Rem realized they were no longer alone.

The locals had been rousted out of their beds. They drifted into the muddy street carrying little lamps or stubs of candle. They were all mages, Rem assumed, though to look at them, one would not mark them so without seeing them here, in their natural habitat. Most seemed pitifully ordinary—middle-aged men and women, some thin, some fat, some just comfortably expanded by time and success. There were a few that were very old and a half dozen or so that seemed very young. Among them were pale-skinned people of the west, as well as foreigners from Shimzaris or Magrabar, to the south—easily distinguished by their olive or copper skin, their almond eyes, their finely oiled or thickly braided hair, and their elegant silk night robes in a rainbow of vivid colors. All of these sleeping mages had heard the commotion, drifted out into the street to see what sort of chaos unfolded below their windows, on their very doorsteps.

They did not seem happy to have found Rem and Torval and their orcish sparring partner among them.

Torval saw them, too. As the dwarf studied the slow-gathering crowd, the orc saw a fleeting chance to put him on his back. It lunged for him.

To Rem's surprise, Torval knew what was coming. As the orc reached for him, the dwarf brought Sheba's meat cleaver down in a swift, hard arc and lopped off half the brute's grasping hand. The cut went through right below its knuckles. In an instant, all four of its pale, thick fingers were limp on the mud and the orc drew its newly shortened hand—just a palm and a thumb now—close to its big, muscled body. It made a sound like a terrified infant, and Rem felt something like pity for the beast.

"I think we're done here," Sheba said, having retreated toward the shattered window of her shop.

"Like hell," Torval snapped in answer. "I want another reading! We can pay for it. We're on the right track now!"

"No, no, and no," Sheba said. "We're done, and that's all there is to it. I don't think you need to come back here for a long, long time, Torval."

"What are you talking about, you blithering hedge witch?" Torval asked, moving nearer to her. "We just saved your life."

The orc moaned, as if in agreement.

"I suppose you could see it that way," Sheba countered. "I prefer to see it this way, though: that orc never would have come here and torn my shop to pieces if you hadn't led it here. It clearly wasn't after me. It was after you."

Torval quaked with rage. "Why, you ungrateful little—"

Sheba held out her hands. "My cleaver?" she asked.

Torval looked to the cleaver in his hands and seemed almost surprised to find it there. He handed it back to her with a frown and a harrumph.

Sheba kept one hand outstretched. "Coin?" she asked.

"Coin?" Torval grumbled. "What for?"

Sheba suggested the shattered front window. "A new window, for starters. Then to replace everything I lost in the shop."

Torval shook his head. "You've got to be—"

"Joking?" Sheba asked. "I don't think so. And if you try to walk away and stiff me, I have a street full of witnesses. Not only can we raise holy hell with the magistrate, we can also see to our own justice. This is a street of mages, after all. You don't want to be on the ill side of a mage and her neighbors, do you, Torval?"

Torval made an animal sound in his throat, a purring snarl that Rem took as both a curse and a capitulation. Rem struggled to his feet and reached into his pocket. He drew out his little sack of coin and threw it to Sheba.

"There," Rem said. "We're square."

Sheba nodded. "Now," she said, "get out of here. Before one of us turns the pair of you into toads."

Rem started to retort, then noted all the unhappy, unfriendly faces around them and thought better of it. He took Torval by the shoulder and urged him on.

"I think we should go," Rem said.

Torval's shoulders slumped. "Bloody mages," he grumbled.

They lingered just long enough to pay a pair of the gawking mages for some good, stout hemp rope and a sledge. Once the pale, now-crippled orc was tied and secured, they rolled him up onto the sledge and each curled a lead line over their shoulder. Thus, when Rem and Torval left Mage's Alley, they left hauling sixteen stone of still-sniveling orc flesh behind them, cutting a track with their laden sledge through the muddy streets of the Fifth Ward toward the city's North Gate and Orctown beyond.

Rem had no idea what hour of the night it was when they finally reached the palace of Gorn Bonebreaker, the orcish ethnarch. Their visit began much like their last, with Torval using his badge of office to gain entry, a brief wait in the low, dark vestibule, and finally, an audience at the behest of that familiar, hunch-backed little orc with the shifty look about him. Rem was amazed that the orcish ethnarch always seemed so willing to entertain guests at such late and random hours, but Torval assured him it was not so unusual. Orcs didn't sleep the night through like humans, nor even during the day, like true nocturnal creatures (or watchwardens on the night shift, for that matter). Instead, they were in the habit of a morning-to-midnight sleep/wake cycle that usually consisted of several hours of wakefulness followed by a shorter period of sleep, on and off through the day and night.

Clearly, Torval knew his old enemies well. Unfortunately, it seemed to Rem that such familiarity had only added to Torval's already considerable contempt for the creatures.

Throughout their journey and their waiting in Gorn's vestibule, Rem stole glances at their orcish charge, curious that it now seemed cowed and strangely docile. A few times, it seemed to have actually fallen asleep, since it snored raggedly and seemed completely at ease. At other times, the brute just lay there, looking all around it, its red eyes betraying a strange, primitive fear and lack of understanding that struck Rem as odd compared with the malign intelligence and crafty ill intent that he'd seen in the eyes of that orc he'd tried to arrest in the Pickled Albatross. On two or three occasions in their journey, Rem even suspected that their prisoner was crying, for its body shook with the ragged tremors of an inconsolable toddler, accompanied by a miserable, high-pitched whimpering that keened out of it for several minutes at a time. By the time they were ushered into Gorn's presence, still dragging the heavy sledge with the tied-up orc upon it, Rem was starting to suspect that maybe, just maybe, their prisoner wasn't really evil or malevolent at all, but simple and childlike, susceptible to easy manipulation.

He broached none of this to Torval, however. Rem knew, instinctively, that his partner's deep-set hatred for the whole orcish race was thoroughly rooted in the attack on his family, and that the same bitter enmity would prevent Torval from

finding understanding or mercy within his heart for their prisoner. The dwarf's hatred ran too deep for that.

Once more, they found Gorn squeezed into his too-small
throne, this time in the midst of a midnight meal. In one large
hand was gripped a great aurochs horn, spilling something
frothy—mead or ale, Rem could not tell—without regard for
the mess it made around the throne. In the other hand, the
Bonebreaker held a joint of meat—Rem guessed it was a goat
haunch, or maybe mutton—which he tore at with relish as Rem
and Torval dragged their prisoner into his presence. Only when
they had proceeded to the place where they would address him
from did Gorn finally deign to toss his victuals and drink onto a
nearby sideboard, wipe his hands on his rough-spun tunic, and
address them.

"Twice in one week," the Bonebreaker said. "Tongues will
wag, my diminutive comrade."

"I'm no comrade of yours," Torval answered.

"No," Gorn said, his thick lips curling at their corners. "Of
course not. But you are a mess. Why all the mud and blood,
master dwarf? Mating again?"

Torval looked like he could have cleared the space between
where he stood and Gorn's throne in a single bound if he'd so
desired. The hate in his eyes practically lit up the dim, torchlit
room, and the whole of his muscular little body shook with
rage. Rem thought he might have to subdue him, but then
realized that, even if he thought it necessary, he could not.
Torval would tear right through him. Instead, he decided to
interrupt.

"Gorn Bonebreaker," Rem said, perhaps too loudly and
officiously, "we come before you with one who's broken the
law, and wants punishment."

Gorn seemed puzzled by Rem's addressing him. For a moment, he stared at Rem, studying him, head to toe.

"Obsequies," Gorn said.

Rem struggled to remember the words Torval had offered the last time they'd visited the ethnarch's shabby little court. "Hail, Gorn, called Bonebreaker, Bane of the Minefolk, Scourge of Men, and chosen Harbinger of his People's Destiny. I present to thee this prisoner, for his use, his mercy, or his wrath, however the majestic Bonebreaker sees fit to use him."

Gorn, seemingly satisfied, rose off his throne—having to strain a little to extract his narrow hips from its narrower breadth—then took two steps down from the dais on which he sat. He was trying to get a better look at the tied-up prisoner. When Rem realized that Gorn was studying their perp, he stepped aside and silently urged Torval to do the same. Thankfully, the dwarf obliged.

The albino orc on the sledge—slashed head to toe and stained with purple-red streamers of dried, crusted blood, which stood out savagely on his milk-white flesh—craned his neck around uncomfortably to get a look at Gorn. The Bonebreaker circled the sledge and the bound bundle of flesh and bone borne upon it. Finally, he gave a sharp command in his own tongue. The two nearest bodyguards hulked forward. Rem watched as they lifted the bound prisoner upright, then slashed at his bonds with their belt knives to set the albino orc free. Opposite Rem, Torval tensed, ready for the bound orc to go beastly when freed, but thankfully, that didn't happen. Instead, the orc simply sagged there on the sledge, on its knees, shamed and ruined before its fellows, loath to meet their contemptuous gazes.

Gorn barked a few more orcish words at the trembling prisoner. The pale orc heard the words, but did not seem to understand them. As Gorn barked the same phrases and a few new ones in rapid succession, the albino orc only opened its mouth dumbly to speak, found no words, then settled for shaking its head and lowering its eyes. Finally, Gorn Bonebreaker strode forward, gripped the unbound orc's wide, square chin in one great hand, and forced it to look at him, face-to-face, eye to eye. After a long, pregnant silence passed between them, Gorn finally stepped away.

"This is an imbecile," Gorn said. If Rem were not mistaken, he detected a note of sadness in the orc's deep, rumbling voice.

"How's that?" Torval asked.

"Look at him," Gorn said. "Look in his eyes. No fire of lust or desire or understanding burns there."

Torval stood behind their prisoner, and could not look into its face, but Rem could. And he felt vindicated when Gorn Bonebreaker confirmed the very suspicion that Rem had started to harbor. Their prisoner was a simpleton—probably no more cunning or malign than a child. Perhaps, just perhaps, they could convince him to aid them in their investigation?

"My people did not raise this," Gorn said.

"What does that mean?" Rem asked.

"It means," Torval broke in, "that if an orc maid living in the wild gave birth to a pale, simple beast such as this, she probably would have taken it to a high, cold place and left it for the wolves."

"Look at his body," Gorn said, sneering. "He's large by your standards, manling, but he's scrawny by ours. And look at his frame—one shoulder almost a hump, one arm shorter than the other..."

Rem stared. He had never truly noticed those qualities before now, but he saw them clearly under Gorn's guidance. It was true: the albino orc was big and frightening by human standards, but next to Gorn and his bodyguards, he looked like a twisty, stunted runt—a leafless tree bent by a lifetime on a wind-racked hill.

And then there were those eyes—so empty, so frightened now that they were not filled with murderous rage.

Gorn approached the prisoner again. "Have you a name?"

The prisoner said nothing.

Gorn pressed, snarling. "Your name, milksop! You are commanded by Gorn, the Bonebreaker! Make yourself known or I shall crush your skull where you kneel!"

The orc was shy. Rem saw it clearly. The poor creature understood Gorn's words, more or less—but he was too frightened to answer. All at once, Rem felt a deep, sharp pang of pity for the creature.

Gorn lunged, roaring in the prisoner's face. "Your name!"

"Lock. Dumb."

Rem threw a puzzled glance at Torval. Torval was just as amazed.

"What was that?" Gorn pressed.

"Lock dumb," the prisoner whimpered.

"Lugdum," Gorn said.

Lugdum, Rem mouthed silently. *All this while, our tracker and nemesis had a name . . .*

"And who is your master, Lugdum Milksop?" Gorn asked.

Lugdum shook his head.

Gorn roared and drove one enormous fist into Lugdum's skull. The prisoner hit the floor with stunning force and cried out, a pitiful sound that actually brought all of Rem's gathering pity to the surface.

"What is your master's name, you fool?" Gorn shouted, towering over the fallen prisoner. "Tell me now, or so help me, I'll have you skinned and deboned, one morsel at a time, from the feet up!"

Lugdum shook his head again, vehemently this time. He even tried to speak, but only a hoarse, voiceless groan came forth from his throat, as if he wanted to tell his captors—his torturers—something of importance but that he had neither the voice nor the words to truly communicate. Rem saw the pale orc's eyes began to water. Within moments, tears cut tracks down his blood-encrusted white cheeks, and Rem felt a sickening stir in his gut—the gathering realization that this creature, however dangerous he had been when he was set upon them, was now both helpless and deeply frightened.

"Dumb," Gorn Bonebreaker pronounced, looking to Rem, then Torval. "Dumb, imbecilic, stunted, weak, and childish. This is no orc, but an abomination."

"I don't understand," Rem said. "How has he survived this long? Why is he so intent upon us?"

"Isn't it clear?" Torval offered. "Someone who wasn't an orc came upon him when he was a foundling. They kept him and raised him and made a servant of him—a loyal one, too—but all the while, he was the perfect cat's-paw, because, even if caught, he couldn't squeal on them."

"This is most distasteful," Gorn grumbled, moving away from the increasingly troubled Lugdum and urging Rem and Torval to follow. They did as the orcish ethnarch bade, and all gathered some distance from where Lugdum knelt on the sledge. "I cannot bear this pitiful creature's grief any longer."

"Is there nothing we can learn from him?" Rem asked.

Torval shook his head. "Nothing. You see. He's dumb. No doubt, he and his master have some means of communicating—hand signs or something—but clearly it's something only they know, and only they can make sense of."

"But with time," Rem began.

"You should go," Gorn said with finality.

"Go?" Torval asked.

"Go," Rem repeated.

"This beast is mine to deal with. Let me deal with him."

"Deal with him, how?" Rem asked. "The two of you have already said—"

"There's no place for him here," Torval said. It wasn't a question.

"Here, nor anywhere," Gorn Bonebreaker sighed. "Rest assured, his end will come quickly and without suffering."

Rem stared at the orcish ethnarch, then swung his gaze to Torval. Was he really hearing what he thought he was hearing? "So that's it?" he asked. "Once we're gone, you'll just murder him? In cold blood?"

"'Twould be a mercy, Watchwarden," Gorn Bonebreaker said. "He has no one. He belongs nowhere. He is weak, crippled, set apart—"

"He's like a child!" Rem protested. "He barely understands what's happening to him!"

"Need I remind you," Torval said, "that it's been following us? That it just tried to kill us both?"

"Under orders, Torval!" Rem snapped. "Hasn't our little attempt at an interrogation proven that? He's as feeble and trusting as a babe. No doubt, his master gave him commands and he followed them, because that master is the only family this creature's ever known! We don't just put people down like crippled horses because they're different, or less than useful—"

"*You* do not," Gorn said gravely. "But that is our way. An orc who cannot fend for himself or herself once their fledgling years are past is no orc at all—that is why the weak and enfeebled are abandoned when they are yet infants—to keep the whole of our tribe strong and—"

"To the sundry hells with strength!" Rem shouted. "Where is your compassion? Your mercy?"

Torval moved closer. "Those aren't qualities these brutes know, lad."

Gorn's deep-set eyes narrowed. "Watch your tongue when insulting my people, you stunted little pickmonkey."

Torval lunged at Gorn. Rem had to catch him. This was becoming untenable. Gorn was impatient—and now, insulted. Torval, with his naturally inclined hatred toward the whole of the orcish race, was not disposed to argue on their prisoner's behalf, nor to be gracious to Gorn in an effort to find a softer fate for the very confused Lugdum.

Rem stole a glance at their prisoner, still kneeling on the sledge. He looked sad and lonely and miserable and hurt, a lost child scanning a battlefield for the corpses of its parents. The sight of him filled Rem with a terrible pity—a pity that he had never imagined he could even feel, especially for something that wasn't even human.

But, those eyes. He saw humanity—deep feelings, true fear—in those small ruby-red eyes.

"Go," Gorn commanded. "You have taken up enough of my time and done what you came to do."

"We brought him here so that you could help us get answers," Torval said. "And we leave with none."

"That," Gorn Bonebreaker said, with notable relish and smugness, "is not my problem."

Rem studied the orcish bodyguards in the throne room. Their eyes were no longer on the pitiful, weeping Lugdum but on Rem and Torval themselves. Weapons were in hand, at the ready. They scowled and glared, all awaiting a final command from their master.

"We need to go," Rem said to Torval.

Torval did not answer him, nor did he take his eyes off Gorn Bonebreaker. But he did hawk a ball of phlegm up from his throat and spat it on Gorn's flagstone floor. Then, he broke out of Rem's grasp and headed for the twin doors that would grant them egress. Rem followed, willing himself not to look back over his shoulder at the doomed Lugdum.

"It is my sincere hope that we won't meet again anytime soon!" Gorn thundered as they made their exit. "Even a ward-watchman can wear out his welcome in my court!"

They cleared the doors, and those same doors were closed behind them. They were once more out into the night. For a long time, all through the streets of Orctown, in fact, until they had almost reached the North Gate to reenter the city, both Rem and Torval were silent.

It was Rem who finally spoke. "I know you hate them," Rem said, "but the thought of that poor creature simply being... put down—it sickens me."

"Me too," Torval grumbled. "I hate to admit it, but once we realized it was just like a wee bairn headwise..."

He said no more then. Finally, he added, "Well, there's nothing for it. Once more, we're back where we started, knowing little more than that some winesink called the Moon Under Water might hold answers. I've never even heard of the place. Sheba's probably sending us on a hare chase."

Rem shook his head. "I don't care. We'll follow the lead and we'll see what it has to offer. I want him dead, Torval."

Torval looked up at him. They were inside the North Gate now, back on the winding streets of the Fifth Ward. "Want who dead?"

"Lugdum's master," Rem said. "Whoever's behind all this. To use such a simple, helpless creature and abandon him after his service...the man that would do that is a monster, Torval. And I want to be the one to put him down and watch the life bleed out of him."

Torval stared at him for a long time. Little by little, a predatory smile bloomed on the dwarf's broad face.

"There's the partner I've been searching for all along," Torval said. "So glad you've finally arrived."

CHAPTER TWENTY-THREE

Rem and Torval walked for a long time in silence. They were covered in mud and blood, lighter of purse, and no closer to solving the mystery of the strange little bauble stolen from the fleet fingers of Ginger Joss. Eventually, they ended up at the King's Ass.

It was past midnight, but the place was far livelier than it had been during the day. A curly-haired young minstrel played lute while a curvy wench with black hair and dark, playful eyes sang of love and loss, courage and despair, heroism and cowardice. Games of chance unfolded in every corner and ale and mead were quaffed in vast quantities. The air was redolent of honest sweat, sour malt, stewing onions, and whatever meat turned on the spits in the kitchen.

Despite their rough appearance, Torval led Rem right up to the bar and there greeted the burly, smiling fellow who was in the midst of serving and hosting the patrons. He seemed quite happy to see Torval—albeit puzzled at the great amount of mud and blood that the dwarf tracked in with him. Rem couldn't hear their conversation—the room was too loud, too boisterous—but he noted that the smiling barman and Torval only exchanged a few pleasantries before the barman finally cocked his head, indicating that Torval should follow him into the back. Torval tugged at Rem's sleeve. The two of them trailed behind their host.

He led them to a room off a corridor behind the bar. Once

ensconced in the cozy little space—the desk, balance, ledgers, and many barrels and casks around them suggested it was part office, part storeroom—Rem and Torval were left alone with their wounded pride and bruised bodies, the noise of the main room reduced to a dull roar once the door was closed.

"Where's Aarna?" Rem asked.

"He's fetching her," Torval said, not looking at him.

Rem felt like he could sleep for a week if he could only lie down. "Who was he? The fellow behind the bar?"

"That's Joedoc," Torval said. "The brewmaster. As I told you, he works nights. Gives Aarna a break, since she handles the day shift most of the time."

The door to the little room opened then. Aarna swept into the room, studying the two scrappy watchwardens and giving them a look somewhere between concern and incredulity. A serving girl was at her elbow, lingering in the doorway, trying to get a good look at the two mud-encrusted ruffians in the office.

"What on earth happened to the two of you?" Aarna demanded.

Torval opened his mouth to answer. Aarna stopped him and turned to the serving girl. "A bowl of hot water, some rags, and two mugs of Joedoc's Old Thumper." The girl disappeared to do as she was told. Aarna sat down. Before either of them said a word, she told Torval that his sister and children had made it to the King's Ass safely, and that they were presently in a room upstairs, probably fast asleep.

Torval smiled warmly at the news. He stared at Aarna with eyes full of want and wonder. "You've done me a great service," he said.

Aarna shrugged and smiled that bright, broad smile of hers. "Anything for my closest friends, which you're counted among. Now tell me—what the hell happened to the two of you?"

Torval told their story.

To Rem's surprise, Torval told Aarna almost everything: their investigation, Joss in Freygaf's chambers, the little medallion, the trips to the Creeper's and the Nightjar's, and finally, their foray to Mage's Alley. It was as he regaled her with a reconstruction of their fight with the albino orc that the serving girl returned with the hot water and rags. As Torval's tale unfolded, Aarna bade both of them strip their shirts.

"You're both a mess," she said. "I'll clean you up."

And so she did. They stripped their cuirasses and shirts, and Aarna wiped away the dried mud and blood. She tended their wounds with tinctures and herb pastes that she kept handy for just such emergencies, then disappeared once more to try to find the two of them some clean shirts, for she had a seamstress and laundress who used the King's Ass as her office and who usually kept some spare bits of clothing around to sell to the needy or the roughhoused.

While Aarna was gone, Rem decided he would broach a question that had been on his mind ever since their run-in with the orc.

"That wasn't just self-defense or the prosecution of duty," Rem said. "You hate them, don't you? You really, truly, deeply hate them. Orcs."

Torval threw Rem a sour glance and shrugged. "What of it?"

Rem drew a deep breath. Let it out. "They're not all bad, you know. They're rough and belligerent and sometimes quarrelsome, but there are some who come down out of the mountains—just like you did—wanting nothing more than to find some work and pocket some coin. They get tired of fighting, too."

"Save it," Torval said. "I don't really know who you are or

where you come from, boy, but I'll wager you haven't spent as much time around those slag-skinned brutes as I have. And I'm here to tell you, *they're no good*. Not a one of them. The world would be a better place if we could wipe them all from the face of it."

Rem decided not to argue any further. Best let things lie.

Aarna returned. She bore with her a pair of shirts: one large, for Rem, the other smaller, for Torval. Each of them took the offered frock and slipped into it. Rem found his shirt a little baggy, but it fit more or less. He wasn't terribly pleased by the ruffled sleeves and collar, but what could he do? Go shirtless?

Torval's shirt was clearly made for a child, and his broad shoulders almost split it open. But, assuming he moved very little in it, it seemed to meet his needs. Rem thought the roses and vines embroidered around the collar and shoulders a nice touch and couldn't help but laugh when he saw it on his belli-cose little partner.

"You've got to be joking?" Torval said to Aarna.

"You're welcome to wear nothing at all," Aarna said, a self-satisfied smile on her face. "These were all she had that would fit the two of you."

"But...roses?" Torval whined.

"How do you think I feel?" Rem asked. "Just look at these bloody ruffles?"

"They make you look dashing, young sir," Aarna said, and she only appeared to be half joking. "Honestly, the two of you look better now than you did when you came in. Stop com-plaining or I'll make you pay for those frocks."

Torval harrumphed. Rem threw up his hands in a gesture of surrender. Each of them took long swigs from the mugs Aarna had provided. Joedoc's Old Thumper—a special, signature brew of the brewmaster's—rolled down their throats, filled their bellies, and settled their nerves. It was good, strong stuff, and Rem fancied he could probably swill a barrel of it if only one was provided.

"So," Aarna began, "what next for you two miscreants? Ready to raid one of the patriarchs' palaces? Maybe a sweep through the whorehouses quayside? Or perhaps you'd just prefer to wade into Orctown calling 'huffer' and 'mudknuckles,' marauding as you go?"

"None of the above," Torval said. "We've a lead and we have to follow it. Sheba told us of a gaming house or tavern of some sort—the Moon Under Water. Have you heard of it?"

Aarna nodded. "Certainly. It's quayside, Fourth Ward."

"Fourth Ward," Torval muttered.

Rem immediately understood. "Frennis."

Torval nodded grimly.

"Another journey into our favorite prefect's jurisdiction," Rem muttered. "Ondego will be pleased."

"To hell with him," Torval shot back. "If we break this case and find Freygaf's killers, Ondego won't give a damn that we stepped on some other prefect's toes—least of all a puffed-out twat like Frennis."

"May I remind you," Aarna interjected, "that if this Moon Under Water place is in the Fourth Ward and hides some terrible secret, it's probably under Frennis's protection. And if the two of you could prove that—"

Rem and Torval both stared at Aarna for a moment. She stared back, hands on her hips. "But I'm sure the two of you already thought of that—pair of brilliant sages like yourselves."

Rem smiled a little and raised his mug to her. "I like the way you think, milady."

"As do I," Torval said, following suit and raising his own mug. As Rem sipped, he stole a glance at Torval. Even as he upended his mug and gulped, the dwarf never took his eyes off Aarna. Rem fought an urge to smile.

"If I'm not mistaken," Aarna said, "the place is on Pike Street. But I could be wrong."

"That'll do," Torval said, rising and stretching. His face and shoulders were still covered with bruises and scratches, but at least he was no longer crusted in mud and old blood. Rem felt fresher as well, although simple weariness was starting to catch up with him. It had been a hard night, and he had a feeling it was far from over.

"One last thing," Torval said to Aarna. "Did you get a package today? Something I asked to be delivered here?"

Aarna nodded. "I did, in fact."

"Fetch it, lass. Then we'll be on our way."

Aarna lingered, staring at Torval as though he were a child. "The magic words, Old Stump?"

Torval looked genuinely baffled. "Now?"

Aarna raised an eyebrow.

Torval seemed to hit upon the right words. "If you please?"

Aarna smiled. "No trouble at all." She bustled off.

"So, what now?" Rem asked.

"We go to the Moon Under Water," Torval said. "As soon as Aarna returns with my parcel."

"What's the plan?" Rem asked.

Torval shrugged. "We beat the bouncers senseless, get inside, and take a look around. Someone will tell us something."

Rem drew a deep breath. He ached all over. "Might I suggest, Torval, that we try something a little less...direct?"

"Like what?" Torval asked.

Rem shrugged. "I don't know...maybe, being polite? Perhaps a little subterfuge? Not announcing ourselves as watchwardens right at the outset?"

"I don't understand," Torval said, and he looked like he truly didn't.

"Have you ever heard the adage 'You'll catch more flies with honey than with vinegar'?"

Torval shrugged. "Heard it. Never cared for it. You don't catch flies, you swat them."

Rem shook his head. If he was going to convince Torval, he needed a plan. With the two of them running all over the city, chasing leads and getting into fights, there was a good chance that the guards at such a shady establishment might already be expecting them. If they could just find a different angle of approach...

Aarna returned then. She carried something long, slender, and heavy, wrapped in a cotton shroud. "Who gets this?" she asked.

Torval pointed to Rem. "It's his," he said.

Rem was puzzled. His? What was Torval talking about?

Aarna handed him the parcel. Rem knew what it was the moment she placed it in his hands—the heft and weight of it made it clear. He felt a smile creeping onto his face as he unwrapped the shroud and found himself staring at a well-made but unostentatious Estavari short sword, complete with a scabbard and baldric. It was the sort of weapon a mercenary might invest in—not so finely tooled or gussied-up as a knight's or a lord's weapon, but made of better steel and with better balance than the sword of a farmer or man-at-arms. Rem held the blade out and peered down its length. Straight and true. He thumbed the edges. It was sharpened and well oiled.

He looked to Torval. "What's this for?"

"It's yours," Torval said. "You said you were good with a sword. I expect you to prove it."

"A gift?" Rem asked, truly floored.

"Not precisely," Torval said. "You can pay me back for it if you wish, at your leisure. I just wagered it would be easier if I bought it for you from the Ward stores, rather than letting you try to run a gauntlet of teases and naysayers if you picked one out for yourself. And if this day has proven anything, it's that you need a good sword at your side. Does it suit you?"

Rem nodded. He wanted to be out in the street with the blade, so that he could truly test its balance and grace. "You chose well, Torval. You're a good matchmaker between warrior and weapon."

Torval shrugged. "Always fancied so. Shall we be on our way?"

Rem turned to Aarna, having a sudden inspiration. "Aarna," he asked, "should we be on our way?"

Aarna stared at Rem for a moment, not sure what he was suggesting. Rem studied the bar matron and his partner, then leaned on his new sword.

"I don't understand," Aarna said.

"Neither do I," Torval added.

"We need a new strategy," Rem said. "If the two of us approach the Moon Under Water, Torval, we'll probably be recognized and turned away. Then, our only way in is by force."

"So?" Torval asked.

"There are other ways," Rem said. "So, listen…let me lay this out before you dismiss it."

He told them.

Aarna was delighted.

Torval, not so much.

CHAPTER TWENTY-FOUR

They left their watchwarden cuirasses behind and wore their badges inside their shirts. They might need to make their warden status clear at some point, but to start with, they would approach as normal patrons, out for games, some drinks, maybe a roll in the hay. To complete their subterfuge, Aarna found a fresh jerkin for Rem—borrowed from one of her taproom patrons—and Torval got a leather vest for himself from the clothing that Osma and the children had brought with them to their rooms at the King's Ass.

Thus, somewhat refreshed, their wounds tended, Rem, Torval, and Aarna set out from the King's Ass and headed toward the Moon Under Water. It was, according to Aarna, over in the Fourth Ward, on a ridge of bluffs above the merchant docks. Climbing the gentle slopes into that bawdy and boisterous quarter, it took them almost no time to locate the Moon Under Water, backed up against the bluff's edge and overlooking the moon-drenched harbor beyond. There, they ensconced themselves in a dark alleyway adjacent to the tavern's front entrance. They watched for a time as patrons came and went, debating their options. Despite a few more objections from Torval, Rem insisted that they stick to his plan.

"I don't like that plan," Torval countered. "That plan entails you taking Aarna into that place, and we don't know what we'll find in there. It may not be safe."

"Pishposh," Aarna answered. "I'm a big girl, Torval, and I'm here of my own free will. The boy's plan is a good one, and it certainly carries fewer risks than would the two of you approaching the door and trying to bluff your way in. If someone involved in this conspiracy really *is* connected to that place, they may have already warned those two guards out front to be on the lookout for a red-maned youngster and a dwarf."

Torval grunted.

"Are we in agreement?" Aarna asked.

Rem was taken aback. The lady certainly knew her own mind. Here she was doing the two of them a favor by tagging along, and she'd already taken charge of the expedition.

"She's right," Rem said to Torval. "We'll be more conspicuous together, less so apart."

"So what am I supposed to do?" Torval asked. "If you use Joss's bauble to get through the door, I won't have it to get myself in."

"You just act like a customer," Aarna said. "Reel a bit. Act drunk and randy. See if they'll let you in if they think you've got coin to spend."

Torval spat. "I still don't like it."

Aarna bent over, threw her arms around the dwarf, and kissed his bald head. "Ooooh," she said agreeably, "you'll see. It'll work well. It'll be fun."

Rem saw that Torval smiled when Aarna embraced and kissed him, no matter that the gesture was meant as an encouragement between friends. Then the dwarf was all seriousness again. He looked to Rem and scowled, brows lowering above his blue eyes.

"You keep her safe," Torval said with all seriousness. "You're the watchwarden. She's just a civilian. If anything happens to her—"

Rem patted his sword. "Safe as houses, Torval. You have my word."

"Are we going or aren't we?" Aarna asked, then threw her arms around Rem, planted a sloppy kiss on his cheek, and laughed long and loud, the laugh of a drunken moll answering a joke from her well-paying jack.

"What the bloody hell . . . ?" Torval breathed.

Aarna shrugged. "Just getting into character. Come on, dear boy"—she yanked at Rem's arm—"let's carry on into this den of iniquity."

Rem looked to Torval and raised his eyebrows. Once more, he understood well Torval's attraction to the bar matron. Torval, for his part, did not look amused.

Rem and Aarna stumbled out of the alley. Rem did his best to seem good and soused, well into his cups, and Aarna did a spectacular job beside him. Clearly, spending most of her adult life serving drunks had taught her how to impersonate one. Rem, for his part, was reminded of the very few times he'd joined troupes of traveling mummers on stage for performances at his father's court. His father had never cared for his literary or theatrical proclivities and chided him often for 'making a fool of himself,' as he put it, whenever the mummers were passing through. That memory—the joy of performance, the weight of his father's shame, Rem's eventual decision to simply watch the performances and not try to insert himself—almost drew him right out of the performance he should have been putting on at that moment. Then Aarna laughed again beside him and Rem yanked himself back into the moment, laughing as well. The two of them kept up their act all the way across the muddy street, the Moon Under Water looming closer and closer in their vision as they lumbered and lurched this way and that, told each other silly jokes, and laughed too loudly in answer to them.

The Moon Under Water itself hardly seemed sinister. It was

two-storied, with porches below and above, shuttered windows, and wooden shingles on the peaked roof. It was one of a number of warehouses, inns, and taverns that lined this particular quayside avenue, and it seemed wholly unremarkable in every way. It didn't even have the customary red lantern out front to indicate that it doubled as a sporting house. As they approached, the front door opened and a fresh bouncer appeared to relieve one of the two burly sentries who flanked the door. When the door opened, Rem caught a glimpse of the smoky, crowded interior of the common room downstairs. Whatever dark secrets the place possessed, they were buried beneath the jostle and energy of what seemed to be a pretty normal—if large and crowded—tavern.

Aarna loosed another loud, cackling laugh, threw her arms sloppily around Rem, and gave him another kiss. Her open mouth fell on his and pressed firmly. Rem, not sure what he should do, muttered through pursed lips.

"What are you doing?" he whispered.

"Just staying in character," she said as she kept kissing him. "Don't be such a prig."

Rem surrendered and kissed her. Her mouth tasted of basil and strawberries, quite pleasant. She ran her fingers through his hair and pulled him close. Rem decided to up the ante and laid one hand on her ample buttocks. He gave her bottom a good squeeze. Aarna responded by breaking the kiss and descending into a giggling fit.

When Rem pulled away from her, a dopey, un-unfaked smile on his face, she whispered to him. "Are they watching us?"

He dared a look at the bouncers. "They are. But they don't seem terribly interested."

"Perfect," Aarna said. "Let's go."

They lurched on, right up to the front door. When they got there, Rem stood waiting for the bouncers to either ask his business or open the door for him. They did neither. Meanwhile, Aarna hung off him, licking his ear and breathing on his neck. He sincerely hoped Torval understood that all her attentions were faked, for the purpose of getting them through the door.

"What's your business here, lovebirds?" one of the bouncers asked.

"Business as usual," Rem answered, smiling cheekily. "Mind getting the door for me?"

"I mind indeed, sir," the bouncer responded. "This here's a private club, and you don't look familiar to me."

"Did you hear that?" Rem asked Aarna. "This sod says I don't look familiar to him!"

"You bloody barmpot!" Aarna brayed. "Don't you know who this is?"

The two bouncers exchanged incredulous looks. "No," they both said.

Rem decided to go for it. He reached into his pocket and pulled out the little bauble that they had lifted from Ginger Joss. "Does this help?" he asked, holding the medallion by its chain.

The bouncers studied the pendant. One moved for the door. The other stopped him with a raised hand. "Who gave you that?" he asked.

"Joss," Rem answered, doing his best to sound annoyed and impatient. "You know him, don't you? Ginger Joss? He's a kinsman of mine." Given Rem's red hair and freckles—a different shade than Joss's but still similar—he hoped that explanation would suffice.

The incredulous bouncer kept staring. The other one lingered, hand on the door handle. Finally, the suspicious fellow cocked his head. The other one opened the door.

"Welcome to the Moon Under Water," the doubter said as Rem and Aarna moved past. "Upstairs and to the back, as always."

Rem feigned annoyance again. "I know my way, you prat."

In they went, and the noise and smoke and close air of the common room beyond surrounded them.

Rem studied the place, Aarna still beside him, her arms still draped around his shoulders. It was an upscale taproom and gaming house, not unlike the others he'd seen recently, but of a different caste entirely in its particulars. For one, every prostitute that he saw in the room—clearly working professionals, with premium prices attached—were all stunningly beautiful—even the painted and perfumed men. There wasn't a wasted, wormy, toothless urchin among them. Secondly, it was clear from the lacquered chairs, polished tables, velvet tapestries, and shiny bronze lamps that the owner and operator of the Moon Under Water was wealthy and of a far more elevated caste than the owners of most of the city's whorehouses. The place was furnished as finely as a lord's house—in some ways more so—and the clientele, though not entirely made up of the best of Yenaran society, nonetheless seemed to be on their best behavior. The place was lively and loud, but not chaotic. It probably helped that more bouncers were spaced around the room, huge men with bulging muscles, burning stares, and idly crossed arms, waiting for trouble, daring anyone to break the peace.

"Promise me," Aarna whispered in Rem's ear, "that if you close this place down and confiscate its contents, I get this furniture."

Rem smiled. "You have my word."

"Come on," Aarna urged, back to business. "Upstairs and to the back, like the man said."

Rem nodded and the two of them wended their way through the crowd toward the stairs, a double flight, all the way at the rear of the common room. When they reached them, they once more showed their pendant to a bouncer guarding the foot of the stairs, were cleared, and climbed to the second floor. At the top, they found themselves at the head of a long, narrow corridor lined with doors and guarded by yet another bouncer.

This one did something strange, though: he barely noted the medallion, but he took a long, appraising look at Aarna. In truth, Rem didn't care for the length or closeness of the fellow's appraisal. Finally, though, the guard smiled lasciviously and stepped aside.

"Late summer instead of bright spring, but buxom indeed," he said. "Go to the third room on the right. Your service will begin shortly."

Rem nodded. He and Aarna continued down the hall, arms still around each other, all the way to the door suggested. The door stood open and they ducked into the waiting room without hesitation. Once the door was shut behind them, the world was far quieter.

They studied their new surroundings. There was a bed, a wealth of pillows and cushions strewn about one corner of the floor, a large elaborate Shimzari water pipe, and a table on which waited a pitcher and two cups. There was wine in the pitcher.

Rem started to circle the room, examining the plank walls for signs of spy holes. Occasionally, he would knock upon them, hoping to hear the deep, telltale resonance that suggested a hollow space behind them.

Suddenly, rapping on one of the inside walls, Rem got the

sound he'd been anticipating: a deep, hollow thumping, like a drum. He turned to Aarna, rapping on the wall again with his knuckles. "Hear that?"

"Hollow," she said.

Rem examined the planks before him, peering upward toward where they met the roof beams, then down, to where they disappeared behind the edges of the floorboards. "No sign of hidden joints, though. Maybe it's just a space in the wall."

"Or maybe," Aarna said, "their secret architects are better at keeping their hidden panels hidden than you'd like to admit."

Rem scowled at her. "Unkind."

He moved to the water pipe and studied its smoke chamber. It was loaded with a brick of something dense and sticky.

"What is that?" he asked Aarna, assuming that a woman who owned a tavern of her own might instantly know.

She took a quick glance. "Cured witchweed."

"So that's what it looks like," Rem muttered.

"Some like it dried—still green—others like this cured stuff, pressed into bricks. I don't allow it at the King's Ass because it brings a cartload of trouble along with it. Fights, weeders gone comatose. And orcs, of course."

"Orcs? Are they partial to it?"

Aarna shook her head. "Not at all. It doesn't even work on them. But they know humans like it and they're the ones that bring most of it into the city. Orc maids cultivate it up in the mountains; war bands trade with the orc maids for food, shelter, and breeding; then the bucks bring the witchweed down to the city and trade it for ale or weapons or whatever they might need. Sometimes they just keep it handy as a peace offering if they're stopped by orc slayers or bounty hunters—a little something to grease the wheels of understanding and help them carry on their way."

Rem thought of the drunken orc that he and Torval had arrested on his first night walking the ward—the one bearing a bundle of witchweed on his person. Rem clearly remembered the smell—funereal incense, burnt cloves, and pitch—and when he took a great, deep whiff of the brick packed into the water pipe, the same pungent scent stung his nostrils.

The stench brought an image of Gorn Bonebreaker to Rem's mind: the arrogant, absurd orcish ethnarch sitting on his too-small throne, eyes betraying the briefest, barest hint of worry when he saw that fat bundle of confiscated witchweed in Torval's hands. Could that parcel have been bound for this very sporting house, for use in these very pipes? Was the dual loss of revenue and a satisfied customer what gave Gorn Bonebreaker that evident, momentary pang when he saw that bundle of contraband in Torval's little hands?

"Is it illegal?" Rem asked. "Selling witchweed, that is?"

Aarna smiled crookedly. "You tell me, good watchwarden."

Rem cocked his head. "Third day on the job. Throw me a bone, eh?"

Aarna relented. "Like everything else, it's perfectly legal if you have a license. Some taverns and innkeeps get licensed and do regular trade in it. Some eschew the licenses but let swaps and smoke-ups go on in their establishments anyway, so long as they get a cut and it all stays quiet."

Rem nodded and said a silent prayer of thanks. Aarna was turning out to be even more helpful than he'd hoped. He supposed that shouldn't surprise him, given the fact that she herself was a tavernkeep and businesswoman, and probably knew more about the ebb and flow and undertow of Yenara's nightlife than Rem and Torval combined.

Aarna stepped away from the water pipe and back to the jug

of wine on the table. She poured some of the wine and sniffed it. Satisfied, she tasted a portion with her tongue.

"What are you doing?" Rem asked.

"Spiked," she said. "Poppy milk, maybe."

"Poppy milk in the wine," Rem muttered, "and witchweed in the pipe. How powerful is this stuff, compared to the poppy milk in the wine?"

"Ten times more powerful," Aarna said. "Or so I've heard. So, we can assume the purpose of this room is to get blinkered sideways and robbed blind?"

"Maybe," Rem said. "It seems so clumsy for such a slick operation. All this secrecy, the medallions, the bouncers, all so a patron can come back here, smoke themselves loony, and get pickpocketed?"

"It doesn't make much sense, does it?" Aarna placed her hands on her wide hips. "Well, brave watchman—what now?"

Rem moved back to the door. He opened it, just a crack, and peered out into the hallway. "I want to take a look around," he said, "if I can slip out without the bouncer seeing me. Check out some of the side corridors."

"And what will I do while you're poking around?" Aarna asked.

Rem turned to her. "Stay here. Just wait. I'll be right back."

"Yes, sir," Aarna said in an affected city dweller's accent. "As ye please, sir. I'll wait right here for ye, sir. Shall I warm the wine and turn the bed down for the night?"

Rem raised an eyebrow. "I know you're strong and capable, Aarna—but if you suffer even a scratch, Torval will rip me limb from limb."

Aarna gave him a crooked, mordant grin, clearly indicating that she understood. "Fine. Go have all the fun and leave me here."

With that, he was gone.

★   ★   ★

Not six feet from where he stood, the corridor split into two different directions. Rem hove to the left, then peered back around the corner to make sure he wasn't followed. The bouncer at the far end of the corridor—the one guarding the head of the stairs—still stood with his back to Rem, arms crossed, staring down on the proceedings in the main room below with affected boredom. Rem nodded, satisfied, and padded slowly, quietly, down the corridor he now moved in. At each door he stopped, pressed his ear to the door, and listened. At the first two he heard nothing. Behind the third, he heard voices.

What they said was impossible to discern, but this he could tell: there was a man and a woman, the woman did a lot of giggling, and over the course of the many moments that Rem stood there, listening, her voice and speech seemed to stretch out, growing ever more hesitant and sluggish. The acrid smell of witchweed was in the air, wafting from beneath the door. Rem was afraid that if he stood there too long, he would start to feel its effects.

So, as slowly and quietly as he could, Rem turned the knob on the door. When he felt the latch disengage, he gently pushed the door open, just a crack, and peered inside. The smell of witchweed was immediately stronger, making his eyes water and his tongue dry.

Through the tiny crack that he had allowed for his spying foray, Rem saw a room not unlike the one that he and Aarna had been in. A man and a woman reposed within, the man older, his face pitted and pockmarked by time, his shirt and breeches half-undone as though he and the girl had been ready to engage in some sexual activity. The girl, meanwhile, looked far younger than the man—surely not far into her twenties, and quite beautiful. The laces on her bodice were mostly undone, and her red-rimmed eyes and loose manner told Rem that she'd imbibed quite a bit of the witchweed and the poppy-laced wine. She was swaying where she sat, looking in danger of collapsing at any moment. She sucked eagerly on the pipe nozzle, smoke puffing out of her nose and the corners of her mouth, then suddenly spat the nozzle out as a coughing fit racked her. In the midst of her coughing, she laughed.

"There now," the man said. "That's better."

"I think this is going to my head," the girl said sluggishly, staring at the nozzle as though it were some alien implement she didn't entirely recognize. "I can't...I can't..."

"You can," the man said with a smug and satisfied grin, "and you will."

The girl shook her head, but the gesture was distant and feeble. Even as she did so, she was already putting the nozzle back in her mouth, sucking to get another good cloud of the witchweed in her lungs. She blinked, her eyes glassy, her pupils wide enough to make her eyes look like two black marbles.

The girl's mouth worked as she tried to form another coherent thought, as she tried to prove that she was still in charge of her own mouth, her own limbs, her own body. Then, as if giving up the ghost, she simply let the nozzle drop from her hands and pitched sideways. She landed on the pillows that surrounded her, curled up in a tight little ball, and settled in for a long, deep sleep. Across from her, the man stretched out one foot and firmly prodded her prone form.

"Darling," he said. "Darling girl, are you huffing out on me?"

She muttered something, completely incoherent, then shifted slightly. She was fast asleep, snoring. The witchweed had finally overtaken her and done its work. Nothing could wake her now...not for hours and hours.

As Rem watched from the other side of the door, the man

did something strange. He reached up one hand, made a fist, and knocked on the inner wall of the chamber. The knock was coded, and after it had been given, another coded knock came in answer. Then, to Rem's great surprise, a panel of the inner wall slid aside and two men stepped into the room. They were thick and burly and they made straight for the girl lying unconscious on the floor cushions.

One straddled her and turned her onto her back. The other grabbed her limp wrists. The one straddling her smacked the girl's cheek a couple times, as though trying to wake her. She muttered but remained unresponsive. The girl was deeply asleep, and would not be awakened. The two men threw the third fellow on the floor rapacious looks, then bent to lift the girl. Before taking her ankles to help his partner lift her, the man straddling the girl flipped the man on the floor a small object that looked like a coin or a gambling chip.

"Redeem downstairs," he said.

"Good doing business with you gents," the man on the floor said amenably. "As always."

The two men muttered polite replies, lifted the girl, and slowly removed her from the room, back through the secret panel they had come through. The man on the floor struggled to rise and began lacing up his breeks again. Rem gently closed the door and backed away. He studied the intersecting corridors again. When he was satisfied that no one was nearby, he padded quickly back to the room he had left Aarna in.

So, that was their game! They lured beautiful young women here, plied them with witchweed and poppy-laced wine, then, when they were good and knackered, they spirited them away. But to where? And for what purpose? Was it just some adjunct of the slave trade, dealing in shadily acquired young women of free birth? Or was it something more sinister? Worshippers of dark gods looking for sacrificial lambs? Vivisectionists or physicians looking for bodies to experiment upon? A rich potentate from the east adding to his harem? And how did poor, dead Telura Dall tie in to it all? Or Freygaf, for that matter?

Or Indilen! Could this have been her fate? Sent here on an errand, drugged and spirited away?

You're imagining things, Rem thought. *Indilen ducking you probably doesn't have a thing to do with all this. Stop mooning over her. You've got work to do.*

Rem wondered, but felt something else as well. He was filled with a strange sort of indignant rage. To think—an unsuspecting girl accompanied a man to this place, allowed herself to be plied, and then, after passing out, woke up in a dungeon beneath them, or on a slave ship, already cutting the seas far from the land of her birth. There really was no end to human cruelty and depravity, he supposed.

And that was why they had to stop it, no matter what.

As Rem turned the knob of the door to the room he'd left Aarna in, he sincerely hoped that Torval had found a way to infiltrate the Moon Under Water. If not, the dwarf would just have to take Rem's word for what was happening there, and forgo seeing it for himself. Either way, they were onto something here, and they needed backup: the other watchwardens would have to be called out and a raid undertaken.

Just as soon as they managed to flee the place with their hides intact.

Rem opened the door.

For just a moment, Rem felt embarrassment, as though he had stumbled upon something he had no business seeing. Then he realized that he should not be embarrassed, but horrified.

There was Aarna, locked in a rough embrace with an unshaven fellow who held a knife at her throat, one dirty hand clamped over her mouth.

And there was a second man, just three steps off to Rem's right, also with a sharp, rather unpleasant-looking knife in his hand.

The men seemed stunned by Rem's sudden entrance.

Aarna screamed behind the man's filthy hand and her brown eyes went wide with pleading terror.

Rem went for his sword.

CHAPTER TWENTY-FIVE

All that Rem could think about in that moment was that something terrible was about to happen to Aarna, and that he was the only one present to thwart it.

But there was no apparent line of attack that he could work out in the moment. If he went for the man off to his right, the man holding Aarna could draw his own blade across her throat and kill her instantly. If he tried to engage the man holding Aarna, even to distract or bargain with him, the knifeman on the right could easily slide in and get the drop on Rem while Rem was so engaged. And here he stood, fallen into an on-guard stance, sword in hand, as useless in that moment as a bouquet of flowers.

The man on his right moved a little. Rem pivoted so that he now stood with each potential adversary before him, each only about forty-five degrees off his central line of vision. That slight movement froze the knifeman in his tracks. Satisfied, Rem kept his eyes on the man with his knife to Aarna's throat and his hand over her mouth.

"You're not a regular," the man holding Aarna snarled. "So, who are you?"

"You wouldn't believe I'm the pox inspector?" Rem asked.

To his surprise, the man holding Aarna smiled a little. "Funny boy. Talk," he pressed his blade against Aarna's throat, and Rem saw the first red glint of blood drawn, "or this one bleeds."

Rem noted that the man on the right was closing in again. One step. Then another.

"Tell him to back off," Rem said, suggesting him with his free hand but never moving his gaze. "You may have time to bleed her and this one may get one good stick in me, but I promise you, no matter what you do to her or me, I'll take at least one of you down to the ghast pits with me. That's a promise."

"I'd like to see that," the hostage taker said, his smile widening again—then he started to scream.

For a moment, Rem had no idea what was happening. Then blood started to seep wetly from between the man's fingers, clamped as they were over Aarna's mouth. She had managed to get her teeth around one of them and she was biting, hard. The man tried to yank his hand away, but the grip of her teeth was far too tight. Shaking, desperate to save his finger, the man's knife hand drifted away from Aarna's throat.

Rem was just about to plunge in and see if he could plant his sword point in the man's arm—even a slight wound might get him to draw farther away from her—but already he saw the killer on his right lunging for a strike. The man's momentum carried him quickly, and Rem knew that he was already far inside the reach of his blade. But that didn't mean that Rem was entirely helpless. He swung backhand, toward his oncoming attacker, and the heavy steel pommel of his blade connected hard with the man's right temple, knocking him sideward. The point of the would-be killer's stabbing blade nicked Rem's right shoulder blade, but his strike was solid. The man groaned and toppled, crumpling toward the floor. Rem let his backhand strike carry him around in a full circle and he came back to where he started, now facing Aarna and the man that threatened her.

Aarna's teeth were still dug deep into the man's bloody finger. He had drawn away from her, still trying to yank free, but his knife was high and poised for a downward strike now. Rem could only think of one way to get Aarna safely away before the blade fell and likewise clear a path for him to make his own play to end their bloody little duel.

So, acting purely on instinct, desperate to save Aarna's life, Rem lunged and kicked her square in the stomach.

With a loud *whoof*, Aarna's teeth finally disengaged from the knifeman's finger and she went tumbling backward, toward the open space in the wall that the two men had probably emerged from. The knifeman's plunging blade sliced the air where she'd stood just a moment earlier as the man yanked his bleeding, finally-freed hand close to him. Before he could shift his stance or raise his blade to meet Rem's charge, Rem already had him squarely in his sights. Before the fellow could defend himself, Rem straightened his arm, driving his sword blade before it with terrific force. The blade sliced right through the man's middle, barely resisting the sharp point and the arm's length of steel behind it. The knifeman stared down at the blade, a look of puzzlement and agony on his ruddy face. A mass of blood bloomed beneath his shirt, then came pouring forth down his middle and onto the plank floors of the chamber. He fell to his knees, skin already turning an ashen white. From the floor, he made one weak attempt at a swipe with his blade, but it came nowhere near Rem's body.

Rem withdrew his blade from the man's middle. Without hesitation—without remorse—he drove it in again, this time through the man's heart. He nicked ribs on his way in. The blade buckled the slightest, for the barest of instants, then straightened and slid on. When it pierced the man's heart, the knifeman stopped moving altogether, face frozen in an awful, almost comical mask of wonder and discomfort. Rem withdrew his blade and stared for a moment at the great glut of blood dripping from its tip and leading edges.

He looked to Aarna. She was just yanking herself out of the little alcove behind the secret wall panel, hands braced on the wall struts to either side of her. She had her would-be assassin's blood all over the bottom half of her face. Rem moved to help her up.

"Aarna, please, forgive me—"

She reached one hand toward him, to accept his help and regain her feet—then screamed.

"Rem, look out!"

Rem turned. The other knifeman—the one he'd thought was suitably unconscious because of that hard knock he'd given him with his sword pommel—came flying toward him. Rem tried to get his sword between them, but it was too late. The man hit him and down they went. Rem's sword flew from his hand.

The two of them hit the floor with stunning force, a tangle of arms and legs and curses. Desperate for advantage, Rem threw a bevy of punches—aimless, directionless—in the hopes of stunning his opponent or knocking him out cold. To his horror, his attacks seemed to be useless.

They rolled across the floor. Rem blocked the knife half a dozen times as its wielder tried to get in close to slide it in. In desperate snatches, Rem searched the nearby floor for his fallen sword, knowing that he could air the fellow out if only he could get his blade in hand, get back on his feet, and get a little distance from the bastard.

But at the moment, that would have to wait. They were too close, breathing in each other's faces, spitting and gnashing and groaning as they grappled. Blood dripped from the man's temple where the pommel of Rem's sword had split the skin. And that damned knife in the intruder's hands kept falling toward Rem—threatening his face, his exposed throat, his heaving chest. Time and again, Rem managed to deflect the blows and dodge the blade, but he wasn't sure how long he could maintain his good fortune without some distinct advantage.

Rem tried to dismount, but the assassin held on and they tumbled sideward. Rem was underneath now, his attacker on top. The villain raised his knife for a powerful, killing blow. When he stabbed downward, however, Rem managed to catch his arm and deflect it, keeping that ugly, pointed blade from plunging right into his chest. Rem tried to use one knee or the other to get a clean shot at the assailant's balls, but he couldn't quite manage the right angle. Likewise, the assassin was aware that his jewels might be exposed and kept bending his body, left and right, to avoid the substratum attack. In all of their rolling, they ran into the edge of the secret panel in the wall, hard. Rem's head took a mighty blow. He saw stars, but he kept struggling to hold the knife at bay, to somehow get himself back on top.

As Rem's star-strewn vision cleared, he saw Aarna run forward, poised for a strike. She had something big in her hands: the central column of the chamber's water pipe! The smoking hoses and nozzles hung from the great tin trunk like vines from the limb of a forest tree. Aarna lifted the unwieldy assembly and brought it crashing down on Rem's adversary. Rem felt the force of the blow through the man's strong, corded arms and writhing body. The water pipe bounced off his hunched shoulders. In the instant that followed, as the fellow bent forward and blinked, trying to maintain his composure atop Rem in the wake of such a fierce blow, Rem saw his opening. He drew back one fist and punched the rogue in the face. Once, twice, a third time for good measure. Spittle and blood fell down into Rem's eyes. He was momentarily blinded.

But he felt the weight upon him relieved. Rem threw his whole body away from the wall, finally slipping out from beneath his would-be killer. When Rem blinked the blood and spittle away and looked, he saw the fellow scrambling on all fours for the shallow chamber beyond the secret panel. Rem's first thought was that the scoundrel was fleeing...and that he couldn't allow that to happen.

Rem threw himself onto his attacker, hands grasping at his belt and trousers and throwing him to the floor. Then Rem was up, ready to drive an elbow or a knee into the man's back to immobilize him.

But Aarna beat him to it. She brought the body of the water pipe down again, right onto their adversary's head. Rem heard a wet, sickening crunch, saw the man's skull collapse a little under all that weight, and felt the man's body give a convulsive shudder beneath him. This time, Aarna could not maintain a grip on the water pipe. It fell with a great clang and rolled across the floor. Aarna, dripping with sweat and tears, blood smeared on her face, body shaking from a sudden rush of fear and fury, stared at the man whose skull she'd just crushed. Rem did as well.

When the two of them were sure he wouldn't rise again, Rem struggled to his feet and swept Aarna into his arms. He pushed her sweat-matted hair away from her face and tried to wipe off all the blood around her mouth with his sleeve. Aarna let him clean her up. Just as he seemed to have wiped all the blood away and was taking a moment to assess her, to make sure that she was not wounded or nicked, Aarna shoved him away.

"Enough," she said. "I'm fine."

"Are you?" Rem asked. "Are you certain?"

"After you kicked me like a stray dog? Certainly, boy. Peachy."

"I'm terribly sorry about that," Rem said, moving closer again.

Aarna stepped back, doubled over, and drank the air deeply. No matter how much she gulped, it seemed she could not get enough. Still, she held up one hand to keep Rem at a distance.

"I'm fine," she wheezed between lungfuls. "Honestly. It was a fine gambit. Got me clear and surprised the sundry hells out of that one." She indicated the man Rem had impaled, now lying in a spreading pool of his own blood on the floor.

"You're sure you're all right?" Rem asked. "I thought he cut you."

"Just a nick," she said, voice starting to sound almost normal again, neither so wavering nor so breathless. "Aemon's bones, I wish that wine wasn't spiked. I can still taste that foul bastard's blood and filthy hands in my mouth..."

Rem snatched up his sword. First things first. They had to make sure they were truly safe. He peered into the dark spaces behind the wall where the secret panel had slid aside. No one seemed to be back there. Rem assumed that if these two men had backup, they had not called for it. What had brought them here? Pure chance? A quick look through a peephole and curiosity about why Aarna was left alone in the room?

No, that wasn't it at all.

"Sundry hells," he muttered. "I brought them. My knocking on the walls..."

"How's that?" Aarna asked.

"I saw it in another room," Rem said, disgusted with himself. "After the girls are drunk and unconscious, the men who've brought them knock on the walls—a coded knock—and that brings the likes of these two to snatch the girls and spirit them

away. They must have heard me knocking when I was looking for hollow spaces. They must have known right away that
someone was in here looking for a secret passage with no notion
that anyone might be waiting behind the walls. If I hadn't left
you—"

"Quiet," Aarna said. "We made a lot of noise in here. Someone might be coming from the main hall already."

Rem's eyes went wide. She was right. Gods of the Panoply—
how could the two of them slip out of here if more hired hands
arrived outside the chamber door? There were no windows,
and there were probably more knifemen waiting in the maze of
secret passages behind the walls.

Don't panic, Rem thought. *Deal with the situation. One problem
at a time. Go and check the hall to see if anyone's coming.*

Rem hurried to the chamber door. He pressed his ear against
it. To his great surprise, all he heard was a great and thunderous
clamor—outside.

"What is it?" Aarna asked.

Rem urged her to be quiet with a silent gesture, then slowly
opened the door. Through the crack, he heard the great row
that seemed to drift up from the common room, down the
stairs at the end of the hall. He peered into the hall and saw no
one around, so he threw their door open wide and stepped out,
all the caution having fled from him.

There was a commotion down the hall, beyond the stairs.
It came from the common room. Patrons alternately screamed
and cheered. Feet thumped across the wooden floor, tables and
chairs scooted, clay cups fell and shattered. It was a cacophony
of voices and noise, and amid it all, the vague clang of weapons:
wood on steel, steel on steel, iron on wood.

A brawl, then—and by the sound, a big one. The bouncer at

the head of the stairs was nowhere to be seen—probably down amid the tumult, trying to maintain order. Rem counted himself very lucky. He grabbed Aarna's hand and yanked her out of the room.

They hurried up the corridor. When they reached the gallery rail that looked down into the common room, they saw the source of the furor. A great brawl had indeed broken out. Among the knots of adversaries at one another's throats and the throngs of bystanders trying to clear the way and get to safer ground, the bouncers waded into the fray in an attempt to dispel the fight, or at the very least, get it under control.

At the center of the melee, Rem saw two unequal figures locked in combat.

One was a bearded Estavari bravo wrapped in a flowing cloak, sporting a sharp, rather malign-looking sword of exquisite make.

The other was a bald-headed four-foot-tall sculpture of thick muscle and bone armed with an iron maul and a broken chair leg.

Oh yes, Torval had made it inside ... and already, someone was trying to kill him.

Rem drew his sword again. "Stay up here," he said to Aarna, then went pounding down the stairs and thrust himself into the melee, eager to save the dwarf's life and see just what sort of skills that greasy southern bravo had to offer with his blade.

Pressing through the surging crowd wasn't easy. People hove this way and that, joining the fray or fleeing from it. At one point, one of the familiar bouncers saw Rem approaching Torval and the Estavari bravo and tried to head him off. Rem saw the bouncer's approach, changed course slightly to put a knot of scrapping longshoremen between him and his would-be adversary, then struggled on, jostled by the fray surrounding him.

Torval saw Rem just before he arrived on the dwarf's right, and tried to wave him off. "Forget about me!" Torval called above the din. "Get Aarna out of here!"

Sorry, Old Stump, Rem thought, *I've come too far now to turn back. Besides, if I've learned anything tonight, it's that Aarna can take care of herself—and me, for that matter.*

He thrust himself right into the midst of Torval's contest with the sword-wielding bravo, colliding with Torval, knocking him clear, and immediately taking his place in an on-guard stance, body narrowed, blade leveled.

Torval started to protest and charge back into the fight.

"You finally put a sword in my hand," Rem snapped, without taking his eyes off his adversary, "so let me handle this!"

He sized up his opponent. He was Estavari, all right—olive skin, black, oiled hair, a well-trimmed beard. His clothes were common, but his face and bearing were noble—a strange combination, but not unheard-of, Rem supposed. Hadn't everyone he'd met in Yenara recognized the same quality in him? More troubling, though, Rem recognized the fellow: it was the same Estavari bodyguard that they had noted at the house of Kethren Dall, the one in the employ of the elf merchant, Mykaas Masarda.

Then Rem noticed another small detail as the Estavari prepared himself for their contest of blades: a long, thin cut—freshly scabbed—ran up the Estavari's left bicep, matching precisely the wound Rem had given the mysterious assassin who had infiltrated Torval's home in an attempt to kill them while they slept.

So, this bravo—this olive-skinned southerner with his regal sneer and his rough raiment—had already tried to kill them once that day.

By Masarda's order? Or someone else's? Or was the bravo the mastermind behind this whole, rotten kidnapping business?

Too many questions for the here and now. Presently, there was only one concern: crossing swords with the bastard and walking away with his life.

Rem felt the familiar mental calm and spring-loaded tautness of the expert fencer spread over him, the product of all his youthful training. Mind supple, body taut—that's what he'd been taught in his youth. That's what would keep him alive.

He hoped.

"So," Rem said to the bravo, "ready for another round?"

"Your last," the swordsman answered through a smirk.

Their blades flashed, and the duel began.

Rem didn't open with his strongest moves. Instead, he tested his opponent, trying to get some sense of his style and capabilities. He feinted and thrust, parried and riposted, dared attacks with edge and with point, each carefully modulated and formulated to expose his opponent's strengths and weaknesses.

The Estavari was very good. He parried every thrust with subtle movements, blocked Rem's slashes, thrusts, and passes with practiced calm. He might be dressed as a common sellsword, but his blade work was fluid and elegant—clearly the product of a courtly education.

A strange, fleeting thought flashed through Rem's brain, unbidden and dangerous, coming as it did in the midst of a life-and-death duel. *What if he's like me?* Rem thought. *What if this murderous, shifty, smirking bastard is nothing but a runaway child of privilege looking for a new start, like me?*

Look what's become of him.

Look what could become of me.

He shoved those thoughts away. There was more weighty business at hand—the sort that could get him killed if not attended to. Save all other ruminations for later.

Just as Rem made the decision to stamp down his conscious

thought and press his advantage in earnest—that it was time to engage his adversary head-on, up close, and bring the duel to a close—the Estavari redoubled his own attack and struck mercilessly. He advanced on Rem with a lunge, and brought his own sword—longer and heavier than Rem's—down in a series of sweeping overhand chops that nearly broke right through Rem's clumsy parries. The Estavari's attacks were swift, strong, crushing. They drove Rem back until he ran into a table and had nowhere left to retreat to.

On came Torval, charging from the bravo's right with his iron maul high. But the dwarf barely proved a distraction for the seasoned swordsman—the Estavari simply threw up his cape in Torval's vision, then raised one boot, and shoved the dwarf off again. But that moment of distraction gave Rem a fleeting opportunity to reset himself, and that was all he needed. In an instant, Rem had pivoted sideward, giving him a better angle on the bravo's open left flank. He attempted a long lunge and daring underhand thrust designed to end the whole match.

But the Estavari had seen him sliding into position. He spun back toward Rem, sweeping his sword out to parry Rem's thrust, then gracefully brought his sword point up out of the parry into the perfect position for his own thrust. Before Rem could slide clear, he felt his opponent's cold, sharp sword point biting into his right forearm. He withdrew clumsily. The wound wasn't deep, but he was bleeding now.

The Estavari's smirk widened. He was quite pleased with himself.

Over his adversary's shoulder, Rem saw Torval again. The dwarf was retreating, rushing toward the door, for what purpose Rem couldn't guess. Somewhere behind Rem, there came a terrific crash, the sound of two strong bodies colliding with a table, shattering it. A beer mug flew across the room at the edge of his vision.

This is a bad spot for a sword match, Rem suddenly realized. *I'm surrounded by pure chaos. Someone could slam into me at any moment and give this son of a whore the opening he needs—*

"Ready for another lesson, whelp?" the Estavari asked, and drew a new blade from an unseen sheath at the small of his back—this one a long, broad dagger. He adopted a new stance now—longsword thrust out in his right hand as a forward defense, dagger floating farther back, in his left hand, ready to parry or snatch a lucky strike. That was a classic position for a two-handed match, and any doubts Rem had as to his adversary's noble background evaporated. The longsword and the dagger gleamed in the murky light of the common room.

Rem prepared himself. He had only ever matched two or three opponents in tourneys who used both hands and two weapons. The results hadn't been favorable for him.

The bravo attacked.

Rem's defensive instincts were put through merciless paces. Using his single short sword to block feints from dagger point and thrusts from the bravo's blade forced him to constantly open himself to hazard, not to mention tiring him out quickly. Worse, the oily Estavari was a whirlwind with both blades, in some ways better in this mode than he had been with only his sword. Something about the two-pronged attacks that the double armament made possible, combined with the added defensive postures he could adopt, made him bolder, surer, more audacious. Still, Rem kept his cool—albeit barely. Offense went out the window and defense became the order of the day. He blocked, he parried, he riposted. Every now and again, he managed a deft feint, but he couldn't seem to break through the Estavari's defenses or put a scratch on him.

Not good.

He needed some advantage, some distraction, some means of ending the contest. If he could find his own second blade, even something to use as a block or a buckler, then perhaps he'd have a chance. But his opportunities to search for such a shield were nil under the unending barrage of thrusts and cuts from his opponent.

Then he heard the howl of brass whistles, the thunder of boot-heels. A new slurry of combatants entered the fray, pouring in through the front door, spreading out around the room, a bevy of hard men in boiled-leather cuirasses sporting lead badges, armed with all manner of weapons—swords, axes, mauls, and maces.

It was the ward guard—men Rem recognized as guardsmen of the Fifth, as well as strangers he assumed to be the men of the Fourth—and Torval was among their number. The brawl must have raised an alarm. Rem saw them all—familiar faces and new, as they poured into the room and spread out to engage with the various life-and-death matches unfolding around the room.

Torval charged the Estavari that Rem stood toe to toe with.

The Estavari gave Rem a mordant grin, then pivoted side-ward and hooked a toppled chair with his foot. With a swift kick, he sent the chair skittering toward Torval. It collided squarely with the onrushing dwarf's pounding feet, and Torval went sprawling, his momentum carrying him forward.

Right toward Rem.

Rem had no time to dodge. Torval's compact but consider-able bulk slammed into him with crushing force and the two of them hit the floor, a tangle of arms and legs. Rem's sword flew from his hands. As they came to rest, Rem raised his head, in search of their adversary. The Estavari was already far across the

room, making his escape, wending a path through the brawling chaos toward some back corridor and rapid egress.

On top of Rem, Torval struggled to plant his hands and
push himself up.

"Where is he? Where is that shady bastard?"

"Get off me," Rem urged. "He slipped away. If you hadn't
come barreling in, I might have had him!"

Torval stood, straddling Rem. "Well, you're quite welcome," the dwarf countered. "See if I come rushing to your aid
at the last minute any time soon!"

Rem sighed. At least he was alive to fight another day.
Should he be upset about that? He thought not. He held out his
hand to the dwarf. "Help me up," he said.

Torval obliged.

"Give me something good!" a husky voice barked out of the
chaos.

Rem and Torval turned to see Ondego marching toward
them, followed by Djubal and Klutch, the two watchmen no
doubt eager to see Rem and Torval get a reaming from their
prefect.

"How did you all get here?" Rem asked, honestly confused.

"I sent a runner after you came inside," Torval said. "Figured we might need backup. And they arrived not a moment
too soon, I'd say."

Ondego looked angry enough to chew them out, but
focused as well—intent on some prize. Rem decided it would
be best to give Ondego something at the outset to placate him.

"We should hurry," Rem said.

"Hurry where?" Ondego asked.

Rem cocked his head toward the stairs. "Up there," he said.
"There are secret passages—at least a dozen of them! They're

drugging the young women they bring here, then taking them into those passages—"

"Go, then!" Ondego barked. "Go now! Frennis is on his way, and if he gets here before we've gone into those tunnels—"

Rem looked to Djubal and Klutch. "Back us up?" he asked.

Djubal's dark face was split by a puckish grin. "Delighted, Gingersnap."

Torval called for torches and the four of them went bounding up the stairs.

CHAPTER TWENTY-SIX

Rem, Torval, Djubal, and Klutch entered one of the secret passageways via a sliding panel in the first chamber at the head of the stairs. The narrow little corridor beyond was tight, the air close and stale. Torval had acquired one of their ubiquitous watchman's lamps—the sort made of iron and tin that all the watchwardens carried on night patrol—and the little oiled wick within was all that lit their way. In single file—Torval, Rem, Djubal, and Klutch—they followed the twisting, turning passage built into the walls of the tavern.

After two or three bends in the passage, they reached a narrow stairwell and began their descent. The stairs were rickety and rotten, but the space seemed largely clear of cobwebs and dust, indicating regular foot traffic from top to bottom. Down and down they went, the stairs bending in a square spiral as they took them from the second floor of the tavern down past the ground floor, then into a vast cellar, probably cut right into the earth of the bluffs about the harbor. The stairs were separated from the cellar proper by a flimsy wooden door—access, along with secrecy—but continued downward beneath even the level of the cellar. The deeper they got, the more pronounced the smell of salt water and low tide became. The watchwardens continued, Rem sure that the others were just as edgy as he was. They were in a terribly vulnerable position. The stairway was too narrow to effectively defend themselves if they were beset from above or below—or, worse, from both directions at once.

Still, Torval seemed little concerned. He took the stairs two at a time, bounding down, down, down, lamp in one hand, maul in the other. A few times, Rem asked the dwarf if he saw anything, but Torval never answered. He would just grunt and keep moving.

"And here I thought you came to our fair city to escape the mines!" Djubal said.

"Keep your sauce boxes shut and be ready!" Torval barked in answer.

Rem shot a glance at Djubal. The ebon southlander's face betrayed little worry, just quiet bemusement. "Right behind you, Old Stump!" he called.

Deeper. Deeper still. The smell of salt and rotting fish grew stronger.

Finally, they hit bottom. The stairs terminated in a cramped chamber with packed dirt walls shored up by wooden planks and struts. Beyond the little chamber lay a long, bending passageway, hewn out of the limestone of the bluffs and reinforced with skeletal wooden supports. Dim little miner's lamps lined the passage, some still flickering, others extinguished. From the far end of the passage, Rem thought he heard voices and the hurried sough of boots, but he couldn't be sure.

"Do you hear that?" he asked his companions. "It sounds like there's someone up ahead."

Torval huffed in the affirmative, then broke into a dead run down the passage.

"Is he mad?" Rem asked.

"Always," Djubal said, and swept past him.

Rem set off at a trot, right on the southlander's heels. Klutch brought up the rear.

After following the snaking passage for some distance, Rem finally saw a broad portal ahead of them that opened into a larger chamber beyond. Torval and Djubal hurried through, already shouting as they did.

"Blast!" Torval growled.

"Empty," Djubal spat.

Rem burst out of the narrow passage into the vast chamber beyond. It was a cave of not-inconsiderable size, sporting a number of wooden piers and platforms, a wealth of shipping barrels, a few simply cobbled structures that probably acted as office, sleeping, or storage space, and, down in the little black lagoon that stretched into the cave, a single long, flat barge— the sort used to punt goods around the canals of the city and across the harbor to waiting ships. The place was in a state of disarray, clearly bespeaking a sudden and hastily undertaken migration. Rem guessed that, once upon a time, many boats had graced the little piers that stretched into the lagoon. Now, of course, all the men who toiled down here while life went on above had made their escape, unconcerned for what they left behind, intent only on flight before the wardwatch penetrated their secret passages.

Torval kicked an overturned barrel in fury. "Blast!" he shouted, his voice echoing in the vast, open space of the cave. "Just moments too late!"

"This must be where they brought them," Rem said, studying a collection of barrels and coils of rope near the wall where he stood. "They brought the girls through the passages and down the stairs and then ferried them somewhere else from this cave. I'm assuming that lagoon gives out onto the harbor?"

"Appears so," Djubal said.

"But where did they take them?" Klutch asked. "And how? Certainly the dockmasters would notice barges laden with unconscious young girls sliding back and forth across the harbor?"

As if in answer, a strange thumping began off to their right. Rem heard it first, but the other three followed suit soon enough. It was irregular, alternately weak and strong, coming at no set interval. It came from a convocation of barrels pressed into a storage alcove. It could only be made by something alive.

Rem moved nearer the alcove, readying his sword.

"Careful, lad," Torval warned.

Rem moved slowly around the loose gathering of barrels. Even though the casks were piled three high in some places, their arrangement was haphazard and there were numerous empty spaces among them. He half expected to find some holdout hiding among them—some piratical knave, desperate and cornered, abandoned by his fleeing fellows, a dirk in his eager hands. But there was no one. Even as the thumping continued, he could see no one hiding among the barrels—no one cornered and waiting to make a valiant last stand.

Then he realized that the strange thumping was coming from *within* one of the barrels before him. Rem sheathed his sword, moved to the nearest barrel, and lifted off its unfixed lid. It was empty. The one next to it was the same, and the one after that.

Rem began tearing the lids off every barrel before him, sure that he would soon lift a lid and find some hapless, living soul crammed into one of the damned things, thumping hard on its inner skin, desperate to get out.

Twenty barrels in, he found the source of the thumping. It was a young girl, no more than fifteen summers old. She was crammed into the barrel in such a fashion that she could find no leverage to lift herself out. Her legs were bent up under her chin, her arms at her side. There was enough room for her to breathe, for some air to be left in the barrel when it was shut, but little more. Rem called for his companions. All four helped the girl out of the barrel.

She was groggy and panicked, half mad with fright and probably still high on witchweed. She was lovely and ragged and the thought of someone lifting her out of one of those rooms above when she was in a stupor, then stuffing her into one of these barrels, made Rem so furious that his whole body shook with the force of that fury. When he looked to Torval and saw that his partner was trembling in the same fashion and wearing the same stunned expression, Rem knew that he was not alone.

"Bastards and knaves," Torval grumbled.

"Who would do this?" Rem kept asking. "Who *could* do this?"

They sent Klutch down to the lagoon to fetch some water. It was salty, true, but they could at least wet the girl's face and try to bring her out of her stupor. While Torval and Djubal tended to her, Rem began climbing among the barrels remaining. Most were empty, but in two he found another young girl and a handsome boy, each packed just like the girl they had rescued. It was too late for these two, however: they were stone-dead, clearly having suffocated because they were packed too tightly into their barrels. Whatever precautions normally taken by their captors to keep their cargo alive had, in their sad cases, been overlooked.

"What did you find?" Torval called from his perch beside the groggy girl.

"You don't want to know," Rem said, completely at a loss. Could such things truly be? Could men be so fantastically cruel and careless?

A bauble's glint caught Rem's eye. He clambered over the barrels he'd been searching, thumped down onto the wooden floorboards on the far side, then swung around a corner into a shallow alcove. There were shelves and crates there, all overflowing with a wealth of sundry, mismatched knick-knacks. There was jewelry of all sorts, from the finest to the most modest, items of clothing good for trade or resale such as silk scarves, beautiful shawls and wraps, one or two evening cloaks, even a pair of hastily folded silk gowns finely beaded and embroidered, no doubt stolen from a pair of the girls that passed through here on their way to the gods knew where. Clearly, this was where the kidnappers gathered every little thing of value they could filch from the victims they subdued, be it rings from their pale little fingers or the very clothes from their backs. All that seemed to matter was that the items were undamaged and that they might be worth a few silver andies in trade.

As Rem studied the cache of stolen goods—broaches, torques, fine leather slippers, combs of silver, gold, or tortoiseshell—a certain something suddenly caught his eye. His gaze almost swept right by it, but some dim, unbidden recognition rang a tiny little bell in his rage-fevered mind. For a moment, he stared at it. As he reached out and drew it from the shelf where it lay amid silks and lace and a storm of polished ivory bangles, he willed for it not to be what he suspected it was. But then, once it was in his hands and he stared at it long and hard, the memory of his market encounter with Indilen just a few days earlier returned to him with clarity and force. He was not wrong, and that realization made him vaguely sick to his stomach.

Torval appeared at his elbow.

"What's all this, then?"

"Stolen goods," Rem said, eyes never leaving the object in

his hands. "From the victims, I'd assume. Anything the bastards could sell or trade."

Torval nodded at the item Rem held. "And that?"

Rem's hands gripped an oblong, finely tooled leather box. Upon the face of that box, amid delicate silver chasing, lay an ornate medallion, also of silver, emblazoned with a single letter of the old Horunic alphabet: the letter "I."

"This is a secretary set, custom-made. Quills with finely wrought tips. Bottled ink. A phial of sand and a blotter. A few sheets of paper."

"You look like you've seen it before," Torval said.

Rem nodded. "I have, Torval. Remember the girl I was searching for? Indilen? This belonged to her. I remember it well because I commented upon what a handsome piece it was, and she opened it to show me all it contained." Finally, Rem managed to stop staring at the secretary set and looked to his diminutive partner. "She's passed through here, Torval. These bastards took her."

Torval laid a rough hand on Rem's shoulder. "Then hold on to that secretary set," he said quietly, "and you can give it back to her when we find her."

For just a moment, that thought gave Rem a deep and abiding satisfaction—a bright, warm hope in the center of him that he wanted—nay, needed—at that very moment. But only a moment later, another thought occurred to him, terrible and unsettling.

What if he held on to this small memento of that girl and never, ever saw her again?

A moment later he heard Ondego's unmistakable rasp from one of the platforms above.

"Well?" the prefect demanded. "What have you lot got for me?"

"Slavers," Torval shouted in reply. "And bodies."

Those words froze Ondego and Hirk on the stairway. If the prefect had been silently celebrating their infiltration and raid on the Moon Under Water before that moment, all the bravado and exaltation left him. It was subtle—a squaring of the shoulders, a lift of the chin, the impression of a frown—but even at his present distance from the prefect, Rem noted the change.

"Did we nab any?" Ondego asked, then once more began his descent of the stairs.

"Not a one," Djubal said bitterly. "They'd all fled before we reached the cavern."

"Well, then," Ondego grumbled, "it's a good thing I've already dispersed the watchwardens upstairs to inform the city guard at the gates and wharves. Ten to one, our slavers will try to slip away quick and quiet-like with the warm bodies they already have. Let me see what you've found here."

They walked him through. They showed him the barrels, the stolen merchandise, sorted for resale, the two dead prisoners in their casks. Finally, Ondego knelt and studied the half-conscious girl that Djubal and Klutch attended to. Rem was amazed to see true pity and sadness on the prefect's normally inscrutable face.

"Who's responsible for this?" Rem finally asked, not sure if he was addressing anyone. He bent to Ondego. "Did you get any of the men above to talk—"

"We caught two," Ondego said grimly. "But they haven't talked yet."

"Then let us make them talk," Torval growled.

Ondego studied Torval for a moment. He then looked to Rem. There was a strange sort of concern on his face. "Think you can handle it, Bonny Prince? Some up close and personal interrogation?"

Rem spat onto the salt-washed rocks of the cave floor. "Gladly, sir."

Ondego nodded. "Then get back upstairs and get to work. Frennis could be here at any moment, and he'll probably chase us out. I've already got an inkling that bastard is tied up in this somehow. If we can get one of those men upstairs to talk—"

Ondego didn't have to finish. Hirk cocked his head—an indication to follow. Rem and Torval set out after him, hurrying back through the passages and up the stairs.

Hirk led them to one of the upstairs rooms, where two men of the Fifth—fat Demijon and the Tregga horseman Brogila— stood guarding one of the two prisoners. The fellow sat on a wooden chair, leaning casually, as though he were waiting for some friend to finish his tryst so the two could be on their way. He was a hard-looking fellow, probably past forty years but still well-muscled and fearless in aspect. When Hirk, Torval, and Rem entered the room, the prisoner smiled a toothless smile and barked harsh, grating laughter.

"Look here, now!" he said. "A pretty-faced lad and his half-pint fool! You are a motley band, aren't ya?"

Rem almost lunged for the prisoner, but Torval beat him to it. The dwarf swept right past Hirk, and hove up to the hard-faced prisoner without a moment's hesitation.

"Gonna dance for me, li'l fella?" the prisoner asked.

Torval brought one of his thick, oversized feet down on the prisoner's left foot. Just before the fellow started screaming, Rem swore he heard bones crack. The prisoner drew his foot up off the floor and reached out for it with his hands. The sound he made was childish and hysterical and not at all what Rem would have expected from such an apparent roughneck.

Then Torval struck again. Before the fellow could even

grasp his raised foot in pain, Torval drew back with one fist and punched him three times, hard, square in the face. The prisoner's screams were swallowed in the rattle of breaking teeth and the gurgle of blood and saliva as he choked and snuffled. Down he went, toppling heavily out of his chair and onto the floor, where he curled up in a fetal ball, broken foot twitching, hands covering his now-ruined face and bleeding nose.

"You bastard!" he snuffled. "You bloody little stump!"

Torval stood over the prisoner. He was only four and a half feet tall, but from where that fellow lay, the dwarf probably looked like a giant. The fury on his face even put a knot in Rem's belly. There was a great reserve of righteous indignation in Torval for those who were preyed upon. That reserve was now alight and burning in the center of him, red hot and approaching white.

"Do you have any idea what you're mixed up in here?" Torval asked his prisoner. "Kidnapping free citizens of this city and shipping them out—in gods-damned barrels—for slave labor on some foul foreign shore? A public disemboweling and flaying is probably in your future, my friend."

"What difference does it make?" the prisoner grated, still sobbing over the broken bones in his foot.

"Talk," Torval said. "Tell us everything."

The prisoner tried to prop himself up on one hand to better face Torval and defy him. The moment his hand touched the plank floor, Torval brought his maul's hammerhead crashing down. Rem heard the suspect's fingers crack like pine logs on a fire. The prisoner drew up his ruined hand and fell back hard, head thumping into the floor.

Torval loomed over him again. "Talk, or I'll be here all night breaking bones, one after the other."

The prisoner was not just screaming now, or snuffling and

choking on his blood and snot. He was crying, sobbing like a switch-scolded child.

"Please," he muttered. "Someone get him away from me..."

"Sorry, friend," Hirk said. "Torval here's the officer in charge at the moment."

Torval kicked the prisoner's ribs, hard. He doubled up where he lay on the floor.

"I can't hear you," Torval snarled.

"All right, gods, just stop!" the man bawled. "What do you want to know?"

Torval lowered his maul, brandishing the hammer and spike in the suspect's face. "Keep talking," he said. "Where are they bound for?"

"Aadendrath," the bawling, bleeding villain said. "They sail before dawn, from North Harbor! That's what we were told, at least...now, please..."

"Shut your gob!" Torval barked, then looked to Rem. His face was caught somewhere between anger and terror. "Aadendrath," he whispered.

"The elf isle?" Rem asked, thoroughly confused.

"Yarma's cunt," Hirk sighed. "That *is* a bloody mess, and no mistake."

Torval turned back to the sobbing prisoner. "That doesn't make any bloody sense. Elves don't keep slaves—everyone knows that."

Rem had an unbidden memory of that handsome, muscular man on a leash in the Lady Ynevena's pleasure garden.

Elves didn't own slaves...everyone knew that. Just as everyone knew that dwarves never left their caves or undertook pursuits forbidden by their lawgivers. Just as everyone knew orcs were nothing more than pitiless, mindless, war-mongering beasts, or that children of power and privilege never ran away from that privilege in some blind, idiotic quest for independence or total reinvention. What was it that Torval himself had said to the elven ethnarch? *There are wormy apples on every tree in the orchard.* Maybe it was true that elves, by and large, weren't the sorts to keep slaves. But there were those rare rotten apples, weren't there?

Aemon's bones, hadn't they even met that rarest of rare birds, an elven merchant who lived and worked among men in a sprawling city with nary a forest or placid lake in sight? Where else but in Yenara—

And then, almost at once, Rem thought he understood. When Torval asked his next question, Rem suspected he knew the answer.

"Who runs this place?" Torval demanded.

The prisoner shook his head. "He'll have my soul. I can't—"

Torval bent down and snatched the man up by his tunic. "I'll have your head!" Torval growled, "But not before I've taken you apart from the feet up! Who is he? Who's the rotten son of a whore in charge around here?"

"It's Masarda, isn't it?" Rem asked. "Mykaas Masarda."

Torval turned and stared at him, mouth agape.

So did the prisoner, as though Rem's speaking aloud that name would doom them all.

"You know the fauneys practice black magic," he whispered, his hysteria suddenly bound by pure terror. "When he finds out that I betrayed him..."

Rem turned to Torval, eyes wide. "Did you hear that? Almost exactly what Joss said to Frennis before he fed him to the sharks! 'He'll kill you for this, Frennis. He'll not just have your skin, he'll have your soul.'"

Torval stared at the prisoner, nodding. "Because everyone assumes those bloody tree huggers wield magic of some sort or another..."

"Who is this Masarda?" Hirk demanded.

Rem threw a glance at Hirk. "You know him," Rem said. "We all know him."

Torval dropped the man. He studied Rem. "He was the one who came to us with news of Telura Dall's disappearance," Torval said, "offering that reward. How did you come to that conclusion, Bonny Prince?"

Rem nodded to the man on the floor. "What he said about their ultimate destination is a good start. Could anyone but an elf peddle kidnapped slaves to other elves? And then there's the presence of his bodyguard, downstairs. The same man that I just crossed swords with in the common room stood by Masarda's side at the Dall wake, and tried to kill us while we slept earlier today. I saw the wound on his arm plainly."

Torval's eyes widened. "Did you now...?"

"Think of your own words to me, Torval: there are all sorts under the sun—and wormy apples on every tree. If his thorning scar is a sign that he was once a slave, wouldn't enslaving the sons and daughters of the very people that stole his life and identity from him make for a fine revenge?"

Torval seemed to quietly consider all that for a moment. "Aye," he finally whispered. "That would be a fine vengeance, indeed."

"Care to place coin on the fact that he was Lugdum's unnamed master? That that poor creature was only following us—and finally threatened us—because Masarda commanded him to?"

Torval nodded. "Makes sense..."

Hirk shook his head. "The sundry hells it does—"

Rem ignored their sergeant and knelt beside the prisoner. "Which wharf?" he asked.

The knave only bawled and bled. A rope of pink, bloody

snot hung from one nostril. His probing tongue found a tooth rolling loosely around in his mouth and he spit it out.

"Which wharf?" Rem demanded.

The fellow had no words left.

And that's when the door to their erstwhile interrogation room burst open. Standing outside was a familiar copper-haired fellow standing beside a scowling Ondego. Frennis had arrived. Rem said a tiny prayer that there were no sharks at hand for this suspect to be fed to.

"What the bloody hell is all this?" the prefect of the Fourth demanded.

Hirk looked to Ondego. Ondego shrugged.

"Interrogation," Hirk said. "Sir."

"Give us five more minutes, Frennis," Ondego asked. "I'd give you the same, and you know it."

Frennis's glaring eyes locked on Rem and Torval. "These two again? Twice in one night?"

Torval scowled back at Frennis, never mind that the prefect of the Fourth was twice his height and twice his mass. "Perhaps if you'd helped us the first time..."

"Shut it," Ondego said, but there was no urgency in the order, just a weary hope that Torval would not make things worse.

Frennis's glare became a foul, cruel smile. He turned to Ondego. "I'll be going to Black Mal with this, Ondego—you can count on it. If you're lucky, he'll only strip you of your badge and your command."

That challenge didn't sit well with Ondego. At first, Rem had clearly read the weary resignation on the prefect's face—clearly saw that Ondego was not interested in challenging Frennis, but simply in controlling the amount of damage done by their interference with ward protocol. But that threat from

Frennis had a different effect—an unexpected effect—than what Rem wagered Frennis intended.

On the floor, the suspect continued to cry and whimper. He displayed his hand for the two prefects and asked for the aid of a surgeon. Torval kicked him in the gut and stole his breath.

Rem, meanwhile, watched his commander closely. Ondego, though a good handbreadth shorter than Frennis, hove up nose to nose with his rival prefect and glared right back at him.

"Last time I checked, we had taken the same oaths and were fighting the same nightly war," Ondego said through gnashed teeth. "I beg your sincere pardon for the suspension of protocol, but now that we know what we're dealing with—"

"And just what is that?" Frennis pressed. "Do tell, Ondego."

Ondego almost answered in full, then Rem saw the change come over him. The decision to challenge the burly prefect; the decision to interrogate him, right here in front of everyone.

"I think you know all too well," Ondego said quietly. "And I swear to you, I *will* prove it."

Rem studied Frennis carefully. The prefect's face remained stony, cross, inscrutable, but Rem thought he saw the barest hint of something hitherto unseen. A frightened narrowing of the eyes. A twitch at the corner of Frennis's wide mouth.

Finally, the big man turned and surveyed the interrogation room again. He spoke calmly, quietly. "Looks like you've overstayed your welcome. I want you and your men out of here, now."

"Frennis, don't you dare—"

"Take it up with Black Mal and come back to me with a mandate," Frennis hissed. "Until then, get out of my ward and leave all your prisoners with my men."

Ondego snapped his fingers. "Out. All of you. Leave him."

Rem rose and followed his fellows out of the room. As he

left, he heard the suspect mewling and trying to weakly hawk a ball of phlegm out of his throat.

As they approached the stairs, Torval hurried up abreast of Ondego.

"Mykaas Masarda," he said flatly. "Sailing off with the dawn."

"Then we'll find him," Ondego said quietly, "and we'll burn his ship down around him."

CHAPTER TWENTY-SEVEN

Rem was relieved to find that Aarna was alive and well, waiting in the common room under the watchful eye of some of their fellow Fifth Warders, but he was equally a little ashamed to realize that, after running off to Torval's aid, he had completely forgotten that she was present or that she might need protecting. Before Rem could inquire after her of his own accord, however, Torval rushed to her and lifted her up in a crushing bear hug, eliciting a scream of surprise from her. Thankfully, she seemed unscathed and grateful for the excitement.

Soon enough, Ondego and Hirk were leading their men out of the Moon Under Water, moving the lot of them southeastward, toward the border of the Fourth and Second Wards, their pace quick and deliberate.

As they marched, Ondego and his executive officer made plans, plans that Rem overheard because he and Torval stayed close on their commander's heels the whole way. Ondego would take half the Fifth Warders present with him, to double-time it across the city and approach North Harbor from the landward side. Meanwhile, Hirk and the rest would hurry down to the Third Ward wharves and cross the harbor in launches. Ondego wagered that by the time his men were in place on the landward side, Hirk and his men could have Masarda's ship in their sights. The squads in their launches then need only wait for the landward forces to storm the berthed ship.

It was there, on the borders of two wards, as the men of the Fifth separated and sped to their separate duties, that Aarna quickly offered both Torval and Rem kisses of gratitude and farewell, then separated from them and headed back toward the King's Ass. Rem left Indilen's secretary set in Aarna's keeping, voicing the not-too-convincing hope that, if they yet found her alive, he wanted it returned to her. Aarna offered a smile full of silent assurance: they would find her, that smile said. All would end well. Rem wasn't sure he believed that, but he appreciated Aarna's uncanny and sincere ability to make him think he believed it, if only for a fleeting moment.

If he was not mistaken, he thought he saw Torval looking like a love-struck pup as they watched Aarna begin her stroll back to her tavern and home.

But the lovesickness afflicting both of them, man and dwarf, would have to wait. Presently, they had more pressing concerns, and Rem had every intention of being involved in the reckoning to come, one way or another. Having seen what Masarda and his conspirators had done to those they had taken prisoner in the Moon Under Water, he could not countenance the thought of not being instrumental in the pointy-eared bastard's swift seizure and punishment. Truth be told, if there was a killing blow to be struck, he half-hoped he might be the one to strike it.

And what of Indilen? Would she still be among the prisoners awaiting transfer, or had her ship already sailed? If she was already gone, what were their real chances of ever finding and recovering her again?

Comport yourself as if you will find her, Rem told himself, *as if you must find her.* Let nothing shake your resolve.

"Hurry now," Torval said, and Rem suddenly realized that he was standing idle, lost in his thoughts, while the rest of their company jogged down toward the wharf. Rem fell in step behind them.

Thus, Hirk led Torval, Rem, and the remaining men at his disposal down to the docks of the southern harbor, where they piled into four commandeered launches and began a swift, silent glide across the waters toward the quayside wharf where Masarda's ship with its odious cargo prepared to sail.

Their crossing, to Rem's eager spirit, was painfully slow. Surely, their transit from one harbor to its neighbor would take no more than a half to three-quarters of an hour—relatively swift, Rem supposed, since every man in the launch—he included—worked an oar. But that did not settle him. His blood was up. His mind was fevered. His heart was eager. He wanted this bloody business to be done with. He wanted every one of those prisoners yanked out of their barrels and safe. He wanted Indilen to know that even if she never wanted to see him again, someone had cared enough to seek her out and find her and make sure she was safe. In the same circumstances, Rem would have wanted as much.

But here, now, all that he could concentrate on was the infernal slowness of their glide across the waters of South Harbor and the fog-shrouded river toward North Harbor on the far side. All he could seem to think of was how soon the sun would rise, how soon the tide would bear Masarda and his unlucky cargo out of the harbor and beyond their reach forever.

He felt a heavy hand on his shoulder. It was Torval's.

"Too fast," the dwarf said quietly. "You're out of step with the rest of us."

Rem nodded. "Sorry," he said over his shoulder, as quietly as he could. "I'm just...eager."

"We all are," Torval answered, and there was a curious warmth in his voice. "Just bend to your oar, lad, and get in step with the rest of us. We'll spill blood soon enough."

Rem did as he was told. Strangely, he found comfort in the regular rhythms of lifting and drawing his oar, doing his part to move the launch across the swift current of the Embrys.

Soon enough—far sooner than Rem expected—they passed Gaunt's Point, the spit of land that marked the mouth of North Harbor. Almost as soon as it had materialized out of the fog, the point receded back into it again and they were once more in diaphanous darkness.

Then, slowly, the dim light of torches and lamps material-ized out of the inky-night mists, gradually painting the outline of the smuggler's ship for them, complete with the distant echo of barked orders from the first mate and a flurry of movement upon its decks. It was a sixty-foot caravel, double-masted, tied to a hundred-foot dock with no other berths in use. In the fog the lights of torches and lamps from the deck of the ship made strange, bright blotches on the face of the murky night, and the forms that moved on deck took on a dreamlike quality, drifting like ghosts, casting strange, deformed shadows on the curtains of mist that separated the approaching watchwardens from their quarry.

Hirk received orders from the captain of the launch—a salty bargeman impressed into service with the wardwatch and seemingly enjoying the excitement—and relayed them to Rem and Torval.

"They answered our signal lamps," he whispered, "so they're already in place and ready. We'll approach from the ship's star-board side, grapple on, and climb over the gunwales onto the deck. We'll be the first party to reveal ourselves. When the crew tries to cut and run along the dock, Ondego's squad will be waiting for them."

Rem and Torval nodded their assent. It seemed like a sound-enough plan, though Rem was more than a little troubled by the notion of trying to slide up alongside that berthed ship and clamber over the gunwale on a grappling line like a pirate. He supposed it was a good thing that his father had insisted, all those years ago, that he learn to swim. At least if he fell into the waters of the harbor, he knew he wouldn't drown.

Although, there were always the sharks to contend with. After devouring Ginger Joss, the sea beasts might have decided that they had a taste for redheads.

Oh well. Nothing for it now. In for copper, in for gold, as the sages said. All he could hope to do now was to acquit himself bravely and uphold the honor of his ward. If he died, he died in a cause of his own choosing, at the time of his own choosing—the master of his own destiny. Perhaps, just perhaps, what he did now could save Indilen—or one of the many prisoners in the same predicament.

There was some comfort—however small—in that thought.

The launches slid closer, closer. Though it was neither the largest nor the handsomest vessel Rem had ever seen, the caravel nonetheless had a hulking, imposing quality, a great, looming leviathan of wood, hemp, and canvas all alone in the middle of the darkness, ghostly figures moving on its deck, a terrible, living cargo in its hold. The closer they got, the steeper and higher those gunwhales seemed. Climbing them would be no mean feat.

Now they were less than fifty feet from the ship's starboard side, all of them crouched low in the keels of their launches, oars shipped to allow them to silently drift the last, short span between them and their destination. As the overloaded launches skated nearer, the watchwardens all held their breath, afraid that, so close to the ship, any movement, any minute sound, could give them away and ruin their advantage. The lead men of each launch readied grappling hooks on stout hemp ropes. The ship's hull loomed perilously nearer and nearer in Rem's vision...

Then, someone up on deck gave a shout. Another answered it. The crew had spotted movement on the dock. The light above shifted, torches and lamps shuttled portside to improve visibility. Then, Rem heard the call.

"Wardwatch on the docks, boys! It's a raid!"

Damn. Ondego's band had been discovered. Rem thought he heard the twang of a bowstring, followed by a sudden shout and the sound of something heavy hitting the deck. After that, there came the bellicose hiss of steel drawn from scabbards and a rebellious whoop from the sailors on deck.

"So much for surprise," one of Rem's companions muttered, then tossed his grappling hook up over the gunwale above. He yanked his rope taut and the hook held fast. From the other launches, more grappling lines were tossed and couched. Rem felt someone tapping on his shoulder.

"Go!" they said. "Go now!"

Rem, without hesitation, grasped the hemp in his hands and began a mad scramble up the side of the caravel.

The climb seemed to take an eternity—though he was sure he had only drawn three or four breaths in the interval. He scurried over the gunwale, tripped, and nearly landed on his face. Rolling and regaining his feet, he saw that most of the crew were on the port side of the deck, repelling Ondego's boarding party, readying any advantage against them. One knot of sailors hauled a cauldron of steaming pitch toward the side to dump onto the invaders. Others scrambled out of the holds with surplus cutlasses, pikes, and any other hand tool capable of being used as a weapon. With a quick glance, Rem saw that members of his own raiding party were already joining him on deck. He might have been the first over the gunwale, but he was no longer alone.

Then he saw their true quarry: Mykaas Masarda, face a mask of shock and fury, up on the aft deck. His Estavari bodyguard stood close by, fine sword already drawn. Master and servant watched the mad scramble on the port side of the ship as the hired crew hurried to repel the invading watchwardens from the dock.

Scanning the deck, the Estavari swordsman saw Rem and his fellow watchwardens newly arrived at the starboard gunwales, and drew his master's attention to them. Rem thought he saw Masarda's fair skin flush crimson, his fury rising.

"Behind you, you fools! There are more of them!"

They had been seen. When one of the sailors on deck shouted that there were boarders to starboard, Rem knew that their brief element of surprise had evaporated. Now they would only come out on top by force of arms. As his fellow watchwardens—including Torval and Hirk—fell in beside him, a number of the ship's crew crowding the port gunwales turned and studied the new arrivals at the starboard railings.

There was a long, pregnant moment when near silence reigned. Some of those at the port gunwale still busied themselves with repelling Ondego's dockside party while many of the rest simply studied the new arrivals starboard.

Then someone sounded a bloodcurdling yawp. War cries rose from both sides and the watchwardens and pirate crew charged toward one another, converging center-deck in a clash of swords and cutlasses, pikes and axes. In seconds, the deck was engulfed in bloody chaos, the watchwardens fighting with grim determination, the pirate crew answering them with savage efficiency and pure, brute strength. Everywhere there were blood, screams, and the sounds of men mortally wounded and slowly dying. Rem said a little prayer to the gods that, if his end were upon him, it might come quickly, in the heat of battle, and leave him no time to lie bleeding and contemplate what had gone wrong, how unfair his death might be, what rewards or punishments might come next.

Rem had never been in a pitched battle before, but now here he was, right in the heart of one. And on a ship's deck, no less! What would his father think of him now, seeing him blade to blade with ruddy-faced Loffmari and Thorian sailors, his sword flashing, swiping, and thrusting before him as he fought off clumsy attacks from men wielding clubs and swift, sure onslaughts from more skilled men with sabers or axes?

There seemed to be a great breadth of skill and experience among the sailors, but quickly Rem realized that none of his opponents could be underestimated. Every one was dangerous, desperate, willing to cut him down where he stood to secure safe passage out of that harbor. Thus, Rem did his best to silence his racing mind, to quell his rising fear, to simply exist in the bloody moment. He let his sword and his reflexes do his thinking, for if he stopped to consider what a perilous, chaotic juncture he'd come to, he might never regain the wherewithal to escape it.

Ondego's squad now stormed the port side of the ship, using grappling hooks and the tie ropes from the pilings to scramble over the gunwales and onto the deck. Men dueled with swords and spears. Rem caught sight of the Fifth Ward's single elven watchwarden—Queydon, was it?—slicing a deadly path through any and all who faced her, the elf maiden's sword hand and the elegant blade she wielded little more than a blur in the murky, misty darkness. Near him, Djubal and Klutch fought, back to back, as tight a pair of combat partners as Rem had ever seen. Knots of men brawled at the foot of both the main and mizzen masts, and when a few tried to flee to the forecastle, they found their way blocked by armed troops from Ondego's party, the watchwardens fanning out in wide formations to surround and fetter the desperate sailors.

Rem blocked an overhand strike from a lumbering, bearded Kosterman, then plunged his sword deep into his opponent's gut. The Kosterman's face screwed up terribly, the fair barbarian looking almost comically puzzled, then down he went. In the instant when his opponent fell, before anyone else engaged him, Rem stole a glance at the stern. Masarda lingered there, watching the chaos on deck with cold cunning and not a little satisfaction. But where, Rem wondered, was his Estavari bodyguard? He saw the master, but not the servant.

Rem searched the melee and caught sight of him, his familiar opponent hurrying down the steps from the stern deck to the main deck, dark eyes fixed on Rem.

Strangely, in that moment, Rem felt no fear, only a strange sort of elation.

Come on, then, he thought.

Not content to wait for his adversary to reach him, Rem began to hack and slash his way through the roiling fray.

This is no game, he reminded himself, closing in. *If he wins, you die. It's as simple as that.*

So, I shall simply have to win.

"Where are you off to?" Torval shouted from Rem's left.

Rem stole a quick sideward glance. The dwarf was surrounded, bloodthirsty sailors nearly encircling him, armed and murderous. Torval stood on guard, unafraid, with a deck hatchet in one hand and his maul in the other. He looked more than equal to the men threatening him. Rem swung his gaze forward again and found his approaching adversary, now just a stone's throw from him.

But Rem couldn't leave Torval, could he? The dwarf was his partner, facing down a six-on-one battle with deadly stakes. True, the little bastard was probably delighted by those odds— but as much as Rem wanted to carry on and enter his deadly duel with Masarda's Estavari bodyguard, he knew, also, that he could not abandon his partner. Torval, he imagined, would do the same for him.

And so, Rem fell in on Torval's right, sword leveled, ready to join the impending brawl. Torval's opponents seemed to sour when they realized that they wouldn't be ganging up on the dwarf alone.

Torval gave a gruff laugh. "Now we get to see just how good you are with that blade," Torval growled.

"Just remember to save a few for me," Rem countered. "You grandstanding little shit."

Two of the closing sailors charged, one going for Torval, the other coming right at Rem. Part of Rem wanted to watch Torval work in the heat of battle—his speed, his assurance, his ferocity—but Rem knew that his own opponent should be his only concern. Smooth as flowing water, his sword rose and fell, glided side to side, parried, blocked, thrust, and slashed. In moments, after trading equal, well-matched blows with his opponent—a determined, near-toothless Loffmari with a cutlass—Rem managed to find an opening. He thrust. His sword point sank deep into his opponent's gut, probably skewering the cur's liver. The Loffmari crumpled to the deck, groaning—and on came another crewman, this one looking as though he hailed from the Far East, skin the color of copper, hair as black as pitch. The Easterner wielded a pilot's hatchet, and did so with deadly efficiency. Rem, enjoying only a momentary victor's rush, immediately fell back a step to better situate himself, then began his contest.

Beside him, Torval repelled all comers. Rem only got glimpses from the corner of his eye as he fought, but it was clear that nothing could stop the ferocious little dwarf once he let his inner berserker out of its cage. The hatchet whistled, the maul rang. Blade bit flesh as hammer and spike shattered bones, dislocated limbs, dashed blood and brains onto the gently rolling deck of the moored ship. As Rem downed his second opponent, Torval was tearing into his fourth—the little crowd around the two of them growing by the moment. It was as if their determined teamwork and Torval's savagery actually attracted opponents instead of scaring them away. Every time one more man fell to their blades, another seemed close at hand to take his place.

Then, through the pandemonium, Rem saw a familiar figure. It was Masarda's bodyguard, skirting the fringe of the little crowd of would-be challengers surrounding them. His sword and poniard were drawn and he was clearly studying Rem's every move. He paced with a tigerlike mix of patience and presentiment, watching intently as Rem drove his knee into his latest opponent's groin, bent him double, then sent him sprawling to the deck with a blunt blow from the pommel of his sword.

Would he join the fight or wouldn't he?

Would he assume that Rem was sufficiently distracted by the stream of challengers and flee?

Or was he just waiting for Rem to grow tired?

That was it, Rem wagered. The sailors came, one after another, with their bale hooks and their hand hatchets and their rusted, long-unused cutlasses. Rem fought them, one after another after another, and each took a little more out of him.

He could not sustain such a furious pace under such deadly circumstances. Already he could feel his limbs growing sore and stiff, his breath grating in his chest, his movements growing less fluid, more ragged, often desperate and wild.

If Rem allowed these fools who kept challenging him to take the best out of him, he wouldn't survive two minutes against Masarda's sellsword. He had to challenge the villain here and now, while he still had all his wits and most of his strength remaining.

So Rem brought the cross guard of his sword sweeping up into the face of his present opponent—a freckled young wretch with horrible breath. The boy's nose crunched sickeningly and blood poured from his nostrils. Down he went, limp as a sack of onions, and Rem made straight for the waiting Estavari bravo. On his approach, he snatched up a discarded cutlass from the deck: his opponent wasn't the only one with two-handed fencing experience.

The oily Estavari smiled when he saw Rem snatch up the cutlass, then fell into a defensive posture, front leg poised, back leg bent, forward hand holding his dueling poniard, back hand leveling his sword along his eye line.

Rem took a guarded stance of his own. For a moment, the two stood still, sizing each other up.

"Are you sure you want to do this?" the Estavari asked, his voice almost friendly. "I'll neither beg nor bestow quarter."

"Stop talking," Rem answered, "and have at me."

The Estavari obliged. Instantly, his blades flashed forth, poniard jabbing uncomfortably close to Rem's face, forcing Rem to lean backward as his opponent's sword blade thrust forth toward Rem's exposed shoulder. In midretreat, Rem managed a clumsy parry followed by a weak reprise, but his blow touched only air. The Estavari gave him a breath to recover, then followed with a savage eruption, blades slicing the air around Rem, sharp points and keen edges seeking Rem's joints and kill zones, pressing all advantages, chipping away at Rem's defenses and confidence with surgical precision and ferocious, merciless intensity.

Steel sang and clamored as the two fell into the rhythm of their duel. The Estavari was good—marvelously so—and it took every ounce of self-control and focus that Rem was capable of to meet and counter his attacks. Rem drew blood once or twice—a cut here, a glancing thrust there—but soon enough, Rem feared that the Estavari had the advantage. He was faster, more assured, and he had joined the duel fresh, whereas Rem had already been fighting for his life for an interminable span before the two ever touched blades. Increasingly, Rem noted that his own movements grew wanton and careless, and that his opponent, emboldened by that fact, affirmed his supremacy by affecting ever more detachment from their contest. His delighted smirk had disappeared, and if Rem was not mistaken, the bastard wasn't even sweating. Rem's eagerness to meet his smug nemesis sword to sword had long ago been replaced by an abiding hope of slipping away when his enemy wasn't looking and living to a ripe old age.

Time and again, as the Estavari's blades licked close to Rem's bare flesh or vital bits, Rem had grim visions of the outcome to this contest. He could not win against this man. He had been a fool to test himself so. Rem would end the night on the deck, one more corpse, bleeding out, fading away. No doubt, he'd have the same surprised, embarrassed look on his face that all men seemed to adopt when slain without warning.

No. He couldn't give in to that sort of despair. That was how duels were lost. Just as his father's master-at-arms had taught him, Rem had to drive away the desire for a given outcome—*the lust of result*, he used to call it. There was only the moment. Only necessity, opportunity. As Rem parried yet another blow that thrust too near to his exposed throat, then blocked a feint from the Estavari's poniard that dove for his right flank, he pressed all desire and hope away from himself. There could be no hoped-for outcome, no preferred end: there was only blocking the Estavari's attacks and launching attacks of his own. Thrust, parry, feint, block, riposte. Lunge, thrust, block, retreat. Back and forth they went, the two of them oblivious to the chaos and bloodshed all around them, two contestants locked in a contest for the ultimate prize: life itself.

And miraculously, Rem once more seemed to gain some advantage, however tenuous. He blocked three thrusts, then drew blood from his opponent's left flank with a hasty pass of his own. The Estavari's apparent shock at that reversal gave Rem an instant that he exploited. He pressed his opponent, driving him back with a series of fierce blows in succession from both short sword and cutlass. Back and back the hired swordsman retreated. On Rem came, determined to press his coup until he could land another cutting blow.

Success! Rem saw that the retreating Estavari was just about to run into a fallen corpse on the deck. If Rem could press him, send him tumbling backward over that fallen sailor, then Rem might have a chance.

Then something heavy slammed into Rem from the left—a wardwatchman, reeling from a broad, bloody wound across his middle. From the corner of his eye, Rem saw this wounded ally, hands pressed to his bleeding gash, too stunned to watch where he was stumbling. He and Rem fell in a tangle of limbs and curses and hit the deck hard. When Rem landed, both swords went clattering from his hands. Indifferent to the wounded watchwarden's groans, Rem kicked free of the fellow's bent frame and tried to scramble for one of his fallen blades.

The Estavari charged as Rem dove. The bravo drove his own sword's point right into the deck before Rem's grasping hand. Rem managed to draw his hand back just in time, nearly losing his fingers. His sword was out of reach. The Estavari—and his very deadly blades—stood between him and it.

Rem raised his eyes. The bravo lowered his sword point to Rem's throat. The blade lingered, sharp and deadly.

"It was a good contest," the bravo said, smirk returning, his tone almost wistful. "When next I drink, I'll drink to you, lad."

CHAPTER TWENTY–EIGHT

Rem prepared to feel the cold bite of the bravo's blade in his throat, the sudden outrush of hot blood and the quick ebb of life into the cold darkness of death. Above him, the bravo drew back his blade and prepared for the killing thrust.

Then a small bulky form came soaring out of the fray, describing a long, shallow arc through the air toward Rem's would-be killer. It was Torval. He held a battle-ax—newly acquired from a fallen foe, no doubt—and with both of his thick, strong hands he brought the blade crashing down.

The blade bit deep into the bravo's skull from behind, cleaving his black-haired head in two, the weight of the blow and Torval's falling form driving the bravo's suddenly rag-limp body to the deck right on top of Rem. Rem cowered and closed his eyes as the dead man, the deadly blade, and the tumbling dwarf all plunged toward him. A moment later, Rem was crushed under the weight of two bodies and felt hot blood sheeting over his face. He opened his eyes and saw the dead man's staring eyes and the leading edge of Torval's blade just an inch from the tip of his own nose.

From atop the fallen bravo, Torval sat up.

Rem blinked.

Torval yanked on the ax handle. The blade stuck fast in the bravo's skull, so it brought the whole limp body with it. Torval shoved the corpse aside, and Rem was suddenly free, albeit covered in his would-be murderer's blood.

Torval offered Rem a hand. "On your feet, lad. This bloody business isn't over yet."

Rem took Torval's hand and found his feet again. Quickly, he snatched up his fallen sword and studied his slain adversary.

"Pity," Rem said. "I really think I had him."

Torval gave a grim smirk, then reached behind himself and drew out his maul, which was tucked in his belt at the small of his back. "Thank me later, then, when you've come to your senses."

Rem surveyed the deck quickly. The watch was winning, only a few belligerent pirates and crewmen still in the fight, the rest stone-dead on the deck, nursing wounds, or already bound and ready for incarceration. They had not won the night yet, but all apparent signs pointed to a rapidly approaching victory.

"Rem, lad! At the stern!" Torval shouted, and pointed toward the aft deck. Rem followed Torval's pointing finger and immediately saw what had Torval so agitated.

Masarda, seeing his bodyguard cold on the deck and the tide of battle turning in the watchmen's favor, was slinking toward the port side of the ship, a look of angry panic on his thin, pale face.

Masarda was making a run for it.

In silent accord, Rem and Torval gave chase.

The chaos on the deck around them was still thick, despite the fact that the standing watchwardens now outnumbered their still-fighting adversaries. Rem could have sworn that when they boarded, he counted no more than twenty sailors on deck. But more had been waiting, perhaps in the hold, perhaps in the rigging, for there were certainly just as many joined in the fray at the present moment, while almost two score—sailors and watchwardens—lay scattered around, lifeless or nursing wounds or trying to keep from being stepped on by their battling compatriots.

As Rem and Torval wove a zigzagging path through the calamity, they were nearly skewered, axed, speared, bludgeoned, chain-whipped, and tackled. They pressed on, nonetheless, intent on being drawn no further into the melee. They had their eyes on their quarry: Mykaas Masarda, the villain whom all this bitter business hinged upon, who even now hurried down the stern-deck stairs, made his way along the port gunwale of the caravel, then, when the moment was right, leapt over the rail and down onto the pier. Rem and Torval reached the gunwale mere moments behind him. Down below, Masarda had landed hard and rolled. He now regained his feet, and dashed off toward the darkness that was shrouding the storehouses and customs stations beyond the pier along the waterfront. Rem knew well that if Masarda reached those dark labyrinths with any considerable lead on them, he would probably escape.

Torval didn't hesitate. Short or no, the dwarf leapt right up onto the gunwale, then launched himself into space. He landed square on his feet, making a loud thud, as though someone had dropped a heavy chest laden with gold and lead, then took off in a sprint after their suspect. Rem hove himself over the gunwale and followed.

The world grew strangely quiet as the turbulence and tumult of the battle on the ship's deck dwindled and the torchlight and lamplight of the ship's deck receded. The tenebrous fog that shrouded the waterfront engulfed them. All Rem heard was the thumping of their feet as they ran, the pounding of his own thudding heart in his ears. Rem saw Torval about fifty feet ahead of him, and beyond Torval, the fleeing Masarda, his rich silk and velvet robes flowing behind him like a harlequin cloak. The elven flesh peddler seemed to be angling toward a broad, ill-lit alley between two customhouses.

"Torval!" Rem called. "Don't let him—"

"I know!" the dwarf shouted back over his shoulder, never breaking stride.

The darkness swallowed Masarda. Rem couldn't believe how thick, how palpable that darkness seemed to be. One moment the elf was there, fleeing; the next, he was gone, swallowed by the lurid, lightless abyss between the two looming customhouses. Pounding nearer, Rem thought he saw the elf's furtive form moving fleetly among stacked crates and scattered detritus in the dark alleyway, but he couldn't be sure.

Ahead of him, the same darkness swallowed Torval.

Damn! Both of them vanished, swallowed by the shadows! Rem summoned a little more strength, a little more speed, and went hurtling into the malign darkness after them. When the murk swallowed him, Rem dug in his heels and scuffed to a halt. Everything was indistinct and still, the world around him a sinister patchwork of gray blacks and blue blacks sewn onto and thrown into relief against even deeper blacks. The walls of the customhouses rose on either side of him, baleful and ominous. What he thought might be empty crates and discarded pallets littered the darkness like the bones of old mammoths and dragons strewn on a blasted, moonless moor. Not only was he very nearly blind, he was also moving into a narrow passage cluttered with obscured obstacles, replete with places to hide or from which to mount an ambush.

And Rem guessed that an elf, even one no longer capable of using his mind alone to communicate, probably had better night vision than he.

He heard heavy footsteps ahead and off to his right, but no answer came.

Rem drew a breath. Blinked. His eyes were adjusting to the darkness, but it availed him little. He just saw the crowded world before him in more subtle shades of black and gray. When he finally decided to press on, he took three steps, then tripped over something that stretched and shifted with his passage. He caught himself before falling on his face, and felt what had caught him with his hands: it was a span of discarded fishing net, its hemp coarse and dry from long abandonment. Rem managed to stand and tried to disentangle himself. He freed one leg, but the other held fast. When he finally managed to yank that leg free of the net's grip, he lost his balance and went tumbling backward into a heap of splintery old crates. Something atop one of the crates fell when he nudged it. When it hit the stony alley floor, it rang like metal, then thumped like wood.

"Poor, blind manling," a silky voice purred from some deep corner of the inky blackness.

It was Masarda, hiding somewhere in the shadows ahead, waiting for him. Rem tried to pinpoint where the voice came from, but his fear and the darkness made it impossible. Knowing that he needed some advantage—any advantage—Rem turned, used the crate as an anchor, and crouched toward where he'd heard the fallen object land. He felt about in the darkness. His hands finally found a long, slender shaft, damp and cold in the night air, pocked with rust. It was mounted atop a thick wooden pole.

That's what he had knocked over when he thumped into this crate, then: an old whaler's harpoon.

"I should warn you, boy, that you have no hope of besting me, hand to hand or blade to blade. One of my owners saw little value in me as a laborer, but ample opportunity for me as blade fodder in the blood-sport ring. No one was more sur-

prised or delighted than he when I survived that first match—
and almost two dozen thereafter."

Rem let his fingers slide along the harpoon's length, seeking
its spear tip. The shaft was old and rusted, slightly bent, but the
tip still felt somewhat sharp, deadly enough. Rem decided that
in such close quarters, unable to see anything around him, it
might be a good idea to have a throwaway weapon that could
work equally well as both a wide block and a leverage against
bodily attacks. Thus, he lifted the old harpoon, couched it in
his grip like a spear, and regained his feet. He slowly advanced
into the inky night, his sword swinging in its scabbard at
his hip.

"I earned my freedom with blood, boy—can you say the
same?"

"I thought elves were a silent folk," Rem snapped in
response. "Shut your mouth and make your move, if you're so
bloody dangerous."

Surely Masarda heard the trembling in his voice, the fear
underlying the bravado, even if being thorned meant he
could no longer read minds. Rem couldn't even fool himself
into thinking he wasn't worried about the outcome of this
misadventure.

"Quake in fear, Watchman. Your time will come."

Rem moved forward, caution making his legs stiff and his
feet heavy. "Torval?" he hissed, trying to locate his companion, finding no sign of him. Wan light seemed to bloom
above him and descend like slow-falling rain, drawing out the
contours and gilding the leading edges of the detritus littering the alleyway. For a moment, Rem wondered just what was
happening, then realized that, above them, the clouds must
have drifted, revealing the slim crescent moon that hung in
the sky and giving them, even through the considerable mists

that shrouded Yenara at this hour, some small increase in light. Something moved off to his right, fleet and low, and set his heart hammering in his chest. He swung the harpoon toward the moving shadow. When he blinked and tried to focus on its movement, he realized it was too low to the ground to be his elven adversary. It was only a stray cat, green eyes flashing in the dark.

"Tilting at phantoms," Masarda taunted. "Your dread is pitiful."

There was a quick, soft sound off to his left. A heavy foot crushing loose sand and gravel beneath its weight. Rem turned toward the sound and there, in the diaphanous darkness, he thought he saw his partner's low, broad form materializing out of the moon-silvered fog.

Rem fought the urge to say something, assuming that Torval, like most dwarves, had good enough night vision to know that his partner was just ahead of him. Of course, Torval could see him clearly, and would be at his side in moments—

Then steel whispered from a scabbard. In the murk, Rem saw a lithe figure separate itself from the deepest shadows and spring toward Torval. Only the sudden movement of the two figures drew them out of the darkness and made them distinct in Rem's vision. Rem thought he saw the flash of steel in the moonlight and cried out, barely able to help himself.

"Torval, behind you!"

The dwarf half turned, but Masarda was already on him. The long, curved dagger in the elf's hand flashed—its blade clearly visible because it caught the pallid moonlight—and dug deep into Torval's muscled flank. Torval roared, enraged, and Rem saw the maul in the dwarf's hand rise for a killing blow.

But Masarda had the advantage. His lithe form swung behind the dwarf, out of the path of his maul, as he simultaneously twisted the knife in Torval's side. Torval's maul fell to the ground with a ferrous clatter. Rem charged toward them, bent and rusted old harpoon ready. As he neared, he realized that there was another blade in Masarda's second hand. That blade hovered at Torval's throat. Both figures were still.

Rem edged closer, blinking. He held the harpoon low, ready for an underhand thrust. He tried to get a better image of the two shadowy figures before him, but they were little more than moon-edged silhouettes, just like everything else in the alleyway: ghosts of themselves, half-effaced by gloom and fog.

Nonetheless, Rem thought he saw precisely what was unfolding. Masarda was behind Torval, crouching a little so that the dwarf's short, broad body protected his own. One slender elven hand kept the first dagger planted in Torval's left flank, just below his ribs, while the other hand held a similar curved blade to Torval's thick throat, ready to slice it at a moment's notice. Although Rem could not be sure, he thought he caught the glitter of Masarda's almond-shaped elven eyes in the shadows, studying him, daring him to edge closer.

"Another step," the elf said, "and the Stump dies."

Rem did not drop the harpoon, but he did raise a single hand in deference.

"Drop the harpoon, clumsy weapon though it is," Masarda said. "I want both of your hands where I can see them."

Rem nodded. "Fine," he said, "just don't—"

"Don't you do it, lad," Torval growled.

"Quiet!" Masarda hissed, jerking the hovering blade closer to Torval's throat and digging the other deeper into the dwarf's flank.

Everything that happened next happened quickly.

Rem saw Torval, still howling from the pain of that twisted knife in his side, pivot and wrench away from Masarda's grip.

One thick-fingered hand rose, grasped the arm holding the dagger close to Torval's own throat, and yanked. Masarda tried to compensate and return the dagger to its previous position, ready to cut Torval's throat and bleed him like a pig, but the moment gained by Torval yanking the dagger away was enough. Torval sounded a low, bellowing battle cry, bent forward, then jerked his head backward with all the force he could muster. Rem heard Masarda's nose break, saw moonlight glinting on a sudden rush of blood sheeting down the elf's long, narrow face.

Then Torval collapsed. Masarda stood unprotected, a clear target.

Rem's instincts seized him. He lifted the harpoon, took the length of a single, in-drawn breath to aim down the slightly bent shaft, then hove the awkward iron-and-wood pike as hard as he could. The harpoon sailed in a long, flat arc. There was a grunt, a groan, then Masarda's legs folded beneath him.

Rem rushed forward. Torval, nearer to the fallen elf, rolled toward him and disarmed him, clumsily swiping each dagger from Masarda's grip in turn. Rem blinked, trying to get a good look at Masarda in the dark. If he was not mistaken, the elf's eyes were still open wide. His face was covered in a glut of shiny black blood, all gushing from his newly broken nose. The harpoon had skewered him just below the ribs, passing through cleanly and gleaming out the far side of him. It probably hurt like the sundry hells, but it didn't look like a killing wound.

At least, not right away.

"Your whistle," Torval said.

"What?" Rem asked.

"Your whistle," Torval said again, weak and wheezing. There was agony in the dwarf's voice, and the sound of that agony gave Rem a terrible fright. "Blow your whistle."

Rem suddenly realized that Torval was talking about the little brass whistle that Rem wore—that *all* the watchwardens wore—about his neck. He reached into his shirt to fetch it.

That's when Torval exhaled a long, rattling breath and seemed to go limp on the dirty floor of the alleyway.

Rem blew his whistle. The sound was shrill and vulgar in the still night air. Moments later, he started screaming. Amid the pounding of bootheels coming nearer and voices crying out in the dark, he thought he also heard Mykaas Masarda laughing where he lay.

CHAPTER TWENTY-NINE

A party arrived with torches. There was Ondego, along with the silver-haired healer that Rem did not know by name, and a few other Fifth Warders. Under the undulating glare of their torches, Rem could finally see that Torval's face was ashen, that the pool of blood spreading beneath him was large and growing larger. Torval's blood looked black in the torchlight. The sight of it made Rem feel ill and helpless, like a child.

Ondego took charge of the scene instantly. He set three of the watchwardens on Masarda, to heave him to his feet, bind him, and see him quickly back to the dockside. Then, with the quick, sure hands and eyes of a surgeon, Ondego rolled Torval over to get a better look at his wound. It was deep, still seeping dark blood. Rem imagined the dwarf's liver had probably been punctured. If that was the case...

"Minniver?" Ondego asked, addressing the mage.

The very same healer that had mended Sliviwit's broken ankle that evening in the watchkeep slid forward. She had an air of assurance and confidence about her that set Rem at ease a little: her eyes were deep, dark pools of indigo and her mouth never betrayed emotion, be it fear or concern or even undue pride. Her young, smooth face and mane of silver hair were alien and incongruous, making it impossible for Rem to guess her age. As he watched, she examined Torval's bleeding wound, then gave a curt nod.

"I think I can save him," Minniver said, then looked to Ondego again. "But I need someone to draw from."

Ondego looked to Rem.

Rem blinked. "Draw...?"

"His life force is dwindling as he bleeds out," Minniver said, never taking her eyes off Torval's wound. "I need to take life from elsewhere to give his body enough energy to close the wound and start replenishing his blood supply."

"Take life...?" Rem repeated dumbly.

Minniver threw a cold glare at him. "Will you or won't you? You're young and strong, so you're the best—"

"I'll do it," Rem interrupted. "Just tell me what I need to do."

Minniver took one of Rem's hands in one of hers, then placed her free hand on Torval's bleeding wound. The dwarf groaned a little, but barely stirred. He was right at the edge of consciousness.

"Hold him still," Minniver told Ondego. "This will hurt."

Ondego held Torval's shoulders. Another watchman held his legs. They were ready.

Then it began.

It was the strangest feeling that Rem had ever known. As if he could feel the heat and vitality of his body—its most latent energies, so easily taken for granted—flowing away through his palm and his fingers into Minniver...flowing away and leaving him weak, cold, tingling all over as though he had just awakened from a too-long nap under a snow-capped tree. Rem felt himself start to tremble, felt his skin begin to prickle with moisture and gooseflesh.

Beneath Minniver's hands, Torval groaned and suddenly stiffened. Ondego and the watchman on Torval's legs both held him still. Clearly, something was happening, a pain that cut right through Torval's deathly stupor and snatched him back toward the surface of consciousness. Likewise, Minniver kept her hand pressed against the wound, never losing contact. Rem realized she was muttering something—incantations in an ancient tongue, no doubt some component of the magical transfusion ritual she was enacting.

Then Rem's vision started to fill with a broad, black cloud. Upon that cloud there were whirling stars and fireflies. He heard a buzzing in his ears.

"Prefect," he said, his voice sounding far away.

"He's going white," he heard Ondego say, also from far away.

"Just a moment longer," Minniver answered.

Torval suddenly howled in pain. Rem blinked away the fireflies for a moment and saw the dwarf's compact little body buck and arc. Then the darkness and the fireflies returned, and Rem felt himself drifting away again.

Finally, Minniver let go of him. That vague feeling of having something sucked away from him, something that his body needed and could not live without, subsided almost instantly. Despite the relief he felt, Rem couldn't help but collapse. He toppled backward onto the earthen floor of the alleyway and gulped air, desperate to regain his vision and his senses. Vaguely, he heard Ondego shouting at him from very far away, shouting his name and slapping something, again and again.

Ondego was slapping *him*. Once, twice, three times the prefect's rough hand whacked Rem's face. Rem felt a heat rising in his cheeks in response to the hard strikes, and found himself vaguely delighted that he could feel something again. When Ondego moved to strike him a fourth time, Rem raised one hand weakly.

"Please," he managed. "I'm here. I'm awake."

Ondego did something then that both encouraged and unnerved Rem: the hard-faced prefect smiled. It was a warm smile, a genuine smile, but seemed strangely out of place on Ondego's face. "Good lad," he said. "I knew you wouldn't desert us."

He helped Rem to sit upright. Rem's vision was finally clearing. In the torchlight, he saw Minniver bending over Torval. The dwarf lay on his side, his wound clearly visible.

Or rather, the place where his wound *had been* was clearly visible. There was still a great deal of blood smeared all about the lower part of Torval's flank and back, but if Rem's eyes did not deceive him, the dwarf's wound was now fully closed, marked only by a rough drawn-in patch of scar tissue. It looked like a wound that had been closed for weeks, not just moments. Minniver, for her part, was exhausted and haggard. Nonetheless, she attended Torval kindly, whispering to him, asking him how he felt and whether or not he thought he could sit up. Rem saw Torval nod, and then Minniver helped him sit. The dwarf was deathly pale, but there was something like the rose of life blooming in his cheeks once more, the light of life seeping back into his small blue eyes.

Rem lay there, held up by Ondego, staring at Torval, who was held up by Minniver. The young man and the dwarf smiled at each other.

"You look like the sundry hells warmed over," Torval croaked.

"You're welcome," Rem countered, and the two managed a round of weak, relieved laughter.

CHAPTER THIRTY

After a time, the watchwardens present helped Rem and Torval back onto their feet and led them—providing support along the way—back to the dock where Masarda's ship lay berthed. It felt like they had been here hours ago—days ago—but, in fact, they had only left the ship and taken chase after Masarda less than a half hour earlier. In that short span, Rem felt as if he had lived three or four lifetimes, and turned into someone he barely recognized any longer. Were such things truly possible?

The surviving members of the caravel's crew, now in custody, were being sorted by country of origin, so that their local ethnarchs could be contacted and, presumably, offered the option of arguing on their behalf. Rem guessed there would be no pardons for them—pirates and smugglers all—the sort of men who were often left to fend for themselves and find their own way through a cruel world, a harsh fact that only made them crueler. Meanwhile, Masarda himself was perched on an assemblage of barrels near where the pier met the quay. The harpoon had had to be delicately removed from his torso by a field surgeon while he'd been held by six watchmen whose job it was to keep him from floundering around in pain and at the same time prevent him from trying to make a run for it. Rem overheard someone say that an oxcart was on the way to collect the prisoners and take them back to the watchkeep. He suspected that he and the rest of his fellow watchwardens would feel safer when that finally occurred and this lot were all locked away in the same dungeon that Rem had inhabited just a few days ago.

Up on the deck of Masarda's caravel, Rem saw freed prisoners drifting among the watchwardens milling about on deck. The new arrivals were mostly young women, but there were young men among them as well. All were pale, haggard, and wandering about in a fog of confusion, but otherwise of generally attractive countenance.

"How many are there?" Rem asked. "How many survived?"

Ondego sighed. "Dozens," he said. "So far, we've extracted them all from their shipping barrels alive. Bless the Panoply for small favors, eh?"

Freed would-be slaves, all alive. Knowing that gave Rem a feeling of satisfaction he could not give words to. He had not simply helped his partner, and rendered honorable service to his ward, he had saved lives. Real, young, hopeful lives, forever altered because he and his fellow watchwardens did their duty and brought them out of peril safely.

It was a good feeling, better than any he had ever known.

Then Rem caught a glimpse of someone on the deck. A familiar face. Large brown eyes under disheveled auburn hair. Her high, pale cheekbones and fair, freckled skin were burnished gold by the light of the torches and lamps burning along the gunwales of the caravel. Could it be? Was he dreaming?

Rem stepped away from the two watchwardens who supported him. They protested, and he nearly stumbled, but then he caught himself and pressed on right toward the gangplank, climbing on shaky legs toward the deck. He was winded before he reached it, but nonetheless, he called out a name, hoping against hope that the apparition before him answered to it.

"Indilen!" he called.

The girl in his sights blinked and slowly turned toward the sound of her name. Rem said it again, louder. Her foggy eyes finally focused on him as he approached. For just a moment, the young lady looked confused, as though she were struggling to summon up a memory. Then, like dawn breaking over a darkened horizon, the light of understanding filled her bleary eyes. Her mouth spread in a wide, delighted grin and her eyes shown with a new unfettered light: life, hope, relief, understanding.

"Rem?" Indilen said. "Is that really—"

She did not finish because Rem did not let her. He swept the girl into his arms, held her tightly, then planted a series of heavy, relieved kisses on her pale freckled cheeks. To his great relief, Indilen did not pull away from him. In fact, she seemed just as happy to see him as he was to see her.

Indilen studied the deck of the ship, the many bodies milling about, the gathering of ne'er-do-wells on the dock, all bound and ready for incarceration. She looked to Rem for answers.

"What's happening here?" she asked. "One moment, I was in a tavern—Cupp sent me, told me a fellow there might have a job for me transcribing a contract. I had a cup of wine, then... nothing."

Rem held her close. "It's all right," he said. "You're safe now. Soon I think we'll be able to explain everything."

"So strange," Indilen said against him. "I dreamed of you. I thought you would think I stood you up. Knowing that grieved me... I don't even know why it grieved me so."

"Would you believe," Rem asked, "that I've been looking for you all this time?"

She looked puzzled. "All this time? How long has it been?"

Rem almost answered but then thought better of it. Finally, he shook his head. "Let's not worry about it," he said. "Follow me. We'll get you some water and food. You must be famished."

Fetching an old wool blanket from a pile of sailors' bedding on deck, Rem wrapped it around Indilen's shoulders and led her back to the gangplank. As they slowly descended to the dock, Rem saw Torval approaching. The dwarf had also left his assistants behind, hobbling slowly, warily, like a drunk feigning sobriety. No doubt, his wound still pained him, healed or no, while blood loss left him half-delirious.

"And who is this?" Torval asked, as Rem led Indilen toward him.

"This is her, Torval," Rem said. "This is Indilen."

The look of surprise and delight on the dwarf's face was priceless. He seemed to study the girl and accept her as a long-lost member of his own family.

"The cause of all your troubles," Torval said with a grin. "It's good to meet you at last, milady. This young sod's done nothing but moon about you since I met him."

"Troubles?" Indilen asked, genuinely baffled.

Rem held her close. "Later."

Rem and Torval were present for most of the interrogations, and worked tirelessly with Ondego to try to tie all the loose threads together. It took two days of questioning, the work of a half dozen translators, and several hours of well-applied torture, but in the end, the watchwardens got a more-or-less complete picture of Mykaas Masarda's vile plans, and how both Freygaf and the unfortunate Telura Dall were woven into them.

Masarda was a flesh peddler, plain and simple. His primary innovation was the acquisition of chattel through the use of poppy-laced liquor and powerful witchweed—evidenced by those chambers in the Moon Under Water where Rem had seen that young woman smoked into waking oblivion, then carried away through the passages in the walls. Masarda had

had a number of "talent scouts" always scouring the city for pretty young things, male and female. Freygaf, desperate for coin to pay gambling debts, was one of them. These accomplices were issued medallions—the strange little bauble that Ginger Joss had tried to filch from Freygaf's effects—and those medallions were their entry passes to the upper rooms of the Moon Under Water. These men would bring their prospective "talent" to the tavern under false pretenses, get their victims to drink a cup of wine or enjoy a puff of witchweed, then, when they were good and blinkered, they'd be spirited away to the packing house in the caves below. There the drugged victims were shoved into those barrels for transit. Eventually, they were loaded onto ships and spirited overseas, their destination always the same: the elven isle of Aadendrath, in the west.

"So, it's true, then," Torval had interrupted, as the captain of the pirate caravel informed them of this one and only destination. "This pointy-eared bastard has been selling humans to elves as house slaves?"

The pirate captain shrugged. His arrest and eventual fate seemed to worry him little. "Not simply house slaves," he said. "His customers were often more particular in their requirements. Looking for playthings. Slaves of a far more *intimate* sort."

He smirked lasciviously. Torval sprang across the interrogation table, thick hands grasping for the captain's throat. It took four watchwardens to drag the dwarf off the smirking whoreson and out into the hall to cool down.

Rem understood well how Torval felt, but he also knew that this single boat captain was not primarily to blame in this. He was just a merchant of sorts, hiring out his ship for the transportation of illicit cargo. Masarda was the real mastermind—the real villain. And if there were truly elves on Aadendrath keeping human slaves for who-knew-what horrible purposes—well, that was a blatant violation of the ancient treaties between human and elf-kind, treaties signed in the age when even Yenara was a young city, and not half so deadly or jaded. Violation of those treaties was not simply a broken law or breached trust: it could be taken as an act of war. Now the Lady Ynevena, elven ethnarch of Yenara, would have to be involved in Masarda's prosecution and punishment, as would the Council of Patriarchs. If they could keep the bitter business quiet and avoid its relay to the countryside or neighboring cities—avoid stoking the fires of fear and fury that always burned in the bellies of the general populace—then there was a slim chance that human-elven relations could remain intact. If they could not, the whole world as they knew it might shatter like an overturned cartload of eggs.

Yet, even as the *how* was gradually illuminated for them, Rem found himself continually returning to the *why*. Why risk so much—centuries of peaceful coexistence and trade, the honor of an entire race, the stability of an always-precarious social system—simply to line one's pockets? Could Masarda really be so base, so selfish, that he would risk a human uprising against his own people just to fill his already-fat coffers with silver and gold? Ondego and the rest of the wardwatch seemed unconcerned with that question—why?—but Rem could not ignore it, no matter how deeply he tried to bury it in his own psyche.

And so, when Rem suddenly found himself alone in the interrogation room with Masarda while waiting for Ondego and Hirk to confer with some officials from the Council of Patriarchs in the hall, he decided that he would ask that very question. He had not been forbidden to speak with the prisoner, after all. And he was a watchwarden, wasn't he? Surely, trying to glean his own answers from their prisoner could not undermine the progress already made?

Rem studied the elf in the lamplight. His downcast eyes. His implacable face, narrow and chiseled, like the work of an ancient sculptor. Masarda looked no more troubled over his present state than a tavern patron might waiting a little too long for a mug of ale. There was no anxiety in him, no sense of loss or defeat, only mild impatience and boredom.

"Do you care to tell me why you did it?" Rem asked.

Masarda raised his eyes. The look of contempt he summoned for Rem was unnerving. "Are you speaking to me?"

Rem forced himself to meet the elf's gaze. "I just asked a question. I wondered why you did it."

Masarda seemed quite puzzled by the question itself, let alone that Rem would be forward enough to ask it. Finally, he lowered his eyes, as though he could forget Rem were even there simply by not looking at him.

"I have a theory," Rem continued, "but I should like to know how close to the truth I came in formulating it."

"And what is your theory, good watchwarden?" Masarda asked, still not looking at him.

"I'd like to hear it from you first," Rem said.

Masarda finally raised his eyes again. There was a malevolent light in them and a strange, almost exultant smile on his finely sculpted pale face. The star-shaped thorning scar on his forehead caught shadows from the undulating lamplight. It almost looked like a crater.

"You humans," he said. "You always want to *understand*. As if knowing why a single creature in this world turned cruel somehow explained all the cruelty in all of creation."

"I'm not asking about the world," Rem said. "I'm asking about you."

"When I was a child—probably a century or more before you were born—Loffmari slavers raided the little woodland village I called home. They took all of the children—myself among them—raped our mothers and sisters and grandams before putting them all to the sword, then dashed out the men's brains with maces and stones. Every hut was put to the torch. The great, ancient trees that bounded our enclave were licked by flames and reduced to ash. And the two dozen of us captured as prisoners were taken away, in chains, for thorning and sale. Every one of us felt the bite of the iron spike, and lost in an instant the supraliminal sight and sensitivity that was our birthright.

"Then, on to our new masters. Some became house slaves. Some were sent to mines, to navigate the narrowest and most dangerous of veins. Still more were installed as whores in brothels, flesh chattel for human males who thought the violation of elven flesh good sport indeed. I ended up as a bath servant to a rich young lady for a time. Then a body servant to her father. Then his...plaything."

Rem was stunned when Masarda's description of his plight faltered on that single word. He would not have guessed there was any pain—any true shame—left in the elf's clearly fractured soul. But he heard it in his voice when he spoke that word—*plaything*. He heard the sadness, the bitterness, the contempt.

Masarda continued, trying to hide his pain beneath a mask of condescension, as though he were telling a tale to a dull-witted child. "Eventually, I could take no more of his attentions and murdered him in his sleep. I was tried and bound for the gallows, but a fellow from the southlands—dark and bloodthirsty and with a flair for the theatrical—bought me for use in his blood sports. He thought throwing an elf dressed in a ridiculous forest dweller's costume into the arena to be torn to shreds by leopards or spitted on a spear by a pit fighter would be good drama. Instead, I slew every adversary they sent against me. He realized then that I had a value of another sort, and I spent the next ten years fighting for my life, three or four times a week."

Rem was starting to understand now. He could hardly imagine anyone emerging from such an existence with their soul and—dare he say it, humanity—intact. Part of him wished that Ondego and the rest would return, soon, and end Masarda's tale. Another part of him prayed they would not.

"Eventually, I bought my freedom, and I could go where I liked. But, of course, there was nowhere for me to go. My own kind would not have me, and your sort just looked upon me as a sad curiosity. They saw a pitiful freed slave or a displaced woodlander or a sort of road-bound orphan with no home to call his own—but they never saw me as a person—a sentient being—a creature worthy of their attention or affections. In time, I managed to make a living for myself buying exotic junk from the sunlands or my elven brethren and reselling it to gullible human buyers as fine imports and wondrous sylvan handicrafts. You copper-gobblers do love to commoditize the world—you sell with abandon, you buy as though your very lives depended upon it.

"By and by, I was fairly well-to-do. I spent decades wandering from place to place, buying, trading, selling, amassing a fortune, putting on the veneer of respectability—but never once was I truly embraced or accepted. I was—and remained—an orphan. A creature without a country or a tribe."

"It was vengeance," Rem said. "Wasn't it? Vengeance upon men? And upon your own people?"

Masarda gave a sad, wistful little smile, as though nursing a bittersweet memory. "Perhaps it was, at that. Why not snatch the young and beautiful and hopeful from among your sort—the people that snatched and enslaved me—and sell their bodies and their futures to the very worst of my kind? And why not feed the unutterable vices of my fellow wood folk, be they here, on the continent, or off upon our isle of refuge? Even if there were not so many in search of my peculiar merchandise, their appetites and coffers both seemed bottomless. Let them do as they liked with your youngsters—I would reap the rewards, and watch, bemused, as human lives were destroyed and self-satisfied elven morals were tainted and debased—all while I fattened my purse. There was elegance in it, I thought. A serendipitous reciprocity that never failed to put a smile on my face."

And with those words, Masarda did, indeed, smile. That smile made Rem shudder and feel vaguely sick. He had never been so sorry to be right in all his life.

But questions remained. He pressed on.

"The orc? Lugdum? What part did he play?"

Masarda shrugged. "Just a longtime companion. I bought him out of a blood-sport pit when he was young. He was so grateful—and so simple—that he followed my every order thereafter. Even when I required nothing of him, having his considerable bulk beside me in dangerous situations was a kind of security. And, if need be, I could set him loose on any who dared threaten me."

"You had him follow us," Rem said.

"Just so," Masarda answered. "We spoke a private language between us—simple but effective. He was not terribly bright, but he was a good observer. More than once over the years I've sent him into the streets to surveil my enemies. Or my friends."

"Do you know what became of him?" Rem asked, vaguely

sickened by the memory of how he and Torval had abandoned the crippled orc to Gorn Bonebreaker.

Masarda shook his head. "Nor do I care. Clearly, he had outlived his usefulness—poor, pathetic beast that he was."

Now Rem felt the urge to cross the table and beat the smug elf bloody. To use Lugdum for so many years as bodyguard and errand boy was one thing. But to be so indifferent to his ultimate fate? To care nothing for what became of him?

There really was a great, black hole in the center of this creature before him. Staring into that abyss, Rem had the unsettling feeling that the abyss itself stared back at him. It left him cold and covered in gooseflesh.

"Are you satisfied, Watchwarden?" Masarda asked. "Have you plumbed my depths and uncovered the truth at the heart of the riddle that you sought?"

He was teasing him. Rem did not appreciate that.

"You've been most candid with me," Rem said slowly. "I thank you for that."

"It was the least I could do," Masarda said with a bent grin, "for one so young and ignorant of the world's ways. Pray you never find such a bottomless well at the center of your soul, boy. We can run from many things in this world, but we can never run from our true selves."

The door of the interrogation room opened. Torval, Ondego, and Hirk returned. Within moments, a more formal interrogation resumed.

It was Hirk who took the lead, with Ondego occasionally interjecting an inquiry of his own. Rem and Torval stood by, watching, listening, but both kept their mouths shut while their superiors teased answers from their lackadaisical prisoner. Rem noted that Masarda seemed to have lost the relish he evidenced when speaking to Rem alone. Likewise, the elf never acknowledged him. It was as though Rem had ceased to exist the moment the other watchmen returned. The elf answered almost every question posed to him, but usually with few words and little emotion. Rem had sensed a nasty delight in the elf's confession when the two of them were alone in the room; now he saw only a creature eager to end a tiresome chore and once more be left alone. The idea that Masarda had taken some special interest in answering Rem's questions—in baring his own fractured soul and exposing the true depths of his own evil and antipathy—gave Rem no comfort, but rather, left him more than a little shaken.

Why me? Rem wondered. *Why did he deign to talk to me with such delight, while he now treats Ondego and the rest of them like beggars?*

They questioned him about everything: the logistics of the operation, the profits generated, the ultimate destination of his victims and the uses they were intended for, even the nature and number of his associates. Masarda's answers remained curt and brief, offered with a slow-gathering annoyance. After quite some time, with a great deal of information having been extracted, Hirk finally threw a glance at Torval, gave him a little nod—as if in warning or silent agreement—then asked a new question, wholly unlike the others.

"What about Freygaf?"

The name seemed to stir something in Masarda's reticent character. "Freygaf?"

Hirk nodded. "Barbarian. Northerner. Had a pentacle tattooed over his right eye."

Masarda searched his memory for a moment, his attempts to couple face with name apparent. Then a slight smile crept onto his lips. He kept his face down, but he raised his eyes and met Hirk's gaze. "Oh yes," he said slowly. "A friend of yours?"

Rem looked to Torval. The dwarf's face was set in a deep frown. His jaw was clenched so tightly it seemed he might grind his own teeth to dust. Anger was rising in him. He was struggling mightily to suppress it.

"He was a watchwarden, wasn't he?" Masarda asked. "Yes, I do recall him saying something to that effect before we dispatched him."

"So you confess to his murder?" Ondego asked.

Masarda held up his dainty, slender hands. "I see no blood, good prefect."

"Cut the cack," Hirk snapped.

"If you mean did I kill him myself, the answer is no," Masarda said, sitting back comfortably and looking again, to Rem, like a man gladly about to share unpleasant information with an unprepared audience. "Though I'm afraid sending him home to his mountain gods was my idea. Others simply saw it through."

"Why?" Torval suddenly spat, as though he could manage to eject that one word and no others.

Masarda's icy sapphire gaze turned on Torval. "Because he was a fool," Masarda said. "That blundering barbarian found poor Telura Dall in a winesink, out drinking with some low-class companions, flirting with sellswords and gamblers. He managed to talk her into accompanying him back to the Moon Under Water. When I saw that he had delivered us the daughter of one of my closest—and richest—social acquaintances, I knew he had to be made an example of. The girl was killed because she could not be allowed to live—she could have connected your late friend to our operations, after all. I ordered her drowned while still unconscious, her body dumped in the Fifth Ward, as far from her home as possible. Freygaf, meanwhile, was dispatched as a lesson to my other talent scouts—to urge them to pay closer attention to who they deemed fit for service. Generally speaking, rich young ladies with influential parents are to be avoided."

Rem did not watch Masarda as he spoke. Instead, he watched his partner, Torval, and saw clearly the pain and grief and fury in the dwarf's eyes. He thought that Torval would try to kill the self-satisfied elf, but Torval somehow remained silent and still all the while. Perhaps his anger was directed at Freygaf, for his deceit. Perhaps it was simply driven inward, at himself, for not seeing through his partner's mask of friendship and virtue.

Everyone in the room was silent. A question suddenly bloomed in Rem's mind and bade him inwardly to speak it aloud. Without thinking, he posed it.

"How could you?" he asked. "You were clearly close to the Dall family. You knew Telura—"

"From her birth," Masarda confirmed.

"Then how?" Rem pressed. "I simply don't understand."

Masarda shrugged. "Business, boy. If I ever called anyone of your kind my friend, it was only because he was useful to me, putting money in my purse or lending me the respectability necessary to move in wider and richer social circles to maintain my position. Were my sentiments, earlier confided to you, not clear enough?"

This indication that he and Rem had spoken earlier caused Hirk, Ondego, and Torval to all turn their puzzled gazes on Rem. He waved them off. "Later," he said, "when we're out of this room."

"Did you know," Masarda broke in, and all eyes turned back to him, "that your compatriot tried to convince me that he was only working for my operation in an effort to fully expose it and dismantle it? That he had already made notes regarding it and that those notes would be delivered to you lot if anything happened to him?"

Ondego and Hirk exchanged glances. Rem looked to Torval. Torval glared at the malevolent elf.

"Then again," Masarda added, "he made those claims after enduring a beating from Lugdum, whilst staring at the point of good Rhaegir's dagger—Rhaegir being my bodyguard. You remember him, don't you, boy? The one who nearly skewered you on the deck of my ship before your diminutive little friend there so unceremoniously split his skull?"

"Don't change the subject," Hirk said. "Just what did Freygaf tell you about this investigation of his?"

Masarda shrugged. "Just what I told you."

"That doesn't corroborate anything," Ondego muttered.

"But that was precisely my point," Masarda said. "The poor fellow was under duress and facing certain death. Perhaps his claims of investigating my operation with the intention of exposing it were simply desperate attempts at forestalling the inevitable. In any case, his throat was cut and Lugdum took the body through the sewers to be rid of it."

The door to the chamber opened. The Fifth's elven watchwarden, Queydon, stood there accompanied by a familiar vision of unearthly beauty and immortal desire, whose presence Rem found terribly jarring in the close, coarse confines of their watchkeep. He actually smelled her before he saw her, a cloying, heady waft of lilies and lilacs that made Rem's vision go gray and his cock stand at attention. Thank the Panoply she was wearing actual clothes this time and not that sheer, diaphanous gown that she'd been draped in when they called at her pleasure garden.

The Lady Ynevena recognized him. She smiled, and Rem thought he might cry at how lovely she was, how desperately he wanted her.

Witch, he thought, ashamed of his own unbidden bodily responses to the elven ethnarch's mere presence. *Torval was right about you all along.*

"Watchwarden Remeck," the elven matron said, stepping into the chamber. "What a pleasant and most unexpected surprise. When last we met, you found me in my native habitat, and now, I get to see you in yours."

Rem stood and faced her. He knew why she was there. Ondego and some of the other watchmen had already groused about it. She would question Masarda, she would argue for his swift rendition into the custody of his own kind, and then she would spirit him away to Aadrendrath or some other elven enclave, never to be seen by human eyes again—perhaps, not even punished for his crimes.

He wanted Ynevena to feel his disdain for her. He wanted her to see that despite the fact that he wanted to throw her down on the table that separated him and Masarda and ball her elven brains out, he also thought she was a rank weed in the garden of decency and civilization.

Ynevena studied him. Smiled again. She read him thoroughly, and she did not care.

When she spoke, it was to everyone, though her eyes never left Rem's. "Good watchwardens, I beg your leave for a private audience with my kinsman. Leave a guard in the hall and I'll make it known when our exchange is completed. No one should enter this room before that moment."

Rem moved to grant her wishes. She stopped him, one soft hand falling on his forearm. "My invitation stands," she said quietly.

Rem left the room in a hurry.

He found Torval lingering in the corridor outside, a stunned, sour look on his broad little face.

"I'm sorry you had to hear that," Rem said. "But at least you know that Freygaf tried—"

"Bollocks," Torval growled, not turning to face his young partner. "I know nothing. I know what he told me. He could be lying. Or telling the truth, and Freygaf was lying, just trying to buy himself a few more breaths."

"Or," Rem countered, "Freygaf was telling the truth. Maybe he wasn't innocent, entirely . . . but it could be that what he discovered while trying to scrape up some extra coin in Masarda's employ moved him to finally remember who he was and the service he was sworn to. He could have been compromised, yet still trying to find a way back—a way to redeem himself."

Torval kept staring at the floor.

"There are always the necromancers in Mage's Alley," Rem said quietly.

"No," Torval said with finality. "Whatever the truth, he needs to rest now. The gods knew, his life was hard enough."

"But the truth, Torval . . ."

Torval raised his eyes to Rem. There were tears in them, glinting and ready to roll down his broad, ruddy cheeks. "The truth is, I'll never know about his end. I only know that despite his many faults, he was a good mate. And now he's gone."

An awkward silence fell. Rem and Torval remembered that they were not alone. Both turned toward Ondego, still standing not far from them with Hirk at his elbow. The warden and his second had strange expressions on their faces: set mouths with ghostly bends at their corners—the merest shadow of smiles—along with narrowed eyes suggesting a conspiratorial bend to whatever they were about to say.

Silence persisted between them. Finally, Torval spoke.

"What is it?" he asked. "If you're about to tell me I can't

be alone with that elf any longer, I'd wager you were dead right—"

"We need two hands," Ondego said. "We think the two of you will do nicely."

"Two hands for what?" Rem asked.

"Another interrogation," Ondego said, then turned and walked back down the hall. Hirk followed. Rem and Torval, intrigued, brought up the rear.

In moments, they were down in the dungeons. The standard chorus of begged pardons and offers of remuneration began the moment the prisoners all saw Ondego's face.

Prefect, sir, there's been a terrible mistake . . .

Prefect, sir, someone must have spiked my ale, because the last thing I remember, I was enjoying an evening out with some mates . . .

Prefect, sir, I've a chest of treasure waiting back at my rooms at the Rusty Gibbet. A golden cup full of rubies and emeralds is yours, if you'll just let me out of here . . .

Prefect, sir . . . Warden, sir . . .

Over and over again. The old litany almost made Rem feel at home.

Ondego and Hirk proceeded to a certain corner cell, where a fat, familiar face awaited beyond the cell bars. Rem felt a smile creeping onto his face and had to struggle to keep it from blooming. He looked to Torval. The dwarf's own satisfied scowl was his version of a smile, and Rem knew he was delighted.

"What the bloody shit is this?" Frennis, the former prefect of the Fourth, barked as Ondego and Hirk stepped up to his cell. "Ondego, when Black Mal gets word—"

"He got word," Ondego said. "He got it from those salty dogs we seized on Masarda's ship and from Masarda's hired hands captured at the Moon Under Water. He even got testimony from the Nightjar, who was very happy to finally divest himself of his knowledge of your criminal conspiracy with that pointy-eared scum upstairs."

"I don't know what you're on about," Frennis said, but Rem could see clearly that he *did* know what they were on about. And for the first time, Rem thought he saw fear in the onetime prefect's jowly face.

Ondego nodded to Hirk, who unlocked the cell. Rem and Torval, knowing now why they'd been enlisted, stepped into the cell, each took one of the prefect's arms, and began the slow, laborious work of dragging him out again.

"Come on, Ondego, you know me," Frennis pleaded. His fear seemed to have sapped his normal, considerable strength. He struggled, pitching his body from side to side, but it was a weak struggle—a futile one. "This isn't necessary," he said. "I can assure you—"

"'Fraid so," Ondego said. He indicated their destination with a nod. "The chair, lads."

Rem and Torval obliged. It took some doing, but they finally got Frennis perched on the chair in the torture pit—a chair almost too small for his big frame—and shackled in place.

Ondego descended into the shallow pit. He made his usual rounds: the font, the brazier, the table, with its array of nasty surgical implements and blunt objects.

Rem smelled something. He lowered his eyes. Frennis had pissed himself.

"Ondego, my partnership with Mykaas was lucrative. What say we make a deal—"

"No deals, Frennis," Ondego said, reciting holy writ. "Not now, not ever."

"Bollocks," Frennis spat. "So what's it gonna be, Ondego?

A rusty bone saw? Thorns beneath my fingernails? A red-hot poker in my arse?"

"Nah," Ondego said, letting his eyes dance from Hirk to Rem to Torval, then finally back to their prisoner. "Bare fists."

Frennis drew a deep breath, preparing himself.

"Who shall do the honors?" Ondego asked, looking to Rem and Torval.

Rem was eager for the first go at the fat former prefect, but he deferred to Torval's seniority.

CHAPTER THIRTY-ONE

Ultimately, it played out as Ondego predicted. After the Lady Ynevena held two private meetings with the Council of Patriarchs, Masarda was remanded into her custody. She swore on the spirits of all her ancestors and any progeny to come that any and all of his victims still held in bondage on Aadendrath would be returned to their homes, and that Mykaas Masarda's crimes, being of the most heinous and terrible sort, demanded swift and terrible justice. But that justice, she assured them, would be dispensed by his own kind, not by any wardwatch, city guard, or executioner of Yenara. If the Council of Patriarchs insisted, Masarda's head could be returned to them, after his long punishment was done and perdition finally claimed him. But Masarda could not be left in the hands of human authorities. That would simply not do. Elves did not hand over elves for execution by human hands, after all, no matter how terrible their crime.

Ondego assured Rem and Torval that this was the way of things: how it always had been, how it always would be. It chapped his dangly bits, to be sure, but what could one do?

Thus, Torval and Rem watched as a squad of elven guardsmen from the Lady Ynevena's house came to claim the criminal, the kidnapper, the flesh peddler, the murderer Mykaas Masarda to accompany him to an elven ship waiting in Yenara's harbor, and from there to spirit him they-knew-not-where to some unknown, unseen justice. Rem assumed their odds of seeing Masarda again were minuscule to none, whether he was punished or not. When he said as much to Torval, the dwarf agreed.

"But," Torval said, "that's the job. Sometimes you're the edge of the sword or the boss of the shield, and sometimes you're just a cog in a mill."

That did not sit well with Rem, but he supposed he had little choice but to accept it.

Their reward for being the pair that captured Masarda and solved the case: three full days off the rosters. Ondego urged them to get some sleep and enjoy the comfort of their idle holiday, because when they returned, he would once more expect them to jockey for the honor of the best watchmen in his ward. No resting on their laurels. To start their days of rest, Rem and Torval decided to mount a little celebration, just for themselves and their loved ones.

So, on his first morning of respite, Rem went to visit Indilen at the House of Healing, where she now resided, under the physical and spiritual care of the Holy Sisters of the Panoply. He had visited her there on every one of the three days since her liberation, and agreed with the Sisters that she should stay there until she felt equal to striking out on her own again. She confided that she suffered frightful dreams nightly and that when they woke her in the dark, she often suffered a momentary panic, not knowing where she was or how she got there. These feelings were fleeting, she said, but nonetheless harrowing in the moment. Rem, understanding why such an experience might leave such a horrible scar upon Indilen's heart and mind, did all that he could to put her at ease. He brought her good food from the markets and street stalls that he passed on his way to visit her; flowers once, which the sisters happily arranged in a bronze vase at Indilen's bedside; and even her secretary set, so that she could see that it had been recovered.

"It's waiting for you," he assured her, "as soon as you're well enough to leave this place."

She thanked him in myriad small ways, each of which thrilled him: squeezing his hand when she held it; sometimes tousling his forelocks and making fun of his rusty-red hair; and, at the best of times, simply staring at him and smiling and saying, "I've never known a kindness like you've shown me."

"I could do no less," Rem responded whenever she said that to him. "You dropped into my life so unceremoniously and made such a great commotion that I could not let you leave it the same way."

The day of their impromptu celebration, Rem asked Indilen a hundred times if she really thought herself up to the strain. Should she not stay in bed? Should she not rest and continue her recovery? Indilen assured him, again and again, that not only would she love a brief respite from those restful but dreary chambers and their somber attendants, but that she also would not be stopped by anything—illness, incarceration, not even death—that stood in the way of celebrating Rem's victory and what it meant for both of them. Satisfied, Rem promised the Sisters he would have Indilen back in her bed by the midnight bells, then led her to the Third Ward and to his favorite taproom: the King's Ass.

It was early evening, rolling toward night, and the tavern was lively. Joedoc, the brewer, and lovely Aarna were both behind the bar. That curly-haired lute-player and buxom brunette lass harmonized from their little corner stage. Soon enough, Torval arrived with his entire family in tow: sister Osma, daughter Ammi, sons Tavarix and Lokki. They all took a great, round table in an alcove near the bar, and Aarna served them.

The feast was fulsome. Tav and Lokki drank goat's milk while

Osma and Ammi swilled cider, but Rem, Indilen, and Torval all partook of Joedoc's Old Thumper and Indilen agreed that it was the best ale she'd ever tasted. Rem worried silently about just how well he and Indilen would get along, now that she was no longer in mortal danger and he was no longer haunted by the question of her disappearance, but their conversations were effortless and smiles were frequently exchanged. Indilen had a good appetite, was a fearless drinker, and loved to laugh—qualities that made Rem admire her all the more. But nothing moved him quite so much as when he caught her staring at him over the rim of her ale mug, or smiling in his general direction when she didn't think he was looking. Rather than play coy and look away, Rem decided he would meet her gaze, stare right back, and hoped that perhaps, just perhaps, this little infatuation of theirs—rudely interrupted, now luckily reengaged—could lead to something true and long-lasting and wonderful.

Only time would tell.

At one point in the evening, Aarna approached the table with a full pitcher of Thumper to refill their cups. She poured one for herself as well, then raised it toward Rem and his diminutive partner with that familiar, broad smile that Rem had come to love. Before she spoke, Rem stole a glance at Torval, and saw how sweetly and longingly the dwarf gazed at that woman who was two feet taller than he and of a separate race altogether. Rem did not know if a dwarven widower could ever win the heart of a human taverness, but he thought that if any dwarf could manage it, the unstoppable, unflappable Torval—so desperate to make his own way in the world, and not have it made for him—might.

"To Rem and Torval," Aarna offered, "and their well-earned days of rest. May your mutton be hot, your ale cold, and your beds always warm—though, hopefully, not with each other."

Laughter all around. They drank, even the little boys with their goat's milk. Rem saw Torval upending his mug, determined to down its contents in a single draught. Rem kept gulping from his own mug, intent on doing the same.

They finished together and slammed down their mugs, then clasped hands and roared at one another like a couple of drunken Kostermen.

There was a sudden clamor from a far corner of the tavern. Chairs scraped across floorboards, then pitched over backward with a series of wooden thumps. Steel blades slid from their scabbards and oaths were exchanged—the sort that Torval probably did not want his children hearing. There was the brief ring of blade on blade—a swift, short exchange of blows and parries. Someone swore. A woman screamed.

Then the violence began to spread. Two men at adjacent tables urged on the duelists. Three more set to arguing about who started it. Four others were doused with flying ale when one of the fighters upended the table that stood between him and his opponent.

More blades were loosed. More curses tossed. Those unwilling to join the fray scattered.

"Bloody hell," Aarna muttered. "It's to be one of *those* nights..."

Rem caught Torval staring at him. The dwarf was probably half-crocked, or close to it. So was Rem. But he knew what that look meant.

"After you," Rem said, and rose on watery legs.

Torval slid down off his chair and went swaggering toward the escalating brawl. His iron maul swung in his hand at his side. Rem followed, hand on the pommel of his sheathed sword.

When Rem reached Torval's side, the dwarf gave a long,

shrill whistle. The dozen brawlers all froze where they stood and turned toward the terrible sound. Rem wondered what they were thinking, staring at the two of them: some red-haired, freckled youngster with a sword, a bald and whiskered dwarf with a maul. Two lousy challengers against a dozen or more, one only four feet tall.

They probably think we're mad, Rem thought.

In fact, they probably were.

"Right," Torval barked. "Let's stop this before it even starts, shall we?"

A muscled Hasturman in the midst of the would-be brawlers sneered. "And just who in the sundry hells are you, little man?"

Torval spat on the floor. "Tell 'em, lad."

"We're the wardwatch," Rem said.

It wasn't their ward.

Nor was it their watch.

But this lot didn't know that, did they?

The story continues in the next Fifth Ward adventure,

The Fifth Ward: Friendly Fire

ACKNOWLEDGMENTS

Long is the way and hard that out of hell leads from Chapter One to The End (I think Homer said that... or maybe Lester Dent). But that climb is never, ever undertaken alone—not entirely anyway. I'd like to take a moment to thank everyone who offered their personal support and assistance while *First Watch* grew from an amorphous daydream into a published novel.

First, my sincere thanks to my beta readers, Keith Gouveia and Doug Cherry, whose enthusiasm and pointed critiques kept me afloat and pushed the book toward its last, best form.

My deepest appreciation to Matt Peters of Beating Windward Press, whose unwavering friendship, faith in my work, and first-rate editorial skills kept me going through some dark times, unleashing my first published novels upon an unsuspecting world and proving that an audience was indeed out there.

I cannot say thank you enough to my loyal and tenacious agent at Fuse Literary, Emily Keyes, who's stuck with me through more near-wins and disappointments over the years than I can count.

Unending gratitude to my editor at Orbit, Lindsey Hall, for her rigor, her kindness, and her steadfast support. I couldn't have asked for a more engaged and supportive guide for my journey through the process of making *First Watch* the best book it could be, and on toward the next chapters in the adventures of Rem and Torval.

And finally, mountains of love to my son, Gabriel, my parents, Jim and Carol, and my beautiful partner in this world, Liliana. Their faith and acceptance remind me, constantly, that I have something to offer the world, above and beyond the words I write and the stories I tell.

To all of you who walked Yenara's streets with me and enjoyed the visit: my heartfelt thanks and best wishes. 'Til next we meet to roll the bones or quaff a pint, keep your eyes open, your firsts clenched, and your backs to the wall.

Dale Lucas
December 2016

extras

www.orbitbooks.net

about the author

Dale Lucas is a novelist, screenwriter, and film critic from Saint Petersburg, Florida.

Find out more about Dale Lucas and other Orbit authors by registering online for the free monthly newsletter at www.orbitbooks.net.

if you enjoyed
THE FIFTH WARD: FIRST WATCH

look out for

KINGS OF THE WYLD

by

Nicholas Eames

*Clay Cooper and his band were once the best of the best —
the meanest, dirtiest, most feared and admired crew of mercenaries
this side of the Heartwyld.*

*But their glory days are long past; the mercs have grown apart
and grown old, fat, drunk — or a combination of the three.
Then a former bandmate turns up at Clay's door with a plea
for help: his daughter Rose is trapped in a city besieged by an
enemy horde one hundred thousand strong and hungry for
blood. Rescuing Rose is the kind of impossible mission that only
the very brave or the very stupid would sign up for.*

*It's time to get the band back together for one last tour
across the Wyld.*

if you enjoyed
THE FIFTH WARD: FIRST WATCH

look out for

KINGS OF THE
WYLD

by

Nicholas Eames

Chapter One

A Ghost on the Road

You'd have guessed from the size of his shadow that Clay Cooper was a bigger man than he was. He was certainly bigger than most, with broad shoulders and a chest like an iron-strapped keg. His hands were so large that most mugs looked like teacups when he held them, and the jaw beneath his shaggy brown beard was wide and sharp as a shovel blade. But his shadow, drawn out by the setting sun, skulked behind him like a dogged reminder of the man he used to be: great and dark and more than a little monstrous.

Finished with work for the day, Clay slogged down the beaten track that passed for a thoroughfare in Coverdale, sharing smiles and nods with those hustling home before dark. He wore a Watchmen's green tabard over a shabby leather jerkin, and a weathered sword in a rough old scabbard on his hip. His shield—chipped and scored and scratched through the years by axes and arrows and raking claws—was slung across his back, and his helmet...well, Clay had lost the one the Sergeant had given him last week, just as he'd misplaced the one given to him the month before, and every few months since the day he'd signed on to the Watch almost ten years ago now.

A helmet restricted your vision, all but negated your hearing, and more often than not made you look stupid as hell. Clay Cooper didn't do helmets, and that was that.

"Clay! Hey, Clay!" Pip trotted over. The lad wore the Watchmen's green as well, his own ridiculous head-pan tucked in the crook of one arm. "Just got off duty at the south gate," he said cheerily. "You?"

"North."

"Nice." The boy grinned and nodded as though Clay had said something exceptionally interesting instead of having just mumbled the word *north*. "Anything exciting out there?"

Clay shrugged. "Mountains."

"Ha! 'Mountains,' he says. Classic. Hey, you hear Ryk Yarsson saw a centaur out by Tassel's farm?"

"It was probably a moose."

The boy gave him a skeptical look, as if Ryk spotting a moose instead of a centaur was highly improbable. "Anyway. Come to the King's Head for a few?"

"I shouldn't," said Clay. "Ginny's expecting me home, and..." He paused, having no other excuse near to hand.

"C'mon," Pip goaded. "Just one, then. One drink."

Clay grunted, squinting into the sun and measuring the prospect of Ginny's wrath against the bitter bite of ale washing down his throat. "Fine," he relented. "One."

Because it was hard work looking north all day, after all.

The King's Head was already crowded, its long tables crammed with people who came as much to gab and gossip as they did to drink. Pip slinked toward the bar while Clay found a seat at a table as far from the stage as possible.

The talk around him was the usual sort: weather and war, and neither topic too promising. There'd been a great battle fought out west in Endland, and by the murmurings it hadn't gone off well. A Republic army of twenty thousand, bolstered by several hundred mercenary bands, had been slaughtered by a Heartwyld Horde. Those few who'd survived had retreated to the city of Castia and were now under siege, forced to endure sickness and starvation while the enemy gorged themselves on the dead outside their walls. That, and there'd been a touch of frost on the ground this morning, which didn't seem fair this early into autumn, did it?

Pip returned with two pints and two friends Clay didn't recognize, whose names he forgot just as soon as they told him. They seemed like nice enough fellows, mind you. Clay was just bad with names.

"So you were in a band?" one asked. He had lanky red hair, and his face was a postpubescent mess of freckles and swollen pimples.

Clay took a long pull from his tankard before setting it down and looking over at Pip, who at least had the grace to look ashamed. Then he nodded.

The two stole a glance at each other, and then Freckles leaned in across the table. "Pip says you guys held Coldfire Pass for three days against a thousand walking dead."

"I only counted nine hundred and ninety-nine," Clay corrected. "But pretty much, yeah."

"He says you slew Akatung the Dread," said the other, whose attempt to grow a beard had produced a wisp of hair most grandmothers would scoff at.

Clay took another drink and shook his head. "We only injured him. I hear he died back at his lair, though. Peacefully. In his sleep."

They looked disappointed, but then Pip nudged one with his elbow. "Ask him about the Siege of Hollow Hill."

"Hollow Hill?" murmured Wispy, then his eyes went round as courtmark coins. "Wait, the Siege of Hollow Hill? So the band you were in . . ."

"*Saga*," Freckles finished, clearly awestruck. "You were in *Saga*."

"It's been a while," said Clay, picking at a knot in the warped wood of the table before him. "The name sounds familiar, though."

"Wow," sighed Freckles.

"You gotta be kidding me," Wispy uttered.

"Just . . . wow," said Freckles again.

"You *gotta* be kidding me," Wispy repeated, not one to be outdone when it came re-expressing disbelief.

Clay said nothing in response, only sipped his beer and shrugged.

"So you know Golden Gabe?" Freckles asked.

Another shrug. "I know Gabriel, yeah."

"Gabriel!" trilled Pip, sloshing his drink as he raised his hands in wonderment. "'*Gabriel*,' he says! Classic."

"And Ganelon?" Wispy asked. "And Arcandius Moog? And Matrick Skulldrummer?"

"Oh, and . . ." Freckles screwed up his face as he racked his brain—which didn't do the poor bastard any favours, Clay decided. He was ugly as a rain cloud on a wedding day, that one. "Who are we forgetting?"

"Clay Cooper."

Wispy stroked the fine hairs on his chin as he pondered this. "Clay Cooper . . . oh," he said, looking abashed. "Right."

It took Freckles another moment to piece it together, but then he palmed his pale forehead and laughed. "Gods, I'm stupid."

The gods already know, thought Clay.

Sensing the awkwardness at hand, Pip chimed in. "Tell us a tale, will ya, Clay? About when you did for that necromancer up in Oddsford. Or when you rescued that princess from . . . that place . . . remember?"

Which one? Clay wondered. They'd rescued several princesses, in fact, and if he'd killed one necromancer he'd killed a dozen. Who kept track of shit like that? Didn't matter anyway, since he wasn't in the mood for storytelling. Or to go digging up what he'd worked so hard to bury, and then harder still to forget where he'd dug the hole in the first place.

"Sorry, kid," he told Pip, draining what remained of his beer. "That's one."

He excused himself, handing Pip a few coppers for the drink and bidding what he hoped was a last farewell to Freckles and Wispy. He shouldered his way to the door and gave a long sigh when he emerged into the cool quiet outside. His back hurt from slumping over that table, so he stretched it out, craning his neck and gazing up at the first stars of the evening.

He remembered how small the night sky used to make him feel. How *insignificant*. And so he'd gone and made a big deal of himself, figuring that someday he might look up at the vast sprawl of stars and feel undaunted by its splendour. It hadn't worked. After a while Clay tore his eyes from the darkening sky and struck out down the road toward home.

He exchanged pleasantries with the Watchmen at the west gate. Had he heard about the centaur spotting over by Tassel's farm? they wondered. How about the battle out west, and those poor bastards holed up in Castia? Rotten, rotten business.

Clay followed the track, careful to keep from turning an ankle in a rut. Crickets were chirping in the tall grass to either side, the wind in the trees above him sighing like the ocean surf. He stopped by the roadside shrine to the Summer Lord and threw a dull copper at the statue's feet. After a few steps and a moment's hesitation he went back and tossed another. Away from town it was darker still, and Clay resisted the urge to look up again.

Best keep your eyes on the ground, he told himself, *and leave the past where it belongs. You've got what you've got, Cooper, and it's just what you wanted, right? A kid, a wife, a simple life.* It was an honest living. It was comfortable.

He could almost hear Gabriel scoff at that. *Honest? Honest is boring*, his old friend might have said. *Comfortable is dull.* Then again, Gabriel had got himself married long before Clay. Had a little girl of his own, even—a woman grown by now.

And yet there was Gabe's spectre just the same, young and fierce and glorious, smirking in the shadowed corner of Clay's mind. "We were *giants*, once," he said. "Bigger than life. And now..."

"Now we are tired old men," Clay muttered, to no one but the night. And what was so wrong with that? He'd met plenty of *actual* giants in his day, and most of them were assholes.

Despite Clay's reasoning, the ghost of Gabriel continued to haunt his walk home, gliding past him on the road with a sly wink, waving from his perch on the neighbour's fence, crouched like a beggar on the stoop of Clay's front door. Only this last Gabriel wasn't young at all. Or particularly fierce looking. Or any more glorious than an old board with a rusty nail in it. In fact, he looked pretty fucking terrible. When he saw Clay coming he stood, and smiled. Clay had never seen a man look so sad in all the years of his life.

The apparition spoke his name, which sounded to Clay as real as the crickets buzzing, as the wind moaning through the trees along the road. And then that brittle smile broke, and Gabriel—really, truly Gabriel, and not a ghost after all—was sagging into Clay's arms, sobbing into his shoulder, clutching at his back like a child afraid of the dark.

"Clay," he said. "Please... I need your help."

Chapter Two

Rose

Once Gabriel recovered himself they went inside. Ginny turned from the stove and her jaw clamped tight. Griff came bounding over, stubby tail wagging. He gave Clay a cursory sniff and then set to smelling Gabe's leg as though it were a piss-drenched tree, which wasn't actually too far off the mark.

His old friend was in a sorry state, no mistake. His hair and beard were a tangled mess, his clothes little more than soiled rags. There were holes in his boots, toes peeking out from the ruined leather like grubby urchins. His hands were busy fidgeting, wringing each other or tugging absentmindedly at the hem of his tunic. Worst of all, though, were his eyes. They were sunk deep in his haggard face, hard and haunted, as though everywhere he looked was something he wished he hadn't seen.

"Griff, lay off," said Clay. The dog, wet eyes and a lolling pink tongue in a black fur face, perked up at the sound of his name. Griff wasn't the noblest-looking creature, and he didn't have many uses besides licking food off a plate. He couldn't herd sheep or flush a grouse from cover, and if anyone ever broke in to the house he was more likely to fetch them slippers than scare 'em off. But it made Clay smile to look at him (that's how godsdamn adorable he was) and that was worth more than nothing.

"Gabriel." Ginny finally found her voice, though she stayed right where she was. Didn't smile. Didn't cross to hug him. She'd never much cared for Gabriel. Clay thought she probably blamed his old bandmate for all the bad habits (gambling, fighting, drinking to excess) that she'd spent the last ten years disabusing him of, and all the other bad habits (chewing with his mouth open, forgetting to wash his hands, occasionally throttling people) she was still struggling to purge.

Heaped upon that were the handful of times Gabe had come calling in the years since his own wife left him. Every time he appeared it was hand in hand with some grand scheme to reunite the old band and strike out once again in search of fame, fortune, and decidedly reckless adventure. There was a town down south needed rescue from a ravaging drake, or a den of walking wolves to be cleared out of the Wailing Forest, or an old lady in some far-flung corner of the realm needed help bringing laundry off the line and only Saga themselves could rise to her aid!

It wasn't as though Clay needed Ginny breathing down his neck to refuse, to see that Gabriel longed for something unrecoverable, like an old man clinging to memories of his golden youth. *Exactly* like that, actually. But life, Clay knew, didn't work that way. It wasn't a circle; you didn't go round and round again. It was an arc, its course as inexorable as the sun's trek across the sky, destined at its highest, brightest moment to begin its fall.

Clay blinked, having lost himself in his own head. He did that sometimes, and could have wished he was better at putting his thoughts into words. He'd sound a right clever bastard then, wouldn't he?

Instead, he'd stood there dumbly as the silence between Ginny and Gabriel lengthened uncomfortably.

"You look hungry," she said finally.

Gabriel nodded, his hands fidgeting nervously.

Ginny sighed, and then his wife—his kind, lovely, magnificent wife—forced a tight grin and reclaimed her spoon from the pot she'd been tending earlier. "Sit down then," she said over her shoulder. "I'll feed you. I made Clay's favourite: rabbit stew with mushrooms."

Gabriel blinked. "Clay hates mushrooms."

Seeing Ginny's back stiffen, Clay spoke up. "Used to," he said brightly, before his wife—his quick-tempered, sharp-tongued, utterly terrifying wife—could turn around and crack his skull with that wooden spoon. "Ginny does something to them, though. Makes them taste"—*Not so fucking awful*, was what first jumped to mind—"really pretty good," he finished lamely. "What is it you do to 'em, hun?"

"I stew them," she said in the most menacing way a woman could string those three words together.

Something very much like a smile tugged at the corner of Gabe's mouth.

He always did love to watch me squirm, Clay remembered. He took a chair and Gabriel followed suit. Griff trundled over to his mat and gave his balls a few good licks before promptly falling asleep. Clay fought down a surge of envy, seeing that. "Tally home?" he asked.

"Out," said Ginny. "Somewhere."

Somewhere close, he hoped. There were coyotes in the woods nearby. Wolves in the hills. Hell, Ryk Yarsson had seen a centaur out by Tassel's farm. Or a moose. Either of which might kill a young girl if caught by surprise. "She should've been home before dark," he said.

His wife scoffed at that. "So should you have, Clay Cooper. You putting in extra hours on the wall, or is that the King's Piss I smell on ya?" *King's Piss* was her name for the beer they served at the pub. It was a fair assessment, and Clay had laughed the first time she'd said it. Didn't seem as funny at the moment, however.

Not to Clay, anyway, though Gabriel's mood seemed to be lightening a bit. His old friend was smirking like a boy watching his brother take heat for a crime he didn't commit.

"She's just down in the marsh," Ginny said, fishing two ceramic bowls from the cupboard. "Be glad it's only frogs she'll bring home with her. It'll be boys soon enough, and you'll have plenty cause to worry then."

"Won't be me needs to worry," Clay mumbled.

Ginny scoffed at that, too, and he might have asked why had she not set a steaming bowl of stew in front of him. The wafting scent drew a ravenous growl from his stomach, even if there were mushrooms in it.

His wife took her cloak off the peg by the door. "I'll go and be sure Tally's all right," she said. "Might be she needs help carrying those frogs." She came over and kissed Clay on the top of his head, smoothing his hair down afterward. "You boys have fun catching up."

She got as far as opening the door before hesitating, looking back. First at Gabriel, already scooping at his bowl as if it were the first meal he'd had in a long while, and then at Clay, and it wasn't until a few days after (a hard choice and too many miles away already) that he understood what he'd seen in her eyes just then. A kind of sorrow, thoughtful and resigned, as though she already knew—his loving, beautiful, remarkably *astute* wife—what was coming, inevitable as winter, or a river's winding course to the sea.

A chill wind blew in from outside. Ginny shivered despite her cloak, then she left.

"It's Rose."

They had finished eating, set their bowls aside. He should have put them in the basin, Clay knew, got them soaking so they wouldn't be such a chore to clean later, but it suddenly seemed like he couldn't leave the table just now. Gabriel had come in the night, from a long way off, to say something. Best to let him say it and be done.

"Your daughter?" Clay prompted.

Gabe nodded slowly. His hands were both flat on the table. His eyes were fixed, unfocused, somewhere between them. "She is . . . *willful*," he said finally. "Impetuous. I wish I could say she gets it from her mother, but . . ." That smile again, just barely. "You remember I was teaching her to use a sword?"

"I remember telling you that was a bad idea," said Clay.

A shrug from Gabriel. "I just wanted her to be able to protect herself. You know, stick 'em with the pointy end and all that. But she wanted more. She wanted to be . . ." he paused, searching for the word, ". . . great."

"Like her father?"

Gabriel's expression turned sour. "Just so. She heard too many stories, I think. Got her head filled with all this nonsense about being a hero, fighting in a band."

And from whom could she have heard all that? Clay wondered.

"I know," said Gabriel, perceiving his thoughts. "Partly my fault, I won't deny it. But it wasn't just me. Kids these days . . . they're obsessed with these mercenaries, Clay. They worship them. It's unhealthy. And most of these mercs aren't even in real bands! They just hire a bunch of nameless goons to do their fighting while they paint their faces and parade around with shiny swords and fancy armour. There's even one guy—I shit you not—who rides a manticore into battle!"

"A manticore?" asked Clay, incredulous.

Gabe laughed bitterly. "I know, right? Who the fuck *rides* a manticore? Those things are dangerous! Well, I don't need to tell you."

He didn't, of course. Clay had a nasty-looking puncture scar on his right thigh, testament to the hazards of tangling with such monsters. A manticore was nobody's pet, and it certainly wasn't fit to ride. As if slapping wings and a poison-barbed tail on a lion made it somehow a *fine* idea to climb on its back!

"They worshipped us, too," Clay pointed out. "Well *you*, anyway. And Ganelon. They tell the stories, even still. They sing the songs."

The stories were exaggerated, naturally. The songs, for the most part, were wildly inaccurate. But they persisted. Had lasted long after the men themselves had outlived who (or what) they'd been.

We were giants once.

"It's not the same," Gabriel persisted. "You should see the crowds gather when these bands come to town, Clay. People screaming, women crying in the streets."

"That sounds horrible," said Clay, meaning it.

Gabriel ignored him, pressing on. "Anyhow, Rose wanted to learn the sword, so I indulged her. I figured she'd get bored of it sooner or later, and that if she was going to learn, it might as well be from me. And also it made her mother mad as hell."

It would have, Clay knew. Her mother, Valery, despised violence and weapons of any kind, along with those who used either toward any end whatsoever. It was partly because of Valery that Saga had dissolved all those years ago.

"Problem was," said Gabriel, "she was good. Really good, and that's not just a father's boasts. She started out sparring against kids her age, but when they gave up getting their asses whooped she went out looking for street fights, or wormed her way into sponsored matches."

"The daughter of Golden Gabe himself," Clay mused. "Must've been quite the draw."

"I guess so," his friend agreed. "But then one day Val saw the bruises. Lost her mind. Blamed me, of course, for everything. She put her foot down—you know how she gets—and for a while Rose stopped fighting, but..." He trailed off, and Clay saw his jaw clamp down on something bitter. "After her mother left, Rosie and I . . . didn't get along so well, either. She started going out again. Sometimes she wouldn't come home for days. There were more bruises, and a few nastier scrapes besides. She chopped her hair off—thank the Holy Tetrea her mother was gone by then, or mine would've been next. And then came the cyclops."

"Cyclops?"

Gabriel looked at him askance. "Big bastards, one huge eye right here on their head?"

Clay leveled a glare of his own. "I know what a cyclops is, asshole."

"Then why did you ask?"

"I didn't . . ." Clay faltered. "Never mind. What *about* the cyclops?"

Gabriel sighed. "Well, one settled down in that old fort north of Ottersbrook. Stole some cattle, some goats, a dog, and then killed the folks that went looking for 'em. The courtsmen had their hands full, so they were looking for someone to clear the beast out for them. Only there weren't any mercs around at the time—or none with the chops to take on a cyclops, anyway. Somehow my name got tossed into the pot. They even sent someone round to ask if I would, but I told them no. Hell, I don't even own a sword anymore!"

Clay cut in again, aghast. "What? What about *Vellichor*?"

Gabriel's eyes were downcast. "I . . . uh . . . sold it."

"I'm sorry?" Clay asked, but before his friend could repeat himself he put his own hands flat on the table, for fear they would ball into fists, or snatch one of the bowls nearby and smash it over Gabriel's head. He said, as calmly as he could manage, "For a second there I thought you said that *you sold Vellichor*. As in the sword entrusted to you by the Archon himself as he lay dying? The sword he used to carve a fucking doorway from his world to ours. *That* sword? You sold *that sword*?"

Gabriel, who had slumped deeper into his chair with every word, nodded. "I had debts to pay, and Valery wanted it out of the house after she found out I taught Rose to fight," he said meekly. "She said it was dangerous."

"She——" Clay stopped himself. He leaned back in his chair, kneading his eyes with the palms of his hands. He groaned, and Griff, sensing his frustration, groaned himself from his mat in the corner. "Finish your story," he said at last.

Gabriel continued. "Well, needless to say, I refused to go after the cyclops, and for the next few weeks it caused a fair bit of havoc. And then suddenly word got around that someone had gone out and killed it." He smiled, wistful and sad. "All by herself."

"Rose," Clay said. Didn't make it a question. Didn't need to.

Gabriel's nod confirmed it. "She was a celebrity overnight. Bloody Rose, they called her. A pretty good name, actually."

It is, Clay agreed, but didn't bother saying so. He was still fuming about the sword. The sooner Gabe said whatever it was he'd come here to say, the sooner Clay could tell his oldest, dearest friend to get the hell out of his house and never come back.

"She even got her own band going," Gabe went on. "They managed to clear out a few nests around town: giant spiders, some old carrion wyrm down in the sewer that everyone forgot was still alive. But I hoped——" he bit his lip "——I still hoped, even then, that she might choose another path. A better path. Instead of following mine." He looked up. "Until the summons came from the Republic of Castia, asking every able sword to march against the Heartwyld Horde."

For a heartbeat Clay wondered at the significance of that. Until he remembered the news he'd heard earlier that evening. An army of twenty thousand, routed by a vastly more numerous host; the survivors surrounded in Castia, doubtless wishing they had died on the battlefield rather than endure the atrocities of a city under siege.

Which meant that Gabriel's daughter was dead. Or she would be, when the city fell.

Clay opened his mouth to speak, to try to keep the heartbreak from his voice as he did so. "Gabe, I—"

"I'm going after her, Clay. And I need you with me." Gabriel leaned forward in his chair, the flame of a father's fear and anger alight in his eyes. "It's time to get the band back together."

Enter the monthly
Orbit sweepstakes at

www.orbitloot.com

With a different prize every month,
from advance copies of books by
your favourite authors to exclusive
merchandise packs,
**we think you'll find something
you love.**